"[ROSS'S] COMBINATION OF LYRICISM AND SENSUALITY IS ON PAR WITH JO BEVERLEY'S."
—*Booklist*

Praise for the novels of Julia Ross

Games of Pleasure

"Beautifully written with intelligent characters . . . and an insightful glimpse into the human heart, this book is one of Ross's finest novels. You'll be captivated from page one."

—*Romantic Times* "TOP PICK" (4 ½ stars)

"*Games of Pleasure* is the kind of book one can sink into . . . While intensely character driven, (it) also chronicles a suspenseful plot . . . replete with wit and sensuality . . . Full of romance and excitement, telling prose and engaging dialogue, and soul-deep characterization, *Games of Pleasure* is another winner." —*Romance Reviews Today*

Night of Sin

"Exhilarating and highly sensual adventure romance . . . Ross's gift for creating masterful plots and memorable characters is at its height."

—*Romantic Times* "TOP PICK" (4 ½ stars)

"A terrific character study . . . Fans will appreciate gutsy Anne."

—*Midwest Book Review*

"One of the most lush and atmospheric books I've read in a long time; I was drawn in and engulfed in the story." —*All About Romance*

The Wicked Lover

"The Georgian period comes vividly to life here . . . I highly recommend *The Wicked Lover* to anyone seeking a romance with rich details, intriguing characters, and a fabulous conflict." —*All About Romance*

"Master storyteller Ross delivers a spellbinding double dose of intrigue and passion in this . . . fast-paced, sensual story brimming over with unforgettable moments and memorable characters. Exquisitely romantic, utterly captivating." —*Romantic Times* "TOP PICK" (4 ½ stars)

"A sensual, sophisticated tale, mysterious, elegant, and lusty . . . The pages heat up with very sensuous passages, passionate without a taint of crudity . . . For a tantalizing novel rich in atmosphere, I highly recommend *The Wicked Lover*." —*Romance Reviews Today*

"Ross's Georgian romances are never what one expects. They have a vein of eroticism, and plots and character traits that push the boundaries of the genre and make for not-to-be-missed reads . . . Twists and turns entwine with sensuality and suspense to make this lush romance a genuine page-turner." —*Booklist*

"An exciting story that sizzles with unbridled sensual desire. Lots of amusing twists and turns, a real keeper." —*Rendezvous*

"A stunning tale of intrigue and passion (with) some of the most beautiful and erotic imagery I have read in a long time . . . I feel very strongly about this book." —*A Romance Review*

The Seduction

"Ross's lush, evocative writing is the perfect counterpoint for her spellbinding tale of a wickedly refined, elegantly attired rake who is redeemed by one woman's love. Ross, whose combination of lyricism and sensuality is on par with Jo Beverley's, skillfully builds the simmering sexual chemistry between Alden and Juliet into an exquisitely sensual romance and luscious love story." —*Booklist*

"A gripping novel starring two wonderfully tainted romantic skeptics as lead protagonists." —*Midwest Book Review*

"Rich, delicious . . . Books like this are treasures . . . Put it at the top of your summer reading list." —*The Oakland Press*

"Magnificent . . . A wonderfully tempting tale filled with unsurpassed sensuality . . . A hot and fast-paced read . . . Completely enthralling." —*The Road to Romance*

"An extraordinary story . . . A superb example of Ms. Ross's outstanding storytelling talents and exceptional writing abilities. Intense emotions and passionate, strong characters are the complement to a complex love story, replete with such dastardly villains as Shakespeare might have crafted."
—*Historical Romance Reviews*

"Wit, lust, and just enough mystery . . . The characters are charming, reckless, and endearing."
—*Rendezvous*

My Dark Prince

"Brilliant! Passionate, complex, and compelling. The best book of any genre I have read in a long, long while. Don't miss this beautifully written, intensely satisfying love story. I am in awe . . . Highly recommended."
—Mary Balogh

"I thoroughly enjoyed *My Dark Prince*. If you enjoy exciting, entertaining, wonderfully written romance, read this book."
—Jo Beverley

"A fantastic cast of characters . . . Julia Ross traps the reader from page one . . . outstanding . . . a breathtaking and mesmerizing historical romance. This is romance in its finest hour."
—*The Romance Journal*

"Lovers of tortured heroes and intense stories will take this one to their hearts . . . *My Dark Prince* has a plot filled with complications and dangers—real dangers . . . I don't think I'm going to forget this one anytime soon."
—*All About Romance*

"A powerful story of the redemptive power of love, with one of the most tortured heroes I have come across in quite a while . . . *My Dark Prince* has loads of danger and adventure . . . the definition of a 'keeper.'"
—*The Romance Reader*

"With this thrilling adventure of the heart, Julia Ross establishes herself as a powerful, distinctive force in the evolution of the romance genre . . . Darkly erotic and sensually stunning, this innovative and spellbinding romance will enslave your heart and fill your dreams."
—*Romantic Times* "TOP PICK" (4 ½ stars)

Clandestine

Julia Ross

BERKLEY SENSATION, NEW YORK

THE BERKLEY PUBLISHING GROUP
Published by the Penguin Group
Penguin Group (USA) Inc.
375 Hudson Street, New York, New York 10014, USA
Penguin Group (Canada), 90 Eglinton Avenue East, Suite 700, Toronto, Ontario M4P 2Y3, Canada
(a division of Pearson Penguin Canada Inc.)
Penguin Books Ltd., 80 Strand, London WC2R 0RL, England
Penguin Group Ireland, 25 St. Stephen's Green, Dublin 2, Ireland (a division of Penguin Books Ltd.)
Penguin Group (Australia), 250 Camberwell Road, Camberwell, Victoria 3124, Australia
(a division of Pearson Australia Group Pty. Ltd.)
Penguin Books India Pvt. Ltd., 11 Community Centre, Panchsheel Park, New Delhi—110 017, India
Penguin Group (NZ), Cnr. Airborne and Rosedale Roads, Albany, Auckland 1310, New Zealand
(a division of Pearson New Zealand Ltd.)
Penguin Books (South Africa) (Pty.) Ltd., 24 Sturdee Avenue, Rosebank, Johannesburg 2196, South Africa

Penguin Books Ltd., Registered Offices: 80 Strand, London WC2R 0RL, England

This book is an original publication of The Berkley Publishing Group.

This is a work of fiction. Names, characters, places, and incidents either are the product of the author's imagination or are used fictitiously, and any resemblance to actual persons, living or dead, business establishments, events, or locales is entirely coincidental. The publisher does not have any control over and does not assume any responsibility for author or third-party websites or their content.

First edition: November 2006

Library of Congress Cataloging-in-Publication Data

Ross, Julia.
   Clandestine / Julia Ross. — 1st ed.
      p. cm.
   ISBN 0-425-21197-5 (trade pbk.)
   I. Title.

   PS3618.O846C55 2006
   813'.6—dc22

                                                 2006022772

PRINTED IN THE UNITED STATES OF AMERICA

10 9 8 7 6 5 4 3 2 1

Acknowledgments

I owe thanks to Bruce Ide and Jay Pfahl for suggesting some orchids that might have been growing in English hothouses in 1829, a time when these glorious flowers were being imported into England from every part of the world.

I'm very grateful indeed for their generous help, though any errors in my choices or descriptions are entirely my own.

CHAPTER ONE

London, June 1829

SHE HAD BEEN SECRETLY WATCHING HIM FOR DAYS.

He moved with quicksilver vitality, as if he alone were vibrantly, brilliantly alive. Love of life radiated from the tilt of his hat, from his long strides, from the creases that marked his cheeks when he laughed.

He seemed to laugh often.

Guy Devoran no doubt had a great deal to laugh about. His uncle was a duke. He could never have known poverty, or fear, or self-doubt.

He was standing now on the stoop of his townhouse, gazing up at the sky as if he read mysteries in the clouds.

Sarah's heart began to hurt, beating agitation against her ribs. Perhaps this quest really was thunderingly foolish, after all: both the hope for help and the hunger for revenge.

Her quarry tipped his hat to the hidden sun, then strolled away down the wet pavement, exchanging pleasantries with passersby. It seemed impossible ever to catch him alone. Others eddied in his wake as if he were royal.

She dodged after him through the throng of carriages and horsemen and into St. James's. He stopped to talk to another gentleman, who had been gazing idly through a wine merchant's window. Tall and lean, both men betrayed the unstudied elegance of power and unquestioned wealth. The other man laughed at something Guy Devoran said.

Letting her bonnet hide her face, Sarah pretended to be examining a nearby shop window. After a few minutes' conversation, Mr. Devoran bowed good-bye to his friend, then strode off as if he owned London.

She followed, keeping several discreet paces behind, until a group of young men burst from a doorway. Arguing loudly about politics, they blocked the pavement. By the time they dispersed, still shouting to one another, Mr. Devoran had disappeared.

Biting back her frustration, Sarah walked rapidly in what she hoped was the right direction, choosing her path at random until she was lost in a maze of unknown streets.

A bookseller's occupied a corner with doors on both sides. She glanced in through the window as she scurried past.

Her throat froze. Her heart hammered as if she were about to be sick.

The glass panes distorted his image, but Mr. Guy Devoran was moving past the stacks inside, examining titles. He tugged off his gloves and thrust them into a pocket, then stepped out of sight around the end of some shelves. No other customers were visible.

Now or never!

A bell rang as Sarah pushed open the door.

The bookshop smelt musty. The young man behind the counter glanced up, then continued writing in his ledger. She nodded to him before she hurried between the stacks. Her breath raced, as if months of ongoing terror had squeezed a cruel hand around her lungs.

The front room splintered through multiple doorways into a maze of inner rooms. Every wall was filled, floor to ceiling, with leather spines, dust, and cobwebs. Passageways linked or led to dead ends. As if the host of words had simply absorbed him, Mr. Devoran had vanished.

Sarah circled the shop again before she retreated into the deepest room, where she sat down on a wooden trunk and tried to calm her pulse. Perhaps there was no need for such elaborate caution, after all. Perhaps she had simply misjudged everything, right from the beginning. Even if she had not, what real hope could she possibly have that this particular man would help her?

A tiny movement disturbed the dust motes. Her head jerked up.

Arms crossed, brass-headed cane tucked against his body, Mr. Devoran leaned one shoulder against the doorjamb and examined her.

Fine olive skin burnished high cheekbones and shadowed the angle of his jaw. Beneath the brim of his hat, exquisitely carved bone defined the harsh arch of eyebrows above dark, liquid eyes.

His gaze was considered, almost daunting.

Sarah stared back, her thoughts hijacked.

A man who might have been crafted in the Underworld to play Theseus stalking through the Labyrinth.

Eyes filled with perilous intelligence met her hot stare, but he smiled and became simply Oberon, lord of gaiety and madness.

Exactly as Rachel had described him. His smile invited only laughter and caresses.

An uncomfortable flush of awareness ran over her body.

"Pray forgive my boldness, ma'am." He stepped farther into the room, doffed his hat, and bowed. "Mr. Guy Devoran, at your service. I fear my sins must demand instant retribution. If I misread your intentions, I beg you'll accept my apologies, but I believe you've been following me?"

"Why should you think—? Yes, sir, I have. How did you know?"

Humor sheened his expression, but he turned away to study the bookshelves. It was much easier to examine the perfect cut of his coat than face that quick gaze. Perhaps he even knew that.

"A lady wandering alone in St. James's is hard to miss, ma'am, especially when she hovers for several days like one of the Furies near my front door."

She felt absurdly close to panic. "The Furies?"

"Greek deities of vengeance and destruction."

A new fear sent clenching fingers through her gut. "I know who the Furies were, sir, of course."

He had folded his hands around his cane, holding it behind his back. His fingers were lovely, sensitive and strong.

"Ah, very well, then!" The broad shoulders shrugged with consummate elegance. "Yet you're a damsel in distress, I take it. How may I assist you?"

A drumbeat rolled in her chest, robbing her of breath. She pushed two fingers over her tight forehead, trying to force herself to relax. "I hope— Yes, I need your help very urgently, Mr. Devoran."

He took down a book to flip casually through the pages. "Mine in particular?"

"Yes."

"Have we met before, ma'am?"

"No, never! But you're very well known in London, sir."

He set the book back and pulled out another. "And I have the unmistakable aura of a knight errant? I trust I may oblige. Yet you didn't think it seemly to knock at my house, or send me a note?"

"I couldn't be certain that no one else would open your correspondence—a secretary or footman, perhaps. And it's vital that I'm not seen to visit you."

"Indeed? I shake at the implications." He did not sound in the least shaken, only mildly curious. He glanced back over his shoulder. "You have my full attention, Miss—?"

Her discomfort had deepened almost to pain. She felt a little faint. "Mrs. Callaway, Mr. Devoran. My maiden name was Sarah Hargreaves. You once met my cousin. She was calling herself Rachel Wren—"

He spun about and caught her by the arm, whether to support her or himself was unclear. Intensity quivered from his strong grip.

"Rachel Wren?"

"It was over a year ago. Rachel said that you asked her—or your cousin, Lord Jonathan St. George, did—to spend a day with you on a yacht. She was free for a few days while her employers were away. Though of course she had reservations about such an indecorous adventure, she was assured of anonymity, and she'd anyway given you a false name. Lord Jonathan wished to escort another lady from town, yet remain unnoticed by his enemies—"

"*I remember.*"

The strong pulse of life emanated from his fingertips. Echoing ripples seemed to spiral down through her body: a kind of hot madness in the blood.

Sarah glanced down as if to shut out black smoke.

"So she wasn't Rachel Wren," he said. "What's her real name?"

"Miss Rachel Mansard." She forced herself to ignore the wild rush of sensation and meet the dark flash of his eyes. "She and I were raised together and have always been close. Though she never saw you again, Rachel never forgot your kindness, Mr. Devoran."

He smiled entirely without mirth. "Was I kind?"

"She thought so."

"Ah!" He released her arm and stalked away. Guy Devoran moved with the grace of a dancer, but there was something lethal in it. "And was today's encounter Miss Mansard's idea?"

"No, indeed not! It was entirely my own." The frantic hammering in her heart threatened to deafen her, but Sarah plunged on, horrified by her clumsy rush of words. "No unmarried lady would impose like this on a single gentleman after one day's acquaintance. Yet though I realize that such a casual episode must have meant very little to you—"

"Quite so! So what brings you to me now, Mrs. Callaway?"

She glanced back toward the main bookstore. "This isn't anywhere near private enough, sir. Someone could come in at any moment."

He strode to the single doorway to glance through, then walked back to guide her by the elbow into the deepest recesses of the room. He was tall and broad-shouldered enough to block out most of the light.

"No one else is here. Yet if your predicament is so confidential, why trust in a stranger?"

"I don't know anyone else to ask."

He stood quietly for several seconds, gazing at her like a man eddying into a void, while her heart beat loudly in her chest.

"But what if I'm some kind of villain?" he asked at last.

"Your uncle is the Duke of Blackdown. Your elder cousin is Lord Ryderbourne. If that doesn't place you beyond reproach, Rachel is certain that you're a gentleman of honor. Is she wrong?"

"That a man's noble relations guarantee his good behavior?" He smiled with real amusement—and the shadows fled as if Oberon might yet command the sun to make the world laugh. "London disproves that idea every day."

"No doubt," she said. "I'm not very familiar with the habits of town gentlemen."

"Yet you come to me, when I'm very much the town gentleman. Do you expect me to drop everything in order to help you?"

Suddenly exhausted, as if the musty ranks of books had robbed her of energy, Sarah plunked herself down on the trunk.

"Why not? I doubt that you have anything much better to do."

"Of course, I'm a member of the idle classes." Wry irony settled at the corners of his mouth. "My time is obviously my own to indulge as I wish."

"Yes, I imagine so."

"And are you always this blunt with strangers, Mrs. Callaway?"

"No," she said. "Of course not. But Rachel helped you once at some risk to herself. Any true gentleman would honor such a debt."

"There is no debt." He tugged out another book and flipped casually through its pages. "Your cousin was very well paid for her services at the time."

"She was paid?" It seemed unreal. Perhaps he meant that Rachel had been given a gift of some kind. "Then I must appeal to your gallantry, sir. I assure you that I wouldn't approach you like this, were I not quite desperate."

"There's no family member or close friend who can help you?"

"I've no living family other than Rachel, and I can't trust any of our acquaintances in this."

"Then there's no Mr. Callaway?"

"Captain Callaway. I'm a widow."

His fingers rested quietly on the leather binding for a moment, before he set the book back on its shelf.

"My husband died two years ago," she added. "He was considerably older than I. He'd been wounded at Waterloo and carried the shards of metal in his spine for twelve years. He lived for only a few months after our wedding."

"I'm so sorry," Guy Devoran said.

The concern in his voice was almost her undoing. Sarah gripped hard at her reticule. "I haven't told you this to gain your sympathy, sir. Merely to explain my situation."

"Condolences can only ever be offered," he said gently. "There's no obligation to accept them. You're not usually a resident of London, I take it?"

Sarah smoothed one hand over her green skirts. To think for even a moment about her past only made this conversation the more bizarrely fantastic. It was absurd, a madness, to imagine that Mr. Guy Devoran would help her.

"No, I teach botany and dancing and geography at a Young Ladies' Academy in Bath."

"But you came up to town specifically to seek me out, because your cousin mentioned meeting me some thirteen months ago?"

"You spent a whole day together," she said, "in most unusual circumstances."

"A day on a yacht, during which we barely exchanged two words. And now you tell me that she was using a false name."

"Only to protect her reputation should you or your cousin prove less than honorable, and spread wild tales about your adventure together."

"Yet now her faith in my good nature—from that one encounter—is so absolute that you're certain I will aid you in whatever so disturbs you?"

Swallowing her trepidation, Sarah nodded.

He met her gaze as if he accepted it, but his smile spoke only of withdrawal. As if beneath a keen natural vigilance he must rein in deeper, more mysterious impulses that she would never be able to fathom: impulses that somehow amused him, but would always scatter his attention.

"You can hardly expect me to believe that," he said.

Betraying color flooded over her cheeks like the tide. He was cousin to a future duke. He was desperately, heart-stoppingly attractive. Yet he belonged to a class that was essentially unknown to her: the hereditary aristocracy of England, who played, danced—and ruled—as if there were no tomorrow.

Young, handsome, eligible, he was the kind of man she would never normally expect to talk to privately, even as the relative of a pupil.

Sarah tamped down her runaway pulse and erratic heartbeat. Unless she risked everything, he would dismiss her out of hand.

"Nevertheless, that is the truth, Mr. Devoran."

He slipped his gloves from his pocket and eased the fine leather onto his fingers. The neat movements were both strong and sensual, as if he took wicked pleasure in the simplest of gestures.

"But why won't your cousin help you herself, Mrs. Callaway?"

Sarah stood up, feeling as if she were about to step—arms outspread—off a high cliff to plummet straight into the sea.

"Because Rachel has disappeared, sir, and I have very good reason to believe that she's been abducted."

CHAPTER TWO

SILENCE SEARED, LIKE THE SHOCKED VOID AFTER LIGHTNING.
He cupped her elbow to drag her back into the corner.

"*Abducted?*" His attention was absolute now. "You have proof of this?"

She steeled herself to face his obvious skepticism. "Rachel's last letter betrayed such fear that I left Bath immediately and caught the next available coach to town. It arrived in London very late, so I took a room in a hotel that Rachel had recommended. But when I went to her lodgings first thing the next morning, she was already missing."

"She was living here in *London?*"

Sarah nodded, disconcerted by his passion. "Yes. Why not?"

"No reason at all, of course. Where were her rooms?"

She felt in her reticule, pulled out a scrap of paper, and gave it to him.

He glanced at the address, then thrust it into a pocket. His gaze was shadowed, as if his eyes had opened on darkness.

"So you went to this place in Goatstall Lane. How long had Miss Mansard lived there?"

"For several weeks, though she hoped to find new employment soon. She's a governess."

"God! A governess! Are you quite certain of all this?"

"Yes. Why? Though they wouldn't let me into her rooms, I thought the location quite respectable."

"No doubt. She lived there alone?"

"Of course—apart from a maid-of-all-work, who came in during the day."

"So you don't think that she fled town of her own accord?"

"Rachel would never have gone away without first sending me her new direction."

He spun about to stalk away. Vitality radiated from his long strides. "And from this you deduce that she's been abducted? By whom?"

"I don't know."

His boots resounded on the wooden floor. "You have great faith in your cousin's reliability, Mrs. Callaway."

"I've known her almost all of my life, sir. Rachel would never have written to me as she did unless she had cause for real alarm."

"So what frightened her so badly?"

Discomfort flamed painfully over her cheeks. "She was being persecuted by a gentleman . . . a visitor to the house where she held her last post."

"When was this?"

"Last spring—in February and March."

He stopped dead, his back taut. "Your cousin was working as a governess *then*? Where?"

"For a Mr. Harvey Penland in Hampstead. He's a widower with six children. Rachel was happy there for almost a year, until this admirer destroyed her tranquillity."

"She described him?"

"Not in any great detail, but Rachel's very lovely, Mr. Devoran. Gentlemen always notice her."

"So I recall." Winter could not have sounded colder. "Did she encourage this man's attentions?"

"When she first met him, perhaps. She even thought she was a little in love—but then he began to frighten her."

His spine like a ramrod, he stared up at the top rows of books. "When did they first meet, exactly?"

"Some time in January, I think. But by the end of March she was quite desperate to escape his notice. Fortunately, the whole family spent Easter in Devon, so Rachel hoped her persecutor would forget about her while she was away. Instead, when they returned to Hampstead, he only became more importunate. So she made an excuse about an illness in her family—though we have no family left, of course—and fled to those lodgings in Goatstall Lane."

A small muscle worked at the side of his jaw. "Yet she was still afraid of this man?"

"He threatened her with . . . with physical retribution. She was sure he would hunt her down."

"And now you think this mysterious villain has *abducted* her?"

His incredulity battered at her, as if the bright, dismissive wave of his disbelief swept the floor from beneath her boots.

"Yes," Sarah said stubbornly. "I do think so."

He stood with his back to her, his head bent, as if he sought answers in the gold top of his cane. Dark hair curled over his ear. A rigid tension marked the line of his shoulder and arm.

The air felt thick with suppressed emotion: fear, anger, grief? Sarah's heartbeat echoed into the silence.

"I cannot find her alone, Mr. Devoran," she added desperately. "I don't have the resources, nor the skills, nor the courage."

"But why the devil come to me?" He spun about. "I think you're not telling me everything, ma'am."

She stepped forward, fingers clenched. "Perhaps not. But then, neither are you, sir."

His nostrils flared. "Really? In what way?"

"You just said that you barely exchanged two words with Rachel that day on the yacht. That's not what she told me."

"Indeed?" Ice seemed to have congealed in his voice.

"It was a whole *day*. Rachel wrote that she chattered on like a magpie. Lord Grail was her employer then, so she'd thought her position quite secure. Yet when the family left her alone in that port while they visited relatives nearby, she feared she'd been abandoned there without funds. She was worried enough to write to an employment agency here in London. You must remember!"

"She's supposed to have told me all this?"

Sarah sat back down on the trunk. "Perhaps Rachel seemed only garrulous and silly to you, but she wrote me a long letter all about it. A letter full of joy and . . . and triumph! Did she in fact make so little impression on you?"

"It would certainly seem so." A shadow cloaked his expression, though his gaze remained fixed on her face. "But none of this explains why you think I will help you now."

"Rachel said you were ineffably kind." Sarah choked back her rush of anxiety and rage, and glanced down at the pile of books on the trunk. "She said you made her laugh."

"Did I? I had forgotten. But our situations are not quite equivalent in this, are they, Mrs. Callaway? You are the suppliant. I am the one being importuned."

"Yes." Feeling stiff and awkward, she picked up a volume at random. The prospect of help was sifting away like dry sand through clenched fingers. "I didn't mean to harangue you, Mr. Devoran. I'm sorry."

"Not at all!" He smiled with a kind of remote courtesy. "You're understandably distressed about your cousin's disappearance. But aren't you at all concerned about the impropriety of approaching a stranger like this?"

"I'm a widow, sir, not a young girl. With Rachel's happiness and possibly her safety at stake, I have very little choice."

He remained silent for a moment, his expression closed, contained, as if he ruthlessly reined in his natural male restlessness.

"So the choices, it would seem, are all mine," he said at last.

The leather cover in her hand was embossed in gilt. The gold outline of a bullheaded monster glowered up at her from one corner.

"Theseus chose to enter the Labyrinth to face down the Minotaur," she said. "He didn't have to do so. He volunteered."

"I beg your pardon?"

Embarrassment burned up her neck. She set down the book and stood up. "I'm sorry. But you mentioned the Furies, sir."

Guy Devoran laughed. "And so invited a deluge of random Greek associations?" He stepped closer to glance down at the cover. "Where are you staying, ma'am?"

"Brockton's Hotel. It's not far from here."

"Yes, I know it."

She almost grasped his arm. "Then you will help me?"

His eyes met hers. Sarah gazed back into a heart of black flame.

A hot disturbance eddied through her veins, a quickening, like an onrushing ocean wave. She felt suddenly light-headed, as if he had mesmerized her, as if loose strands of her hair sang faraway songs of enchantment.

A bell rang.

Voices echoed from the outer shop.

The spun-sugar threads of the spell snapped in two. Though her heart still danced a frenzied fandango, Sarah dropped her hand and stepped back.

He had already looked away toward the sound. "If secrecy is so essential, you must leave right now," he said quietly. "Which room?"

"Room?"

Guy Devoran glanced back at her and smiled. "At Brockton's: a modest but decent establishment, as recommended by your cousin, suitable for young ladies traveling alone."

"The last one in the north hallway at the top."

He turned away to pull down a thick tome. He began to study it, almost as if he were no longer aware of her.

"Then I suggest that you return there," he said, "while I think about it."

She was dismissed. The loss of that vibrant attention stabbed like a knife.

With her blood on fire, Sarah slipped into the main part of the bookstore. An elderly couple was talking to the man at the counter. Using the bookshelves as a shield, she hurried to the other entrance and stepped out into the street.

It was raining. She had left her umbrella at the hotel. For no reason she could fathom, hot tears began to burn down her cheeks.

GUY closed the book with a thud. He thrust it back on the shelf, then stared blindly at the spine.

The scent of green apples dampened by rain—fresh and crisp and sweet to the tongue—eddied among the stuffy smells of the bookstore.

If he glanced up, would he still see her, frowning with apprehension? The green skirts and modest cloak. The proud tilt to her bonnet. The sensually rounded figure. The firm chin and changeable hazel eyes, glaring up at him beneath long, sandy lashes, like the eyes of a tigress.

Mrs. Sarah Callaway possessed a striking face, compelling without being beautiful: the opposite of her cousin, Rachel Wren—no, *Mansard*.

As if to mock his memory of Rachel's cool, pale skin, flecks of brown rioted over Sarah's cheeks to meet in a frantic dance on the bridge of her nose. More freckles cavorted over her perfect little chin to race along her jaw like a flock of tiny sparrows. Even her earlobes were speckled, as if finely crumpled autumn leaves had been mixed into cream.

My maiden name was Sarah Hargreaves. You once met my cousin. She was calling herself Rachel Wren—

Sarah probably had no idea that any man who saw all those little freckles would burn to touch them. From her straightforward manner, she probably thought she was plain.

Rachel, of course, had always known that she was beautiful, even when she carried a mop and bucket.

Guy dragged his palm down over his mouth. He had not even known that Rachel had a cousin. Especially one so very upright and interesting and . . . freckled!

The very proper teacher of botany and dancing and geography possessed very lovely skin, shaped delicately over lush female flesh. For all her lack of flirtation, Sarah Callaway was hiding what he suspected was a wanton mass of hair, not entirely successfully pinned back in a knot beneath her bonnet.

He cursed under his breath. Was Theseus really expected to plunge, sword in hand, back into the Labyrinth?

The hazel eyes had seemed stunningly honest, yet almost every word that she'd told him was a pack of lies. So either the redheaded schoolteacher had not been entirely frank with him, or her cousin had fooled her very seriously. And, as he knew to his cost, Rachel was perfectly capable of skipping out on a relationship without leaving any forwarding address.

Thus he very much doubted the reality of any villainous abduction.

He almost doubted the existence of the room at the end of the hallway at Brockton's Hotel, and even of the late Captain Callaway.

Guy had definitely begun to question the motives of this dappled lady with the self-possession of a queen, who might have danced, like autumn, directly out of summer.

He would, of course, help her anyway.

Though he would make a few inquiries first.

UMBRELLAS sprouted around her like mushrooms as Sarah hurried back to the hotel. She ordered hot tea, then ran up the stairs to her room. It was small and mean, the cheapest the hotel had to offer, and lacked a working fireplace. But the long summer days were busy stealing time from the night, so she did not need a fire.

At least Brockton's was safe and decent, as even Mr. Devoran had acknowledged.

An impeccable reputation was essential, of course, if a young lady with no other prospects was to keep her employment and not starve. Especially a widow who had just run out on her teaching post with no guarantee that Miss Farcey would ever take her back.

Sarah tugged off her bonnet and stared at herself in the mirror. Her eyes were angrily rimmed in red. Her lashes burned like dry grass. The lady of misrule, her hair a damp mass, like a tangle of spun copper.

It was hard to remain respectable when one possessed such riotously wicked hair and skin that betrayed one's every emotion, however fleeting. Without her bonnet she looked like a loose woman who had dipped her head in a dye pot.

When she had first applied for her position with Miss Farcey, she had wet the most wayward strands to darken them, then dragged them back beneath a modest little cap. Yet her hair had always had a life of its own, as if it sparked with hidden electricity.

It was lucky that she was otherwise unremarkable and speckled like a thrush, or how could she have risked accosting a strange gentleman, especially one as intimidating as Guy Devoran?

She made a face at herself and turned away. For Rachel's sake, she would have faced down the devil himself, had she thought it necessary.

Her coat was soaked, so she tugged it off and hung it behind the door, before she sat down on the single chair and pulled a small key out of her pocket.

Rachel's letters lay tucked into the secret compartment of Sarah's writing case. The same hidden drawer that graced any ladies' writing case. With an uncomfortable new awareness, she stared at the mahogany box. It was crafted mostly from thin veneers. Any strong young man could smash it open with one blow.

A shiver ran down her spine.

It was only custom and social disapproval that prevented aristocrats like Guy Devoran from smashing into whatever they desired to take whatever they wanted. A nephew of the Duke of Blackdown was essentially above the law.

That was why she hoped he would help her.

Yet the thought of that potentially unrestricted power yawned its threat: casual and absolute. Guy Devoran and his cousins could play at life and death if they wished, and no one would stop them.

Was Rachel's tormentor just as powerful? Had she been stolen away by a man who knew that no one could touch him, whatever he did?

Sick fear seized Sarah by the throat. Even the thought of tea was nauseating for a moment, though that was what she needed: a nice strong cup of tea.

A rap at the door revealed one of the inn servants with a tray. As soon as the girl left, Sarah poured herself a cup, then read Rachel's last letter through yet again, though she had already committed parts of it to memory:

> . . . *He insisted that I marry him, and he wouldn't take no for an answer. I was obliged to be very firm. Yet I fear that he intends to persecute me, even that he will resort to a most dishonorable solution to his ardor. I'm so afraid. I dare not imagine what he might do if he found me here alone. Please come right away, dearest Sarah!*

This man must know that she and Rachel had no family left to turn to: two young ladies, essentially unprotected in the world. It was despicable. It was also terrifying.

Sarah had rushed up to town to find Rachel already missing. All of her inquiries had run into blank walls. Just this morning she had become certain that a forcible abduction was the only possible explanation for Rachel's disappearance. Otherwise her cousin would surely have sent word by now.

Then she had crashed into the wall of Mr. Devoran's disbelief.

In the face of it, her certainty had almost wavered. Yet the fear in

Rachel's letters was palpable—enough to make Sarah determined first on rescue, then on revenge.

She sorted at random through the earlier letters. Ah, this one! Rachel had written it the previous autumn, when her news had still been only light and amusing, filled with the trivial details of her life as a governess for the Penlands.

> . . . *When I get too bored with all this, especially with having to eat my meals by myself—too exalted for the servants' hall, but nowhere near good enough to grace the family table—I try to recall those long summer days that we spent together as children. I miss it all so much, beloved Sarah! Then sometimes I think of that day on the yacht with Mr. Guy Devoran. I can still hardly believe that I spent all those hours with a nephew of the Duke of Blackdown! Even though it reminds me of everything that we've lost, dear Sarah, it also reminds me that some men are true gentlemen—*

Sarah folded the paper and tucked it back into her writing case. Everything had changed after Christmas, when Rachel had become so euphoric that she often neglected to write. Yet in the spring the tone of her letters had become suddenly frantic, until she had sent that last panicked plea.

The paper split a little as Sarah unfolded the final missive yet again. Her eyes skimmed over the important phrases:

> *A lady alone is so helpless against any influential gentleman. Society always judges a female more harshly than her persecutor, and I fear no one would believe me if I ever revealed his name. But, oh, how I think now about that day on the yacht—one golden, bright memory in my sea of despair! How I wish I might ask Mr. Devoran, the loveliest man I ever met*—Rachel had scratched through the next several lines—*But no, that would never do! What if my enemy found out? All these titled families know each other, don't they? They might even be friends*—

So when she'd denied that Rachel had wanted to enlist his help, Sarah Callaway had indeed been hiding something. But so had he.

Why else had Guy Devoran reacted to her explanation of her cousin's predicament with such vehemence? No doubt he'd been annoyed that Rachel had given him a false name, and perhaps that information had bruised his pride a little, but surely he must be otherwise unconcerned?

After all, they had met only that once. Rachel had adored her day on the yacht, because Guy Devoran—carefully courteous—had neither embarrassed nor propositioned the young lady in his power.

Instead he had made Rachel laugh.

Yet it had all only been to help another young lady named Anne, who was now married to Lord Jonathan St. George, Mr. Devoran's younger cousin. According to the newspapers, the couple had recently returned to England from India, and Lady Jonathan was expecting a happy event any day.

By spending that day on the yacht with Rachel, Guy Devoran had helped Lord Jonathan's future wife to escape her enemies, and made all her happiness possible. He had done it only because he was generous and gallant and compassionate, not because of any personal concern for Rachel.

But what if this time he decided not to help a young lady in distress, after all?

Or worse: What if she had misjudged everything about him from the snippets in Rachel's letters? What if Mr. Devoran was hiding something that really mattered?

RAIN streamed along the pavement. Guy stood in the doorway of the bookseller's with several volumes wrapped in brown paper tucked under one arm. He glanced up and down the street as if checking the weather.

The light-skinned man that he had seen earlier loitering near his townhouse was gone. The man's presence might have been co-incidence, or it might be that Guy was not the only person who had noticed Mrs. Sarah Callaway, captain's relict, lingering in the street with anxiety marking her face like a brand.

Devil take it! If anything truly dangerous was going on, she would have been far safer to have sent him a note. No one in his house would have dreamed of opening his correspondence. Instead, she had delayed her decision to seek his help until Rachel had already been missing for several days.

If she really was missing, of course, and not simply hiding from the disappointed rage of another abandoned lover.

Guy shrugged and strode off. He was indeed well known in London: the duke's nephew who was the friend of so many and the intimate of almost none.

As soon as he was ensconced in the security of his study, Guy sent out several letters. The first to deliver his regrets to a certain lady whom he had planned to escort to the Park that afternoon. The second to Lady Ryderbourne, the beautiful wife of the Duke of Blackdown's eldest son, who had a marked fondness for him and wouldn't hesitate to do as he asked. The third a set of requests to London's ladies' employment agencies, where one might—if one needed such a creature—find a governess.

As soon as his missives were gone, Guy jotted two names on a sheet of paper and stared at them: Lord Grail, Mr. Harvey Penland. He knew Grail, though not well. The name *Harvey Penland* meant nothing.

He glanced at the clock and wrote one more note—in a code they had invented as schoolboys—to his younger cousin, Lord Jonathan Devoran St. George, otherwise known as Wild Lord Jack, so Jack would receive it before he reached London.

With the Goatstall address still burning in his mind, Guy stalked out of his study and called for a thick cloak. Yet as he strode away down the wet pavement, he made no attempt whatsoever to face the riot of hurt and anger that Sarah's news about Rached caused him.

*   *   *

SARAH stared down from her bedroom window to watch the lamp-lighter casting out the night. She had come to stay in town once as a small child, long before the widespread introduction of gas, a few years before she had gone to live with the Mansards. The streets had been pits of darkness then, the sooty glow of the lanterns barely penetrating the murk. The memory made the gaslights seem like a miracle.

Had it been a madness to try to enlist Guy Devoran?

Her stomach rumbled. She glanced at the tray holding the cold teapot. She had spent a good part of her savings already, and she was almost out of money. She didn't dare order any more food until tomorrow. Nor did she dare to go out, in case Mr. Devoran sent word.

What on earth could she do, if he refused to help her?

She had been able to walk to Goatstall Lane, but no one who might have known Rachel there would talk when they learned that Sarah lacked the funds to reward their cooperation.

She glanced at the clock: almost bedtime. Ignoring the gnawing hunger and fear, she began to pace, trying to count her assets and reassess what she knew.

Someone rapped.

Sarah jumped like a startled hare, then stared at the door for a moment. Her heart beat loudly enough to almost choke her, while one man's name seemed to echo into the room: *Guy Devoran!*

The knocking progressed into thumps.

A gentleman would never rattle the panels like that. It was probably some slightly inebriated guest, trying the wrong room. Sarah cracked open the door.

A boy gawked up at her. He held a large package in both arms.

"Delivery for Missus Callaway. By hand to the lady herself and no one else, on pain of a whipping."

Sarah opened the door all the way. "I'm Mrs. Callaway."

The boy grinned. "The gennulman said I'd know if it was the

right lady, because she looks like a mouse had dabbled his little feet in brown ink, then run all over her skin. That's you, right enough."

He dropped the package, touched his cap, and ran off down the corridor.

A flush of mortification warmed her face, but her predicament was far too serious to be upset by such nonsense. Whatever a gentleman might notice about Sarah Callaway, it was certainly not her good looks.

She picked up the package, carried it into her room, and set it on the bed. Perhaps he had sent her some food? At the very thought, she laughed at herself. Apprehension was obviously a more appropriate reaction when a gentleman sent a lady an unexpected gift.

Sarah pulled herself together and cut the string.

The paper fell open to reveal a mass of blue silk. Aware of a renewed flutter of nerves, she shook it out: a blue-and-white fantasy of a peasant dress, at least a hundred years out of date.

Caught by the sheer beauty of the fabric, she stared at the dress for a moment before she unwrapped the next layer: a white-powdered wig, set with bows of blue ribbon and tiny models of sheep—*sheep?*—that decorated a miniature bonnet. A dark-blue mask lay beneath that, wrapped in a white lace handkerchief. A pair of silver shoes and a tiny shepherd's crook set with beetles' wings and glass spangles sparkled at the bottom of the parcel.

Tied with more blue ribbon, a bulky paper was wrapped about the handle.

In spite of the frippery of the ribbon, the note carried a hint of cedar and beeswax beneath its top note of expensive ink: masculine scents that spoke of an elegant study, the private preserve of the man who had so disturbed her composure in the bookstore.

His dark head had bent over this very sheet of paper, a dry quirk at the corner of his lips, his profile perfect as he dipped his pen in the inkwell.

And—if he had happened to glance up—he'd have pinned any observer with eyes so dark that a woman might drown in their black fire.

Her fingers fumbled as she untied the ribbon and unfolded the paper, while a rush of trepidation sent quite definite little mouse feet running down her spine. To her surprise, some coins rattled onto the table. She set them aside and started to read.

Dear Madam,

The recent christening of the infant Lord Wyldshay, the first grandson of the Duke of Blackdown, is to be celebrated tomorrow night with a masked ball. I enjoy the perhaps unfortunate privilege of being one of the baby's godfathers, so I am obliged to attend.

No one will notice an extra shepherdess.

A maid from Blackdown House will arrive tomorrow evening to assist you. You may, of course, send her away, if you wish. However, it would be prudent for you to remain quietly in your room at the hotel until then.

Meanwhile, since the servants will expect their vails from your hand, and Brockton's will expect you to settle your reckoning with a certain generosity, I enclose a small token toward that end.

If you don't wish to accept it, please use it for charity.

Either way, we need not refer to it again.

I remain, dear madam, your most humble, obedient servant,

Guy Devoran

Sarah picked up the coins. Money was such an improper present for any gentleman to give to a lady that she ought to return it with a stiff note. Yet her hotel bill would use almost the last of her cash, and now she could buy several meals, as well as offer the correct rewards to his servants.

She had asked for Guy Devoran's help. It would be idiotic to faint from hunger before he could give it. And, of course, he had very cleverly offered her a way to save face—*please use it for charity.*

So it was just one more small indignity she must suffer for Rachel's sake.

Yet a masked ball?

Sarah had never attended such an event in her life.

The first grandson of the Duke of Blackdown—that would be Lord Ryderbourne's new baby, who enjoyed the courtesy title of Earl of Wyldshay even in his cradle. The birth had recently been announced in the newspapers.

The thought of Mr. Devoran's being godfather to his cousin's new baby was indeed oddly reassuring.

Concentrating only on that, Sarah washed her face in cold water, stripped off her plain green gown, and donned the blue silk. The fit was tight, but passable. The fabric, obviously, was French.

The shoes, luckily, were a good fit.

The entire costume was probably worth several months of her schoolteacher's salary.

It was not easy without the help of a maid, but she managed to bundle her unruly hair beneath the wig. The little bonnet perched above her left ear like a drunken post boy. Using the small dappled mirror above the fireplace, she tried to adjust it. The sheep—all tied together by a length of ribbon—seemed determined to race off down the powdered ringlets to escape over her shoulder. Which only emphasized that the tight bodice was very close to being indecent.

Sarah tucked the handkerchief into the décolletage. One of the sheep entangled itself in the lace edging. She tried to free it and only caught two more of them.

From the sheer absurdity of it—and as if she must at last release all of her worry in open mockery at herself—she began to laugh. She laughed till she cried.

CARRIAGES lined the street. Music echoed into the night.

Beneath the glow of the gaslights, each fabulous equipage moved, then stopped, then moved again. The procession stretched for several blocks as the most glorious members of the beau monde stepped down into the courtyard to sweep in through the grand entry of Blackdown House.

Sarah stood in the shadows and tried to breathe normally, though a rapid staccato beat in her veins. The tall, burly footman who had been sent to accompany her stood at her elbow.

As Mr. Devoran had planned, she was completely hidden beneath a dark cloak, the one worn by the maid who had arrived as promised at Brockton's Hotel. Should anyone be watching, it would appear that the woman had delivered a message, then left again to rejoin the footman who waited for her in the street.

So Sarah felt physically safe enough, in spite of her harshly beating heart and tingling spine. It wasn't simply the prospect of the ball that was so unnerving, not even one given by a duke. It was the idea of surrendering her quest to Guy Devoran's control without guide or anchor.

In spite of the shepherdess costume, or perhaps because of it, whenever he glanced at her with those intelligent, laughing eyes, he was bound to find her wanting.

She took another deep breath.

Some of London's less respectable citizens had gathered at the gates to watch. The grand mansion sat in its own grounds, as if it had been plucked from the countryside to flaunt its superiority over the neighboring streets. As the town residence of one of the most powerful peers in England, perhaps the Duke of Blackdown's London house had reason to boast. After all, he also owned a castle at Wyldshay in Dorset. The facade and setting were intimidating, precisely because they had been designed that way.

Yet Sarah's headgear required perfect posture, as she demanded from her pupils when she taught them to dance. With a wry appreciation for all of her own childhood lessons in deportment, she stared at the glittering home of one of the most powerful members of the peerage and kept her head high.

Already masked, Neptune and Athene—complete with owl—

passed up the steps. Meanwhile Sir Lancelot and Titania were climbing down from their carriage.

The crowd cheered and called out comments, trying to guess identities. A circle of liveried menservants kept them at bay. Yet every member of the rabble was clutching a mug of ale, a meat pie, and a small purse set with blue ribbons. So another kind of party was taking place in the street.

Sarah Callaway belonged to neither of these worlds. Both the watching crowd and the glittering aristocrats were as foreign to her as the men of Patagonia, who were said—or so her geography book claimed—to be of gigantic size.

As if acknowledging her lack of status, the footman hustled her around to the back of the house. The stable yard was another hubbub of activity. The man winked solemnly as he handed Sarah over to the care of a maid, who rushed her into the house past the frantic preparations in the kitchens, then into a small anteroom.

The maid bobbed a curtsy and left. The noise and commotion stopped instantly once she had closed the double doors behind her.

Sarah stood and waited, feeling very alone.

The room cocooned her in silence.

After a few moments of absolute quiet, she looked about. A painting of a bareheaded knight in full armor hung above the fireplace. She walked over to stare up at it.

A breeze from the edge of the world unsettled the knight's hair and streamed through his mount's mane and tail. An imaginary forest rioted in the background, decorated with flowers and wildly curling leaves. A tall keep, flying the St. George dragon banner, rose from amongst the trees. Beyond them lay the sea.

Emphasized by the severe lines of the man's face, dark, compelling eyes gazed back down at her.

An odd longing seized her soul.

Sarah could almost hear the drag of the surf on the shingle and smell the salt-sweet fragrance of the flowers.

Closer to her heart, she could sense the presence of the man, as if the knight might step down from the painting at any moment to offer her his fealty and his sword arm to defend her from all enemies.

"As a portrait, it's entirely imaginary, of course," a woman's voice said with a hint of humor. "It was painted about ten years ago as a present to the duchess. I doubt that the real Ambrose de Verrant was either so handsome or so romantic. Though he was an ancestor of my husband's—and for quite different reasons my baby is his namesake—the first Ambrose was very probably a bit of a brute."

Sarah spun about.

Swinging a black mask from one hand, a dark-haired lady had entered through a door that had been hidden in the paneling. She was breathtakingly lovely, the kind of beauty that could stun both men and women into silence.

"Welcome to Blackdown House, Mrs. Callaway." The woman walked forward. Her entire being seemed lit from within, as if she carried a lamp in her heart. "I'm Lady Ryderbourne, the wife of the present duke's eldest son, and the proud mother of the next in line to the dukedom. I'm afraid that all of this"—she waved both hands— "is in my baby son's honor, poor little mite, though he's not yet eight weeks old. Meanwhile, I don't know whether you can tell that I'm meant to be Nell Gwyn, since I've set down my oranges somewhere. I can't think where. And now, I imagine, someone's eaten them."

Unable to help herself, Sarah laughed. She felt suddenly light, as if she had just met a long-lost sister, instead of a duke's daughter-in-law.

"Ah, that's better!" the new mother said. Her smile warmed like the sun. "For a moment I thought you were about to turn tail and flee. But any friend of Guy's is a friend of ours, so we really do extend our warmest welcome."

Sarah curtsied. "You're very kind, Lady Ryderbourne, but I met Mr. Devoran for the first time only yesterday. I'm hardly his friend."

"Yet you will be, which comes to the same thing. So you mustn't let any of us daunt you for a moment. If it helps, just remember that I was born in a cottage." Her Ladyship waved the black mask again and laughed. "For all my exalted titles, I'm no doubt a great deal less respectable than you are."

"I don't know if any person can claim total respectability when she's wearing sheep on her head," Sarah said, smiling. "Though I'm doing my very best to herd them with the appropriate aplomb."

Lady Ryderbourne giggled like a schoolgirl. "With a rather marked lack of success, alas! Yet I trust you'll forgive me for both the sheep and that ridiculous little hat? It was all I could throw together at such short notice."

Dismay undermined Sarah's courage for a moment. "Your Ladyship chose this costume?"

"I'm afraid so, though Guy helped. I confess that we found all the bits and pieces in the attics. In the end the sheep were Guy's idea. Never mind! Let me help you to adjust them before they run off into seriously unmentionable places."

Sarah swallowed her astonishment as a future duchess stood on tiptoe to wrap the sheep-laden ribbon securely about her guest's headdress.

"There!" Lady Ryderbourne said. "That should survive a whole night of dancing."

Sarah turned back to face her. "But surely I'm not expected to attend the ball?"

"Why ever not? Though it's a terrible fuss for a baby, isn't it? I've left strict instructions that I'm to be fetched should my little son cry for even an instant, whatever King Charles's fearsome mother may have to say about it."

"King Charles's mother?"

"The Duchess of Blackdown. Of course, she's my own mother now, as well, since I married her eldest son last September." One lovely dark eye closed in a wink. "Her Grace insisted that we must celebrate the resulting child in the grand style, and she's probably right. So my husband is dressed as the Merry Monarch tonight. It's a bit of a joke between us."

"That Nell Gwyn was King Charles's mistress?"

"Ah, more than that! But never mind. The naughty Nell Gwyn may have been closely related to some of my ancestors, and since several members of my husband's family were acknowledged as the natural children of kings, Ryder's very probably dressed as an ancestor, too."

Her merry mood was infectious. "And it's very likely that some of my ancestors were shepherds," Sarah said, "so I suppose we're all dressed appropriately."

Lady Ryderbourne laughed and glanced back up at the painting. "Guy's family is also descended from de Verrant, of course. It appears that the rogue made very free with his favors. Alas, now my poor little baby is the heir to all of it. He's sleeping far above our heads with a dozen nursemaids watching over him, and it's the first time we've been apart this long since he was born."

"I'm so sorry," Sarah said. "If I'd known, I've never have kept you."

"Attending my baby's christening ball is a very tiny price to pay for marrying a duke's son, especially when he's the love of my life. Anyway, I promised Guy to take care of you, and I'm more than happy to do so."

"Mr. Devoran did not wish to meet me privately, before it all starts?"

Lady Ryderbourne tied on her mask. "Good heavens! It's already started, and Guy is as essential to the festivities as the duke and duchess themselves. He's not only my cousin by marriage, but he's also a very old and dear friend. I've known him since I was sixteen. If Guy asks for the moon, we Ryderbournes would cast nets to the heavens to catch it for him."

"I'm overwhelmed," Sarah said simply. "I had no idea—"

"Nonsense! It's our pleasure, and you may trust the honor of each of our men implicitly."

"I don't know very much about the finer points of honor among the peerage."

"Though you were married to a captain who fought at Waterloo, I understand," Lady Ryderbourne said gently. "And that's the most honorable title that there is. Ah, I see that I've spoken out of turn. I'm so sorry."

To her intense embarrassment, tears pricked at Sarah's eyes. Yet it was impossible to resist her hostess's charm, and especially impossible to resist the certain knowledge that Lady Ryderbourne understood a great deal about the human heart.

"Did Mr. Devoran tell you that?"

"Guy thought I ought to know, but we'll say no more about it. Here, let me help you with your mask." Lady Ryderbourne took the slip of blue fabric from Sarah's hand and tied it securely. "You look wonderful—so mysterious and sensual. You have very lovely eyes, Mrs. Callaway."

Sarah blinked away her moment of distress and stared at herself in a wall mirror. The freckle-faced schoolmistress had disappeared. In her place stood an enigmatic, long-necked lady with a witty little hat perched on her silver wig.

"Goodness," she said. "Not even my own cousin would ever guess it was me."

"No one knows who anyone is, which is a big part of the fun." The new mother linked her arm through Sarah's. "Everyone is in costume, except the Duke of Blackdown himself and Wellington—and the king, of course."

"The king is here?"

"Propped on a large chair filled with cushions. As for Blackdown and the Iron Duke, it's too far beneath their ducal dignity to cavort about in fancy dress. The duchess, however, is ruling the roost as Queen Elizabeth. Her Grace is even wearing a breastplate, as Good Queen Bess did when she addressed the troops at Tilbury before the Armada."

"Ah," Sarah said. "One of the most famous speeches in history: 'I know I have but the body of a weak and feeble woman, but I have the heart and stomach of a king—and of a king of England, too—'"

"'—and think foul scorn that Parma or Spain, or any prince of

Europe, should dare to invade the borders of my realm,' " Lady Ryderbourne finished with a flourish. She tapped on the massive double doors. "You may take it that Her Grace's armor is appropriate."

"And Mr. Devoran's?" Sarah asked. "Might he be dressed as that knight?"

"I doubt it. Guy's a wonderful dancer, and who'd want to be escorted by a man who'd be clanking around the ballroom?"

"Then how will I know him?"

"I don't know." Lady Ryderbourne grinned as the footman swung the doors wide. "But since Guy suggested your costume and picked out the sheep, he'll certainly know you."

CHAPTER THREE

GUESTS STREAMED INTO THE BALLROOM, A MASS OF WIGS AND headdresses and costumes. Everyone was masked.

A tall man in a splendid curled wig and red velvet coat immediately walked up to join Sarah and Lady Ryderbourne. Though a black mask hid his face, he could only be Guy Devoran's older cousin, Lord Ryderbourne, heir to the duchy.

Flourishing his plumed hat, he swept both ladies a bow, then he pulled his wife into his arms and kissed her on the mouth.

"A buss for your sweetheart, Nell! What the devil have you done with your oranges?"

"I lost them."

"Which explains why Lady Fallay sat on them and created a small social disaster for Queen Bess. Though Her Grace will forgive you anything, sweetheart, now that you've given her a new Earl of Wyldshay to dandle."

Lady Ryderbourne laughed and reached up to kiss him again. "Which is too great a name for such a tiny baby, sir. Ambrose Laurence Jonathan Devoran St. George is mouthful enough. But this is Sarah Callaway, Ryder: Guy's shepherdess."

Sarah curtsied, but Lord Ryderbourne took her hand and raised it to his lips. His eyes were deep green, like the laughing shadow beneath a wave.

"Of course! Very pleased to meet you, Mrs. Callaway. I see my cousin's wicked sense of humor has been at work, yet I'm most partial to sheep. May I ask for the honor of this next dance?"

It was impossible not to smile. "You're very gracious, my lord, but—"

"No, don't refuse!" Lady Ryderbourne said. "If you don't dance with Ryder, Guy will think we've abandoned you."

"And then he'll call me out. My tragic corpse will be found on Hampstead Heath, and my little son will be left fatherless." He tucked Sarah's hand into his elbow. "I pray you'll not pretend that you cannot dance, ma'am?"

She was trapped, so she smiled again. "I'm delighted to accept, my lord. But I assume this is only part of some devious plot of Mr. Devoran's?"

"Most definitely!" Lord Ryderbourne led her onto the floor. "Guy's a great plotter, but only in the most noble of causes. He first enlisted me to shadow you in St. James's, in case you didn't take the right street and he lost you."

Sarah swallowed the shock. "So you were the gentleman that Mr. Devoran stopped to talk to in front of the wine seller's? I had no idea that either of you had noticed me."

"I hadn't, until Guy pointed you out. After that, you were the unfortunate victim of our conspiracy. I followed you as you tracked him, while Guy lay in wait for you in a bookstore. I trailed you again after that—in the most casual fashion—until you had safely entered your hotel. Enlist one of us, Mrs. Callaway, and a small army is at your disposal. I hope you'll find that more reassuring than intimidating, though we can be an overbearing lot, I'm afraid."

Sarah tried not to let her growing alarm show in her face, for the green eyes seemed to miss nothing.

"We?" she asked lightly.

"My brother, Lord Jonathan. My cousin, Guy Devoran. And myself. Plus any of a select group of gentlemen whom we could call upon at any time, and whose discretion we trust absolutely. If you're in trouble, Mrs. Callaway, you have powerful regiments of aid still held in reserve."

Her heart seemed to be skipping every other beat. "How many of those gentlemen know of my exact predicament, my lord?"

"None," he replied, "including me. Guy said only that you'd be here tonight and need our support. So now that you're reassured that you still retain absolute privacy, are you ready to dance, ma'am? Guy will find you later, but meanwhile these are the best musicians in London."

The lines had already formed for the next set. Further conversation was impossible. Sarah stood between Atalanta in her gauzy purple gown, and a swan in a mask and costume of white feathers. Lord Ryderbourne took his place next to Julius Caesar. The ladies curtsied as the men bowed, and the dance began.

Sarah wove in and out, touching fingers with every gentleman as she passed up the line. Almost every partner took the brief chance to flirt. She did her best to respond graciously, though her thoughts raced like leaves in a millstream.

How much had Guy Devoran really told his cousins? And where was he? He must have had some purpose in inviting her here tonight. Whenever the movements of the dance allowed, she glanced about the room, hoping somehow to recognize him among all the centurions and knights and monks.

There was no sign of him.

When the set was over, Lady Ryderbourne introduced her to several more partners. As Sarah was led onto the floor for the second time, a footman approached. Nell Gwyn listened to the man for a moment, then whispered in her husband's ear—obviously the baby wanted his mother. Lord Ryderbourne glanced at Sarah and signed an apology.

Sarah nodded her understanding. The new parents linked arms and walked away.

King Charles's plumed hat briefly touched his wife's shoulder as he bent his head down to listen to something she said—such a simple gesture of intimacy that made all the glitter of the ballroom irrelevant.

Sarah spun back to face the dance floor as some deep place in her heart filled with poignancy. She would never again know the warmth of her marriage, the comfort of touching and being touched with respect and caring, the moments of shared humor and gentleness. And children! She and Captain Callaway had never seized their chance to have a baby, and then his final illness had robbed them both of his life.

She shook herself and smiled as a masked gentleman in monk's robes bowed for the next dance. No one except Lord and Lady Ryderbourne—and Guy Devoran himself, of course—could possibly know who she was. Perhaps somewhere in this sophisticated crowd was the very man who was responsible for Rachel's disappearance.

That was one among many compelling reasons for enlisting Guy Devoran's help. How else could a schoolteacher from Bath mingle so freely with the nobility of England?

Meanwhile, the sense of frivolity was infectious. Not only the dizziness of the dancing itself, but the idea that the St. Georges of Wyldshay had taken her under their protection, for at least this one night.

By the time supper was announced, Sarah had danced almost every measure. She escaped her last partner—a rather dull Alfred the Great—and dodged beneath some palm fronds at the side of the room to catch her breath. Her blood ran hot in her veins.

Laughing and talking, the crowd moved past her toward the supper tables. She tried to study each man as he passed, though she had no idea what to look for. Could guilt be betrayed by posture or gait? Even without the masks, she might see the villain and not know it.

"There's quite a jungle a little farther through here, Mrs. Callaway," a male voice whispered in her ear. "Would you like to explore it?"

Sarah whirled around. A tall man in a crimson mask and silk

turban had silently walked up to stand beside her. His Oriental robes were flamboyantly embroidered with dragons.

Uncertainty fractured her perception for a moment, as if she were thrust suddenly into a fantasy. Her heart had leaped in a shock of recognition at his expressive mouth and the hint of perfect profile, yet the gilt-brown gaze was most definitely not Mr. Devoran's.

This man's eyes were filled with a similar humor and bright intelligence, yet she thought that grim determination—even something of anger—also lurked just beneath the surface.

Sarah smiled with blind courage. "Do I know you, sir?"

"Lord Jonathan Devoran St. George, at your service, ma'am." He bowed his head. "Guy asked me to take care of you, should Ryder be otherwise occupied. Come! You'll like this."

Ah! Lord Ryderbourne's younger brother, Wild Lord Jack, who had recently returned to England from India. Mr. Devoran must have told him, too, about the sheep. Yet Lord Jonathan enjoyed an oddly terrifying reputation in the popular accounts of his adventures in the East.

Sarah dismissed her stab of apprehension and took his proffered arm.

They ducked together beneath the palm fronds and through a concealed doorway. Trees and vines clustered, some trailing long sprays of blossom, their roots bound in enormous clay pots. The floor disappeared beneath a thick layer of tanbark. Far above their heads, night scattered dark reflections between the stone ribs of a glasshouse.

The music faded as her escort led Sarah ever deeper into the rustling jade silence.

They stepped out into a small open space, dimly lit by a scattering of paper lanterns. A moist eddy carried earthy, flowery scents, with a strange undercurrent of danger, like air stirred by dragon's wings.

Lord Jonathan released her arm, stepped away, and slipped off his crimson mask.

"Well, Mrs. Callaway," he said. "How do you like our little domestic jungle?"

Her heart beat hard. Orchids she had never seen before nestled among the other plants.

"It's amazing," she said. "Yet I wonder if a real jungle is anything like this."

"No, it's not." His eyes studied her as if he would peel away her skin. "This fantasy is missing the darker scents, the secrets—and the tigers, of course. The real jungle is neither so pretty, nor so tame."

Prickles danced down her spine as she looked back at him. "It doesn't feel particularly tame to me. It feels quite real, though the water must be piped in from somewhere."

He laughed, though he still seemed on edge. "What a very practical mind you have, Mrs. Callaway! You must be a bluestocking."

A sudden splashing started somewhere nearby, as if someone had just turned on a fountain. Sarah's unsteady pulse skipped a beat.

"We're not alone here, my lord," she said quietly.

"No, but you're quite safe with me, Mrs. Callaway."

Lord Jonathan took her arm again to lead her deeper into the trees. The splash of falling water grew louder.

"So what did you think of Miracle?"

"Miracle?"

"Lady Ryderbourne. Nell Gwyn. Ryder's wife. Miracle is her given name."

"I think it's impossible to resist her."

"Ah! Though fortunately I did. She was sixteen when we first met, but she was magical even then."

"Then you and Mr. Devoran met her at about the same time?"

"Yes, but that was a long time ago, many years before she met Ryder. What counts is that Miracle is among the most honest, compassionate, and courageous of ladies. I'm honored to call her my sister." Lord Jonathan stopped to pluck a blossom. Fragrant white petals offset the golden-yellow heart—*Coelogyne cristata*, the combed coelogyne. Sarah had only ever seen it before in prints. "We all agree that white flowers spring in her footsteps, like Olwen."

"Olwen White Track? The fairy tale—?"

"Beautiful, is it not?" His intense gaze fixed on her face as he twirled the orchid in his fingers. "Yet this plant's a parasite, I believe."

Her sense of threat deepened, as if suspicion or dread underlay every casual comment. Perhaps all those lurid accounts about this powerful aristocrat were true?

"That's not a parasite, my lord," she said. "It's an orchid. It feeds mostly on air."

"The host plant isn't harmed?"

"No, not at all."

"Then I'm very glad to hear it. I hate to think that something so apparently fragile might be dangerous."

"Dangerous?" another man's voice asked with a distinct note of humor.

Sarah spun about as if she were cleaved to the heart.

One booted foot propped on a fern-covered stump, his crossed forearms resting on that taut thigh, a masked corsair lounged beneath a riotously flowering vine. A live parrot sat on his shoulder.

A wave of heat spread down Sarah's spine, tingling into every limb, as if her veins melted beneath the onslaught.

"Mr. Devoran!" She swallowed hard and bobbed a small curtsy.

His open-necked shirt offered shocking glimpses of a powerful male throat and chest, smooth and perilous. A scarlet belt beset with daggers and pistols emphasized his trim waist.

The parrot flew off to perch on a branch several feet away, where it began to preen its feathers.

Guy Devoran stripped off his black mask and bowed. "Good evening, Mrs. Callaway." His eyes held a wild glint, as if he often spoke with angels or demons. "I see you've just had the misfortune to meet my other cousin, Wild Lord Jack. I trust the experience was entertaining, at least?"

Lord Jonathan laughed. The family resemblance was striking,

both in bone structure and intensity—and in that perilous intelligence.

"Yes, indeed." Though she was floundering to understand the strange undercurrents, a little rush of rage straightened her spine. "His Lordship was kind enough to show me a glimpse of the tigers in the jungle."

Lord Jonathan raised a brow. "That was hardly my intention, ma'am."

"Oh, I think that it was, my lord. After all, they say that you can transform yourself into a tiger to kill with one blow."

"Good God!" Lord Jonathan laughed with real gaiety. "Do they?"

Her apprehension and anger almost evaporated. Perhaps her nerves were so frayed that she read menace into everything?

"You're a romantic figure in the penny circulars, my lord. Stories about the St. Georges provide plenty of entertainment for the masses."

"Then may I reassure you, Mrs. Callaway," Lord Jonathan said. "There are no tigers here. Even the canaries are caged. See! Up there!"

Sarah glanced up. Gilt cages swung from the ceiling. A soft twittering trickled through the quiet, then several birds broke into song.

Yet for a split second as she first looked up, Guy Devoran had met his cousin's gaze. Energy sizzled between the two men, as if they shared some terrible, silent dread—and tigers stalked the room as clearly as if they truly gazed out from the greenery.

Sarah sat down on the stump. Her pulse pounded, alarm roaring in flood.

"The birds are charming," she said. "Yet I fear that you haven't yet had a chance to exchange family news with your cousin, Lord Jonathan. I'd be quite content to rest here for a moment."

"Then if you would kindly excuse us, Mrs. Callaway?" Guy Devoran said. "Jack?"

The two men strode away and stopped to talk at the edge of the trees. Cloaked in green darkness, they glanced back at her once. Without question, some gathering peril had become too strong to ignore.

Sarah took a deep breath. Alien orchids bloomed all around her. Tantalizing scents wavered on the moist air. Water droplets fell from mysterious leaves to patter onto her face.

Yet her ears burned, though the noise of falling water drowned every word of that intense conversation. How could she possibly understand these aristocrats? Men with such casual power—but with all that restless energy dedicated, perhaps, only to hedonism?

It had been only ten years since the first exotic orchid had been induced to bloom in England. Since then the decadent plants had become a craze, each new import commanding vast sums at auction.

She glanced back at the men. Concentration and concern stamped each handsome face. Any idea that they were dedicated only to pleasure fled instantly.

Yet they strolled over to rejoin her at last with no obvious sense of urgency.

Sarah stood up, her heart in her mouth, as Lord Jonathan bowed over her hand.

He laughed up at her as if he had never known anything but merriment. "I regret that I cannot further our acquaintance, Mrs. Callaway. My wife, Anne, will bear our first child very soon, so I return home immediately. However, you'll be in equally safe hands with my cousin."

"Thank you, Jack," Guy Devoran commented dryly. "After all that talk of tigers, I'm sure that your personal recommendation will go a long way with Mrs. Callaway."

"I'm honestly not concerned for my safety," Sarah said.

"Then the only question that remains, ma'am," Wild Lord Jack replied, "is whether Guy is safe with you."

The dragon robes rippled as he strode away through the trees.

Mr. Devoran leaned one shoulder against a stone pillar. The parrot flashed back to clutch its feet onto his shirt.

Its bright yellow eyes surveyed Sarah. "Safe with who? Safe with who?"

Guy Devoran laughed and walked the parrot down his arm onto his fist.

"There's no distressing family news, I hope," Sarah said.

"You're kind to ask, but no, not at all, though Jack and I were glad to catch up. Thank you for allowing us the chance."

"Yet I thought—"

"No," he said. "Come, ma'am! I must adjust that loud fountain."

He carried the bird away. Her mouth dry, Sarah followed.

They brushed past some trees into an inner court. Falling water shimmered in the glow of a handful of lanterns. No one else was about.

His shirtsleeves stretched over taut muscles as Mr. Devoran thrust the bird into a cage on a stand, then bent to adjust a valve hidden behind some greenery. The water subsided into a quiet ripple.

"You turned on this fountain to hide your voices?" she asked.

He glanced up. "As a signal to Jack that I'd arrived, that's all. The guests won't wander in here until they've all eaten supper. Then several couples will take advantage of the seclusion to indulge in a little naughtiness with other people's spouses. Are you hungry?"

"Only for some truth," she said. "I don't really like being played with."

"Played with?"

"There's something important that you're not telling me, Mr. Devoran. Was Lord Jonathan truly concerned about my intentions? Did he take me in dislike?"

He dropped a green cloth over the parrot's cage. "Not at all, though Jack certainly wondered if you might not be another orchid."

"Difficult, dependent, and out of place?" She smiled, though her heart felt raw. "Not many of these plants will survive here, will they?"

"Torn as they are from their natural habitat? Probably not." He gazed at a cattleya orchid, then glanced back at her. "But perhaps Jack only meant that you're exotic, lush, and enticingly sensual?"

Surprise shocked her into laughter. "Good heavens! Is that why he asked me if orchids are parasitic?"

Mr. Devoran plucked a hanging blossom and touched her cheek with the cool petals. Transfixed, Sarah gazed up at him, her pulse hammering. She was painfully—absurdly—aware of the beauty of his mouth: the perfect white teeth and firm, expressive lips.

"You truly have no idea of your real effect on men, do you, Mrs. Callaway?"

He trailed the flower past the curve of her ear to stroke beneath her jaw. The petals lay soft and moist against her throat.

She swallowed. "Goodness knows, sir, I'm more like a weed suddenly sprouting between beautifully laid flagstones than anything very exotic. And I'm indeed taking advantage of your goodwill. I cannot deny that. Is that what so bothered Lord Jonathan?"

He tossed the flower aside and turned away. "Never mind. You must be starving. Come!"

She followed him past more citrus trees. A flight of stairs soared away from a dim hallway. His boots thudded into an absolute silence as he led her up several flights, then flung open another door that accessed an elegant little parlor.

A selection of sofas and chairs, picked out in gilt. A new Axminster carpet. Dried flowers filling the marble grate. Four towering blue-and-white vases, which no doubt had once belonged to the fabled emperors of China. A table laden with covered dishes.

Guy Devoran strode up to the table and lifted a silver lid. The scents of mushrooms, warm cream, and savory herbs snaked their way across the room.

Her mouth watered, yet she felt filled with apprehension, as if the very walls concealed secrets.

"My cousin Jack is rather fiercely protective, Mrs. Callaway, as you may have gathered. I hope he did not really discompose you?"

He removed another lid. Turmeric and cumin and coriander: creamed, curried chicken?

Doing her best to ignore the aromatic fragrances, Sarah remained standing just inside the door.

"Protective? Of whom?"

"Of his family, of course. He and I were boys together. We're the same age, and notoriously look very much alike. Yet Jack's experienced more real peril than an average man sees in a lifetime, and his sense of danger is particularly acute."

"Lord Jonathan really thinks that I might be dangerous to you in some way?"

He glanced around and grinned. "Aren't you?"

"Only if the lamb is a danger to the wolves."

He laughed. "If you can trust me, you can trust my cousins, but Jack's heart is very far off at the moment. He's deeply in love with Anne and can't bear to be away from her. Yet he also loves his brother and Miracle, and the duchess required his presence here tonight."

"Because he's also a godfather to the new baby?"

Another cover lifted to release the aroma of minted lamb and saffron rice.

"Exactly. However, if he truly made you uncomfortable, I must apologize on his behalf."

The next dish revealed cakes slathered in rum sauce, and cream pastries with candied violets. Sarah swallowed the saliva that was flooding her tongue.

"No," she said. "Of course not. Please don't! I'm sure my presence was of very little import to him."

Her combined discomfort and restlessness forced her to walk across the room. A strange woman in a powdered wig moved with her in the mirror above the empty grate: a disguise that was obviously redundant now.

She reached up to untie her blue mask. The strings immediately caught in the flock of little sheep, threatening to dislodge the entire headdress.

Mr. Guy Devoran's reflection froze in place, his dark gaze burning with unsettling intensity over her uplifted arms and bent neck.

A tiny runnel of heat crept up her spine.

She was alone in a private room with a man other than her husband for the first time since Captain Callaway had died. An extremely attractive young man dressed in nothing but an open-necked shirt and buckskin breeches, with a black bandanna wrapped rakishly about his hair.

A man who had used the petals of an orchid to touch her face.

Suppressing that shimmer of awareness, Sarah dropped her hands. Several sheep slipped down onto her shoulder. She grabbed at them.

Guy Devoran crossed his arms and smiled at her.

"Then I must at least apologize for those damnable sheep," he said. "It was important that Ryder and Jack recognize you, and there were several shepherdesses here tonight. Otherwise I'd never have picked such a mad costume."

"I really didn't mind," she said, though she thought suddenly that perhaps she did mind, a great deal. "I'd already surmised as much."

She turned her back and struggled again to disentangle the mask.

"Jack's integrity is absolute, and he might have noticed something relevant. After all, he also met your cousin once."

Sarah jerked around to face him. To her mortification, wig, hat, and sheep all slipped a little over one eye. She was forced to put up both hands to steady them.

"But that was a year ago and only very briefly!"

"Nevertheless, he agrees that I must rescue her—though first I'd better rescue you." Guy Devoran grinned as he strode up to her. "I don't think you can salvage that unspeakable headdress. Fortunately, you don't need it any longer."

In one smooth movement he lifted away her silver wig. Some stray pins immediately caught in Sarah's hair, threatening to tug the heavy mass into a miserable entanglement about her shoulders.

She glanced up—and felt as if she'd been unexpectedly caught in a net.

Guy Devoran stood locked in place, looking down at her. A tiny spasm tightened the muscles around his mouth, almost as if he'd received a small blow.

The silence sang, humming like a thin wire vibrating just beyond the range of her hearing.

For the length of a heartbeat they stared at each other, while streamers of heat unfurled in her veins.

Thick lashes rimmed his eyes. Each iris was a perfect dark chocolate, rimmed in the thinnest of black circles. His gaze smoldered—burning with power, and passion, and some dark, wicked knowledge—as if he were willingly consumed for her, as if his very soul were abandoned to desire.

No man had ever looked at her like this, as if he would burn directly into her heart to plumb straight into those confused depths.

Sarah spun away, flushed with the knowledge that her frail skin had already betrayed her.

Her fingers fumbled as she disentangled the remaining pins and set the headdress on a nearby chair.

"Thank you, sir," she said.

Mr. Devoran strode away. For a moment he stood with his back to her, but then he tore the bandanna from his head and laughed.

"I no longer need my disguise either," he said. "You've no idea how absurd I feel dressed up as Sinbad the Sailor." He stripped off his red belt and tossed it onto a side table. The pistols and knives clunked. "With weapons made of wood, no less."

Sarah pinned her wayward hair firmly back into place. "Plus a parrot."

He turned and smiled as if nothing were wrong. "Yes, I thought you'd like Eight."

"Eight?"

"Pieces of Eight—the parrot. That's how high he can count, as well, but he's also a very good watchdog."

"You thought you needed a watchdog?"

He removed another silver lid and lifted out a decanter of wine. Rivulets ran down over the cold surface.

"Eight would have screeched like a banshee if any stranger had approached us. However, you were safely in the company of Ali Baba, a member of his family, and he's known all of us since we were boys."

"So nothing as simple as a costume would have fooled him for a moment?"

"A parrot's a natural companion for any wicked set of rogues." He filled two wineglasses and held one out to her. She thanked him and took it. "Though I'd trust no one better, my cousins can try anyone's patience. It's fortunate that Miracle and Anne have tamed them as much as they have."

"Can duke's sons be tamed by their wives?"

He laughed. "That depends on what you believe needs taming." He gestured to the table. "But now perhaps I may make amends for all the outrages you have suffered by suggesting that you try some of these delicacies before you faint away from either hunger, a well-directed derision, or righteous indignation."

The wine was deliciously cool. Savory aromas saturated her nostrils. Yet any desire for food had disappeared. Sarah's heart was still beating too fast, as if he led her ever deeper into a mysterious forest where at any turn she might be suddenly lost. He had neatly avoided her real question about the parrot, and she felt almost as if she was being—with great subtlety—tested in some way.

"My indignation began hours ago," she said lightly. "When you first sent that footman to fetch me here."

"I trust Paul didn't offer you any real insult? If he did, I'll have his hide."

"Your man certainly demonstrated a most improper level of familiarity, Mr. Devoran. He insisted on wrapping his arm about my waist as if we were a courting couple."

His mouth twitched again, but he frowned with mock gravity. "The duchess's footman—and he was obeying Miracle's orders, not mine. It's well known that Paul is stepping out with Rose, the maid who's now waiting so patiently in your room at Brockton's. Miracle no doubt gave strict instructions: If you were to pass as Paul's sweetheart on your journey back here, you and he had better behave accordingly. None of the Blackdown staff would ever disobey Miracle, principally because they worship the very ground that she walks on."

"The ground that springs into blossom as she passes? Like Olwen White Track?"

"Jack mentioned that?" His eyes darkened as he glanced back at her. "You're familiar with the ancient tales, Mrs. Callaway?"

"This one, certainly! The hero Culhwch fell in love with Olwen's beauty, but her father refused them permission to marry, unless the hero could perform a series of seemingly impossible tasks involving a great many magical creatures—"

"The untamable hound!" He grinned and saluted her with his glass.

Chin high, she returned the gesture. "The boar of fierce bristles—"

"Kings turned into beasts!"

"A giant with a sword—"

"And a hag of terrible aspect!"

"At which point, Culhwch had to enlist the whole of King Arthur's army!"

Deep creases marked his cheeks as he laughed aloud. Sarah stared at him, breathless, as if caught again in that magical net where wonders might soon be laid in her lap.

Yet he turned away with studied casualness. "And thus we learn that not even a hero can win his lady too easily."

"Obviously not!" She gulped down her mad emotions and took a deep breath. "Or not in the face of such dreadful opposition—"

"Because the heart of such stories is always that true love is almost impossible to win." He began to fill a plate with food for her.

"Or at the very least that it can only be found by fighting through a thicket of obstacles."

"I don't know. Surely love isn't a battle? Anyway, Olwen was really only a goddess of flowers—"

"No, she was a woman in love." He glanced up, apparently deadly serious. "Why else would she sow a path of white petals as she walked?"

"I don't know." Her stomach contracted into a knot of trepidation in the face of his intensity. "I don't know what you mean."

"Never mind! These particular tales are damnably obscure. How did you ever come across them?"

She clutched the stem of her wineglass as if it were a talisman. "When I was a girl, I did nothing much else but read. I had access to a wonderful library."

He gazed a little ruefully at the feast on the table. "Then you must know that in Arthur's court no one may embark upon the banquet until some miracle has been performed."

Sarah stared at his cleanly boned hands, lovely and lean, as he set the plate back down.

"What kind of miracle does it take?"

"I've no idea." He smiled and stepped closer. "I only know that I'm starving—and that one wayward sheep is still caught in your hair. Stand still!"

His fingers smoothed past her ear. Hot awareness flooded. Her pulse launched into its wild race, that deafening, hot surge of desire in the blood. Every strand of red hair leaped into vibrancy.

His throat ran cool and strong to mesh smoothly with the flexing muscles of neck and chest. The shadow of fleeting dimples still marked his cheeks.

Yet his gaze was shuttered, the fire banked, as if he felt nothing but this careful courtesy.

Far more than she had ever wanted any man, Sarah wanted Guy Devoran. His intelligence. His company. But most of all his lean, virile body and clever mouth, his lovely hands and wicked tongue.

She wanted to know him as a wife knew a husband. No, more than that! As a mistress knew a lover—

A long-buried fear crashed through her defenses. However heady, it was madness to allow such feelings. Young gentlemen had never been serious in their attentions toward her. That kind of interest had always only been Rachel's—

The wineglass slipped from Sarah's fingers and toppled, spreading glistening chaos over the supper table.

"My cousin! I'm only here because of Rachel!"

Face hot with embarrassment, she grabbed a napkin and tried frantically to mop up the mess.

As if burned, Guy Devoran strode away to the fireplace, then whirled about. "Leave that, please! You're not a maid who must clean up spilled wine."

Sarah dropped the cloth and faced him. "No! When my mother died, Rachel's parents raised me as if I were their own child. I owe the Mansards everything. But now that their orphaned daughter so desperately needs my help, I dance away the evening, while you—"

"Go on, Mrs. Callaway!"

Her anger sustained her, though she felt almost faint. "There's no reason for us to discuss the romantic tales. They were *my* secret passion. Rachel was never interested in them. Nothing about Olwen and Culhwch will help us to find her. What's really going on here, Mr. Devoran? Are you testing me in some way? Do you still doubt my honesty, or—"

"God, no! It's not that!"

"Then what are you hiding—you and Lord Jonathan? Why did you think you needed a parrot to play watchdog? Why bring me up here to this private room? What do you dread telling me, sir? That you won't help me, after all? That—"

"No!" He paced to the window. "I wished only to set you more at ease, so that you would trust me a little further."

"Trust you with what, sir? With my integrity? So that I should forget why I came here? And thus allow us both to overlook my awkward pleas on Rachel's behalf? I recognize that I had no right to demand your assistance and I'm sure that you don't—"

His fist struck the folded wooden shutter, making it boom. Her blood thinned into water.

He spun around, his gaze stark. "You must have far more faith in me than this, ma'am, if I'm to continue to search for your cousin."

Goose bumps rose on her arms. "You've *already* tried to find her?"

"How do you think I spent most of yesterday? Why do you suppose I was so late arriving here tonight, and thus had to enlist Ryder and Jack? I've done nothing but hunt for Rachel Mansard since you left me in the bookshop. I thought you'd have surmised as much."

Fear clenched in her stomach. "And you've discovered something terrible?"

"No! God! Nothing to immediately alarm you, or I should have broken the news right away." He strode back across the room as if demons nipped at his boot heels. "I have every reason to believe that Miss Mansard is perfectly safe. She certainly wasn't abducted. So, yes, perhaps I have been testing you. Why not? Why should I accept the unproven word of a stranger? However, you may rest assured that I'm absolutely convinced now of your honesty."

"So you have been hiding something?"

His gaze might devour shadows. "I simply hesitated to tell you how many of your assumptions about your cousin are misplaced."

The implications broke and scattered in her mind. "You mean to suggest that Rachel ran away voluntarily? Or even . . . *eloped*? That's impossible! Why would you even suggest such a thing? She feared and hated this admirer!"

"I strongly suspect that the man she described doesn't even exist."

"You think she was lying to me?"

He stopped again at the fireplace. Dried flowers shredded in his fingers to rain into the cold grate. "Devil take it, but I know of no way to soften this!"

"I remember," Sarah replied with rigid determination, "when Rachel and I were caught outside once in a summer squall. Black clouds ripped suddenly across the blue sky. Our picnic baskets bowled away. Our dresses flapped liked flags as we tried to hold on to our bonnets—until hail obliterated all of our gaiety. That's how I feel right now, as if I were drenched once again in that icy downpour. You don't need to spare my sensibilities, sir. I'm a widow in my mid-twenties. Please, tell me the truth!"

His eyes darkened, as if Oberon, too, had just seen his bright kingdom swept away in a gale.

"Then pray sit down, ma'am! I don't believe that Miss Rachel Mansard is in any direct danger at the moment, but neither is she quite what you think."

CHAPTER FOUR

❧

SHE DROPPED ONTO A SOFA AS IF HE HAD CUFFED HER, YET SHE looked up at him with unbending courage.

"In what way, sir? I think I can claim to know my own cousin. Please, tell me exactly what you believe you've discovered."

Guy paced back to the window. "Even if that might require me to tread the uncomfortable path between deception and unkindness?"

"I need to hear everything, sir, whether or not you believe it is kind."

His veins thrummed with the triumphant intensity of hot male blood. He had touched her three times. The first through the medium of the orchid petals. The second just to remove her headdress. The third to allow his fingertips to caress her hot, naked skin and bright hair.

He had needed to distract her before she stumbled too close to certain truths, but she had responded as a cat responds to the sun: torn between basking and seeking the cool of the dark, acutely tuned to sensation.

Yet something about Sarah Callaway disturbed him far more deeply than that sensual recognition.

Reflections wavered on the glass as if myriad candles floated outside in the darkness. Dancing, counterfeit flames. He would not lie to her, but he most certainly could not tell her the whole truth, even though he needed every scrap of information she could give him. It was going to be like walking a tightrope.

"Very well." He turned to face her. "I'm afraid your cousin's letters have been misleading you for most of the last eighteen months."

"But that's nonsense! Rachel and I have always shared everything."

"Do you really want the truth, ma'am?"

She flushed. "Yes, of course. I'm sorry. Please, go on!"

"Then let's begin at the beginning," he said, "on the yacht on that spring day last year. She wrote that she was still a governess at the time?"

"Yes, for Lord Grail. He'd just returned from a visit to France. That's why Rachel and the children and Lady Grail were staying in Dorset, and not in town as they had the previous May. A friend of the family found her the position right after Mr. and Mrs. Mansard died."

"Which would have been in the April of 1827—a little over a year before I met her?"

Wariness darkened her eyes, though that had been simple enough for him to discover.

"Yes. I was most relieved that she had found such a good place. Why?"

"Her parents' death left your cousin in reduced circumstances, I take it?"

"There were unexpected debts." The apricot brows drew together in a small frown. "Yet once Rachel had recovered from the shock, she wrote the most amusing letters about Lord Grail's household, letters full of wry observations—"

"And falsehoods, I'm afraid."

Indignation marked her cheeks with a quick flush of color. "In what way? She wrote to me from Grail Hall all that summer. And though I'm sure that she in fact spent a miserable, cold Christmas, she made it all sound most amusing. It's a huge old house—"

"Yes," he said. "I've been there."

"Then you'll understand why Rachel was beyond glad when the family removed back to town the following spring. Perhaps she embroidered things a little to make her letters more interesting, but how could you possibly know?"

Guy strode across the carpet to take the seat opposite hers. He leaned forward, hands clasped in front of him, forearms braced on his thighs, as if he could convince her by sheer force of will.

"Because, although she may have told you that she worked for him for the best part of a year, your cousin left the earl's employment after only seven months."

The flush in her cheeks flamed to scarlet, then died as if a red lantern had been extinguished. "No, that can't be true!"

He watched her carefully, as if he still needed to prove to himself that she was absolutely honest. Rachel had always lived like a queen bee in a hive full of lies.

"The truth is a mansion of many rooms," he said gently. "We don't need to open every door, but—"

"Is the path between deception and cruelty proving so much more bitter than you feared, sir?" she interrupted defiantly. "Please, explain how you know all this!"

"Grail's a member of my club. It never occurred to me before to interrogate him about his children's governess. Why would it? However, he was perfectly straightforward when asked. Yes, he employed Miss Rachel Mansard after her parents died. She was wonderful with the children, the best governess he'd ever had. But she walked out without warning just before that Christmas—a good five months before Jack asked her to accompany me on the yacht."

The freckles stood out harshly against her white skin. "Five months? So how was she living all that time? Had she found another position and not told me? I don't understand. If she was not employed by Lord Grail, what was she doing when Lord Jonathan met her?"

He wanted rather badly to offer her some physical comfort. The mad thought uncurled that he could sweep away all of her distress if he kissed her. But there was no viable way to sugarcoat the truth, and perhaps he already respected her enough not to try.

"I'm afraid that—far from being employed as a governess—your cousin was presiding over a bucket."

"A bucket?" she repeated blankly.

"An instrument used to wash floors. Jack found her in the kitchen of an inn called the Three Barrels not far from the docks. Though a decent enough place, it was not the most highly regarded in town. Your cousin was working there as a common scullery maid, Mrs. Callaway."

"But that's incredible!" Her hands closed into fists. "Why would Rachel do such a thing?"

He picked his words carefully, making sure that each one was exactly, literally true.

"As I already told you, we barely exchanged two words that day. Your cousin didn't confide in me, nor tell me why she'd chosen such an unfortunate occupation."

She turned her head to stare at the stone urn, rooted now in its drift of broken petals. Shadows settled in the poignant, vulnerable hollow where her throat met the curve of her jaw.

"But she wrote that you made her laugh."

"Perhaps I did. But only because Jack—through me—paid her enough to live in style without any responsibilities for the next several months. It was obvious that your cousin would have been in desperate straits otherwise."

Her eyes became suspiciously bright. In a flurry of blue silk she stood up and walked away.

"And Lord Jonathan would confirm everything that you've told me?"

Guy rose to his feet and strode back to the table to refill his wineglass.

"Not what happened on the yacht. He wasn't there. But he can certainly confirm how he first found Rachel Wren."

She stopped at the window, a silhouette against the London night. "Then there must be some misunderstanding, that's all."

"What exactly do you question, Mrs. Callaway?" he asked. "Lord Grail's word? Jack's? Mine?"

She rubbed one hand over the shutter, as if to remove the invisible impact of his fist. A few strands of haphazardly pinned copper hair had escaped to trail over one blue silk shoulder and straggle down to the curve of her waist.

"Even if Rachel did deceive me about those five months," she said, "do you also suggest that all of her letters since then have been lies?"

"I don't know," he said. "I've not read them."

"No, it's impossible!" She spun about. "The very idea is ridiculous!"

Guy swallowed wine. "Then you think I am lying, Mrs. Callaway?"

"No! I don't know! I don't know what to believe—and perhaps I misunderstood about her still being with Lord Grail—but Rachel would *never* have worked as a scullery maid. Not for five months. Not even for a day. What did her hands look like?"

Genuinely taken aback, he glanced up from his glass. "Her hands?"

"Yes, her hands!" She stalked back across the room, her skirts flowing like water. "Were they red and chapped? Sore? Clumsy? Like the hands of a female who was used to scrubbing floors?"

"I don't know." He closed his eyes for a moment as he tried to remember. *Rachel, mysterious, defiant—and lovely enough to blot out the sun.* "She was wearing gloves."

"Then was she distressed? Upset? Surely you can recall every detail of her appearance, Mr. Devoran? Gentlemen always do."

He set down his glass. How very neatly she had unwittingly confronted him with the heart of his dishonor!

"Your cousin's charms are difficult for any gentleman to ignore," he said with stark honesty. "However, she spent that whole day standing alone in the bow, gazing out across the whitecaps toward France. If I had been forced to guess at her state of mind, I'd have said that she was more relieved than upset."

"Relieved? About what?"

"Presumably because she knew I'd be rewarding her in gold for her time. As soon as Jack and Anne were safely away, I delivered your cousin back to shore, where she caught the next coach to London."

"Exactly!" Her eyes shone. "Where that agency had found her new employment with Mr. Penland in Hampstead."

"I doubt it," he said. "No ladies' employment agency in town knows of a widower with six children with any such name."

Sarah sank back onto a chair. "But Rachel received all of my letters at his address—and replied to them—throughout almost the whole of last year. The nursery was upstairs, near the roof. In February it was hard to heat, and the children—two boys and four girls—shivered as hoarfrost flowered on the windows. I remember that particularly, because Rachel wrote later that Jack Frost only mimicked the ice in her heart, for that's when she began to be afraid of her persecutor. She cannot have made up all of that!"

At the moment he'd rather be anywhere than in this room with Sarah Callaway. Rachel had certainly seen ice on the windows in Hampstead in February, but not in Mr. Penland's nursery.

"Why not?" he asked. "We've already established that your cousin dissembles."

"No!" she said. "Whatever Rachel was doing in the five months before she met you, she couldn't have invented those six children, nor the man she met after Christmas. Her emotions about that were far too real."

"Which emotions?"

"When she almost fell in love," she said. "When her admiration turned to loathing. When he began to terrify her."

His gut contracted as if he'd been punched. The metaphorical rooms in that elaborate mansion of truth echoed and boomed as he slammed closed every last door, but one.

"Nevertheless," he said, "your cousin was not abducted."

Her fists clenched as if she would strike him. "I still don't see how you can be sure of that!"

Exasperation burned in his blood and set him pacing the room. Almost as if convincing her of this would solve everything, when he knew it was only the first turn of a terrible labyrinth.

"If I weren't absolutely certain of everything I'm telling you, Mrs. Callaway, I'd never burden you with such uncomfortable facts. Your cousin lied to you last year about continuing to work for Grail. I strongly suspect that this Penland and his six children don't exist. But either way, Rachel Mansard just left London voluntarily."

"No." Her skin had become chalky, insubstantial, as if she were fading into a phantom with bright, burning eyes. "I don't believe it. After writing as she did, she'd never have abandoned me like this without a word. No! Something terrible is going on, and I cannot fathom what it is."

Guy strode back to the table where he refilled his glass, with brandy this time. His throat felt as if that February hoarfrost still lingered there.

"There are advantages to being Blackdown's nephew. It wasn't hard to get information out of her landlord, her maid, the neighbors who'd noticed such a lovely young lady living in their midst. Your cousin settled her accounts, packed her valuables, and walked to an inn, where she took the night coach to Salisbury. No one accompanied her, nor forced her."

A little shudder passed over her shoulders, as if an undertow of pain dragged through her blood.

"Then I must thank you for your help, Mr. Devoran. Since I'm not related to a duke, no one would give me that information." Her voice was tight, almost prim. "Thus I'm sorry if I wasted your time with my foolish concerns. Yet you've equally wasted mine by not telling me the truth straightaway. I can hardly comprehend why you didn't do so. I think I must return to Brockton's—"

His glass shattered like hailstones among the dried flowers in the fireplace, soaking them.

Fiery color flooded back into her cheeks.

"I said that your cousin left town of her own free will, Mrs. Callaway," he said. "I did not say that her reasons weren't desperate, or—since she slipped away so secretly—that she might not still be in some kind of trouble. Rest assured that whatever uncomfortable truths may emerge, I shan't abandon either you or your cousin. I give you my word on that."

The copper hair shimmered as she stumbled to her feet. "No! All of this was a huge mistake. I regret that I ever involved you. I must have been mad. Why didn't you tell me the truth—about the bucket and the inn, at least—when we first met in the bookshop?"

"Why the devil should I? It was neither the time nor the place—"

"No, I suppose not." Tears broke and fell at last, staining her eyelids. Her nostrils and mouth flamed scarlet. "After all, you had no reason to trust me. So instead you allowed me to run on and on, making a fool of myself. Just as Rachel did with you on the yacht—no, all of that was another fabrication, wasn't it? Thank you for your efforts on Rachel's behalf, Mr. Devoran, but I am happy to free you from any further obligation, and I think I must leave now."

"You may not leave."

She grabbed the back of the sofa. Her face was as fiery as her hair, her eyes blazing.

"I cannot stay here with you, sir!"

"For God's sake, I'm not suggesting anything improper. You'll be Miracle's guest, not mine. I have no doubt that something odd is going on, and you cannot solve it alone. I just don't believe for one moment that some terrible suitor is trying to force your cousin into marriage, or any other relationship."

"Perhaps not," she said with icy dignity. "But I know as clearly as I'm standing here that she's terrified of this man and that her fear is real. If you had read her letters, you would know that. She was excited—almost giddy—by February. Love does that, doesn't it? Yet it all changed as she grew more and more afraid of him, until in the end she had to flee. Rachel may have misled me about some of the facts of her employment. She could never have pretended those emotions."

Had Theseus known this livid grief when he first gazed into the yawning mouth of the Labyrinth? The way was slippery and dark. Somewhere, deep in these elaborate recesses, the Minotaur lurked.

"Even so, your cousin met no one who abducted her."

"But why did she leave town without telling me? And where is she now? You've asked me to accept your word, but now you won't take mine. Rachel fell in love with this gentleman, then later she rejected him. That was foolish; it wasn't criminal. But now he's persecuting her, and she's terrified."

"Perhaps," he said. "But unless your cousin has voluntarily arranged to meet someone, she's alone now. If you'd allow yourself to be shown to a guest chamber, you may also sleep in solitary security until morning. Tomorrow is early enough to take the next step."

"The next step?"

Guy filled another glass and stared into the ruby liquid. He felt like a rat. "To track down the truth about this supposed Harvey Penland and his brood."

"No, they must be real—Rachel received my letters there. But the address is in Hampstead, and I had no way—"

"I understand. I'll ride out there tomorrow."

"Thank you. I'm sorry. You're very kind." She glanced down. "In my distress over your news, I was unfair. You did your best to spare my feelings, and you've been more than generous—"

"No," he interrupted. "I have my own reasons for helping you. I always do. I'm damned if I know why you think me either kind or generous."

She stared at him in obvious puzzlement, her hair unraveling around her face, a pulse beating beneath the skin of her speckled thrush throat.

"You dispute your reputation, Mr. Devoran?" she asked with a flash of amused audacity. "When you're so universally respected and admired . . . and liked?"

He deliberately buried the self-recrimination, and told her the simple truth. "You don't need to like me, Mrs. Callaway. I ask only that you trust in my honor."

Color rose in a pretty flush over her cheeks—a lovely color that made him want to hold out his cold hands to warm them.

"I didn't mean to impugn your honor, sir."

"Then I pray you will trust me just a little further—" Guy broke off as someone knocked on the door. "Enter!"

As lovely as night, still dressed as Nell Gwyn, Miracle walked into the room. A maid stood behind her.

Guy met the question in the dark eyes and shook his head. Miracle walked past him to smile warmly at Sarah, who had dropped a small curtsy.

"Come, Mrs. Callaway!" Miracle said. "You look worn out. If that's Guy's fault, I'll pelt him with oranges until he turns blue."

"No, indeed," Sarah said. "Mr. Devoran has been everything—"

"Mrs. Callaway needs a guest chamber," Guy interrupted. "She'll be spending the night."

Miracle's smile still had the power to smite every man in any room to the heart. "My dear friend, I've already seen to it."

She turned back to Sarah. "It's far too late for you to return to your hotel, Mrs. Callaway. Penny here will show you to your room. I trust you'll be comfortable."

"Thank you," Sarah said. "Your ladyship is very kind, but it's not necessary—"

"Nonsense!" Miracle ushered her toward the door, where Penny, the maid, stood at attention. "If you don't seek your bed right away, I'll have to send for some smelling salts. Though Guy possesses more sensibility than most, gentlemen rarely realize when a lady's had enough."

Guy watched the blue skirts and tousled red hair as Sarah Callaway was swallowed up by the shadows in the corridor.

He glanced back at Miracle to find her studying his face. She met his gaze and smiled with real affection.

"I thought at least one of you might need to be rescued. I hope I wasn't wrong?"

"No." Guy flung himself into a chair. "God, no! Of course not!"

"Good, because Her Grace would like you to dance attendance downstairs, before any more of her guests assume that you, too, don't approve of me."

He laughed. "It's beyond my aunt's comprehension, I suppose, that I might not wish to dance?"

"The company simply needs to be made aware of the presence of my most charming cousin." Miracle strolled to the fireplace. "You're Ambrose's godfather, after all. Meanwhile, I'm forced to wonder why you couldn't bear to let Mrs. Callaway defend your character or motives just now. She was obviously about to do so. What's the matter, Guy?"

"Nothing." He glanced around for his abandoned pirate headband and fake weapons.

"No, of course nothing's the matter." Miracle ignored the mess on the table and poured herself a glass of wine. "You bring waifs and strays to Blackdown House on a regular basis, after enlisting my servants in all kinds of strange subterfuges, then ask *both* Jack and Ryder to play bodyguard until you can take over."

"Sarcasm doesn't suit you, my dear friend," Guy said. "Though I'm grateful for your help tonight."

"Because you and Jack believe that Mrs. Callaway might be in some kind of danger?"

"I'm not sure. Some concerns are better kept to oneself." He stood to offer her his arm. "But she's safe here, and we can't keep the duchess waiting."

She caught his fingers in hers, then stared down at his upturned palm.

"You really have the most wonderful hands, Guy," she said. "Jack and Ryder do, too, of course. But I'm damned if I can read your future here. In what way is Sarah Callaway a part of it?"

"I've undertaken to help find her missing cousin, that's all, a young lady who was living in hiding in Goatstall Lane, then suddenly fled town."

Miracle glanced up into his eyes, a small frown marking her forehead, as she released his hand. "And you fear there's foul play?"

"Very probably, though not the kind that Sarah Callaway dreads."

"But you feel some duty or obligation to help, something far more personal than disinterested courtesy. Why?"

He moved restlessly, glancing up at the paintings: several landscapes, a portrait of an ancestor. "Because of a truth that I cannot tell her."

"So you're being forced to dissemble, and now you're feeling as soaked in dishonor as those petals are in the duke's best brandy. On the other hand, you didn't tell her any deliberate falsehoods, did you?"

"*Prevarication* is only another word for lying."

She picked up his discarded mask and pirate weaponry. "Guy, I love you more dearly than my own brother and have absolute faith in your honor. If the alternative is to abandon Mrs. Callaway when she most needs your help, I fail to see where that's dishonorable in the least."

"That's because you're female," he said. "Ladies take a more practical view of such things."

"No," she said. "It's because, unlike you and Ryder and Jack—with all your gentlemanly codes—I was born in a hovel. Such a background helps one to be realistic."

"I assure you that I'm feeling particularly realistic at the moment."

She placed his disguise in his hands. "Will you need to enlist Ryder in this any further?"

"Sweetheart," he said. "Now the duke's aging, Ryder's effectively the head of the family. He'll never agree to be left in the dark, but he knows where his priorities are."

"Yes, I know," she replied. "That's why we both love him."

Guy strapped on the wooden pistols and tied the black cloth about his hair. "You only remind me that I was damned foolish to let you slip away from me all those years ago."

Her gaze searched his face. "Love isn't hard, Guy. We thought it was when we first met and were little more than children, but really, it's not."

"Yes, it is," Guy said. "But the duchess and her guests are waiting." He slipped on his mask and grinned at her. "How do I look?"

"Rakish. Demonic. Piratical. And handsome as the devil. Almost as desirable as my beloved husband, who trusts your competence absolutely and wouldn't dream of interfering in your affairs any further than you exactly requested."

Guy laughed, lifted her fingers to kiss her wedding ring, then allowed Lady Ryderbourne to lead him from the room.

SARAH lay awake for a long time. Every possible need had been met with unobtrusive efficiency: a warm drink, hot water for bathing. A maidservant had carefully combed out and plaited her dreadful hair. The same girl had taken away the blue silk shepherdess costume and laid out a nightgown and robe.

Warm and safe at last, Sarah had finally fretted into exhaustion the news that Guy Devoran had given her. Rachel had lied. For a good part of the last two years. She had worked as a scullery maid. If it hadn't been for the money she'd earned for that day on the yacht, she'd have been in desperate straits.

Yet she hadn't once asked for Sarah's help, other than those little pleas for extra funds when she claimed she needed to purchase some frippery or other.

Life sometimes offered pain that could not be avoided, even great wounds like the loss of Captain Callaway. But this was a hurt of another kind, and it burned with its own intensity.

Rachel's deceptions were almost too great to fathom, as if Sarah stared into a well filled with heartbreak. Yet—with the candles finally guttering—she made herself face some of her more uncomfortable memories.

And then she began to think about Guy Devoran.

GUY slouched in a chair with his legs stretched out in front of him and contemplated the empty wineglass in his hand. Blackdown House yawned about him in absolute silence.

The glass gleamed, shining faintly against the dark grate, as dawn feathered into the room.

Eight bobbed his tail, then sidestepped, feet rasping on the perch.

"Safe from who?" the parrot murmured, bright eyes fixed on the closed door. "Safe from who?"

Guy glanced without alarm over his shoulder. "Enter!"

The knob turned. Wearing a long robe over his shirt and breeches, Ryder closed the door behind him, then strode into the room.

"Good morning," Guy said. "I think there's some wine left."

Ryder ignored the invitation. "You bade me come in before I even had a chance to knock? But, no—I see you have Eight with you."

The parrot lifted both wings. "She's a miracle, sir! Eight! Eight! Pieces of Eight! Tar 'n' feather 'em, Your Grace!"

"Not quite 'Your Grace' yet," Ryder said dryly. He tossed a cloth over the bird's cage, then plucked the glass from his cousin's hand and set it on the mantel. "You felt in need of warning if a stranger approached?"

"Perhaps. Dawn tends to dull the senses. So to what do I owe the honor of this visit? No one else will be up before noon."

"I've not been to bed yet either." Ryder dropped into a chair. "Ambrose was fussing. Miracle's fast asleep now, but you and I need to talk."

Guy closed his eyes. "About what? The extraordinary circumstance of Lord and Lady Ryderbourne allowing their infant son to disturb their rest, even though Lord Wyldshay has a dozen maids to attend his every whim?"

"Don't be obtuse," Ryder said. "Miracle would never leave our baby to the mercy of the maids, however well qualified. She grew up in a different tradition."

"Which is exactly what's set London by the ears." Guy winked. "Considering all of that, you have my congratulations that the ball went off so well."

Ryder crossed his long legs at the knee. "Mother certainly considers it a triumph, though there were still a few families who refused to come—"

"Yes, the Duke of Fratherham's faction, who'll always remain implacable enemies of parliamentary reform. The rest will soften in time—"

"—as long as Miracle and I continue to live happily at Wyldshay most of the year, and we don't embarrass them in town too often."

Guy laughed. "It's not every day that a duke's heir marries in a way guaranteed to give such joy to our political opponents. So the duchess was moderately brilliant to hold a costume ball with masks."

Ryder's eyes shone green with amusement beneath his lowered lashes. "Since they could pretend not to recognize her, it definitely meant that certain ladies didn't have to choose whether or not to cut Miracle dead in public."

"Yet they still came."

"In spite of my radical politics, I'm just a little too exalted to ignore, as is Mother. It's one of the advantages of our position."

"And a terrible dilemma for the high sticklers," Guy said with a grin. "Disregard an invitation from the duchess, or appear to condone immorality. Do you think that such pettiness bothers me?"

"No, except that you can't bear to see Miracle slighted." Shadows raced as Ryder stood up and walked across to the window. "If you or Jack had married so shockingly, society would never have forgiven it, but—"

"—but you are the favored son of Zeus. I truly have no regrets,

Ryder, except insofar as I could never have loved Miracle as you do." Guy dropped his head against the chair back and allowed himself another dry smile. "Though if you ever fail to defend your exquisite wife, I'll ride like Lancelot straight to her side."

Daylight gleamed in Ryder's hair as he turned around. "I've never been tempted to knock you down before," he said mildly, "but if you weren't already sprawled in that chair, three sheets to the wind, I'd be damned tempted to do so right now. I promise you I'll never fail her. But enough about Miracle! I came here to talk about your present predicament. Jack thinks—"

Guy bolted upright. "Jack found time to talk to you?"

"A brief alert, that's all. My brother can never lose the habits of close observation. When a man has survived mountain tribes and desert bandits, he tends to develop a damned shrewd ability to assess human nature. God, I'm tired! I'd better call for some coffee."

Ryder strode to the bellpull and yanked it.

"So what did Jack observe?"

"You with Sarah Callaway," Ryder said. "Mrs. Callaway with you."

Guy laughed. "And it's Jack's considered opinion that Mrs. Callaway is the soul of honor, but that she's hiding dark passions. He therefore believes that she may be far too susceptible to my charms. The result will be broken hearts and ruined reputations. She'll be forced to retire to a nunnery, while I'll shoot myself from shame."

"Not exactly in those words. Though Miracle also said it was as if you two struck sparks from each other."

"We did," Guy said. "But much as I love you both, I would suggest that you and Miracle mind your own bloody business when it comes to my ramshackle heart. As for Jack, I'll stop by Withycombe Court one day to stab him in the back, since no one could kill him if he had even a moment's warning."

Ryder laughed. "As I know to my cost. He knocked me down last summer."

"Because you were foolish enough to take him by surprise. But what the hell's the cause of all this family concern about Sarah Callaway? Yes, I find her attractive. Yes, I'd like very much to take her to bed. But for what it's worth, I'm not so dead to honor that I intend to act on any of that."

"No one questions your honor, Guy. Of all of us, you're probably the finest drawn. But even if Miracle worries about your heart, that's not why Jack's concerned and you know it. You'd be mad to ignore his instinct for danger."

"I'm taking Jack's instincts as seriously as you could possibly wish. I've just spent the last six hours or so thinking about them. What did he tell you?"

Ryder opened the door to take a tray from a footman. He dismissed the man and set the tray on a side table.

"No details. There wasn't time. He was desperate to get back to Anne—"

"—and I'd already delayed him far longer than I intended. I'm sorry for that."

"Jack was more than happy to help, though it put him in rather a hurry, of course. So he simply dropped a few witty comments on his way out and said that you'd tell me the rest. So what's happening? When you asked me this afternoon to welcome Mrs. Callaway here, her problem didn't sound so terribly perilous."

"No, it didn't—not then. I'd simply agreed to help find her missing cousin."

"You spend too much of your life solving other people's problems," Ryder said. "Why not hire a man from Bow Street?"

"Because this time there's a personal responsibility, as well. The missing lady's name is Rachel."

Ryder's hands froze on the coffeepot. "Not the same Rachel?"

"Unfortunately, yes," Guy said. "Exactly the same Rachel."

"I see." Ryder calmly filled two cups. "The mysterious beauty who helped Jack and Anne escape safely to Wyldshay last year, then became your mistress in February—until she walked out without warning as soon as you left to go home for Easter. Of course, Mrs. Callaway knows none of this. And of course you can't tell her."

"It's disgusting to be obliged to lie to her, even by omission. Yet Sarah Callaway truly believes her cousin to be an innocent. Though I had to disabuse her of some of her illusions, I can hardly reveal all of reality's rooms—certainly not the secret passages and hidden bedchambers."

"—which is bound to involve you in some damnable complications. No wonder Miracle's concerned!"

Guy briefly contemplated the ceiling as he stifled a yawn. "Miracle simply wants to see me with my own babe at my knee. Like all happy newlyweds, she wants everyone she loves to get married."

"Not a bad idea," Ryder said, handing him a cup. "I'm only sorry that my wife doesn't have a sister."

Guy nodded his thanks, swallowed hot coffee, and welcomed the resulting jolt. In the more than forty hours since the bookshop he had hardly slept. The wineglass had been empty for the last six of them. Nevertheless, he felt drunk with fatigue.

"If she did, the simple fact is that I probably couldn't hold her affections, any more than I could Miracle's ten years ago."

"Only because you've not yet met the right lady."

Another gulp of coffee scalded down Guy's throat. "With the exception of Miracle, I think we may conclude that my judgment about the fair sex stinks. Rachel lied—not about trivialities, but about fundamentals, and for at least eighteen months—to her closest childhood companion, the cousin who loves her like a sister."

"Mrs. Callaway didn't know this?"

"No. None of it. Rachel lied to me, also, of course. I always knew it, but I thought that I loved her anyway. Perhaps I still do. Even though now I learn that she fled my protection simply to hide right here in London—in Goatstall Lane, of all places! Obviously, honor demands that I not abandon a lady I made promises to, even if she failed to deserve them. Yet for the last ten years, that's rather been my pattern. I'm not sure that I want to face what that says about me."

"Nothing much, except perhaps that you're a little too loyal," Ryder said. "Jack told me before he and Anne went to India last summer that Rachel was as out of place in that inn kitchen as a rose on a dung pile. You'd not be the first man to be fascinated by that kind of beauty."

"Nor the last, apparently," Guy said. "But either way, Sarah Callaway is more than safe. Any vague threat that I may pose to her virtue and reputation is barely relevant, compared to the reek of what Jack and I suspect is a far more literal danger."

Ryder settled back into his chair and sipped at his cup. "So what does Mrs. Callaway know?"

"She's in no doubt that her cousin is genuinely afraid, but she thinks that Rachel's being persecuted over a failed love affair."

"And you'll continue to allow her to think that?"

"I may have to." More hot coffee burned down Guy's throat. "Even though Rachel supposedly fell foul of her tormentor in February and March—"

"When she was in fact living in perfect security with you in Hampstead?"

Guy smiled dryly at his cousin. "Nice, isn't it?

"You said Rachel lied to you all along, even when she was your mistress? What about?"

"Almost every detail of her past, her identity, her real feelings. I knew it. I just let it go."

Ryder frowned into his empty cup. "I hate to have to ask this, Guy, but could she have been seeing someone else at the same time?"

He had analyzed the idea to death, enough that he was able to smile at his cousin.

"That painful thought obviously occurred to me, so I rode out to Hampstead yesterday to browbeat my staff and pursue some discreet investigations. That's why I was so late getting back for the ball. While she was living with me, Rachel was receiving and sending letters in secret, just as I'd already surmised from what Sarah Callaway told me. One of the maids helped her."

"And?"

"The same girl confirmed that Rachel never entertained visitors, and she never left the house without me—until the day she disappeared. All the rest of the servants swore the same thing, and I believe them. However, according to her cousin, Rachel first went to live in Hampstead as soon as Jack paid her for that day on the yacht, long before she and I moved back there together."

"You know where?"

"Perhaps, though I need to confirm it."

"So if there's really any furiously disappointed swain involved, Rachel must have met him either before or after she lived with you."

"Exactly." Guy stood and poured two more cups of coffee. "The cause of attempted murder is usually one of only two things: passion or money—"

"*Murder?*"

"Possibly. And since I fail to see how this can be about money, Sarah Callaway's story may indeed hold an element of truth."

"Why the devil would any gentleman want to kill a woman, merely because she'd refused his advances? That's too melodramatic to be real."

"I thought so, too, at first." He handed one refilled cup to Ryder. "However, while I followed up on some other leads, Jack visited Goatstall Lane disguised as a workman. We exchanged notes later by the orchid fountain. There's no doubt that Rachel fled London in fear for her life."

"Justifiably?"

Guy paced restlessly to the window and back. "I don't know. Perhaps someone wanted only to frighten her. Either way, something damned unpleasant is going on."

"Sarah Callaway may also be in danger?"

"I'm certainly not taking any chances. That's why I insisted she come here." Guy dropped back into his chair. "I couldn't leave her at Brockton's, and obviously I can't take her back to my townhouse."

"Blackdown House is yours as long as you want it," Ryder said. "I'll help in any way that I can."

Guy shook his head. "Your place is with Miracle and Ambrose. And Jack's already done far more for me than I had any right to ask. Besides, I fear that Mrs. Callaway may insist on helping me herself."

Ryder laughed. "Then by all means send her down to Wyldshay. She can teach my little sisters all about the wickedness of plants, and we can give her a position there for as long as you like."

"Thank you," Guy said. "I may do that, unless I discover in the next day or two that all of my fears for her are groundless. In which case, I'll simply send her back to Bath."

"Will she go quietly?" Ryder asked. "Jack didn't think her a shrinking violet, and neither do Miracle and I."

"God, no! She's an exotic orchid, of course. I already told her that, much to her consternation."

Ryder laughed again. "Why, for God's sake?"

"Because of that bloody spark that so interested Miracle and Jack. In order to discover what's really happening, I must uncover the details of Rachel's genuine past. If I'm to protect Sarah Callaway from the more uncomfortable parts of that, I'd better drive her away as soon as possible."

"By complimenting her?"

"She's not a natural flirt. A little interest from a man like me only makes her uncomfortable, whatever passions she keeps buried."

"So Sarah Callaway need never know the whole truth about her cousin."

"Let Rachel tell her the truth, if she likes."

"Because gentlemen don't kiss and tell. God, it's almost day! I don't question your ability to handle this, Guy, but—"

"I won't hesitate to call on you, if need be. Meanwhile, there's no need for Miracle to know all these details, when the truth is anyway nothing but shadows."

"And is yours to confide or not, as you wish." Ryder rose to his feet and set his cup on the tray. "Though sometimes I think that we try to protect the fair sex far too much. Ladies aren't really the frail vessels our society would have us believe."

Guy folded his arms across his chest and closed his eyes. In spite of the coffee, fatigue swam in waves through his blood.

"Then Miracle's changed your view of women quite a bit in the last eleven months."

"Not only Miracle. Anne may have seemed unworldly, but she's as strongly rooted as any mountain. She didn't hesitate to take off for the Himalayas with Jack last summer."

His nerves jangled as if exhaustion were jerking them. "And let's not forget the duchess. So tell your wife what you will, Ryder. I have absolute faith in Miracle's common sense, her wisdom, and her strength."

"Thank you," Ryder said. "Though, as it happens, I see no need to distress her with any of this. Not because she couldn't handle it, but because it would only make her worry unnecessarily about you."

"Miracle, Anne, and your mother are each exceptional females," Guy said, "with the fortitude to marry one of you St. Georges. But unfortunately in the last ten years I've known quite a few frail vessels, and Rachel Mansard is one of them."

"Though it's Jack's considered opinion that Sarah Callaway has the backbone of a queen."

"That remains to be seen," Guy said. "Though I certainly hope so."

"So do I, because—for all your good intentions—it seems highly unlikely that you can pursue the truth about Rachel without Sarah Callaway discovering that her cousin was your mistress."

His muscles felt as if he had been swimming for three days without rest. The temptation to let the ocean swallow him was almost overwhelming, but he laughed.

"Devilish, isn't it?"

Ryder stalked across the room to jerk the cloth from the parrot's cage. Eight opened his eyes, then closed them again to huddle down into an avian sulk.

"You do realize," Ryder said, "that if there was ever a formula for disaster, this is it."

"Quite so," Guy replied. "I've been entertaining that delightful conclusion all night."

SARAH opened her eyes. A vision of pink orchids, sensual and lush, danced on the bed canopy. She blinked. Not orchids. Just the patterned fabric, dazzling where light poured into her room.

The maids must have folded back the shutters without waking her.

Iron-shod wheels rumbled and clanked somewhere outside, the sound muffled by the walls of Blackdown House. The clock hands formed a neat crook, like the crotch of a tree. Two o'clock! She hadn't slept past six in the morning for years, and it was already afternoon?

Sarah grinned, lay back again, and closed her eyes. The house thrummed with silent energy.

Orchids: *cattleya* and *angraecum* and *catasetum*.

Mr. Guy Devoran dressed as a pirate with a parrot on his shoulder.

That heady moment of recognition when her blood had sung symphonies of delight.

She had even thought that his eyes burned with the same wicked ardor, as if he would tear her dress from her shoulders to bury his open mouth in the curve of her neck.

Yet the real nature of love was the warm sharing of affection she and Captain Callaway had discovered. The sacrifice, given willingly. The gracious acceptance of one-sided care. The gentle humor maintained even in the face of disaster. Not this mad, uncomfortable shivering deep inside.

These young aristocrats were so sure of their power. More sophisticated ladies no doubt took that for granted. If one's father or brothers moved through the world with such confidence, surely that would offer some protection against making a fool of oneself?

And Rachel? How could her cousin have lied for so long about so much?

What terrible collapse of love and trust had prevented her from asking her only cousin for help?

Sarah jerked up in the bed as pain spiked cruel fingers into her heart.

CHAPTER FIVE

UY STRODE BACK INTO BLACKDOWN HOUSE. PAUL HURRIED to
take his hat.

"You and Rose are planning to marry very soon?" Guy asked.

The footman flushed. "Yes, sir."

"Then I wish you both every happiness." Guy handed him his
gloves. "Yet the duchess won't allow her town staff to marry each
other, so you can't keep on here together. Please know that there's always a place for you both at Birchbrook. My father keeps country
manners and has no objection to married staff."

"Very kind of you to say so, sir. But Lady Ryderbourne's already
seen to it that we'll be employed at the Derbyshire house. We're to
have our own cottage."

Guy smiled. "Then allow me to congratulate you on your good
fortune."

"Thank you, sir, but I'd have worked carrying night soil rather
than lose my girl, and Rose would've taken in washing, if that's what
it took to be with me. Yet we're both London born and bred, Mr.
Devoran. We don't know too much about Derbyshire." He wrinkled
his brow. "But love often requires sacrifice, doesn't it, sir?"

Guy met the man's honest brown gaze. He saw no reason not to
honor Paul with the truth.

"I don't know. I'm damned if I can claim to know anything about the true nature of love. Is Rose already back from Brockton's?"

"Yes, sir. Peter Coachman came there this morning, as you required, and Rose carried away all of the lady's things."

"You and Rose remained undisturbed through the night?"

Sweat broke in visible beads on the footman's forehead. "Yes, sir."

"It's all right," Guy said. "I understand that part of love perfectly well."

So no one had seen anything unusual—including the man Guy had posted to watch outside Brockton's Hotel. Though one quiet night proved little, perhaps the pale-skinned man he'd seen lingering earlier had been just a coincidence, after all.

"Yes, sir," the footman said. "I'm sorry, sir. I should mention that Mrs. Callaway is waiting in the Ivory Room. I was that distracted thinking about Rose, I forgot."

To the man's immense surprise, Guy shook him by the hand, forcing him to shuffle the hat and gloves beneath one arm.

"All the best, Paul. Derbyshire's very lovely. You'll like it. And I think you and Rose may expect some rather handsome wedding presents, as well."

"Yes, sir. Thank you, sir."

Beaming, his face brilliant, Paul bowed his head and walked off.

Guy glanced at the marble columns, the Italian stone floors, the gilt and ebony. Blackdown House must be the pinnacle of any footman's career. Yet Paul would have given up everything he'd worked for just to be with Rose.

Now the newlyweds could settle happily into a cottage on the Wrendale estates—part of the vast holdings of the Duchy of Blackdown—where Ryder and Miracle would spend several months with their new baby later in the summer.

It was bloody absurd, of course, to be jealous of a footman, and he loved Ryder and Miracle, and Jack and Anne, far too well to feel envious of them. His cousins' happiness shone like a golden flame of gladness deep in his heart.

So where the devil did this burning indignation at the unjust caprices of Eros really come from?

Guy laughed at his own folly and ran upstairs. He had far more important things to think about than his past failures with women.

Ten minutes later he knocked at the open door of a room on the second floor, where cases of ivory carvings covered one wall. Sarah Callaway was sitting at a desk near the window, a writing case at her elbow, reading letters.

Her red hair was scraped back into a network of tight braids that hugged the neat contours of her skull. A plain gray dress with a high neck encased her from head to toe. She looked every inch the schoolmistress.

"Good afternoon, Mrs. Callaway," he said. "I see Miracle's been taking good care of you."

She glanced up. Sunlight flamed into a red halo about her head.

Guy felt his stomach contract. Something in her open gaze seemed to see straight into his heart, as if she would strip away all of his subterfuge.

Pink color washed into her cheeks. The freckles faded into a dance of tiny shadows.

She rose to her feet and bobbed a greeting. "Everyone's been very kind, Mr. Devoran. Thank you. Lord and Lady Ryderbourne came to bid me farewell about an hour ago. Please, come in. You sent for all of my things from Brockton's?"

"Why remain in a hotel, when you may enjoy the hospitality of Blackdown House?"

Guy strode farther into the room, then stopped as if he'd run into a wall. His pulse quickened. If he raised his hand he could touch the edge of the faint aura that surrounded her. The scent spoke of simplicity and rest, yet it also inflamed some deep desire, as if he'd been offered manna when starving.

With a quiet dignity she sat down and rearranged her skirts. "Thank you, sir. I've had all night to think about Rachel. I'm truly very grateful indeed for your assistance, and for Lord Jonathan's and Lord Ryderbourne's, as well."

He felt desperate to reassure her, so he deliberately kept his tone light. "Not at all. Solving problems is a hobby of mine. I'm glad that you came to me. Please, believe that!"

Glad? It seemed a damned odd word to describe his true state of mind.

Her hazel eyes remained focused on his face. "You've been out again today, sir? Did you find out anything more?"

Guy swept one hand over his hair. "I slept until noon like the rest of the household, then I made another quick call on Grail before he left town. The duke and duchess already left for Wyldshay with Miracle and Ryder, I assume?"

"Yes, they came to say good-bye. I understand that no one else is here, except for the duke's widowed sister, Lady Crowse."

"She's elderly and eccentric and you probably won't even meet her. She'll also leave for the country in a few days, but until then she's your chaperon. Once the House of Lords prorogues for the summer, almost no one stays in London."

She sat back, her eyes thoughtful. "Then Daedalus has probably left for the country as well."

"Daedalus?"

"I've been rereading Rachel's letters." Sunlight warmed her hair to bronze as she looked down at the scattered papers on the table. "This man who's been terrorizing her. I thought it would help to give him a name."

He stepped closer. The scent of green apples enveloped him. His heart thudded as if he were setting a horse at a fence that was too high.

How much sleep now? Five hours in the last forty-eight?

"Then I hope your choice isn't prophetic, Mrs. Callaway. In myth, Daedalus escaped."

As if he were a lamp, her skin glowed. "Yes, I know, but he was still the maze-maker. Perhaps you'd prefer to choose something else?"

"No, Daedalus is fine." Guy grasped a chair by its back and spun it into place, facing her across the table. "You will allow me to read your cousin's letters?"

Pretty color still warmed her cheeks. "Some of them are rather personal, and much of what she writes would no doubt seem only silly to you. But, yes, I think that I must. Some of them anyway." She picked up a large sheet. It had obviously been read many times. "This is the first that's even remotely relevant. It's the letter where she first told me about that day on the yacht with you."

"She wrote it after she had arrived in London?"

"Yes, last June. I can't fathom why she'd lied to me for so long about still working for Lord Grail, when in fact she was scrubbing floors in that inn. I fear something very terrible must have happened to make her leave Grail Hall that Christmas. Yet whatever the truth of that, I'm certain that she was indeed desperate when she met you. Did Lord Jonathan think the same?"

"Absolutely," he said.

"Is that why you paid her so very much for taking a simple pleasure cruise? Enough to keep her without working for several months, you said?"

"Your cousin played a more critical role in rescuing Anne than she really knew. Jack's very wealthy. She was the recipient of his generosity, not mine."

"There's more than one way to be generous, Mr. Devoran. Rachel's fear may not have been over losing her position, but her panic about an uncertain future was real, and you were infinitely courteous and considerate in the face of it."

Discomfort crawled up his spine. "Was I?"

"Yes, I think so. You must have guessed that she'd given you a false name and wasn't used to working in a kitchen, yet you didn't try to pry even once into her odd situation, did you?"

"Why would you consider that to be kind? Perhaps I was merely indifferent."

"Here," she said, holding out the paper. "Now I know what really happened, it's madly disconcerting to read this. Yet I don't think that she made up everything, you see."

Guy felt as if he were suspended in some uncomfortable trap, like a fox snared in a wire. With enough gnawing he might yet get free, though it would probably be at the cost of a paw. Yet if he was to get to the bottom of Rachel's latest disappearance, he was going to have to read her letters.

He flicked open the paper and skimmed through the florid phrases.

Mr. Guy Devoran was such a bright miracle of generosity, Sarah. As you know, I had been feeling quite desperate—

Guy skipped several paragraphs of falsehoods about Lord Grail, until his gaze stopped once again on his own name.

Not only was he incredibly kind, but Mr. Devoran is so very handsome and with such a wonderful smile. He made me think of Oberon. Not some silly fairy king, but the most powerful ruler in nature, all brilliance and light. I'm already half in love!

Guy tossed the letter back onto the table as if he'd been scalded. While he had been searching in vain for Rachel—obsessed with that first meeting—she had been writing all this nonsense to her cousin?

"She was exaggerating," he said. "Most of this is gibberish."

Sarah gazed at him steadily, her color still high. "Yet I'm almost sure that the heart of Rachel's emotions is always true, even though the facts may be wrong. It's the same with all the rest of her letters."

"God! How can one possibly know? Reading that is like swimming just beneath the surface of a pool, caught between the world of the air and the dark undercurrents in the water. Where the two meet, everything is distorted."

"I don't know about that," she said. "Ladies rarely swim."

He laughed and leaned back. "So what's emotionally true about that letter? The relief that she was in possession of a large purse of gold and safely out of an uncomfortable situation, I assume."

"Yes," Sarah said. "And her admiration for you."

"All very flattering," he said, "but I don't recall that she paid me much attention that day."

Her fingers moved rapidly as she sorted through the scattered letters. "Yet the same adulation runs through many of these. Remembering that one day at sea was a bright light in an otherwise dreary existence."

Part of him wanted to believe it. Rachel had said the same when she'd first turned up on his doorstep. *I simply could not forget you, Mr. Devoran.* Yet it couldn't be true! She had disappeared for most of the year before that, hiding herself away even when he had discreetly advertised for her in the newspapers.

"It was the ocean she remembered so fondly," he said. "Not me."

Sarah's skin paled, then flushed all over as if she were being boiled like a lobster, though she laughed.

"Then perhaps you don't realize your real effect on women, Mr. Devoran?"

"I'm Blackdown's nephew," he said carefully. "That brings me a certain amount of attention, even some small glory. Yet I remain, as you see, unattached."

She looked down. "And that bothers you? I thought young gentlemen enjoyed being unattached?"

"Of course," he said dryly. "Like butterflies, we flit from flower to flower—even orchids."

Hot color burned over her cheeks. She began to fold the letters to set them back into her writing case.

"My pulse has been a little unsteady since you first walked into this room," she said. "I have thought it all through very carefully, the benefits and the risks."

He sat upright. "What risks?"

"The minute I first saw you, I guessed that you might flirt a little. Young gentlemen always do, however automatic and meaningless it may be. Yet it's not necessary, Mr. Devoran, and I prefer not be the recipient of any charitable gallantry."

Astonishment pinned him to the chair. "I don't understand."

"No, because you've not thought about it very much. But since I'm not very pretty or eligible, your small attempts at flattery only put me very firmly in my place, as a female and a dependent."

A little flame of anger flared up his spine. "Forgive me, ma'am, but—"

"But I am a female and dependent, of course. I just hoped—" She broke off and dropped her face into both hands. "Oh, goodness! I've only made it ten times worse, haven't I?"

Guy pushed up from his chair and strode away from the table. Jupiter! Of course she wasn't *pretty*, any more than an exotic orchid was *pretty*. But only because Sarah Callaway was the most sensually attractive woman he'd ever met. Enticement frolicked with the freckles on her skin, hiding in shadowed hollows, rioting over her smooth curves.

Though she was not, of course, eligible. She was the cousin of his most recent mistress. For the second day running, he felt like a rat.

"You wish us to work as comrades," he said, "and instead I've made you uncomfortable. I'm sorry."

Sarah dropped her hands and looked up. "No. I should crawl beneath the table and stay there."

He laughed. "Better to have it out in the open. You're quite correct, ma'am. I'm a reformed man as of this instant."

To his immense surprise, she grinned. "We'll see! You mentioned yesterday that you might go out to find Mr. Harvey Penland's house in Hampstead today?"

"If you'll give me his exact address, yes, I intend to ride out there this afternoon. Why?"

"I can ride," she said.

He turned to stare into one of the cabinets. Ivory animals marched along the shelves. Her face was reflected in the glass, wavering in front of the carvings as he moved.

"Jack brought some of these back from his travels," he said.

"The little elephants and birds?" Sarah leaned her chin on her folded hands. "I was afraid that you'd be awkward about this, Mr. Devoran."

He spun about. "Awkward?"

"In spite of your claim to be so reformed, you're not-so-subtly pointing out that feats of derring-do—like gathering ivory from the far side of the world, or riding out to Hampstead to hunt for clues about the mysterious Daedalus—are hardly the purview of the fair sex?"

"I can track Mr. Penland's existence—or lack of it—more efficiently alone, that's all."

"You only insult me by suggesting that I cannot handle the truth, Mr. Devoran."

"What truth?"

She took a deep breath. "I deduced three things as I lay awake last night. The first was that by this morning you'd have decided to exclude me, even though it's my cousin who's missing."

He opened a glass-fronted door and picked up a little white ivory figurine. Her long flowing robe was intricately carved. Her hands and face bloomed like small flowers.

"And the second?"

"That you thought a little flirtatious pressure on a plain schoolmistress would further that aim by helping to drive me away."

Reflections multiplied in the open glass door. The shadows of the ivory figures danced away into both past and future.

"Why should you think that I wish to drive you away?"

"Because you and Lord Jonathan fear now that Rachel may be in real danger, and you want to protect me from knowing that. Am I right?"

"Perhaps." He set the figurine in front of her. "A fragile creature, wouldn't you say?"

"Yes, but she's Chinese. We Anglo-Saxon females are carved from solid chunks of wood and we're much harder to break. I'm wretched with gratitude for your assistance in finding my cousin, Mr. Devoran, but I simply cannot allow you to exclude me altogether. That is what you were planning, isn't it?"

He propped one hip on the corner of the table. The Asian face gazed down at the folds of her dress, her ivory expression bland, though the angle of her head was both coy and flirtatious.

"You're a lady of remarkable intelligence, ma'am," he said. "Even in the face of the most distressing news, you were able to hone in on a critical question: Were your cousin's hands those of a scullery maid? Meanwhile, you're absolutely correct. I'm quite content to pursue this investigation alone."

"She's my cousin, Mr. Devoran. If you refuse to help me on my terms, I shall ask Lady Ryderbourne, instead, and I will not allow you to read the rest of Rachel's letters."

He felt almost amused, though his humor was mixed with the discomfort that, without knowing what she did, she was determined to force him into ever-deeper levels of dishonesty.

"Yet you will first tell me Penland's address?"

"No," she said, putting both hands firmly on the writing case. "I think not."

Guy strode to the cabinet to set the ivory lady back on her shelf. No one knew about the house in Hampstead that Rachel had insisted he rent for her in the spring. They had arrived after dark, and she had never gone beyond the grounds. Nevertheless, he did not want to take Sarah anywhere near it—though it would be far more perilous, of course, if she went out to Hampstead alone.

"Do you play chess, Mrs. Callaway?"

"Yes, I have. I'm not particularly good at it. Why?"

"You teach mathematics?"

She shook her head.

He laughed as he closed the cabinet door. Sunbeams scattered from the glass, obscuring the contents.

"Never mind," he said. "I gave you my word not to abandon this quest, so you know perfectly well that I shan't call your bluff.

Otherwise, you'd never have risked making that last move. Yet I wonder why you show me your strategy quite this soon?"

"Because I fear that you're still keeping something from me, Mr. Devoran. Something important. Something quite other than this vague suspicion of danger."

He froze for a split second, before he turned to face her.

"Yes," he said. "I am."

"Will you tell me what it is?"

"No, I will not."

Sunlight glared around her in an aura of gold. "Is it something that will harm Rachel, or prevent our finding her?"

"No." Guy strode back to pick up the chair and set it in its place by the wall. "You'll simply have to trust me on that, Mrs. Callaway."

"There's certainly no requirement to strip away all privacy, sir, yet you must also trust me. I shan't become hysterical or difficult. I believe I even have some small courage. So I must insist that you not simply dismiss me. There's no good reason for you not to take me with you to Hampstead."

"Except that you told me in the bookstore that we mustn't be seen together," he said coldly. "Was that just the fleeting impulse of the moment?"

"No, not at all. Fortunately, things have changed since then." She looked up. "Firstly, I had no idea then what kind of man you might really be, so it seemed wiser to accost you first in a public place. More important, Rachel was worried that Daedalus might be a friend of yours. If I had come to your house and run into him there, or if I'd been trying to explain things, and he'd arrived—" She stopped and blushed, though she laughed. "Oh, dear! I've entrapped myself, haven't I?"

Guy smiled, though his less noble suspicions had just been unpleasantly confirmed. "So it was indeed your cousin's idea for you to seek me out?"

Sarah rifled around in the box and pulled out another letter. She unfolded it and pointed to a few lines near the end.

How I wish I might ask Mr. Devoran, the loveliest man I ever met. . . .

Guy stared at the scratched-out lines that followed. Only a few stray words were discernible, yet they were enough to see that they contained hints of longing—even love?

The breath left his lungs as if he'd been thrown from a horse.

How dare she!

He strode to the window and slammed closed one shutter to block the sunlight. The iron bar slapped against the wood with a satisfying clang.

If Rachel wanted to ask for his help, why hadn't she come to him herself? Because of *love*? He felt as if Sarah had just lifted out the first of a set of nested boxes, where each one might contain a more devastating truth than the last.

"Why the devil did you prevaricate about this?"

"Because Rachel might have seriously misjudged you. I didn't know."

It would be equally satisfying to thrust his fist through a windowpane. Instead he swallowed the rage and stalked back across the room.

"And you do now?"

"Enough, I think. But I also feared that you might judge her too harshly, if you knew she had wanted to impose so deeply on your generosity after such a short acquaintance."

"So you took the blame for her immodest wishes onto yourself?"

"I care for Rachel as a sister, sir. It's bad enough that you know now how infatuated she was with the memory of meeting you. Any gentleman might judge that improper, unless he also knew how very naïve she could be."

Guy stared at the urns on the mantel, fighting the temptation to smash them into an agreeable mess of broken china.

"How often do you risk your own contentment to protect her like this?"

"I'm a widow, sir, not an unmarried girl. The risks aren't the same for me."

"So you avoided approaching me directly because you feared that might reflect badly on your cousin, though now you've decided you may confide in me, at least this far?"

She glanced down. "Lady Ryderbourne loves you like a brother. I can think of no higher recommendation than that."

He swallowed the caustic rejoinder that sprung to mind. "Yes, we're very fond of each other, which hardly makes her opinion objective. However, in this much you may trust me absolutely: Miss Mansard's reputation won't suffer because of anything you tell me, and I'll certainly bear in mind your assertions of her innocence."

"Thank you, sir. It's very easy for people to misinterpret Rachel's naïveté for something quite different."

"Quite. As for Daedalus, even if he does number among my acquaintances, he wouldn't know that there's any connection between Miss Mansard and myself, and I assume that no one in London is aware that you're her cousin?"

She shook her head. "No. No one."

"So your cousin's fears on that score, also, would appear to be groundless."

He stalked to the window. A bright sun was breaking through the clouds.

It must take considerable courage to swallow any vestige of pride in order to help the cousin she loved. Could he ever find it in himself to be quite that gracious?

Sarah sat down abruptly and propped her forehead on her interlaced fingers. Her face fell into deep shadow.

"I've thought the same, sir. So, just as I think we may join forces now without arousing anyone's suspicions—even if we are seen together—I'm also afraid that you may be right about Mr. Penland. If Lord Jonathan paid Rachel so large a sum of gold, why would she take the first position she could find, especially a place with six children?"

"I'm quite certain that she did not."

Her color still high, she traced one finger over the lid of her writing case. "Yet Rachel must have gone to live in Hampstead right after she left you on the yacht, because her letters were all postmarked from there. So I must go myself, sir. After all, no one knows Rachel better than I do."

"And if I send you away, you won't give me Penland's address."

Her tawny lashes swept up. "I can only bargain with what I have, sir."

"Which includes the threat of aid from Miracle, instead? I see that I'm trumped. So if you'll kindly tell me exactly where your cousin received your letters, ma'am, we may drive out to Hampstead together right now."

She opened the lid of her writing case. "Here," she said, holding out a paper. "I wrote it down for you."

He didn't really need the information, but he glanced at it: *Miss Rachel Mansard, care of Mr. Harvey Penland, Five Oaks, Hampstead.* Exactly what he had already surmised.

It was still a calculated risk to take Sarah there. Less dangerous than he had feared, but dangerous enough.

IT was a triumph, but an empty one. Sarah gazed out across the meadows as the carriage bowled out of London. Guy Devoran's hands were sure and capable on the ribbons. His chestnut team gleamed as if the horses' coats had been beaten from bronze.

A green afternoon in the company of Blackdown's glorious nephew, driving along one of the prettiest roads in England. The scattering of villas, farm dwellings, and wooded hills formed an ever-changing picture.

Yet sorrow yawned in her heart.

This beautiful man had committed himself to her quest as he might have committed himself to a foxhunt: simply for the adventure of it. As a matter of male pride, he'd follow the quarry until it was either lost or pinned by the hounds.

But he only wanted to be rid of crazy, redheaded Sarah Callaway.

She had responded to his radiant presence like a schoolgirl caught in the presence of a fairy-tale prince. Every word of Rachel's infatuation made sense. No female could ever meet Guy Devoran, even for a day, and not remember him for a lifetime.

Yet, as Sarah had surmised in the endless hours of darkness alone in her bedroom, he'd thrilled her with his luminous attention only because he knew it would make her uncomfortable.

Lord Jonathan had no doubt agreed to the plan. The cousins had hoped that an hour of gentle mockery among the orchids would be enough to persuade her to go back to Bath and leave the hunt to the men.

If she did not feel so committed to Rachel, it probably would have done. Nothing could be more humiliating than an attractive gentleman's showing his pity for a plain schoolmistress through insincere gallantry, however flattering.

Yet she was not, for all her self-doubt, as easy to break as an ivory figurine.

Sarah lifted her face to the sun and laughed at herself.

In spite of her racing pulse and general sense of discomfort, she regretted nothing. With Guy Devoran's help, she was bound to solve the mystery and rescue Rachel, whatever the reasons for her disappearance.

Sarah only wished she knew what Mr. Devoran was hiding. In the meantime, she would try to enjoy this outing and what remained of the day.

The horses were fresh and keen, trotting with pricked ears as if they expected a stable at the end of their journey, rather than a return trip back to town.

"You know Hampstead well?" she asked.

"Well enough. It's a great road to let out a good horse. Of course, there was a time when everyone came to take the waters. Many still come for their health, or for inspiration away from the foul air of London."

"Inspiration?"

Tendons flexed in his wrists as he steadied his team. They trotted down a small hill.

"Hampstead is full of lodging houses for artists and writers, as well as invalids. Pony carriages and donkeys still carry visitors out to the Heath."

"Could Daedalus have been one of them?"

"Not if you insist that he met Rachel soon after Christmas. Winter is hardly the time to come to Hampstead for one's health."

The horses began to climb. A redbrick church tower soared above the rooftops of the small town ahead of them. Within a few more minutes they had passed a tollhouse, and Hampstead welcomed them with detached mansions nestled among small groves of trees, then rows of respectable brick houses.

The carriage turned down a side street to pull into the yard of a small inn. The sign had faded to some indistinct green shapes on a background of pale yellow. The tiger swung down to take the horses' bridles.

Guy Devoran leaped from the carriage and held up his hand to help Sarah step down.

"We'll take a little refreshment here," he said, "before we drive back to London."

"But Mr. Penland's address?"

"This is it."

Sarah glanced back at the row of elegant redbrick facades in the street. A nervous shiver trickled up her spine.

"Which house?"

"None of them. This is the Five Oaks."

She met his dark gaze and swallowed. "Rachel lived at an inn? I don't quite—"

"Come, let's take tea and we may find out."

They walked into a small parlor and took a seat. Mr. Devoran ordered tea and cakes.

"I seek one Harvey Penland, Mr. Trench," he said when the innkeeper returned with a tray. "Does he still work here?"

"Bless my soul, sir! The lad upped and left for his folks' place in Norfolk nigh on two weeks ago."

"Norfolk?" Sarah asked faintly. "He *worked* here?"

"That's right, ma'am. Penland's a Norfolk lad, born and bred. Spent a year learning horses in Newmarket, and then drifted here to Hampstead. A smart enough fellow, though cheeky with it. You'll maybe have seen him, sir, mucking out the stables, though I can't imagine that any gentleman such as yourself would ever have taken much notice of the boy."

"No, I don't recall him. Yet might Mr. Penland have run errands for local residents without your knowing?"

"Well, I suppose so, sir. We sent him out on little jobs for the inn often enough. A reliable lad. Trustworthy. I'm sorry to have lost him."

"Then he might have delivered letters by hand and collected the replies to post without anyone else's knowledge?"

"I can't rightly say, sir. I see no reason why not, but only if he was paid smartly, mind."

"Thank you." Mr. Devoran tapped the side of his nose and slipped a coin into the innkeeper's hand.

"Why, thank you, sir. Mum's the word!" The man bowed his head and bustled away.

Little ripples of distress sent cold shivers down Sarah's spine. "So I was sending my letters here to this inn, not to a private house. You'd already guessed as much, hadn't you?"

He leaned back, fixing her with his dark gaze. "Since no one had heard of him, Harvey Penland couldn't be a gentleman. Yet he had to exist. He also had to have access to the mail, plus the freedom to carry letters back and forth. Thus it was likely that he was working in an inn. I just didn't know which one—"

"—until I told you. But you'd have come here and found out anyway, wouldn't you?" Sarah poured tea. The spout rattled against her teacup. "So where was Rachel really living?"

"I don't know for certain, though I made a few inquiries yesterday evening at St. John's. The curate remembers a lady of her description living alone in a rented house called Knight's Cottage near the Heath. She sometimes took long walks by herself on a Sunday, though she never welcomed visitors or went to church."

A sick anxiety buzzed in her head. "And you think that was Rachel?"

Light limned his strong profile as he gazed out of the window. "For what it's worth, yes. I was also able to talk to the landlord last night. This lady paid him several months' rent in gold in advance."

Her hands felt clammy. "Then Rachel was living by herself in a cottage for all those months, while writing to me about caring for six imaginary children?"

"So it would seem."

Sarah took a slice of cake, then stared at it. "Did the landlord say whether she kept any servants?"

"The landlord provides any heavy work and sends a man to maintain the garden, and a housekeeper lives in." Mr. Devoran glanced back at her, his eyes shuttered. "The same woman is still working there."

The hot tea was quaking gently in her cup. It seemed impossible to keep her hands steady. The cup rattled back into the saucer.

"Then she may be able to confirm whether Harvey Penland was bringing my letters. So may we please drive out to this cottage?"

"That's been my intention all along, ma'am."

Sarah took a deep breath and swallowed hard, before she looked back up at him. The black eyes seemed filled with regret, even apology, as if he couldn't bear to distress her, almost as if he despised himself for the necessity.

She opened and closed her fingers beneath the table, then picked up her teacup again. None of this was his fault. She had promised not to be difficult or hysterical.

"Our home was in Norfolk," she said with quiet determination. "Rachel probably noticed Penland's accent. It might have helped buy his loyalty, if they were from the same area."

"I'll send a man to trace him," he said. "But either way, I think we may assume that your cousin used Jack's gold to move here after that day on the yacht. Do you have any idea why?"

Cake crumbled in her mouth like dry sand. Sarah thrust away her plate.

"No. I can't fathom any of it. And why make up all of those stories about still working as a governess?"

"Presumably so you wouldn't ask awkward questions about why she was living here alone."

"I can't imagine what she was hiding. Yet she must have met Daedalus here."

"On the contrary, I'm certain that she met him long before that."

"That's impossible!" Her empty cup clattered back into the saucer. "I'd have guessed it from her letters."

"So you still believe that your cousin can lie about the facts, but not about her emotions?"

"You've not read the rest of her correspondence, Mr. Devoran. If Rachel had met Daedalus before that day on the yacht, I'd know it."

"Would you?" He leaned forward to meet her gaze, as if convincing her of this one point was imperative. "Why did she leave Lord Grail's house as she did? And why the devil did she work as a scullery maid at the Three Barrels?"

Sarah pushed away from the table. "I don't know, sir, because I'm still not sure that she did!"

He stood up immediately and took her elbow to lead her from the room. As soon as they reached a private corner in the inn yard, he released her.

"You promised me no hysteria, Mrs. Callaway."

"I'm not hysterical, sir," Sarah said. "I'm furious. You've manipulated me and hidden things from me, and now you question my judgment about my own cousin's emotions. Yes, something happened to drive her from Grail Hall. Very probably it was Lord Grail himself. She never liked or trusted him—"

"Then your cousin is a damned bad judge of character. Grail's notoriously affable. I can't imagine an easier household in which she could have worked. And from what he told me this morning, visitors came and went constantly that summer."

"But she was the governess, relegated mostly to the nursery."

"On the contrary. Rachel Mansard had plenty of opportunity to meet the guests. You don't think every man among them didn't take the opportunity to flirt with her?"

Indignation made her spine rigid; otherwise she thought she might have folded as if struck.

"Be that as it may, sir, Rachel was an innocent girl who met Daedalus *here*. She fell in love with him here. She became afraid of him here. She fled him after Easter and ended up in Goatstall Lane. This villain persecuted her here in Hampstead, Mr. Devoran, and I can't imagine why you would even think to question that."

CHAPTER SIX

As Ryder had so eloquently predicted, nothing could come of this situation but disaster. Guy glanced away as if simply distracted by the bustle of the inn yard.

He disliked all these machinations a little too intensely. Sarah Callaway deserved better. But not, surely, the news that Rachel could not have fallen in love with Daedalus in Hampstead in the spring, because Guy Devoran was keeping her as a mistress at the time?

"Yes," he said, glancing back at her. "I have, within limits, manipulated you, Mrs. Callaway. I thought it necessary. That was presumptuous. Pray, accept my apologies."

Rage sparkled in her eyes, but she swallowed, and in a sudden, entrancing change of mood, she laughed.

"Oh, goodness! I've prevaricated almost as much with you, sir," she said. "I did so in our very first meeting and several more times since. I am entirely indebted to you, but I do wish you wouldn't try to protect me from unpleasantness by disputing the obvious truth."

Little barbs sank into his heart. Yet Guy smiled back, even knowing that she would see that his smile was empty and rightfully despise him for it.

"We don't yet know the truth, ma'am. So we must agree to disagree for the moment. Now, do you wish to drive out to the cottage?"

"I certainly wish to find out the truth about Daedalus, sir, and thus rescue Rachel. Thank you."

They walked back to his carriage and he helped her into the seat. His tiger swung up behind, and Guy drove out into the street.

He tried to keep his voice gentle.

"Daedalus the maze-maker escaped his own labyrinth in Crete," he said. "You may believe that he met your cousin in Hampstead, but I'm equally certain that we'll find no trace of him here."

"Then I hope you're wrong, sir, because what other clues do we have?"

Guy shook his head and said nothing. If Rachel was indeed the mystery tenant, she had left Knight's Cottage in January, not in April, as Sarah would assume. Yet even if that uncomfortable fact was about to be uncovered, there was no possible way for Sarah to find out that in February he and her cousin had moved back into Hampstead together.

The horses trotted on toward the Heath, straight past the place he had rented for Rachel. Chimneys clustered like a meeting of top-hatted solicitors. The walls flashed in white glimpses through the trees. The few visible windows were shuttered.

Guy had paid the landlord a year's rent in advance and still held the lease, so he knew that the house was unoccupied. Yet as they turned a corner the high oriel window in the bedroom he and Rachel had shared winked suddenly, as if the low sun conspired to bring the house back to life.

An illusion as absolute as her supposed affection for him.

Guy stared straight ahead and ignored the unpleasant clutch of distaste in his gut.

Hampstead Heath stretched away to a sky-laden horizon. Small gangs of men were working here and there with carts and shovels, making the most of the remaining daylight. Guy paid them no attention, looking only toward the whitewashed cottage that the curate had described.

He pulled up his team in front of the garden gate.

It had been almost completely dark when he had been forced to abandon his quest the previous evening to return to town for the ball. Now, in the late afternoon light, Knight's Cottage looked both charming and private.

His tiger leaped down to take the horses' heads. Guy stepped to the ground and held up his hand to Sarah.

"Come!" he said, smiling to cover his disquiet. "This is the place."

She set her fingers on his and climbed down, then she glanced up at him, her apricot brows drawn together. For a split second they stood gazing at each other. Little sparks seemed to fire between them, as if the air sizzled, as if he might give way to a mad impulse to pull her into his arms and kiss her.

Sarah snatched back her hand and looked away.

The gate opened on well-oiled hinges. Sarah stepped aside to let Guy knock at the door. After a long silence, footsteps rapped on tile.

The door opened. A woman in a cap and apron glanced at Sarah, then dimpled a smile as she gazed up at Guy. Dust sheets, brooms, and buckets were visible behind her.

"Yes, sir?"

"You're Mrs. Harris, the housekeeper?" he asked.

"Yes, sir. But Mr. Ashdown—that's the gentleman as had the lease, sir—he went off to Italy. He's an artist."

"No, we're looking for a lady," Sarah said. "She lived in this cottage all last winter, up until shortly after Easter. Did you know her?"

The housekeeper frowned. "Until Easter, ma'am? No, she—"

"Never mind that," Guy said. "The lady we seek first took the lease thirteen months ago, in late May of last year. A boy from the Five Oaks, one Harvey Penland, ran errands for her."

"Why, yes, sir! That's right. And a cheeky lad he was, too. Yes, yes, I remember the lady very well. Sometimes she would sit for hours at a time, just staring from the windows as if her heart would break, or else she wrote letters, pages and pages of them, which the Penland lad took down to the post."

"Did she ever meet any gentlemen, or have gentlemen callers?"

"No, indeed not, sir! Though she sometimes went walking on a Sunday, Mrs. Grant always kept herself to herself."

"Mrs. Grant?"

The housekeeper glanced back at Sarah. "She said she was a widow, ma'am. Such a shame! Such a lovely lady! The prettiest yellow hair you ever saw, and eyes like a periwinkle. I thought she was sad and lonely, but she always said not."

"Do you think she was ever afraid?" Guy asked.

"Afraid, sir? Well, I don't know, but then I wouldn't, would I? I'm just the housekeeper. Mrs. Grant never confided anything to me."

"Do you know where she is now?"

"God bless my soul, sir! I've no idea. She took herself off one day without a by-your-leave, or word to anyone. Just packed up and left. Mr. Langham had to find another tenant in a hurry, I can tell you, and was lucky to find Mr. Ashdown. Now, if you'll forgive me, ma'am, sir, I need to get on. The new tenant's due any day, and the floors need doing over."

"Thank you, ma'am," Guy said with a bow. "You've been more helpful than you know."

Sarah spun about and walked back to the carriage.

Guy forced himself not to follow, not to compound his sins by offering false comfort.

The garden was a pretty retreat with lawns and bushes and flowers, all hidden behind a high hedge. Rachel had lived here alone, until she had knocked on the door of his London townhouse to throw herself at his feet—and into his bed.

That was not, of course, what she had told him.

When had she first begun to spin her web of lies? During the seven months when she had truly been a governess for Lord Grail? Or in the missing five months before Jack had found her in the kitchen and asked her to spend that day on the yacht?

Whenever it had been, Rachel Mansard had caught Guy Devoran as securely as any spider ever caught its first moth. And now—to his infinite self-disgust—he was reeling Sarah Callaway into that net of sticky threads.

Sarah was standing beside the carriage, gazing valiantly across the Heath, her back upright.

Guy shook himself and strode up the path after her, though his blood burned with awareness, of her brave, resolute determination, of the wisps of fiery hair escaping her bonnet to caress her speckled cheek. A lady who spent too much time in the sun, instead of always sheltering her complexion—as Rachel had done—beneath parasols or white plaster ceilings.

She turned to face him. Her eyes were suspiciously bright.

"You've already followed up all possible leads here, haven't you?" she asked. "That's why you didn't want to bother bringing me. Other than that housekeeper—and confirming that Harvey Penland worked at the Five Oaks—you talked yesterday with everyone who might have known anything."

"Yes," he said. "There's nothing more to learn here in Hampstead that will help us find your cousin."

It was, fortunately, the truth.

Guy helped her up onto the seat. Beneath the escaped tendrils of red hair, brown flecks circled the corner of her jaw like the Pleiades, the daughters of Atlas hidden in the heavens to save them from the lust of Orion.

Avoiding his gaze, Sarah arranged her skirts. "And so I see that I'm defeated. Anything that you wish to share, you will share. Anything you wish to hide, I'll never get out of you. But I have no doubt now that I will discover nothing at all by myself."

"Rachel did not meet Daedalus here," he said.

She adjusted her gloves, her face pale. "No, she must have done."

He felt desperate to make amends in any small way that he could.

"Would you like to drive up over the Heath?" he asked. "The views of London are spectacular, and the sun will be setting soon."

"Thank you," she said. "I should like that."

He whipped up the horses.

They drove in silence for several minutes, while the rolling heights of Hampstead Heath opened up before them. Deep shadows filled the hollows. Pink-tinged clouds massed to the west.

"Isn't there anything else you can tell me?" she asked at last.

"Not much. Rachel apparently lived in that cottage with the discretion of a mouse. She never went into society and she never received visitors of any kind. When the curate tried to call, she told him that she wished to be left entirely alone, because she was writing a novel."

"A novel?"

"Yes," he said. "I'm forced to conclude that she was referring to her letters to you."

To his immense surprise, Sarah laughed, though a bright flush raced over her cheeks. "A novel may be fiction, sir, but fiction is only compelling when it's emotionally true."

"Ah," he said. "So we come back to that."

"Everything comes back to it," she insisted. "Rachel fell in love with Daedalus after Christmas, but feared him by Easter. When she came back from Devon in May, she was forced to hide from him in Goatstall Lane. Nothing will ever make me doubt that. So some detail has been missed. If she lived here like a mouse, he must have skulked in the shadows like a cat."

"So you won't concede that Daedalus, as she described him, may have been another product of her imagination?"

She lifted her chin and gazed away at the scenery. "I shall never in a million years believe that, sir, and neither will you, once you read her letters."

"Then you'll still trust me that far?"

"Yes, and in spite of everything, I can't regret involving you. Yet if we fail in our quest, I trust you'll not take it too much to heart?"

The compassion in her voice froze the blood in his veins. "Why do you suppose that I should, ma'am?"

"Because you smile at me as if you're already crushed by disappointment, almost as if you fear that we shall never discover the truth."

He glanced away, his nostrils filled with her scent, his very bones on fire.

"Nothing so very terrible, I trust, Mrs. Callaway. But yes, we may fail. And yes, I should hate that."

It was a small reality, but all he dared offer. The necessity to hide the whole truth roared like an enraged bull in his heart.

Guy headed his team for the loveliest parts of the Heath.

There was, of course, a great irony in feeling so irate about achieving exactly what he had wanted. All the seeds of truth that he thought it possible to share had been sown. After they took root and she saw that the letters didn't sway him, the luminous Sarah Callaway would surely be convinced and agree to let him hunt for Rachel alone?

After which, he would probably never see her wild freckles again.

Enough cause, surely, for a little fury at fate?

SARAH gulped in the clean evening air and tried to breathe out her distress.

It was hard to remain angry when their surroundings were so lovely. It was anyway beyond ungracious to feel anything but gratitude to Mr. Devoran, even if he refused to accept her judgment about Daedalus.

She glanced at his harsh eyebrows and perfect bones. His eyes reflected nothing but some dark grief that she couldn't understand, like the water in a deep well. Nevertheless, both his features and the scenery were a beautiful, storm-tossed celebration of nature. She was privileged to see them.

And how could she blame him? After all, Rachel had created a story of her life over the last two years as sustained and inventive as any work of fiction.

A group of red-and-white cows stood at the edge of a pond. Trees massed here and there in little copses, or bravely straggled out alone to invade the rolling heath.

Mr. Devoran guided his team to a high knoll and pulled up.

"A remarkable view." He gazed up at the high, drifting clouds, already stained by the oncoming sunset. "Yet it's the sky that makes this place so remarkable."

Smooth skin stretched over the hollow where his throat met his jaw: a defenseless place, usually hidden. A wave of heat spread unbidden over her breasts and up her neck.

"Yes," she said, looking away across the valley. White shafts of light broke between the clouds to light up a few chosen spires. "It's almost as if something sacred transpired from the clouds."

He glanced back at her. Dark fire burned in his gaze. "One is certainly closer up here to the vast vault of heaven, but it's Nature herself who feels holy."

"Why is Nature always female?"

"You don't agree that she is?"

"I don't know, though I suppose it's because Nature is the source of all life."

"No, it's because she's fascinating, capricious, and changeable."

"Like a typical female?" she said.

"I didn't say that."

"No, but it's implied, isn't it? Yet Nature is also capable of unpredictable violence."

"True," he said. "The worst of male attributes."

He moved his team forward until they reached another hillock. Mr. Devoran signaled his tiger, who leaped down to take the horses' heads, then he walked around the carriage and held up his hand.

"Come, Mrs. Callaway. The view is best if one walks just a little way up from here."

She took his fingers and allowed him to lead her to the highest point. London lay spread out before them. Shafts of dying sunlight glanced over the great dome of St. Paul's and picked out the silver thread of the Thames.

"The works of man are also lovely," he said. "But sadly enough, usually only from a distance. From here, the rooftops cluster around each church spire like cygnets around a flock of swans. A little closer, and you'd be confronted with all the misery and dirt of a great city."

"You'd also see splendid buildings and statues and art and gardens," she said.

"But nothing, you must agree, anywhere near as inspiring as the setting sun?"

They stood in silence as color bled slowly from the sky, until the bruised grays and blues were shot through with threads of gold and crimson. At last a faint lime green leached up behind the clouds to dissolve away into darkness, piercing only by the Evening Star.

"Venus," he said. "It'll be truly dark soon. We must get back."

Sarah said nothing as he helped her into the carriage. Yet she caught a sudden flash of real concern in his eyes.

Damnation! He had seen that hers were blurred with tears. Pain seared her heart that he had noticed and possibly even cared a little, though she had no idea why.

THE long summer twilight softened the oncoming darkness as they returned to Blackdown House. Lady Crowse expected her guests to share a small supper, but Sarah pleaded a headache and retired immediately to her room.

Guy watched the sway of her skirts as she marched away up the stairs. Sarah Callaway had inadvertently set up a disturbance in his heart and in his loins, like a squall blustering through clouds and threatening rain.

Though he was not in the least hungry, he ate a light meal with the duke's elderly sister, then dutifully played cards until she was ready to retire. He did his best to be amusing, but several times he caught the old lady's gaze shrewdly assessing him, as if she saw the signs of rot at the core.

Eight watched them play, then snapped at Guy's fingers when he carried the parrot up to Lady Crowse's apartments for her. The bird had learned most of his vocabulary, as well as his suspicion of strangers, from the duke's eccentric widowed sister.

Much to Guy's annoyance, Eight grumpily repeated his favorite new phrase at almost every step. "Safe from who, sir? Safe from who?"

The parrot was not interested in having anyone, least of all an untitled cousin, correct its grammar.

Alone at last in Ryder's study, Guy paced like a caged cat, while a knife turned slowly over and over in his gut.

Was Sarah weeping up there alone in her elegant guest chamber? Or was she too angry with him to allow grief? Either way, every encounter with him—and every piece of news that she had received from him since their first meeting in the bookshop—must have caused her nothing but pain.

Meanwhile, Rachel's letters sat on Ryder's desk like the nine holy books that the Cumaean Sibyl had offered to King Tarquin.

Sarah had sent them down with a brief note:

Dear Mr. Devoran,
Pray, read these for yourself, then tell me that I am still wrong about Daedalus.

            I remain, sir, Your most obedient humble servant,
                        Sarah Callaway

Guy cursed, then laughed at himself. Of the nine holy books, six had been burned unread. The remaining three had been said to contain the secrets of the gods. But of course, the Cumaean Sibyl was also the prophetess whom Aeneas had consulted before his descent into the Underworld.

Meanwhile, Rachel's letters lay piled neatly in chronological order. In what sense could they possibly contain any real emotional truth?

Before he wore a track in the carpet, he forced himself to sit down and unfold the first, written soon after she had genuinely gone to live at Grail Hall. The front bore the date and the earl's name, with the stamp "FREE"—one of the privileges of the peerage.

Lamplight washed over the paper, highlighting the creases and the crabbed writing, crossed and crossed again to make all of her news fit onto one sheet.

My dear Sarah . . .

He read through the second, then the third.

The months with Lord Grail appeared to have been essentially uneventful, though Rachel's letters were often witty, with little flashes of a dry humor that she had never shown him.

However, there was no hint that she had met any gentleman of interest there, and nothing to betray why she had fled without notice that Christmas. The same amused tone continued as she pretended to her cousin that she was still working at Grail Hall, when in fact she had gone—where?

He studied the franks and postmarks. The scrawled signature looked identical, the postmarks the same.

Guy looked up for a moment. Obviously, someone had been able to usurp the earl's franking privileges. Presumably, just as she had enlisted Harvey Penland, Rachel had suborned a servant at Grail Hall to intercept and forward her letters from Sarah. But why?

Rachel had spun such an elaborate superstructure of lies, no ancient Greek oracle could possibly have matched her.

Guy pulled out a sheet of clean paper and sketched out a calendar to cover the twenty-six months since Rachel's parents had died. The day when he'd first met her at the Three Barrels to take her out on Jack's yacht fell almost exactly in the center, leaving roughly thirteen months before it, and thirteen months since.

He marked the first seven months after the Mansards' death: *Grail Hall*. Ink spluttered from the pen as he circled the following Christmas and added a question mark. She had certainly left Grail Hall then, but the next five months remained blank.

Guy took another sheet of clean paper and dashed off a quick note to his cousin:

My dear Jack,

I offer the gratitude of the wicked once again for your help the day and night of the duchess's ball, though I am, like Odysseus, still swirling around in unknown seas.

You remember Rachel Wren. Did you notice the state of her hands when you first found her at the Three Barrels—before she dressed in Anne's clothes and we disappeared for our jaunt on the yacht?

I trust to your eagle eye and nose for suspicious detail.

Meanwhile, pray convey my undying adoration to your astoundingly brave and beautiful wife, along with my gratitude for her recent hospitality, especially so soon after your homecoming and so close to her time.

With my most heartfelt affection and in anticipation that I may soon help to welcome your first child into this sorry world, I am

Ever yours very truly,
Devoran

He rang for a footman and sent off his letter, then he ringed the day on the yacht and wrote "Knight's Cottage" across the next eight months, ending when Rachel had fled Hampstead to throw herself on his mercy.

The lamp burned down as he read the dozen letters that covered those months. The fantastic tales about being employed by one Harvey Penland, gentleman. The imaginary children, given names and individual personalities, the descriptions so clear that he could visualize each one.

All of it false.

Rather than call for a servant to refill the lamp, Guy stood and lit candles.

He left blank the few missing days at the end of January, after

Rachel had left the cottage and before she had turned up on the doorstep of his townhouse.

Then came the rest of February and March.

Guy stared at the empty boxes on his calendar, then he wrote "GD—The Chimneys" across the nine weeks during which Rachel had claimed to Sarah that she had met Daedalus and then become afraid of him, though she had in fact been living safely in Hampstead with him.

She had written only three letters in all of that time. Guy picked up the first, which the maid must have handed to the Norfolk stable lad to post for her. It would seem that the lovely Rachel Mansard had been able to inspire devotion in impressionable males everywhere she went.

Walking back and forth in front of the fireplace, Guy flipped open the letter and scanned the first few lines—more nonsense about Penland's imaginary brood—until he found the relevant passages: Rachel's account of meeting the man Sarah was calling Daedalus, the maze-maker, the villain.

> *Thank you for your generosity, once again, dear Sarah. But you'll never guess why I'm so happy lately, my dear, so I'll tell you: I've met the most entrancing gentleman. He's a close friend of the family and often visits. . . .*

His gut drew tight as if he were strapping on a sword, as if he were about to enter a maze to meet monsters.

He skimmed over Rachel's florid descriptions: *I never saw such lovely eyes on a man . . . so very tall a lady might even find him a little forbidding . . . the most compelling . . .*

Nothing identified the man as Guy Devoran, but neither did a single word contradict that idea. Guy forced himself to read it through again. It was hideously disconcerting to know that Rachel had secretly written to Sarah about him, all the while disguising the real nature of their relationship.

His blood churned with something that felt a great deal like rage.

The next letter had been written five weeks later, and there it was again. Buried amongst the fictional news of her life as a governess, Rachel had written another glowing account of her handsome new follower, Mr. Penland's nameless friend.

This was even worse than the last.

We're now able to meet quite often, my dear Sarah, sometimes more than once in a day. So I have very little time left to write, yet I know you will understand and forgive me. His attentions are so flattering that my affections are quite seriously engaged. Indeed, I fear that I may be falling in love.

Guy dropped the paper as if it had thrust out a wavering, forked tongue.

However he tried to interpret these letters, anger uncurled in his gut. He may have thought briefly that he was in love with Rachel. He had never thought for a moment that she loved him in return. How dare she claim otherwise to her cousin?

He leaned back to stare blindly at the ceiling.

He had rented the house with the top-hatted chimneys only because Rachel insisted they live secretly in Hampstead. Obviously that had been so that she could keep using Harvey Penland as her go-between with Sarah. But could it also be that she wanted to be close to an earlier admirer, someone she had indeed met at Knight's Cottage?

Ryder's presence was almost as strong in this room as if he were truly still here: *I hate to have to ask this, Guy, but could she have been seeing someone else at the same time?*

Yet he couldn't doubt the sworn testimony of his servants, and he and Rachel had barely been apart for those nine weeks. Days and nights in the bedroom with the oriel window. Meals shared in the pretty dining room that overlooked the garden. Quiet interludes in the library, when Rachel read novels while Guy took care of the ongoing business of his life.

He had returned to his townhouse on only a few occasions in all that time and had always come back to the house with the chimneys the same day. Rachel had never known ahead of time when he might leave for a few hours, or how quickly he would return.

How could she possibly have entertained another lover?

Yet she had successfully smuggled out her letters to Sarah, and secretly received her cousin's replies. Could she also have been corresponding with another man?

The legs of his chair hit the floor with a crash as he leaned forward to take up the pen. He drew a circle around April 15, the Wednesday before Good Friday—the day he had left to spend Easter with his family at Birchbrook—then another around April 28, the day he had returned to Hampstead to find Rachel gone.

Guy wrung his fingers through his hair and stood up.

How could any man allege that he valued honor, when he had allowed himself to become besotted with a female who flitted through her days in a dream of perjury? Perhaps his dragging pain was caused not by a damaged heart, but only by an enraged, wounded pride?

Yet either way Rachel had sown thistles of self-doubt in whatever claim he'd ever had to the name of a gentleman.

Now, with Sarah Callaway, he was only compounding it.

Guy strode across to Ryder's cabinet and poured himself a brandy. He stared at the fragrant liquor for a moment, then swallowed it in one gulp.

Rachel may have used him, but she had never been afraid of him. He was not Daedalus.

So when had her fear of this unknown man really begun?

He set down the empty glass and walked back to the desk.

The next letter was nothing but a hurried scrawl, apparently written in a terrible panic, after—Rachel claimed—the Penland family had gone to Devon for Easter. Broken phrases and sentences were strung together with dashes, as if she had lost the heart to form paragraphs.

I misjudged everything, Sarah! He's a brute and a tyrant—I'm terri-
fied of him and the truth is that I have been for weeks—I'd so longed
for his admiration, but now I see that I may have wished to ally my-
self with a monster! How very fortunate that Mr. Penland decided to
remove here to Dartmoor for the holidays—

Guy studied the outer surface. The letter was battered and
stained, as if someone had spilled ale that had smeared the critical
postmark. He rummaged around in a drawer for a magnifying glass,
but the name of the originating post office was illegible. Yet the
mileage stamp and charge amount, scrawled above Sarah's name and
the address of Miss Farcey's school for young ladies in Bath, were both
in keeping with the assumption that the letter had been sent from
Plymouth.

Could Rachel really have gone to Dartmoor when she left his
Hampstead house? If so, why?

She most certainly had not remained anywhere in the immediate
vicinity.

Guy read the letter through again. Disquiet deepened into anguish when he noticed another pattern of smudges across the last few
lines. Had Rachel wept as she had written it and had her tears
smeared the wet ink—or had that same carelessness that had obliterated the postmark also seeped moisture through the paper?

And why all this sudden vitriol about a man she had claimed to
love with such passion?

Ignoring his distress, Guy paced as he reread the previous two
missives, concentrating only on Rachel's exact allegations.

At last he folded the letters and gazed down at the empty grate,
his mind racing, then he dropped back into Ryder's chair and drew a
circle with a question mark around the two weeks from Easter till
the beginning of May—*Dartmoor?*

In her next frantic note Rachel announced that she had decided
she must flee her employer's house in Hampstead from fear of her

persecutor. After that, all the rest of the letters were postmarked in London, sent from the post office nearest to Goatstall Lane.

Guy read them one after another, each filled with more panic than the last, until in the end she had sent the frantic demand that had brought Sarah racing up from Bath, resulting in their confrontation in the bookstore.

He ringed that Thursday over and over in black ink. He already felt as if he had known Sarah Callaway all his life. Yet if she ever discovered that he had been Rachel's lover in February and March, she was bound to think that he was Daedalus.

Rachel had made sure of it.

The candles guttered as he pushed away from the table and began to stalk about the room.

Perhaps he had inadvertently broken Rachel's heart, done something unfathomable that had made her flit the minute he left her alone? Yet why the devil, if that were the case, would she deliberately send Sarah to seek him out?

None of it made sense.

Guy folded all the letters carefully, stacked them, and tied them up in a neat bundle. Then he picked up his calendar and held one corner in a candle flame. The paper flared briefly and ash drifted to the floor like dead, blackened leaves.

Only one fact seemed undeniable: Just as Sarah had claimed, whatever mad fictions Rachel had created before then, at some point after Easter she had become genuinely terrified.

Daedalus was real.

A steady rain drizzled down the windows the next day. Sarah paced nervously, unable to concentrate. Orchids hung in sprays or kept secret vigil in the shadows. The fountain was turned off. The birds were gone.

Yet the little hothouse jungle dripped and breathed and whispered, conjuring mysteries impossible to imagine.

She had eaten breakfast alone, attended Sunday Communion alone, eaten a light luncheon alone. And now she paced alone in this alien hothouse, as if she had stepped into a fantasy.

The blooms of a pale epidendrum clustered like a hatching of tiny butterflies. A bird's beak oncidium—*Oncidium ornithorhynchum*—bloomed like a shy violet, though its starburst-yellow heart seemed soaked in honey. The petals of the fragrant cattleya that Guy Devoran had studied the night of the ball had decayed into a moist clump that smelled slightly rancid.

Sarah had seen some of them illustrated in prints. Others were unknown to her, recent arrivals from the far reaches of the world. Yet whether fleshy or delicate, none of the orchids was innocent.

She sat down on an iron chair. The stone ribs in the roof overhead arched beneath an upturned silver bowl of rain.

Boots crunched on the tanbark.

Her heart exploded into life, flashing heat up her neck, as Mr. Devoran strode around a group of orange trees.

He saw her and stopped dead. Dark hair stuck to his forehead. His coat was soaked. Mud splashes outlined maps and harbors on his boots and wet buckskins.

Fire blazed for a moment in his dark gaze, then disappeared as if an iron door had clanged shut over the burning heart of a coal furnace.

He threw aside his riding crop, tugged off leather gloves, then reached into an inside pocket and dropped Rachel's letters onto the table at Sarah's elbow.

"You read them?" she asked.

"Thank you, yes, but good afternoon, Mrs. Callaway." His voice held delicate mockery. "I trust you slept well?"

Hot embarrassment melted her bones. She stood up and curtsied, but then she laughed.

"I'm so sorry. Yes, I thank you, sir. I slept very well. Actually, no, I didn't. But not for want of every comfort."

He smiled with a genuine, gentle mirth. "Then Holy Communion in the Blackdown's private chapel wasn't comfort enough?"

She sat down again and arranged her skirts. "I'm afraid not. And now I fear that I face damnation for the sin of curiosity, unless you agree to assuage it. You've been out?"

He dodged a large yellow-and-white blossom, the petals as lush as a satin wedding gown, the throat an explosion of sensuous invitation, and propped his hip on the corner of the table, his arms crossed.

"Yes, and I must apologize that I've not yet changed and stand before a lady in all my dirt. I didn't know you were in here."

"Did you discover something new?"

"No." This time it was Oberon's smile, the smile that hid all of Nature's secrets, the smile that might summon birds from the skies and force trees shockingly into leaf. "Nothing that justifies my sharing it."

Sarah looked away into the hidden hearts of some tiny pink-brown orchids. Long petals curled about one another in wild loops.

"Then pray tell me what you thought of Rachel's letters."

"I think that your cousin's a little mad," he said.

"Then you still don't believe that she ever met the man we're calling Daedalus?"

"On the contrary. I'm convinced that she's genuinely afraid of him. However, I don't accept that she first met him in January or February."

"But she said—"

He pushed away from the table. "No, she claimed to have met some nameless gentleman then and thought that she was falling in love. Yet though she gave the impression when she wrote to you after Easter that her fear of Daedalus had been growing steadily for several months, there's no trace of it in the two letters before that. If her correspondence had stopped at the beginning of April, any unbiased reader would think that she was expecting a proposal any day."

"Yes, I know, but I don't think that changes anything. She wrote hardly any letters in February and March anyway, so it's not surprising that she didn't reveal all of that until later. Unless you imagine that Rachel had two importunate suitors. In which case, why did she mention only one?"

"I've no idea," he said. "But I've sent a man to Norfolk to inquire after Harvey Penland."

"Just as someone on Lord Grail's staff must have been intercepting my letters after she left there—in which case, that person knows where she really was for those missing five months, doesn't he? Or she, I suppose?"

"No, it was undoubtedly a man," he said. "This person had access to Grail's franking privileges, which limits the possibilities. I intend to go there next. I've also written to Jack."

"Lord Jonathan? Why?"

He stalked up and down for a moment, then dropped into the chair on the other side of the iron table. Masculine undertones of horse and leather and fresh, damp linen assailed her nostrils. Heat ran in runnels beneath her skirts.

"To ask him whether your cousin's hands really were those of a scullery maid."

She stared at the precise lines of his fingers, the square, blunt nails and clean bones. "You think he would have noticed?"

"I'm certain of it. I'm also certain that we'll have his answer by return."

She made herself look up, though the flash of his dark eyes might burn her. "And after that?"

"Dartmoor."

"Then you think Rachel truly did go there in April?"

"Almost certainly." He leaped to his feet and began to pace again. "You might have noticed if that postmark had been wrong. She couldn't have known it would get smudged. And whether or not we agree about when she met Daedalus, she expressed very little panic before Easter and a great deal of it afterwards. Though the six children didn't exist, there's no reason to suppose that she was lying about having traveled to Devon."

"At least we know that she was still living at the cottage until then. Would the curate have noticed when she left Hampstead?"

Mr. Devoran gazed up at the flow of white rain on the glass, as if he stood at the edge of a precipice where one blind step might plunge him to his death.

"He didn't mention it."

"But why would Rachel go to Dartmoor? We don't know anyone in Devon."

"When I go there," he said, "I may find out."

Dark hair was curling on his collar as it dried. The fabric of his coat stretched damply over lithe, sculpted shoulders beneath the tall, rolled collar. The skirts, still creased from riding, flared down over long, muscled legs.

Treacherous heat danced and flared in her heart.

"Then I should like to come, too," Sarah said, "if it could be arranged with propriety."

His hesitation this time was longer, as if he fought some hidden temptation or secret reproach.

"No," he said at last. "I don't think so."

"I cannot insist, of course," she said. "I have not the means to travel there by myself, but—"

He spun about. "Pray forgive my curiosity, ma'am, but why were you sending money to your cousin?"

The hot pulse in her blood moved deeper, resounding in heavy, secret reverberations.

"How did you—? Oh, the letters, of course!"

"You believed her to be working as a governess. Surely her salary was no less than yours?"

A different kind of embarrassment flooded her cheeks. "Yes, but Rachel required so many extra little things to make her life bearable."

"And you do not?"

"I live at the school, where Miss Farcey provides everything I need."

"Whereas Rachel was sometimes invited to dine with the family, and often mingled with the guests?"

"Whatever the truth of that, I knew she needed to dress appropriately and maintain decent standards, and her employment was never all that secure—"

"So she begged you for whatever funds you could spare and you were happy to help, even though it meant you had to forgo any holidays."

"Several charity girls live with us year-round. It's no hardship to remain in Bath with them for the summers."

He broke off an orchid, then snapped the stem over and over, until he held nothing but petals.

"And what of your future, ma'am? You've set aside nothing for yourself? Instead, you sent your handful of extra guineas to your cousin every payday, so she could purchase a new silk dress, or an ivory fan, or the very best shoes."

"Rachel never thought she'd have to work, Mr. Devoran, so it was harder for her. Her life was once nothing but parties and flirtation, but when her parents died so very deeply in debt, her suitors melted away like snow."

"She had an understanding with one man in particular?"

"No real understanding, no, but several gentlemen had trailed after her like puppies and she thought she'd be able to choose between them. I believe she faced her fate with great courage when they all disappeared."

"It was *courage* that allowed a spoiled girl to rob you of your future security? What the devil urge to self-sacrifice made you concede to her demands?"

Though the blood rushed from her face, Sarah surged to her feet. She wanted to strike him.

"You think I'm a fool to love my cousin, sir?"

"God, no!" Shredded petals rained into the lush heart of a white orchid as he spun about. "I think I cannot bear the presence of so much damned nobility, Mrs. Callaway!"

CHAPTER SEVEN

H E SENT HER A BRIEF NOTE OF APOLOGY. ONLY FIVE LINES. Expressed gracefully and sincerely and with genuine shame.

The grate in Ryder's study was filled with the ashes of all his first drafts.

As soon as the footman disappeared with the note, Guy kicked his feet up onto the desk and leaned back to stare at the ceiling, his chair precariously balanced on two legs.

Then I should like to come, too, if it could be arranged with propriety.

No! Never! He must send her to Wyldshay first thing in the morning. Miracle would take care of her, and he would never again have to face that honest gaze and be confronted by his own perfidy. Especially since he had discovered just enough to be genuinely concerned for her safety.

Guy had no idea of Daedalus's identity, but he was damned sure now that the man could be dangerous.

Yet as he had marched through the glasshouse—taking a short-cut from the stables—Sarah had glanced up and pinned him to the heart.

In the silver light her hair had darkened to a deep russet confection of plaits wrapped about her delicate skull. Pale amber lashes fringed her clear hazel eyes. Then that warm, sensuous color had flooded up her cheeks, and for a moment he had forgotten all of his subterfuge and dishonor, and found himself face-to-face with the shock of his desire.

He had covered it, as best as he could, until the end he had lashed out in anger.

Yet he could hardly be petty enough to criticize Sarah Callaway for doing exactly what he would have done, *had* done, by sacrificing everything to help a cousin she loved. Neither Ryder nor Jack would be happily married now if Guy Devoran had not dropped everything in his own life whenever his cousins had truly needed him.

Guy exploded to his feet, letting the chair fall with a crash.

Sarah would read his note of apology and accept it at face value. She need never know that when Rachel had turned up weeping on his doorstep and begged for his aid, he had seduced that frail, broken songbird and set her up as his mistress in the house with the top-hatted chimneys.

Thus Sarah would never need to suspect that Daedalus might be Guy Devoran, though she would still, with any luck, despise him.

That would make it a great deal easier to send her away.

GUY strode into the blue drawing room the next morning with renewed determination. Sarah Callaway rose and curtsied. That entrancing blush washed over her cheeks, and she glanced down as if his gaze burned her.

"Good morning!" He bowed with formal elegance. "I trust you received—"

"No, please don't apologize again, sir! You were absolutely correct. Though my position with Miss Farcey has always felt quite secure—"

"No," he said. "I spoke entirely out of turn."

"I thought that Rachel was unhappy and longing for a little frippery. So you were right. It was foolish of me to risk my own security, when I didn't know yet that she must have actually needed the money for necessities. But that was the case in the end, wasn't it, especially when she fled Daedalus?"

Guy swallowed. Rachel had certainly loved luxury, but she had not been in need of funds when she left his house in Hampstead.

"You're very generous," he said. "Yet I only came to say good-bye. There's more business I need to attend to here in town, so I've ordered a coach to take you down to Wyldshay."

"To stay with the Duke and Duchess of Blackdown?"

"It's Miracle's home, as well. And, as it happens, Ryder and Jack are cursed with three younger sisters, who'd no doubt love to learn a little extra botany and dancing and geography. You may spend the summer within the walls of the most impregnable castle in England—and one of the most beautiful."

In a rustle of skirts Sarah walked to the window. Rain streamed down the panes.

Her nape was both graceful and vulnerable as she stared at the meandering rivulets on the glass. Straggles of red hair caressed the intimate curves of her neck and ear. He suppressed the urge to stride up to her to brush them aside—though his fingertips burned.

"Wyldshay's white towers float in a lake in a river," she said quietly, "or so they say, rather like Avalon."

"And St. George and his dragons snarl from every wall and fireplace and half of the tapestries." He did his best to keep his voice light. "However, the best of modern comfort softens that heart of medieval stone. It's especially lovely in July."

"I don't doubt it," she said. "Yet I don't believe I shall go."

They were interrupted by a knock at the door. Guy strode across and flung it open. Paul held out a silver tray containing a small package.

"One of the lads brought this over from Brockton's Hotel just now, sir," he said. "He managed to intercept it in time to pay the charges."

Guy glanced once at the postmark and the handwriting on the

cover, then turned to face Sarah. He felt clear and cold, as if he were out shooting on a frosty morning in November.

"It's from Plymouth, from Rachel," he said. "Would you prefer that I leave?"

Her face was very white. "No! No, you're welcome to stay, sir, of course."

Guy paced the edge of the room, his pulse hammering, as Sarah carried the package back to her chair and tore it open. She read in silence for a few minutes.

At last she looked up. Her freckles marked her white skin as if fragments of broken seashell had been abandoned by a retreating tide.

"Rachel's living, or rather hiding, on Dartmoor. She doesn't say why or where, but she's sure that she's quite safe now." Sarah brushed her fingers over her mouth. "She says she couldn't wait for me, because it had become too dangerous for her to remain in London any longer."

"In what way?"

"There were accidents. A carriage almost ran her down. Part of a brick wall suddenly collapsed, barely missing her as she walked by. A robber with a knife threatened her on the street, but a group of gentlemen happened to come by and the ruffian ran away." Pink fired around her nostrils, as if she held back tears. "Daedalus was trying to kill her."

"No," he said. "He was only trying to frighten her."

She leaped to her feet. "You already knew about these attacks?"

Guy stopped, his concentration as acute as if partridges had suddenly burst from cover and he must decide where to aim.

"Yes," he said. "Most of them. Not all of the details, perhaps, though I've been investigating this exact issue all morning. May I read that?"

"Keep it, if you like!" Her fingers trembled as Sarah set the letter on the table and turned away. Her shoulders seemed painfully fragile beneath the knot of red hair. "Every word is already engraved on my memory."

Guy read rapidly—several pages of valuable new details—though his heart burned at Sarah's obvious distress.

"Is this why you wish to send me to a castle surrounded by water?" she asked.

Desperate to comfort her, he thrust Rachel's letter unfinished into a pocket. Time to analyze the rest later.

"Yes. I discovered some of it that first day, after you and I met in that bookstore, then more the next day. Jack helped—just enough to heighten my worst fears."

She walked back to the window. "So there really was a tiger in the glasshouse?"

Guy stalked up and down the carpet. He was still balanced on that keen blade of exact truth, trying not to reveal his own vulnerability.

"If you like. Jack and I certainly feared then that someone was trying to murder your cousin. Fortunately, now I'm absolutely certain that her death was never his intent."

Sarah sank onto the window seat, her profile bright against the gray day outside, as if her red hair were the flame of the world.

"And you chose to hide all of this from me?"

"Of course! There might have been danger to you, also—there still may be."

"That seems highly unlikely," she said. "Daedalus can't even know that I exist."

"Devil take it, ma'am! I will not take that risk. Whether or not Rachel's death was his aim, if a rejected admirer is indeed behind such attacks, he must be a madman."

"So you will send me down to Wyldshay?"

"Yes, of course! Fortunately, no one in their right mind would turn down the chance to go there."

She exploded from the seat. "Then obviously I'm not in my right mind! For whether you wish it or not, I shall immediately go down to Plymouth after Rachel. However long it may take, I won't leave any stone unturned until I find her."

"I will not allow that," he said.

High color flooded her cheeks. "I really fail to see how you can stop me, sir."

It was a card he hated to play, but he played it anyway. "How do you intend to finance such a venture, ma'am? You led me to believe that you were at the end of your resources."

"Then you didn't read that letter far enough, sir. Rachel realized that I might have put myself into financial difficulties by coming to London like this. So in recompense for my losses, she sent me this." Sarah thrust out one hand. A bracelet—shining like tiny, brilliant cornflowers dusted with gold—sparkled across her fingers. "A gift from Daedalus, I assume, which I may sell as I will."

Damnation!

Irony this absolute was rare. Guy's anger collapsed in the face of a new self-derision.

He raised a brow. "You're experienced in selling jewelry for cash, ma'am?"

"No, though I'm sure I could manage—unless it's simply paste and worth nothing. But Rachel believes it has value, and surely no reputable jeweler would cheat me?"

"Of course not, but if you walked into Rundle and Bridges with that, you'd first face some damned awkward questions."

She turned the blue jewels over in her fingers. "And you think if Daedalus bought it there, they might tell him, or he might see it and start asking who'd returned it?"

Guy clasped his hands behind his back, despising himself for having to pick his words so carefully—as if he were digging a hole for himself with a silver fork.

"If I thought it wise, I'd happily sell it for you myself. I could have it held for as long as I requested, then sold privately. However, there's nothing to be gained either way."

She walked back to the table. "You think it's worth so little, it won't even buy my coach ticket?"

For a split second he was tempted to pretend to sell the bracelet for her for a few shillings. She would never find out. Then she would have to agree to leave.

Instead, because he couldn't bear what he seemed to be becoming, he told her the truth. "On the contrary, I'm certain that it's worth a great deal more than your annual salary as a schoolmistress."

The bracelet clattered onto the polished table as if the sapphires had burned her.

"Then I cannot fathom why Rachel would have accepted such a valuable gift from a gentleman to start with!" Sarah sat down and propped her forehead on one hand to stare down at the jewels, her long fingers brushing her hairline. "She must have been afraid to either refuse or return it. No wonder she sent it to me! She must hate it."

"No doubt," he said, and wondered with a small pang of rage if that was true.

"Then may I ask if you would indeed sell it for me, Mr. Devoran?"

"Even if I give you its value right now, ma'am, you must still go to Wyldshay."

"No."

"The carriage is ordered."

Passion flashed in her eyes. "If you try to force me, sir, I shall sell this bracelet myself, whatever the risk, and go where I wish."

"And then what?" He ran his fingers back through his hair. "You show regard for neither your safety, nor your reputation. If you run off to Devon, what the devil are your prospects for employment once your funds run out?"

Sarah sprang to her feet. "Short of imprisoning me in this house, sir, I don't see how you can stop me. But before she left for Wyldshay, Lady Ryderbourne promised me that—whatever I do in the meantime—I'll never want for a secure future."

Guy stopped dead and this time found unadulterated amusement. The Fates—being female—were obviously determined to thwart him at every turn.

"So I'm confounded by a conspiracy of ladies! Not only will Miracle keep her word, but the duchess will undoubtedly back her. Her Grace has an unfortunate weakness for radical politics, which translates into a certain tolerance for independent young ladies."

Sarah laughed, with just a small trace of bitterness. "Good heavens! Miss Farcey would give her right arm to gain the patronage of the Duchess of Blackdown. So, if you would give me even something toward the value of this bracelet, Mr. Devoran, I shall travel down to Devon."

"And what exactly will you do when you get there? Announce to all and sundry that you've come to search for Miss Rachel Mansard?"

"I don't care about any risk to me," she said.

"I've gathered as much, Mrs. Callaway," he said coldly. "Yet if you rush down to Dartmoor, you will very likely only increase the risk to Miss Mansard."

A dark flush raced over her cheeks. Her gaze burned. The riot of freckles ran like the Milky Way over the bridge of her nose. Her mouth was unexpectedly tempting.

In spite of the ice in his voice, his blood ran hot.

"If it were your cousin, Mr. Devoran," she said, "what would you do?"

A silent current seemed to pass between them: an entirely unexpected depth of understanding. Some truths were too great to be denied. He was trumped.

"Move heaven and earth, and hazard everything, of course," he said simply.

Sarah stretched the bracelet out on the table. Even on such a dull day, the stones burned with blue fire.

"As must I," she said. "Especially now that Rachel has just secured my autonomy."

She was unraveling his plans like a cat with yarn. Guy faced the chaos of new patterns and rapidly began to weave the only viable solution. He could not force her to retreat to Wyldshay. Neither could he allow her to race unprotected down to Plymouth.

"Very well," he said. "The terms change. Yet you already put your quest in my hands when we met in the bookstore. So I beg that you'll continue to allow me to help you, in spite of our disagreements."

Her eyes searched his face. "Even though there's still something important that you're not telling me?"

"There are a great many things that I'm not telling you," Guy said. "Though you're very busy finding out some of them for yourself."

"Rachel has no one else, Mr. Devoran. If I don't go to Devon, I'd only go mad with worry and I'd be days away from helping her, if she needs me. Though I see the folly in my rushing off without a plan, surely you agree?"

Guy paced away across the carpet. Daedalus had no reason to suspect Sarah Callaway, and the evidence suggested that he had already achieved his goal of driving Rachel from London. So both women were probably safer in Devon than in town.

Yet he felt as if he were falling down a long, dark tunnel toward some particularly horrendous perdition.

"I had already planned to go to Dartmoor," he said. "Though you and I can hardly travel together, Lord and Lady Overbridge host a house party next week. Buckleigh is only a few miles east of Plymouth, not far from the edge of the moor. I can arrange for you to be there."

"In what capacity?" she asked.

"God, I don't know! As a guest, if you like."

She stroked the gems idly with one finger. "That would look very odd, don't you think? Perhaps some lady who's attending might need a companion?"

"No," he said. "I have a better idea." He turned to face her. "Would you be able to entertain the ladies by giving a few seminars about plants?"

Her smile lit her face as if a lamp burned beneath her fine skin. His heart skipped a beat.

"You can arrange that?" she asked.

"With Lady Overbridge? Yes, of course. Botany is all the rage among females these days. Buckleigh boasts extensive new gardens and she's very proud of them. I'll come myself as soon as I wrap up the rest of my investigations here in London. Meanwhile, I trust to your discretion."

"Thank you, Mr. Devoran. If Lady Overbridge agrees, it's an excellent plan."

"In the meantime, if you would allow me to give you something toward the value of that bauble, I'll put it into the duke's safe until you wish to redeem the rest."

She gathered the bracelet in one hand and held it out. "You're quite that sure that this is worth so very much?"

"I'm absolutely certain of it, Mrs. Callaway," he said.

Guy thrust the jewels away in an inner pocket, then strode out of the room. The sapphires burned a hot track into his soul. He knew the bracelet to be solid gold with precious stones, because he had bought it for Rachel himself.

SARAH rode in Lady Overbridge's second coach with the governess and a most superior lady's maid. Her Ladyship had declared it was the most delightful idea she had heard in an age. Everyone raved about botany these days, such a ladylike pursuit, the study of plants. How absolutely charming to include a young lady at her house party to teach her guests all about pistils and stamens and why flowers have petals, at all!

Didn't Lady Whitely agree?

Lady Whitely, who had witnessed Sarah's interview with her future employer, most certainly did.

In fact, that lady had added her own opinion, with a pretty little titter: "And if it ensured Mr. Devoran's presence—*such* a handsome gentleman!—at *my* house party, I would invite a Hottentot in feathers."

Sarah choked back her smile. A little humility before one's betters was always necessary, but that didn't stop her from being genuinely amused as she remembered it.

She glanced out of the coach window at the summer countryside. Their journey would take several days and, ironically, carry her through Bath, where she could collect some more clothes and some books, and explain to Miss Farcey that she was going to take a summer holiday and couldn't be sure when she might return.

Now she was promised the patronage of a duchess, she would always be able to find employment, whatever happened in the meantime, and Miss Farcey would no doubt welcome her back with no questions asked. The freedom of that thought was remarkably heady. As was the knowledge that she carried a nice sum in coins in her reticule: a deposit from Mr. Devoran toward the value of Rachel's bracelet.

Yet real worry still circled beneath that small happiness, as if tired dogs fretted at a treed cat. Rachel was hiding somewhere unknown on Dartmoor, because—even if Mr. Devoran claimed otherwise—Daedalus had attempted to murder her.

Meanwhile, he had remained in London to delve deeper into those so-called accidents. How much danger awaited him from the thugs that Daedalus must have hired to carry out such attacks?

Lady Overbridge and Lady Whitely were not the only females who would be devastated if Mr. Devoran did not come to Buckleigh as promised.

THE street was even dingier than Guy had expected. Shabby terraces of soot-streaked brick and dirty windows in an area that had once housed prosperous merchants, but was now barely clinging to respectability.

He drew back into the deep shadows and waited.

Rachel's last letter was securely folded in an inner pocket. It contained just enough extra detail about the threats to her life that he had been able to follow several new leads. With the additional information he had gleaned from Jack and his own earlier investigations, Guy had a damned good idea of what Daedalus had been trying to achieve.

Now it was time to make sure.

The brick wall that had collapsed so suddenly had belonged to an abandoned building at the end of this street. Rachel had often walked past it on her way back from the post office, before turning into Goatstall Lane. At the beginning of June, the bricks at the top had crashed down, barely missing her.

Such a dramatic event had fortunately had witnesses.

Yet the inhabitants of Lower Cornmere Street would be understandably reluctant to speak to a gentleman. So—though he made no attempt to hide his competence to defend himself—Guy wore some damned uncomfortable filth on his hair and skin, along with an equally dirty jacket, working men's pants, and rough boots.

His normal voice would have betrayed him instantly. Fortunately, as boys, he and Jack had learned as many different accents as they could from the servants at the various duchy properties and at Birchbrook. Then, as wild young men, they had learned to mimic the prizefighters and their cronies, a skill that had since saved Jack's life upon occasion.

Guy trusted it might now save his, also.

A few high-flung stars promised nightfall when the man with a limp finally emerged from the Merry Dogs public house and began to weave his way up the street.

"Stainbull!" Guy hissed as the man drew level. "Ye've bin playing hide and seek wi' me, ye damned marplot!"

Stainbull jerked to a halt. He peered up beneath the brim of his greasy hat and gave Guy a rotten-toothed grin.

"Mr. Uxbridge, sir? Now, sir, ye made it clear when we last met that ye be a man of the world. Ye'll not hold ill with poor Stainbull, sir?"

Guy ignored the stink of cheap ale and raw onions, and grasped the man's collar.

"And as I said then, sir, I want a name, that's all I want. I know who did it. But who paid to have it done?"

"Well, ye be a bright spark, sir! Where's the blunt ye promised me?"

He thrust Stainbull up against the wall and slipped a knife against the man's throat.

"Ye've bin on the drag lay, cully. The name now, then we'll see about the rest. Or perhaps ye fancy a visit with Jack Ketch?"

"God rest us, Mr. Uxbridge, sir! I don't know nothing!"

Guy tightened his grip. "That's not what a little bird told me."

Stainbull stretched his neck, his eyes bulging. "There's no cause for that, sir! The timing was careful, went just as planned. The piece got dust on her bonnet and was taken all a-mort, but walked on home as merry about the gills as you could please. Not a pretty yellow hair on her pretty yellow noddle harmed, sir."

Guy glowered, keeping his lips tight over his suspiciously good teeth, though he had swilled a little thick tea in an attempt to stain them.

"And if a cove wanted to know how to go about getting another job with timing just as careful, a cove knows who to talk to. But what if that cove don't care how it was done, and only wants to know the name of the churl that ordered it?"

Stainbull's eyes darted about. No one else was in earshot. He licked dry lips and squinted back up at Guy.

"Then that cove'd be too late. He's gone."

The tip of the knife threatened to draw blood. "The name?"

"Falcorne, sir! Prig called himself Falcorne! A squat, dun fellow wi' blue peepers."

It was the third time Guy had heard it: no doubt not his quarry's real name. Though the description—short and thickset, brown-haired and blue-eyed—applied to half the rogues in London.

Keeping Stainbull still pressed up against the wall, Guy relaxed his fingers a little.

"And what did this Falcorne do for a living, Mr. Stainbull, that makes you call him a prig?"

"The cove had airs, set himself up like a gennulman, though he was used enough to having his paws in the dirt."

Guy clinked coins in his pocket. "What kind of dirt?"

"Dirt, sir! Ground in, like. Fingernails cracked like a whore's madge, but with the job done and the mort taken off in a fright, you'll not find him here, sir. He'll be gone home."

For a second Guy's blade threatened to cut the man's throat. "And where is that, Mr. Stainbull?"

"My doxy was married to a blacksmith from south o' Dartmoor. Same way o' talking. Look for him there between the moor and the sea, she said."

Ice water trickled down Guy's spine. "What else?"

Stainbull squirmed. "Well, I thought he might be touched, sir. He said in his cups he could tell the Queen of Denmark from Marie Louise, and Charles de Mills from the Old Velvet, and he was very partial to a monk's head or a ruby-lipped cat. Then he cackled like a crow. I don't know any more than that, sir. Not to save my humble life! So you'll not squeal on poor Stainbull, sir, as was born halt and shamble-legged and never did no one no harm?"

Almost numb with shock, Guy released the greasy collar, just as something sharp blurred at the edge of his vision. He twisted instantly and chopped hard with one hand.

He could almost convince himself that he'd imagined the nasty little blade, except that the edge of his palm stung with the impact against its wooden handle. Another second and he'd have been stabbed in the gut or cut across the ribs.

Stainbull dodged aside and grinned, his knife already hidden again in his clothing.

"You're a rum cove, Mr. Uxbridge, sir," he said.

Before he could prevent himself Guy laughed, but he also tossed a handful of coins onto the cobbles.

As Stainbull scrabbled for them he strode away. It was an

amusingly intense way to test his conclusions about what he had learned. Fortunately, no knife came whistling through the air to fell him in his tracks. A slightly hair-raising vindication!

The lame man had knocked down a brick wall with exactly the right timing for Rachel to walk away terrified, but unscathed. Just like the other men hired by Falcorne to carry out the "accidents," Stainbull was a villain, but not a killer.

If Daedalus had truly intended murder, he'd have used different lackeys and Rachel would be dead. Yet who knew if, or when, that might change?

Marie Louise was a pink damask rose.

The paler Queen of Denmark, a recent introduction from France, bloomed with the blush of Sarah Callaway's cheeks during her most agitated moments.

Charles de Mills, a dark scarlet gallica, was a close enough relative of the old velvet roses of the apothecaries, though anyone knowledgeable about flowers could easily tell the difference.

More chillingly, the monk's head and the ruby-lipped cattleya were both orchids: expensive, sensual, exotic orchids.

And the man spoke with a South Devon accent. The most unnerving condemnation of Guy's decisions that Mr. Stainbull could have made.

Falcorne had dirt under his fingernails and had expert knowledge of flowers. Not a gentleman, but a gentleman's gardener, who had been sent up from Dartmoor to carry out the attacks against Rachel, while Daedalus himself remained at home.

And Guy Devoran—gallant cousin to the clever St. Georges— had just sent Sarah Callaway to teach botany to Lady Overbridge's guests at Buckleigh, where the grounds ran right up to the edge of the moor.

THOUGH no one appeared to be watching or following him, Guy waited till full dark to slip into his townhouse from the mews. As soon as he entered the kitchen he ripped off the filthy neckerchief and tossed aside his knife. A basin of water waited. Guy washed his hands, and walked into his study to pour himself a brandy.

A letter waited on his desk. He tore open Jack's dragon seal and unfolded the single sheet. The entire missive was in code.

My dear Guy,
Anne is extremely well, we thank you, and sends her love by return.
    When I found her in that kitchen, the mysterious Rachel Wren's hands—though a little red—still boasted neatly manicured nails.
    Since she barely knew what the bucket was for, it seemed likely— however improbable otherwise—that she was a distressed gentlewoman of some kind, not an actress down on her luck, nor a member of the muslin company.
    Her voice and manner betrayed the same.
    Enough reason—along with her superficial resemblance to Anne—to pick her for the jaunt on the yacht and give her so much gold.
    I only confirm your own conclusions, of course. Why else did you spend the next several months trying to find her?
                     Believe me ever your devoted cousin,
                               Jack St. G.

PS: Anne smells adventure and is concerned for your safety. I've as- sured her of your prowess, but of course she doesn't know quite how much you've secretly achieved for Ryder and me over the years. For that I can never thank you enough.
              Ever yours to command, should you need me—J. St. G.

Guy stared thoughtfully into his glass. He had always known that Rachel couldn't really have been a scullery maid by trade. He just hadn't been sure how long it had been since she had lived as a lady. From Jack's observations, it had not been more than a few days.

So where the hell—and how—had she lived for the five months after she had left Grail Hall, before he first met her at the Three Barrels?

She had fled to Knight's Cottage after that, only to come to him eight months later and allow him to seduce her. They had lived together in the house with the chimneys. Yet Rachel had never trusted him enough to tell him the truth about her identity or her past. Instead she had woven a fabrication of fairy tales, and then she had left.

With that knowledge burrowing like a worm in his soul, Guy rang for his manservant and ordered a hot bath, before taking the stairs two at a time to his bedroom. While he waited for the clang of the cans, he stripped naked and dashed cold water from the pitcher onto his face and head.

Rivulets raced down his body. Rubbing a towel vigorously over his chest, he strode to the dresser to toss clean clothes for the evening onto the bed.

While his man packed what he'd need for a house party in Devon—and commandeered the fastest traveling carriage and horses remaining in the Blackdown House stables—Guy would have a few hours in which to interview the men he had sent to gather any remaining information in London.

He would, of course, do so dressed once again as a gentleman. In that same disguise he would travel night and day down to Buckleigh.

His arrival would result in a great deal of female twittering, though not from Sarah Callaway. She might blush a little, or glance away with that exquisite diffidence, but dignity was as natural to her as breathing.

Meanwhile, tracking down the facts at Grail Hall would have to be delegated. He pulled out a sheet of paper and dashed off another coded note to Jack.

Thumping and banging betrayed the arrival of the servants with hot water for his bath. Guy threw aside the towel and stalked into the attached dressing room.

Though he acknowledged the men's efforts with a smile, eyes black with rage stared back at him from the mirror. A naked man betrayed neither rank nor education. How deeply embroiled in falsehood must such a man be, before he relinquished his right to the title of English gentleman?

Fortunately, no one would doubt his exalted status, or his honor, in Devon, where both Sarah and Rachel were now staying on Daedalus's doorstep.

CHAPTER EIGHT

ᴍ̃R. Devoran!" Lady Overbridge cried, holding out both hands. "We were so afraid that you wouldn't come."

"Quite! Quite!" His Lordship huffed up to join his wife. "Glad to have you, Devoran! Promises to be a bang-up show if this weather holds, don't you know! Excellent pugilist here from Exeter, a half-decent trainer if you've the mind to try your fives against some of the other gentlemen."

"Your servant, my lord, my lady! Delighted!" Guy stopped at a safe distance and bowed.

Nevertheless, Her Ladyship walked up to take his arm. Dark brown ringlets emphasized her white neck. With only the slightest hint of affectation, she laughed up at him to show off teeth that were even and small. As if to echo their beauty, she wore pearl drops in her ears and another on a gold chain around her neck.

Annabella Overbridge was very young and very pretty, and her husband was the kind of strapping sportsman who still believed in female innocence.

"You'll allow me to show you to your room myself, Mr. Devoran," Lady Overbridge said. "The other ladies are all agog to have you join our little party, but of course you must refresh yourself first." She tossed her ringlets. The pearls danced. "I must know every detail of your journey. I insist!"

His Lordship smiled indulgently and turned to leave. "Hear all your news later, Devoran!"

Guy surrendered with good grace. To look about for Sarah Callaway—to betray impatience for that frank golden gaze, the madness of red hair, and skin as dappled as the shade of a young tree— would be the height of bad manners.

Annabella played idly with the single pearl at her throat as they walked toward the stairs. Dancing brown eyes sparkled. Pearly teeth glistened. She chattered brightly about her house party, the weather, and the latest gossip.

Guy ignored most of it, except to make a mental inventory of the other guests' names: five unmarried girls with their chaperons, four young bachelors, not counting himself, and three married couples, besides his host and hostess.

One of those married ladies, a fragile blonde, stepped around a corner, then pretended surprise. She tittered with delight and threw up both hands.

"Why, Mr. Devoran!" Lady Whitely dropped a provocative curtsy and glanced up beneath her eyelashes. The invitation was impossible to mistake. "We ladies have been laying wagers on your arrival, sir! Only I was so completely sure that you would come to Buckleigh that I risked twenty guineas."

Guy bowed with chill perfection. "Then I am gratified that you did not lose your gold over me, Lady Whitely."

She gazed knowingly up at him, then flounced away to gaze up at a portrait. The stance showed off her long neck and elegant carriage. Huge chintz sleeves framed her tiny waist. A pretty woman with a poisonous tongue and a husband who drank too much.

"Well, anyone might have doubted it when you dallied in town for so long, Mr. Devoran," she said archly. "Though if you had other motives than your interest in orchids for wishing to include that red-headed schoolteacher here at Buckleigh, I am sure I have far too much discretion to even hint at it."

"Oh, my dear!" Lady Overbridge clutched Guy's arm and giggled. "How can you say so?"

To her credit—perhaps—Lottie Whitely blushed.

"Certainly, anyone would wonder at such a thing when Mrs. Callaway is so very plain, while Mr. Devoran is so very—" She giggled and glanced back at him. "Well, sir! Have you nothing to say?"

Guy allowed the silence to grow like a thunderhead, before he smiled with all the hauteur of a direct descendant of Ambrose de Verrant.

"Allow me to assure you, ma'am, that I barely know the lady. I was merely the humble messenger of the future Duchess of Blackdown, who thought Mrs. Callaway's presence here might amuse."

Lady Whitely smoothed one hand over her waist, as if to rivet his eyes to her figure.

"Oh, I was only teasing, sir. We all know that you've simply taken pity on a poor hero's widow and asked Annabella to give her a few weeks' employment. All the ladies agree that it's just the kind of thoughtful gesture Mr. Guy Devoran would make."

"And Mrs. Callaway is so knowledgeable about plants!" Lady Overbridge exclaimed. "So interesting! She's become quite the rage at Buckleigh, sir. Though it's our modest little orchid collection that's really brought you down to Devon, I'm sure."

"Not at all," Guy said. "I look forward to spending time with the company."

"Oh, you don't fool me, sir! We all know that orchids are your secret passion." Her smile lit up her pretty face. "I certainly intend to show you mine!"

Lady Whitely twirled a wheaten strand of hair in her fingers and pouted. "All of the ladies have been dedicated to painting watercolors of the gardens. You'll find our efforts very silly, no doubt, sir, but we're all quite delighted with Mrs. Callaway."

A passionate rage had begun to burn beneath his heart. Guy ignored it and bowed his head.

"Alas, I have little knowledge of watercolors, ma'am, though I trust I may enjoy fencing with your husband. Your servant, Lady Whitely."

He spun away to usher his hostess up the stairs. Lady Whitely flounced off in chintz indignation.

Glowing with excitement, Lady Overbridge showed him into a guest suite, where Guy's valet already waited with a hot bath and his luggage. She walked about for a few moments, touching ornaments, checking the towels, as if trying to make sure of his comfort.

Guy crossed his arms and watched her. The fire might be easier to handle than the frying pan. It was certainly less toxic, so he would try to be a little gentler as he doused it.

"You'll forgive Lady Whitely's indiscretion, I trust, Mr. Devoran?" Annabella Overbridge said with a bright glance from her dark eyes. "She means no harm."

"It's already forgotten, ma'am."

She straightened the bed hangings. "We've given Mrs. Callaway a little chamber by the nursery. She and our governess may share meals up there and keep each other company. Will that suit, do you think? I'd so hate there to be any awkwardness."

"Awkwardness, ma'am?"

She trailed her fingertips over the pillows. "Oh, I am being silly! The very idea that you might have taken such a plain creature in any particular interest! Why, it's laughable!"

Very pretty and very foolish, but perhaps her boredom with her marriage was not entirely her fault. It was not hard to find a little compassion for a young woman who was facing a lifetime of disappointment.

Lady Overbridge whirled about and walked to the door, but she stopped in the doorway, not hiding her reluctance to leave.

"Had I truly thought you wished it, sir, I should have placed Mrs. Callaway in a room closer to yours." Her eyelashes fluttered as she glanced away with ladylike delicacy. "But this wing is our very best." She gestured in the general direction of the stairs. "Lord Overbridge occupies that suite at the end of the hall, but my own room is right here"—she blushed scarlet as she pointed—"next door to yours. Lord Overbridge always wishes me to accommodate my guests in every way."

Guy bit back a sudden urge to laughter. He would not be able to leave his room without passing hers—yet he intended such a desperately celibate stay!

The thought caught him out. Why? Because Sarah would be sleeping under the same roof?

He was about to spend the evening with these prettier ladies in their exaggerated dresses. They would surround him like a mass of overblown roses, while Sarah Callaway—the alien, delicate orchid— was relegated to the nursery to have her dinner on a tray.

"Your husband is most kind, ma'am," he said.

"The unmarried ladies and gentlemen are all staying in the opposite wing," Lady Overbridge added, her words tumbling in a rush, "but Lord and Lady Whitely have those two rooms on the other side of the stairs."

"Thank you," he said dryly. "I shouldn't wish to stumble into the wrong bedchamber by mistake."

His hostess touched one pearl earring and giggled before she walked away down the hallway.

Guy closed the door behind her, strode to the window, and threw it open.

He could not reach the stairs without risking a meeting with either Lady Whitely or Lady Overbridge, should either female decide to lay in wait for him. Fortunately, a stone balcony embraced the window opening. He stepped onto it and looked down. The wall was climbable. Thank God for that!

Breathing in the fresh country air, he surveyed the view for a moment. Glinting like a silver ribbon, a sea inlet led away south to the Channel. The heights of Dartmoor dominated the skyline to the north.

Closer at hand, beyond a set of stone-flagged terraces, to the right of the orangery, swans glided serenely beneath an ornamental bridge.

In the room behind him his valet coughed discreetly into a closed fist.

Guy's bath was ready. His fresh clothes were laid out for dinner.

His desire to dive fully clothed into that lake of cold water would have to wait.

GUY heard her voice as he walked into the orchid house the next morning. It sounded cool and restrained, speaking in a quiet undertone, yet his pulse quickened.

He had spent the morning with the other men, obliged to take part in various manly pursuits, while the female guests twittered on the sidelines.

Lord Overbridge, puce with incipient apoplexy, had tried in vain to keep up with the other men in a forced march around the grounds, followed by practice with rapiers.

Lord Whitely, lean and fit and vivid with intensity, had walked and fenced with the passion of a man whose wife did not hesitate to cheer on his opponent, while—as pretty as an apple tree in full bloom—Lady Whitely had regaled her companions with her sparkling wit.

Hadn't Mr. Devoran learned his skills with his cousins at Wyldshay from the best fencing masters in the kingdom? His style was so beautiful, so strong and commanding! His reach was so much longer than her poor husband's! Lady Whitely would wager anyone that Mr. Devoran would flatten her spouse into dust.

For the sake of social harmony, Guy had instead allowed the jealous husband to win. Lottie Whitely had sulked and turned her back, but a little ripple had stirred through the unmarried girls like wind through wheat.

They thought Mr. Devoran's self-sacrifice—for surely that was what it was—noble.

None of them knew the dark impatience that burned in Guy's soul. He wanted only to luxuriate in the presence of Sarah Callaway: sensuous, mysterious, vibrantly colored—and speckled like the petals of a spotted cattleya.

Yet the power of his craving to see her clashed with a dread that he was poised on the threshold of dishonor, that the magic of her voice alone would seduce him from his principles.

"You induced it to bloom like this?" she was saying. "I've never seen one before, not even at Blackdown House. You must be very skilled indeed, Mr. Pearse."

"Well, to be honest, ma'am, it was mostly luck." The gardener's voice was solid, with a strong Dartmoor buzz. "But we're very warm and sheltered here, and Her Ladyship hasn't stinted with the glass. Perhaps that accounts for it."

Guy walked forward, his shoes tapping quietly on the tile floor.

Sarah was bending over two immense purple blooms, her tightly plaited hair a dull orange beneath the wide brim of a straw hat. Long green bonnet ribbons floated over the sleeves of her plain white dress.

Not layered with a frippery of petals like a rose. An orchid. Simply the most sensual woman he had ever met.

She glanced up at the sound of his footsteps, and her color retreated like a tide, making her freckles seem startlingly dark. Yet her eyes shone with light, as if a tiger gazed into the heart of the sun. His entire body quickened.

"Mr. Devoran!"

The man standing beside her tugged at his forelock. "Good day, sir!"

"This is Mr. Pearse," Sarah said, as if she and Guy were close friends who had been apart for only a few minutes. "Buckleigh's head gardener." She pointed triumphantly to the flowers. "Look what he's managed to do!"

Guy tore his gaze from hers to glance down at the flowers bursting up from their container. The lavender-red blooms had exploded above a single leaf, the petals flung wide in open invitation. Their opulent throats shimmered. Intense golden shadows led deep into each secret heart. *Cattleya labiata Lindley.*

"*Cattleya labiata,*" she said. "Blooming now, in July!"

"Commonly known as the ruby-lipped cattleya," Mr. Pearse said proudly, "begging your pardon, sir!"

His blood knew only his deep visceral reaction to Sarah—just the scent of her, just the simplicity of her presence—yet a buzz began in his brain that threatened to deafen him.

"Thank you, Mr. Pearse," Guy said. "Very splendid!"

The gardener flushed, touched his forehead, and backed out of the room.

Sarah sat down on a marble bench.

"Good heavens!" she said. "What was all that about?"

Guy glanced up from the blossoms, their elegant shape defied by the passionate color of the lips.

"All what?" he asked.

"All that thunder! Poor Mr. Pearse must have thought you wanted to run him through with one of his own plant supports. Are you angry that he's proud of his cattleya?"

"Angry? God, no! They're magnificent."

"Then, what?" Sarah Callaway stared up at him with her honest heart in her eyes. "This orchid's not an easy plant to grow."

Guy negated his desires as if he crushed crystal into sand, and dropped onto the seat next to hers.

"It fills me with craving," he said. "Yet I imagine we'll have very little time before we'll be interrupted. I intend to persuade you to leave, after all."

"You found out something more in London?"

"I found out enough to regret having allowed you to come here."

She began to weave a green ribbon between her fingers. He caught the ribbon and pulled it from her hand. Sarah Callaway looked up at him.

"The man Daedalus hired to oversee the attacks on your cousin comes from this part of Devon. Though he was free to travel to London, he also works with his hands. He knows roses, but he more intimately knows orchids. Thus, he's the head gardener on an estate such as this. No one else can afford them."

A pulse beat in her throat. "You think Mr. Pearse could be this man?"

"Perhaps."

"But surely Lord Overbridge cannot be Daedalus?"

"There are only five or six other great houses within reach. Our quarry must own one of them. That's all I know."

"But if he lives in Devon, why did Rachel flee here to escape him?"

Guy glanced at the other orchids. *Cattleya intermedia*, showy and expensive, and pure white at the heart. *Angraecum sesquipedale,* the comet orchid, ghostly, deeply fragrant after dark. Mr. Pearse must possess a touch of genius.

"I don't know, but I believe that Rachel told you the truth. She's safely in hiding, but why so close to her tormentor, I've no idea."

"Meanwhile, this gardener is the only lead that we have? What else did you discover about him?"

"Enough." He looked back at her. "He was calling himself Falcorne, though that's no doubt a false name. I wish you would go back to Bath, or let me send you to Wyldshay."

"You really believe that the danger is more acute than we feared? We're really dealing with a murderer?"

A lie would no doubt be more convenient. Instead, desperate to hold as close to honor as he could, Guy told her the truth.

"No," he said. "The goal in London was most definitely only to frighten Rachel, not to kill her."

"Yet you still think I'll become hysterical, after all?" Her eyes burned as if she stalked through a jungle. "We've been over this already, Mr. Devoran. I shan't leave. Either we cooperate, or I shall try to find Rachel alone. The choice is yours, sir."

Guy sprang to his feet and paced away. Water dripped from the long spur of the comet orchid. He did not believe she was in peril from Daedalus. He wanted her to leave for his sake, not hers.

"I don't welcome danger heedlessly," she added. "But surely I am safe here at Buckleigh?"

"Yes, of course. No one here has any reason to connect you to your cousin. Yet your situation here can only be uncomfortable."

"Nonsense! I believe your situation may be a great deal more uncomfortable than mine, sir."

Guy spun back to face her. "Really? In what way?"

The deep color began then, spreading up her neck and over her cheeks, yet her eyes sparkled.

"The governess and I were bringing the children in from the garden when you arrived. I'm afraid that we overheard every word."

"Ah," he said, choking down a sudden mad hilarity. "Did you?"

"It was impossible to avoid, sir. Of course, matchmaking is one of the purposes of a house party such as this."

As if a jester had turned the wheel of fate and winked at him, Guy laughed aloud.

"Yet you didn't expect the married ladies to set their caps at me quite so openly, before I'd even removed my hat and gloves?"

The freckles scampered as she grinned. "If I didn't, I should have, though I'll admit to a certain discomposure when Lady Whitely dragged my name into the conversation."

"It's absurd to you, I suppose, that anyone could believe that I might indeed be attracted to you?"

In a flow of white skirts, she stood up. The straw hat framed her face. A few red strands escaped from her plaits to caress her speckled cheeks.

The roar of his desire almost flattened him.

"It's obviously absurd that you'd arrange for us both to attend this house party merely to commence an affair," she said.

Guy dropped onto another marble bench and leaned back to watch her. She wouldn't leave. She would stay here to torment him.

"Lottie Whitely's real fear is that I came here to pursue Lady Overbridge."

Sarah crouched over the ruby-lipped cattleya to brush one fingertip over the deep purple–frilled edge. The soft smudges of snow at the sunshine-stained gullet shivered beneath her touch, as if the orchid surrendered to a pollinating moth.

Ardor raced hot and strong through his blood, spreading fire as if a naked woman ran through dry grass trailing a burning scarf at her heels.

"And did you?" she asked.

Guy stretched out his legs and breathed in a great draft of the scented air, trusting to self-mockery to shred his craving.

"Annabella Overbridge is certainly very pretty," he said. "You don't think that she's already my mistress?"

"I don't know," Sarah said. "She might be, I suppose. Yet she looks more hopeful than satisfied."

In spite of his distress, he laughed. "You're very sure that I would satisfy, Mrs. Callaway!"

She kept her back to him, leaving him nothing but the green ribbons trailing over the curve of her back.

"Oh, every lady here is certain of it," she said. "You must know that they're all fighting for your notice like dogs for a bone: the married ladies for your favors, the unmarried for your hand."

"I'm considered a good catch," he said. "It's bloody exhausting!"

The hat brim threw her face into deep shadow, but he knew that she grinned. "And thus your situation is more uncomfortable than mine. Though I'm sure you can cope, Mr. Devoran."

Female voices chirruped from inside the house.

Guy leaped up to block the view of Sarah from anyone entering the orchid room. He seized her elbow to help her to her feet, though the touch of her soft flesh beneath his palm set fire to his blood.

"If you insist on staying here," he said beneath his breath, "we must talk again. It'll be difficult to do so privately during the day. Can you escape your room unseen after dark?"

"Yes," she said. "I believe so. I could use the servants' stair."

"The governess won't wake?"

"Her room is closer to the nursery and farther from the stairs than mine."

"Then meet me tomorrow just before dawn in the Deer Hut. You know it?"

"The little folly made of bark and antlers near the lake? Yes, of course."

Guy gazed down into her tiger-bronze eyes and ruthlessly repressed the insistent pulse of desire.

"Be careful, Mrs. Callaway!"

"No one will notice anything I do," she said. "Unlike you, sir, I'm invisible."

The chatter of female voices intensified, as if someone herded a flock of pigeons. One voice, shriller and more insistent, dominated the others.

"God!" he said. "I fear Lottie Whitely comes to fetch me to show me her watercolors."

Sarah Callaway glanced away through the glass. The hat brim hid her face. "If she does, sir, I believe she's bringing all of her competition with her."

Guy opened his fingers and released her. Sarah spun about and left the hothouse by the garden door.

With the unmarried roses fluttering behind them, Lady Overbridge and Lady Whitely walked into the room arm-in-arm. The gentlemen trailed after them.

A walk to the lake was planned. But they couldn't go without Mr. Devoran! And where was Mrs. Callaway? She must come to teach the young ladies about the plants in the gardens—and thus give them an opportunity to linger where a young gentleman might get the chance to murmur privately into a shell-like ear.

Guy ignored the chattering voices and smiled boldly at Lottie Whitely.

She twirled her parasol and smiled back.

*   *   *

A chill glow glimmered through the trees as Sarah walked rapidly down to the Deer Hut. She wore her green traveling dress and sensible boots. If anyone discovered her, she would say she had come out to see the sunrise over the gardens.

But as she had told Mr. Devoran, no one was likely to care.

Even if Lady Whitely truly believed that Sarah was Guy's lover, Her Ladyship would dismiss it as the equivalent of a quick tumble with a maid. Real affairs of the heart took place between equals. Guy Devoran was the son of an earl's daughter, and nephew to a duke.

Mrs. Sarah Callaway, captain's relict, was a schoolteacher in Bath. Though her father had been a gentleman, her family had been far from being aristocrats. She was determined not to forget it.

Dew glistened on white stone, ghostly as half-melted snow in the dawn light, as Sarah walked through an alley of classical statues. Blackbirds had begun a faint twittering. Ahead of her, the lake spread like a silver mirror, empty of life.

Yet a creature rustled somewhere in the undergrowth: a fox, perhaps, or a badger.

Sarah shivered and wrapped her cloak more tightly about her shoulders.

The Deer Hut nestled among a grove of birches on a small mound above the lake. The path was a little slippery beneath her boots. As she climbed uphill, her heart began to pound.

As if night refused to give way to the dawn, the door of the hut gaped open onto darkness. Sarah stopped and glanced back over her shoulder.

"Come," his voice said softly. "It's all right."

A hot wave raced through her blood. She knew what caused it. She knew how very dangerous it was. Yet perhaps it didn't matter, as long as he didn't guess how she felt.

Guy Devoran lounged casually in the doorway, tall and solid and secure. Laugh lines furrowed his cheeks. Ebony hair tumbled over his forehead. Yet a much darker fire burned in his eyes, as if he, too, belonged to the night.

Her soul singing like a heavenly chorus, Sarah met that hot midnight gaze and plummeted—like a stone into a lake—straight into love.

Giddy and intoxicating and mad, the air sparkled in her lungs like champagne.

Oh, God! Her improper desires were dangerous enough—to fall in love with him would be fatal!

Yet for that moment, as their eyes met, she didn't care. With every fiber of her being—however foolish, however destined for heartbreak—she wanted nothing else but the absolute, exclusive attention of this one man.

Like every other female here at Buckleigh.

The thought sobered her instantly.

"Mr. Devoran," she said with a kind of desperate normalcy. "How extraordinary that we should run into each other like this!"

He laughed and stepped backward into the shadows as he gestured for her to join him.

"This is the strangest little building," he said. "The roof is built mostly of antlers and deer hide. The floor is tiled entirely with little sections of antler, and the walls appear to be pieced together from bark."

"Yes," she said. "I came here on my first day, when I was able to explore by myself. From the window, one may enjoy a stunning view over the lake to the moor."

"And so may two," he replied with a grin. "I took the liberty of bringing a little breakfast and a jug of hot coffee. It's here on the table: a rather painfully rustic contraption, yet serviceable enough. Please, come in! We shan't be disturbed."

Sarah walked through the door into his magic kingdom, where Oberon had commanded his sensual pleasures. The aroma of coffee and the yeasty scent of fresh baking spiraled into her nostrils.

Saliva flooded her mouth as if she might devour the world.

Her heart beating like a child's drum, she swallowed. "You took a detour through the kitchens, Mr. Devoran?"

"Cook appears to have taken a liking to me," he said lightly. "As has the second dairymaid—thus the fresh buns and the butter and cream."

Sarah laughed, though a pang of sympathy for Cook, for the dairymaid—and even for Lady Overbridge and Lady Whitely— pierced her heart. For all the sad females, even herself, who had ever wanted to capture this exquisite man for themselves alone, and never would.

"The lake," she said dryly, "is filled with broken hearts."

A shadow flickered in his eyes for a moment, but he gave her a quizzical smile. "We may certainly admire the view of the water as we break our fast. The lake was designed to be as picturesque as possible. As are the antler table and chairs: charming, pretty, and only a little uncomfortable."

Guy pulled out a chair for her and she sat down.

"Thank you, sir. I'd be very glad for some hot coffee."

He opened a floury white cloth to reveal hot currant buns, dusted with sugar. "And a bun?"

Sarah nodded and they ate breakfast in a companionable silence.

She tried to ignore the vigorous warmth of his presence, radiating comfort into the chill morning. Yet the shape of his hands— strong and square-boned—seared into her consciousness as if she studied a masterpiece of design.

Her nostrils opened on the scent of leaves and leather and clean linen, enticingly masculine scents, mingling with the aroma of coffee and fresh buns.

When she thought he wasn't looking, she glanced directly at his face. The tip of his tongue licked a trace of coffee from his lips and fired cravings so profound she felt almost faint.

At last he set down his cup and leaned back to look at her.

Sarah glanced away to suck a little sugar from her fingers, knowing that a telltale warmth crept up her cheeks as if her skin reflected the banked fire in his eyes.

"I cannot blame you," he said quietly. "If it were my cousin, all the demons in hell couldn't stop me from pursuing her. Yet I would still rest a great deal easier if you'd leave your quest to me."

She set her half-eaten bun back on the cloth. "Because there are many kinds of danger?"

"Yes, if you like." His tone was guarded.

"I promise that you can trust me to be careful, sir. Besides, if we're looking for a gardener, I can surely be of help? No one will think it odd for a botany teacher to ask questions about orchids."

His dark gaze fixed on her face. That deep shiver of desire coursed along her bones.

"Then we're in this together, Mrs. Callaway, come hell, come high water. I'll do everything in my power to shield you, but if you remain here I can't guarantee that the consequences won't be profound. Do you accept that?"

"I embrace it," she said, though her voice sounded strange in her own ears, as if she promised a fairy king her firstborn child, and didn't know it. "Rachel is far more naïve than I am, sir. She's the one we must think of protecting, not me. So, yes, I accept the risks—of every kind—to myself, and I do so willingly. I'm grateful for your help, but the heart of this quest is still mine."

He pushed away from the table to gaze from the window. The faint light, fey, otherworldly, glimmered along his profile.

Falling in love with a man you could never have was agonizing as well as enthralling.

"Falcorne's description fits half the men in South Devon: brown-haired, blue-eyed, not too tall, the local accent. No particular distinguishing characteristics, except for the dirt beneath his fingernails and his knowledge of roses and orchids. However, he was in London for about three weeks, from around the middle of May through the first week of June, which narrows the field considerably."

"Then it can't be Mr. Pearse. He hasn't left Buckleigh all summer. That's how he managed to get the cattleya to bloom."

Guy Devoran glanced back at her. "Are you sure?"

Her heart thumped. She stared down at the table. "Not sure, no. I suppose one of the under-gardeners could have taken over for a few weeks."

"The truth of that should be easy enough to discover—unless everyone here is part of some conspiracy. Did Pearse say where he acquired his plants?"

"No, but I can find out."

"You don't need to do it alone," he said gently. "I've already arranged outings to the neighborhood hothouses. You'll be included, of course."

Sarah looked up. She could not interpret his mood. It was almost as if he surrendered to something inevitable against his better judgment.

"And there's surely no physical danger," she said.

He smiled with a dry self-mockery. "If there is, you may rely on my strong right arm and the blood of Ambrose de Verrant to defend your life and your virtue."

She tried to keep her voice light and knew she would fail. "So you think Daedalus's gardener may be dangerous, after all?"

He glanced back at the lake. A swan was gliding serenely across the gray water.

"Falcorne's probably not a violent man himself. He hired some local thugs to carry out his orders in London. So in this, at least, the risks should be limited."

"I'll be as discreet in my inquiries as a mouse nibbling behind the wainscot," she said. "No one will even notice me. But you've already planned outings? Won't it seem odd if you show such a sudden interest in orchids?"

"Not sudden."

An even faster pulse began in Sarah's blood, as if a new flower opened to reveal unexpected treasures at the heart.

"I don't understand," she said.

Still staring out over the water, he propped his hip on the windowsill to swing one booted foot from the knee. "It's no secret. I first became interested on behalf of my sister, Lucinda. She loves exotic flowers, as does my aunt. Thus, the orchid room at Blackdown House is mostly my doing."

She felt stunned. "But you gave no indication of that when we were there!"

"No, I suppose not."

"Then you really did come to Buckleigh to see the orchids?"

He laughed. "And not Annabella Overbridge . . . or Lottie Whitely . . . or to find a wife among the eligible girls?"

"But Lady Overbridge believes you've arranged these outings for her sake?"

"Probably. I don't know. But while you're conversing with the gardeners, I shall enthuse over the latest imports with the master of the house. As delightfully bizarre as it may seem, it would appear that Daedalus is another orchid fancier. Unfortunately, since orchids are the latest craze, so are half of the wealthy gentlemen in Devon."

"But we're talking about only five or six, aren't we? You said Daedalus must own one of the great houses in the area."

As if driven by restlessness, he strode to the doorway. The sun was breaking through the trees. A shimmer of gold outlined his lean silhouette.

"And if we're lucky, only one gardener will meet all of our criteria, and we'll have him identified within the week. After which, you may safely leave Daedalus to me."

"And Rachel?"

He shrugged. "I trust we'll soon discover the key to her whereabouts. In the meantime, you and I will need to meet privately again to exchange information. I'll let you know when and where."

"Thank you," she said. "I know that you could still have sent me away, if you'd wished. In spite of the bracelet, you didn't have to allow me to come here."

"No," he said. "Perhaps I did."

Sarah stared up at him in bewilderment.

Cool sunlight traced his dark hair and broad shoulders and traced lovingly over the perfect lines of his face. The soft cooing of doves echoed through the trees. Blackbirds twittered from hundreds of red throats. Seemingly no longer aware of her, Guy Devoran stood encased in silence, his head tipped and his eyes closed, as if he exalted in the sound.

A deep disquiet trickled up her spine, as if the birdsong called up the ancient spirits of the woods, ready to strike stark awe into any mortal heart.

The pain and ecstasy of unrequited love pierced like a rapier. Sarah stood up and swept the crumbs from the table into one palm, then tipped them from the window.

Three swans, their necks arched, now sailed on the quiet water.

"Do you know, Mrs. Callaway," Guy Devoran said suddenly, "that you are quite simply balm to my soul?"

Her heart lurched as she spun back to face him, though she tried to laugh. "I am? Why?"

He leaned one shoulder against the jamb and crossed his arms over his chest. His dark eyes were watching her with that burning intensity. Awareness of a new kind of hazard started to hammer beneath her corset, robbing her of breath.

"Because, though I keep reminding you of the perils of this venture," he said, "I detect no flutter of female hysterics."

She stepped around the table, her hands busy gathering cups. "I assure you that inside I'm feeling every ounce of womanish trepidation that you could wish, Mr. Devoran."

"Then don't," he said. "There's no reason for Daedalus to suspect you. I wanted to send you away for my sake, not yours."

Sarah tied up the cloth and tried to speak lightly. "I can't think why!"

Yet the pulse was pounding, deep in her gut, making her giddy.

The Deer Hut was tiny, the floor uneven. As she hurried, her heel caught on a high piece of antler.

She stumbled. The cloth bundle thumped back onto the table.

He caught her by both arms.

Sarah tried to step back. With the grace of easy strength Guy Devoran set her at arm's length, but he did not release her.

She looked up and was instantly consumed by his black fire.

Even though it burned with something of bitterness—

Even though she thought that he despised his own desires—

Even though she believed his ardor to be entirely random—not personal, not for *her*—Sarah knew with every fiber of her being that she wanted him to kiss her.

Hot flames burned over her skin at the certain knowledge that he wanted it, too.

She had never gathered men's attention for her prettiness—that was Rachel's gift, not hers—yet that shameful sensuality had always lurked at the core, like the dark, sticky heart of a monk's head orchid.

For a moment they stood as if locked in mortal combat, then his hands dropped away.

He spun about and seized the tied cloth from the table. His boots struck hard as he strode to the doorway.

He hesitated for only a second on the threshold to glance back at her.

"Yes," he said. "There are indeed many kinds of danger, Mrs. Callaway."

CHAPTER NINE

*I*T RAINED STEADILY FOR MOST OF THE NEXT DAY, A WARM summer rain that soaked the gardens and streamed over the glass. Sticky air hung oppressively over the orchids. No one felt like taking an outing in a carriage. Since the gentlemen were also trapped inside, the ladies declared themselves bored with painting flowers. No one needed Mrs. Callaway.

So while the guests played cards and games of dice, or read, or strolled up and down the long gallery, Sarah visited Mr. Pearse in his cottage in the grounds.

Mud tracked from her boots as she came back into the house. Feeling damp and disheveled, she dropped the hood of her cloak and brushed a few wayward strands of hair from her forehead. Frizzy curls always sprang annoyingly about her face whenever the weather was wet.

She turned to go up to her room and stopped dead.

Guy Devoran was lounging against a statue of Minerva. His dark eyes bored into hers for a moment, then his gaze settled on her lips.

As if he held a cool flame to her skin, heat brushed her mouth.

Sarah gathered her wits and glanced away. He stepped back to allow her to pass, but as she did so he leaned down to whisper in her ear.

"Tonight. An hour after midnight. The box room at the north end of the corridor that leads to the schoolroom."

Her pulse raced, with alarm, with awareness of every kind of danger, as she glanced up at him.

The dark fire burned, leading into unfathomable depths.

Without waiting for her answer, he spun about and strode away.

GUY climbed hand over hand up the wall above his bedroom balcony, swung onto a ledge, then up the slightly more difficult facade above that. Ornamental stonework was useful as well as decorative!

He climbed easily over the roof to the nursery wing. The slates were slippery with moss, but it had stopped raining several hours before, and bright moonlight was shredding the clouds.

As he had ascertained earlier, the latch on the window was broken. He slipped silently over the sill into the dark box room.

"Good heavens," Sarah Callaway said. "You came over the rooftops? I'm impressed."

She was sitting on top of what appeared to be a seaman's chest from the previous century. Her plain, dark gown disappeared into shadows, but her hair was combed back from her forehead to be confined severely beneath a white lace cap.

The lace glimmered a little in the moonlight. For a moment a vision intruded of the nimbus of copper hair that had encircled her face like a halo when she'd come in from the garden—though his visceral reaction to that had been anything but saintly.

Guy closed the window and propped his hips against the sill, keeping the safety of several feet between himself and Sarah Callaway.

"When I arrange clandestine meetings after midnight," he said, "I owe it to melodrama not to simply walk along corridors and open doors."

"You also owe it to discretion," she replied. "If you were seen in any of those corridors, each lady would only assume that you were visiting the bedroom of her rival. Then everyone would be cross."

"Except me."

Her little chuckle floated softly on the night air. "Yet it would still create unfortunate social tensions."

Guy breathed in the scent of green apples. "No doubt. Especially since tomorrow promises to be fine. We shall take five carriages to visit Mr. Barry Norris, whose orchid collection may be interesting. Meanwhile, I managed to find out from my chambermaid that Lord Uxhampton's gardener is a doddering old fellow with white hair, and that Uxhampton hates anything exotic. Molly's not a particularly garrulous girl, but Uxhampton's man is her grandfather. He grows neither roses, nor orchids. Thus he may be dismissed from our search."

"And Mr. Norris?"

"I don't know. Did you discover anything from Mr. Pearse?"

His eyes were adjusting to the dim light. Faintly tawny against her pale skin, her brows drew together in a small frown.

"Not really. He'll talk freely about how he grows his flowers, but there's an odd wall of reluctance should one venture into any other topic."

"A reluctance that seems general," he said. "None of the servants is eager to talk about anything that goes on in this part of Devon."

"Mr. Pearse even seemed annoyed when his wife let slip that he'd not left Buckleigh all year, though I'm certain that's the truth. All I learned in the end is that his new orchids came from Conrad Loddiges and Sons in Hackney."

"Loddiges is a major importer, so there's no surprise there. Pearse wouldn't say who fetched them?"

Sarah's fingers stroked idly along the iron bands on the trunk, as if she were embarrassed not to be able to offer him more, then she looked up. Desire rose in his blood like a tidal wave. God! For what? To seduce the cousin of his latest mistress?

"When I asked him directly, he changed the subject as if I were asking for the secret of the Gordian knot. I didn't dare press him, so I had to let it go."

"That's all right," he said. "I never thought Pearse was Falcorne, because I'm damned certain that Overbridge isn't Daedalus. Why would he persecute your cousin for her favors, when he's besotted with his wife?"

"I agree," she said. "That seems impossible."

Guy paced to the fireplace. "That is who we're looking for, isn't it? Either an unmarried man, or a man who'd go mad over another woman?"

"If Rachel's letters are to be believed," she said. "But you're the one who proved how untrustworthy she can be."

He laughed then, because for all the intensity of his desire, he also took the simplest of pleasures in her quick mind.

"Of course. We've no real idea of anyone's motives in all this."

"Could this Mr. Norris be Daedalus?"

"Barry Norris is certainly an odd fish. All bluff manner and heartiness, but there's a shrewdly calculating brain behind it."

"And he collects orchids?"

"Yes, but not seriously. Norris buys a few plants because they're the fashion and he can afford it. Now we've eliminated Uxhampton, our only other real suspects are Lord Moorefield and Lord Whiddon. No one else in the area has the necessary resources, though Moorefield's a pretty minor collector."

"And Lord Whiddon?"

"Is quite manic for orchids. He's also a bachelor and a recluse. It won't be easy to get an invitation to visit him."

"So you think he might be our main suspect?"

"Except that he doesn't seem the type to persecute a woman."

"Does he ever send his gardener to London to buy his plants for him?"

Guy turned from his desperate contemplation of the cold grate to stare at the scudding clouds outside. "Of course, though that doesn't mean it's the same man."

Sarah slipped from the chest and stood up. Moonlight cast her in shades of silver and gray. Her skin gleamed like the surface of a pearl.

"Can't you simply ask Lady Overbridge who brought her orchids back to Buckleigh?"

"I already have. But Annabella has no more idea of how her gardens and hothouses are maintained than she does of the little girls who embroider her ball gowns, or how her meals appear on the table."

"You sound as if you don't quite approve," she said.

Guy stalked to the window. "Of a lady who takes no care for the conditions of the people who sustain her pretty lifestyle? No, I don't."

"Good heavens," she said. "You're a radical, Mr. Devoran?"

He laughed. "Why the mockery, Mrs. Callaway? I suspect you share my opinions in this."

"Yes, but I've been forced to earn my living—"

"Whereas I'm merely idle and useless? I've not forgotten."

Even in the shifting light, he knew that hot color raced over her face. Yet she bit her lip as if to prevent herself from laughing aloud.

"I was a little rude in the bookstore, wasn't I?"

"Very," he replied. "But we were strangers."

"Which only makes it all the worse," she said. "I behaved very badly."

"Then we should not remain strangers."

She plunked herself back onto the seaman's chest and tipped her head as she gazed at him. "Is this revenge?"

"No," he said. "Simple justice—though you're under no obligation to oblige. I'm just curious."

"I don't have any secrets, sir. What do you wish to know?"

Guy tried to keep his manner casual, though a battle waged in his heart. His determination to remain detached fought valiantly with his burning desire to learn all about her—and lost.

"How did you come to marry Captain Callaway?" he asked. "You said he was some years older than you?"

"Fifteen, to be exact. He courted me and I accepted him. He owned a little house near Yarmouth, where he maintained warehouses. Everyone thought it a very good match."

"You didn't love him?"

She smoothed a fold of her skirt with one hand. "Not at first. But in the end, yes, very much."

"I'm sorry," he said. "I have no right to pry. I didn't mean to distress you."

The curve of her shoulder and neck glimmered in the moonlight. She gazed down at her moving fingers.

"No. I'd rather like to be able to tell someone. If no one ever speaks of him, it's as if he never existed. But I didn't marry him for love. I married for security."

Guy sank onto his haunches and leaned both shoulders against the wall. He had asked, because he desperately wanted to understand her. Yet it was as if he had carelessly lifted the lid of an ornamental box expecting to find the usual contents—scissors or sealing wax— and instead found himself staring into the depths of a profoundly painful honesty.

"Tell me whatever you wish," he said quietly. "Nothing you say will ever go beyond these four walls."

Sarah Callaway dropped the pleat of fabric and stood up. Her skirts rustled softly as she walked back and forth.

"I had no other real prospects and I wanted a home of my own. So when John—Captain Callaway—offered for me, I said yes. But we'd been married for only a few weeks when he went to Norwich on business, and was brought home in a cart. He'd collapsed suddenly on Elm Street."

"He couldn't walk?"

She shook her head. "He never walked again. He'd carried some fragments of metal in his spine ever since Waterloo. The doctors said there was nothing they could do."

"So you nursed him?"

"Yes, for three months. I knew he was in excruciating pain, but he was kind and funny and clever, and he never complained. I'd never imagined that anyone could be so brave. That's when I fell in love with him."

"Then he was a lucky man," Guy said.

"Lucky to die so painfully?" Her voice cut harshly across the cool air.

"No. Lucky to have won your love honestly and die knowing that."

"Yes," she said. "But I wasn't honest."

Guy carefully studied his boots. "Why do you say that?"

Her skirts rustled as she moved restlessly in the dark. "Because while John lay ill a fire swept through our warehouses, and I didn't tell him. People innocent of any wrongdoing lost everything they had stored there, and they had to be compensated right away. Meanwhile, the bill for the insurance lay lost among piles of other papers, because I had neglected to pay it."

"You cannot blame yourself for that."

"No? When John had worked so hard? In spite of his pain, he tried to teach me how to run the business. Yet a lifetime of work had already turned into debts, because of my mistake, and everything was already lost!"

"There are times when kindness must outweigh honesty," he said.

Silence breathed quietly for a moment. Moonlight dappled her rigid back. A softer light gleamed on her cheek, where a few strands of hair had escaped from her cap.

"Was that my excuse? I suppose so. I was forced to sell the house a few weeks before John died, and it was only luck that enabled me to keep that a secret. The buyers didn't need to take possession until after the funeral."

"Yet he died knowing that you loved him."

"Was that enough?" she asked.

"God, yes!"

Her shoes rapped as she stalked across the room. "I don't know, Mr. Devoran. You see, John knew that I was hiding something, and it worried him. One day he tried to ask me what was wrong. Yet the moment he saw my distress, he made a joke and changed the subject: out of kindness to me, his silly wife, who'd allowed his life's work to go up in flames."

"Because she was nursing him and had grown to love him," Guy said. "And knew where her highest priorities lay—as he did."

Sarah hesitated by the door with her hand on the knob. Moisture gleamed faintly silver on her cheeks.

"You're very kind, sir," she said. "I know the truth of what you say. I don't berate myself so very much. That's only another form of self-indulgence, isn't it? Anyway, what would I have done with warehouses and a shipping business? I'm far better suited to be a schoolteacher, and I've made a perfectly good new life. Yet please don't think that I'm always honest. I'm not. No more than anyone else."

"Yes, you are," Guy said.

Her knuckles tensed on the knob. "I'm glad to have been able to tell someone," she said. "Not even Rachel knows how much I was at fault."

"And afterwards—?"

"The Mansards blamed only Captain Callaway for what had happened. That's the general way of thinking, isn't it? That a man who leaves any business decisions to his wife is a fool."

Moonlight traced across the backs of his hands, throwing stark shadows between his fingers.

"I can only honor any man whom you have loved," he said. "John Callaway doesn't sound like a fool. He sounds remarkable."

Sarah opened the door. Her shoes rapped softly away down the corridor.

Guy sprang to his feet to fling open the casement.

Night cast black shadows in a gray world. The lake lay still and dark, like a great expanse of wet slate. Yet where the moonlight reflected off a bank of low-lying mist to glimmer across the water, it looked like the White Lady walking.

Who was that—one of the heroines of Celtic myth—the lady who'd come walking over the sea to her lover?

Sarah Callaway would no doubt know, because she had escaped a painful girlhood by losing herself in books. And then she had escaped again to find a joy that was only seared by more pain in her brief marriage.

He wished—quite insanely, but with a profound intensity— that he could wipe all of that pain away to find the girl she had also once mentioned, who had worn a straw bonnet and enjoyed carefree picnics with her cousin.

—until hail obliterated all of our gaiety.

Guy swung rapidly down the wall and strode off across the grounds.

I'm glad to have been able to tell someone—

Someone! She had told him precisely because he meant nothing to her, because she imagined that he was a perfect gentleman, because she thought therefore that he was always absolutely trustworthy and honorable, like the man she had married.

The White Lady shimmered in the mist, trailing tears across the water.

Guy shrugged out of his clothes as he walked, leaving garments strewn across the damp grass. At the edge of the lake he tugged off his boots and breeches.

He dived naked into the cool moonlit water.

Impossible to shed dishonor as easily.

Faint phosphorescence fringed his shoulders and arms as he swam, but clouds moved to drop a black cloak over the lake. The mist vanished into darkness. The White Lady disappeared.

Impossible, always, for any mortal to compete with a ghost.

FIVE carriages bowled along the leafy lanes, each one carrying its bouquet of parasols. Sarah sat in the last carriage with the governess and the children, and tried not to watch Guy Devoran. Most of the gentlemen had chosen to accompany the carriages on horseback, as had Lady Whitely.

Mr. Devoran controlled his spirited blood bay with unobtrusive skill: lithe, restrained, and a magnet for every female gaze. Lady Whitely rode beside him on a showy chestnut mare. His dark head bent a little toward her as she chattered. She glanced up at him and laughed, her blond ringlets caressing her lovely face, her neat figure displayed to perfection by her fashionable habit and elegant feathered hat.

Sarah forced her gaze away. A sharp, dark pain stabbed beneath her corset, as if she had the right to be wounded by his paying such careful attention to a beautiful woman.

Why on earth had she told him the truth about John? Not even Rachel had really known why she had broken off her mourning so precipitately to take up a post as a schoolmistress—and then the Mansards had died, and Rachel, too, was cast unprotected into the world.

Yet how could a duke's nephew ever understand any penniless gentlewoman's plight? And how absurd that she had stared at herself in the mirror that morning and wondered if he could ever find her lovely! Yet Sarah had agonized over her appearance. She was not beautiful. She was even freckled like a currant bun, because—never really caring before—she had spent too much time in the sun.

She reached deep into her heart to try to find acceptance, doing her best to laugh at herself, yet the pain still hurt.

BARRISTOW Manor sat in a small fold of hills between the moor and the sea. Mr. Barry Norris and his wife welcomed their guests with wine and cakes, before they broke up into little groups to explore the gardens.

Sarah walked with one of the younger girls and tried to explain the botanical structure of the flowers. Yet Mary Blenkinsop, interested only in one of the younger men—since she considered Mr. Guy Devoran far too far above her touch—simply giggled.

"Is this really quite suitable, Mrs. Callaway?"

Sarah looked up. Mrs. Barry Norris stared at her over the end of her long nose and sharp chin.

"The gentlemen have retired to the glasshouse," Mrs. Norris added. "Your opinion is wanted. Such pursuits may be acceptable, I suppose, for a widow, but certainly not for a young girl. Miss Blenkinsop may remain here with me."

Sarah smiled her thanks and hurried away. As she entered the orchid house, a voice boomed.

"Stole m' head gardener, sir!"

"Really?" Guy Devoran said. "My heart bleeds, sir."

"Ever since the man left, the demmed plants have been dying. Ah! Here's your little botanist! What do y' think, m' dear? Not hot enough in here for orchids?"

Sarah had stopped just inside the doorway, but Mr. Norris marched up to seize her by the arm.

"Take this bloody thing!" He pointed to a sad clump of brown roots in a pot. "Never bloomed once. Cost me a fortune! What the devil do ye know about making orchids bloom, ma'am?"

"Nothing at all, sir." Sarah bit back a grin. "I'm very sorry if you've been led to believe otherwise."

A similarly repressed mirth was dancing in Guy Devoran's eyes. "But I thought you knew orchids, Mrs. Callaway? How foolish of me!"

"I know them only from prints and from books, sir," she said. "I've never grown one."

Barry Norris dragged her deeper into his hothouse. "But tell me what you think of these, ma'am! Only things blooming."

He pushed aside some greenery and pointed to a handful of small flowers.

Seven orchids burst from the shade of a mass of spear-shaped leaves. Snowy outer petals spread open in erotic surrender.

Eria rosea.

At the heart of each blossom, blush-pink lips frilled around a small round knob, like a golden pearl.

"M' wife thinks the blooms shocking," Barry Norris said with a guffaw. "Remind a man of things he ain't supposed to think about."

Obviously fighting an incipient outbreak of hilarity, Guy Devoran coughed into a closed fist. "Tricky things, orchids," he said.

Afraid that she would burst out laughing, Sarah swallowed hard and walked away to gaze out at the gardens.

"I'm so sorry to hear that you lost your head gardener, Mr. Norris," she said as soon as she could trust her voice. "I trust the poor man wasn't taken ill?"

"God, no! Moorefield stole him. Chap by the name of Croft."

"Croft?" Guy asked. "The same fellow Moorefield just hired this spring?"

Barry Norris gave Guy a sharp glance, as if beneath the crude, jovial facade he concealed a set of razors.

"That's no secret, sir. Clever chap with flowers. Moorefield's been wanting the man for years, and he got him only a few days after the fellow got back from London in May."

Guy stroked the white petals with one gentle finger. "Then I'll wager it's exactly the same man that beat mine to the punch at Loddiges."

"Could ha' been." Norris kicked idly at a pot of greenery, his mouth pursed.

"A shipment of some particularly fine orchids had just come in," Guy said. "Annoyed quite a few of us, sir, when the pick of the crop was whisked out from under our noses and sent down here to Devon." The *Eria rosea* trembled slightly as Guy dropped his hand and turned to face his host. "These are very fine specimens, sir. I believe I must meet your Mr. Croft."

"Then you'll find the fellow at Moorefield Hall. But if these plants were the best to be had, I was cheated."

"Then perhaps another Devon gardener carried off the main prize?"

Norris hesitated for a moment. "Damn me, if you're not right, sir! If it's rare orchids you're after, you should talk to Hawk, not Croft."

"Hawk, sir?"

"Whiddon's man . . . went up to town at the same time as Croft—after orchids, you understand—and the rogues traveled back together. Now there's a chap who can grow things!" He turned and grinned. "Better not take ladies into his hothouse!"

Norris cackled at his own wit and stomped off to the doorway.

His arms crossed over his chest, Guy Devoran leaned his shoulders against the wall, threw back his head, and laughed.

Something in the set of his nostrils and the creases at the corners of his mouth poured through Sarah's heart like molten gold—as if she were a rare coin and he were the furnace.

Hating that vulnerability, she walked past him to the door.

Mrs. Norris was shepherding the other ladies back toward the house. Trailing behind them, a nurse carried a golden-haired child in her arms. Norris's expression softened as he gazed at them.

"That's my son," he said proudly. "Damned smart little lad! Never cries! Never makes a fuss! Not even when a stranger surprised the governess in the garden last month."

"A stranger, sir?"

"Just some vagabond fellow! Frightened the life out of the nurse, so she ran back to the house. Yet my little boy never set up so much as a wail, for all he's still in skirts, though of course I've given orders she's not to go so far from the house ever again."

"Very prudent, sir," Sarah said. "The countryside contains far too many poor souls looking for work, or a little bread."

"Nonsense, ma'am! Wastrels the lot of them! No patience with that!"

Barry Norris hurried off across the grass to join his wife and child. The toddler saw his father and reached out with both arms. Mr. Norris plucked him from the nurse and swung him, until the toddler screamed with laughter.

Sarah's heart constricted at the sight of them. A child was the one gift she had hoped for when she'd first married John and what she had longed for as she grew to love him, but thanks to her own choices, she had been left bereft.

Determined not to succumb to self-indulgent melancholy, she walked back to Guy Devoran. He was watching her carefully, the glint of mirth in his eyes now shadowed by concern.

Her heart skipped a beat, sending another ripple of mad awareness through her blood. With the dappled sunlight caressing his dark hair and highlighting the pure lines of his face, he seemed both brilliant and a little feral, like the King of Faerie. Yet that wild heart also seemed infinitely open to compassion.

She immediately reached for levity, for a return to uncontaminated, uncomplicated laughter. "You see, sir, that I am indeed invisible to Mr. Norris. Since I don't really exist, sights that would ordinarily shock a lady may safely be shown to me."

"Ah," he said, grinning. "You refer to Mrs. Norris's concerns? But surely flowers are among the most innocent of God's creations, so how can any of them be improper?"

Sarah walked back to look again at the orchids: *Eria rosea*, so lovely and delicate, and so perilously erotic.

"No, Mrs. Norris is right," she said. "These flowers are most unsuitable for the eyes of unmarried young ladies."

"So why aren't they considered dangerous for the eyes of young men?" He glanced down at his boots. "Such indiscreet blooms might certainly inflame improper male desires."

"Only for a male insect," Sarah said. "And a Chinese one at that."

He smiled as he glanced up at her beneath his lashes. "Ah! In that case, I must banish all thoughts of wantonness, though I'm still left with the image of moths pollinating orchids."

She turned away, giddy. With this man, even laughter was dangerous.

"Which brings us back to gardeners," she said. "You already knew that Lord Moorefield had hired a man named Croft?"

The humor disappeared from his face. "Yes, Molly told me this morning. After all, it's hardly a secret. But now we also know that Croft went to Loddiges in May with Whiddon's man, Hawk, so we have two names."

"And you think one of them is Falcorne?"

"I think it highly likely."

A tremor of apprehension slid down her spine. "Which would confirm that either Lord Moorefield, Lord Whiddon, or Mr. Norris is Daedalus?"

"Exactly."

"But if it's Mr. Norris, why did he tell you anything at all just now?"

"Because it would have been more suspicious if he'd been too cagey. He told me nothing that wasn't easily discovered."

"Yet you think he's hiding something."

He strode to the doorway, keeping his back to her. "Norris is a vain man and a dangerous one, but somehow I can't imagine his sending his gardener to London to order those accidents."

Sarah hugged herself, trying to dispel her shivers. "Yet he's a man who could be intimidating, I think."

Guy Devoran gazed across the lawn at the group now entering the house. "Norris married his wife for love, they say. She wasn't especially wealthy or well-placed, and he's obviously besotted with his little son."

"Yes," Sarah said. "I do think that's real. He was drawn to the child as if a moth were beckoned by a flower."

"And one with an exclusive hold on his attention, like the comet orchid for the one insect that pollinates it."

"*Angraecum sesquipedale?*"

He turned to smile at her. "Have you ever seen one?"

"Only in prints, though I've read that the nectar spur at the back of the flower is almost a foot long. You think there's a unique insect to match every orchid?"

"In the case of the comet orchid there must be, and something with a twelve-inch proboscis specifically designed for that uniquely strange and fabulous flower."

She gazed at the seven *Eria rosea* flowers, and found herself—absurdly—blushing as she tried to imagine the moth or fly that might pollinate them.

In spite of her fears for Rachel and her hot awareness of this one man, a warm bubble of laughter rose in her throat. Something in his dry voice and wicked wit reached out to surround her in a cocoon of safety, as if he could rescue her from all anxieties.

"But we don't usually associate faithfulness with flora," she said. "English plants and insects are nearly always promiscuous."

"Then the reproductive habits of flowers are indeed very shocking," he said. "In which case, botany truly is a most unsuitable subject of study for young ladies."

She laughed aloud then, her blood resounding with a newfound confidence, and spun about to face him.

Tall and lean, Guy Devoran lounged casually in the doorway, the sun at his back, watching her. And Sarah knew that if she took one step toward him, she would fly into his arms to press her mouth onto his.

Ardor roared in her ears. She felt faint.

"We must go," she said blindly. "The others will wonder—"

"No, they won't."

He spun about and strode outside. Common sense returned as if a cloud had darkened the sun.

Had she really thought she had fallen in love with a nephew to the Duke of Blackdown? If so, it was only because he possessed a charisma that drew every female as a lamp drew every moth. Always fatal and always indiscriminate.

Surely Sarah Callaway, who had nursed a man as solid and real and kindhearted as her John, was—if she looked into her heart— immune to that glamour?

Yet the lure was still powerful: the shining, dancing flame, always moving, always dazzling, whatever flower each moth had originally been designed for.

Sarah walked out onto the grass.

"The gardeners, Mr. Croft and Mr. Hawk?" she asked. "When can we talk to them?"

Guy Devoran stared away into the far distance, almost as if he couldn't bear to look at her.

"We're all to attend a picnic at Moorefield Hall tomorrow. There will be gaggles of children. It shouldn't be hard to get away to talk to Croft."

"Children?"

"Lord Moorefield, also, is sickeningly proud of his son and heir. And Annabella has decided that she'll appear to best advantage as a domestic goddess, the model of maternal devotion."

"Best advantage to whom?"

His mouth quirked. "To me, I'm afraid."

"Lady Overbridge believes that the sight of her with her children will help win your affections? I don't understand. Won't such a reminder of her marriage vows have the opposite effect?"

He glanced down to smile at her with renewed humor.

"Not at all. She both demonstrates that she is safely available, and hopes to tug at my heartstrings."

Calling on every reserve of courage, Sarah tried to make her voice tease, as a sensible widow might do with any friend.

"Is that difficult to do?"

He gazed up at the sky. Sunshine poured over his dark hair and broad shoulders. The impeccable tailoring. The spotless linen. The body beneath the gentleman's clothes, supple and powerful and remorseless in its masculinity.

Desire for him, frank and hot and carnal—for his touch, for his exclusive attention—burned in her blood.

"Not difficult enough, alas," he said lightly. "So—if I'm not to be embroiled in a lethally unethical entanglement—it would seem I must learn to harden my heart."

CHAPTER TEN

~~~~~~

OOREFIELD HALL LAY IN A GRACEFULLY LANDSCAPED
park. Blessedly alone for a moment, Sarah walked into a
little private garden surrounded by dense yew hedges. A life-size
stone lion slept on a plinth at the center. She sat down on a bench
and watched some sparrows hopping about in the hedge.

The picnic was over. The ladies and gentlemen were now
strolling about the grounds in pairs or small groups, exclaiming over
the perfection of a vista, or the delight of a folly.

Guy Devoran was no doubt keeping company with Lady
Whitely or Lady Overbridge, two beautiful ladies with dresses and
manners designed to captivate any impressionable male.

Meanwhile, Sarah Callaway in her plain schoolmistress frock was
extraneous to the celebrations, like a poor relative who was barely
tolerated.

She tipped her face to the sun and swallowed her ignoble impulse to self-pity—it was, really, quite absurd! She would enjoy the
rest of this beautiful day and be grateful for help in finding her
cousin. No more. No less.

Something crunched on the gravel, then thudded down with a
little cry. Sarah glanced around in alarm. A toddler had stumbled
into the hedged enclosure, tripped on the edge of the path, and

thumped heavily onto the grass. Round blue eyes scrunched shut in preparation for a wail.

Sarah immediately forgot all of her troubles and leaped to her feet, but a pretty young nursemaid dashed through the yew archway. Hefting the child in both arms, she bobbed a curtsy, her face red.

"I'm very sorry indeed if he disturbed you, ma'am! I'll take him straight in."

"No, please don't! I'm glad of the company. Is he all right?"

The nurse nodded, pushed soft gilt hair from the baby's round forehead, and kissed him. His pink mouth trembled, but he caught sight of Sarah and gave her a wobbly smile, before he held out one hand.

"Hallo," Sarah said. "All better now?"

"He's a brave little lad, ma'am." The nursemaid glanced nervously back at the archway. "Though once he's been shown off to the company, he's not allowed to bother the guests."

"Good heavens, I'm not a real guest!" Sarah sat down again on her stone bench. "Yes, I came here this morning with the visitors from Buckleigh, but only in the governess cart. Thus, I ate my lunch by myself and didn't already meet your little charge. Now, as you can see, I'm hiding here quite alone." She smiled at the little boy. "May I know his name?"

"Lord Berrisham, ma'am, Lord Moorefield's son. I've been with him since he was two months old." The nursemaid shifted the child to brace his weight against one shoulder and curtsied again. "My name is Betsy Davy, ma'am."

"For a moment I thought he was Mrs. Norris's little boy," Sarah said, "but Lord Berrisham's hair is a much paler gold, I think. Yet they must be about the same age?"

"Yes, ma'am, though I believe Tommy Norris is a few weeks older. He'll be seventeen months old this coming Monday, or so I believe."

"Then when they're older, perhaps they can play together?"

Betsy Davy looked puzzled. "Well, I don't know about that, ma'am. Lord Moorefield and Mr. Norris—Well!"

Lord Berrisham wrapped two chubby arms about his nurse's neck and chortled. "Behssy!"

"What a clever boy!" Sarah said.

Betsy smiled proudly. "My name was his first word, ma'am, but he can say several other things, too. Tell the lady, Berry!" She nodded toward the lion on its blocky granite plinth. "What's that?"

The little boy pointed a stubby finger. "Dog!"

"No, it's a lion. Can you say *lion*?"

"Line."

"That's right! *Lion*." Betsy turned to nod at Sarah. "And can you say *lady*, lambkin? This is a *lady*."

Lord Berrisham pointed at the lion again. "Dog!"

Sarah laughed.

The nurse set her charge down on the grass and bent to rub the muddy stains from his dress. His ringlets shone in the sunshine like the petals of primroses. The stone lion reclined lazily.

As his nurse straightened, the toddler held up both arms. "Berry up!"

"What's the matter with the boy?" hissed a man's voice. "Can't he stand on his own two feet?"

Betsy glanced around, turned bright red, and dropped a deep obeisance. The child ducked behind her to hide his face in her skirts, his little mouth frozen in a tight line.

The Earl of Moorefield stood beneath the yew arch. Sarah had met him briefly when she had arrived earlier that morning, though he had barely acknowledged her existence. There was something in his eyes that seemed arctic, as if he always stared through other people to see nothing but infinite wastes of snow.

Fragile, watery, the countess had followed her husband. Sleeves the size of pillowcases emphasized her tiny waist. Her pale skin seemed almost translucent beneath wheat-gilt hair and ivory silk parasol.

Lord and Lady Moorefield now blocked the only exit.

Sarah curtsied respectfully, but they both ignored her.

The earl marched forward and bellowed at the nurse. "Take the boy into the house! Why is he still out here in the gardens when I have guests?"

Betsy tried to turn around to pick up the child, but two tiny fists had locked onto her apron.

"And he has stains on his dress." Her Ladyship's pale blue eyes dampened further, as if she suffered a personal affront to her delicate nerves and could only whisper her indignation. "Lord Berrisham is not to soil his clothes, Betsy. He shall go without his supper."

"Devil take it! He's not to hide behind his nurse's skirts!" Lord Moorefield towered over his baby son. "He shall step out and make his bow to his father like a man."

Betsy leaned down to whisper in the toddler's ear and tried to push him forward. His chin quivered. His baby boots dug into the grass.

The earl's lip curled in clear exasperation. "God! If he cries, he's to have a whipping."

Sarah stepped forward, horrified. "If I might be so bold, my lord?"

Lord Moorefield whirled about to face her. His eyes held nothing but ice, as if he would freeze her where she stood.

Sarah fluttered both hands like a simpleton. "Lord Berrisham is very clever for so young a child, my lord. Such a credit to you! He knows how to say *dog* and *lion*, and he's such a handsome boy and so very brave. I believe he resembles you, my lord, above anything—"

As if a glacier had just cracked beneath his boots to spread chaos to the horizon, the earl spun on his heel. Taking his wife by the arm, he stalked out of the yew enclosure, snapping one last command over his shoulder.

"You'll do as I say, Betsy, or you may look for another post."

Unable to contain his white terror, the toddler collapsed to sit on the grass in round-eyed silence. His blue eyes filled with tears. His nurse crouched down and hugged him to her breast.

"There, there, Berry! It's all right, my lamb, but you must be quiet now. Don't cry! Please, now! For your Betsy! See, there's a bird!"

A sparrow hopped along the lion's back, then perched on its stone mane. The child gulped down his sobs and turned to look at it.

Betsy glanced up. "I'd best be taking him in, ma'am, before we get into any more trouble," she whispered.

"But he will get his supper, won't he?"

"Not his own supper, ma'am, no. The kitchen would know about that and tell Her Ladyship." The nurse gave Sarah a conspiratorial wink. "But Berry can have what he likes of mine."

Betsy Davy swooped the little boy into her arms and hurried away.

Her heart filled with rage and desolation, Sarah sat down. The bright day blurred behind a sudden rush of tears. With angry fingers she tore apart the ribbons beneath her chin and tossed her straw hat onto the bench, so she could lift her naked face to the sun.

If the angels were supposed to match each child's soul to the right parents, they had been interrupted this time by demons from Hell.

"It's only me," a voice said softly. "Your harmless coconspirator."

She blinked away the moisture and looked up. Guy Devoran stood beside the lion. Sunlight shimmered in his dark hair. His coat gaped, deliberately left unbuttoned to reveal a snowy cravat and white silk waistcoat, the skirts caressing the backs of his long legs.

He must have walked past her, his boots silent on the grass.

The idea that such a tall, athletic man could move so quietly, could observe her without her bonnet—while she had been oblivious to his presence—sent a wave of panic through her blood. Hot, uneasy feelings, as if she were prey and had just caught sight of a faraway eagle.

"Harmless?" she said a little bitterly. "I hope not—or at least, not to our enemies."

He smoothed his palm along the lion's spine. Sunlight glanced off the fine bridge of his nose and his high cheekbones.

"Something has happened to distress you, Mrs. Callaway?"

She shook her head. "You were able to speak with Mr. Croft?"

The lion's mane harbored mosses. Guy Devoran's long fingers traced the spreading shapes of some lichen. "I was. A difficult character, not given to idle chatter."

Sarah looked away to hide her distress—in case he thought it was only for this—and tried to make her voice light. "Yes, but he's also brown-haired, blue-eyed, and a local man."

Concern lurked in the black depths of his eyes, but it was instantly masked, as if he drew a curtain over any deeper emotions.

"And so fits our description of Falcorne. You also spoke with him, I understand?"

"I did try, but he was almost rude."

"Even though it's no secret that he went to London in the spring."

She picked up her bonnet, running the ribbons through her fingers. "Yes, he did admit that, but I was afraid I might raise his suspicions if I was too persistent, so I retreated here into the grounds. Did you do any better?"

Abandoning the lion, he walked up to the bench to sit next to her. His waistcoat hugged the taut lines of his chest. Another hot disturbance washed through her blood, as if he brought the sun with him and nothing could shield her from its merciless rays.

"Lady Whitely insisted on accompanying me, herding most of the other ladies and gentlemen ahead of us."

"I feared as much." Sarah tossed the bonnet aside. "So you weren't really able to talk to Mr. Croft, either?"

"Not privately, though I still learned something. But first, what did you say to Moorefield—or rather, what the devil did he say to you? Do I need to call him out?"

At the small mockery in his tone, her pain twisted into a blind, unhappy fury. "On my account? I'm flattered, Mr. Devoran, but the fault was all mine."

He tipped his head back, lifting his face to the sun. His profile was as pure as a warrior god's.

"So you were flagrantly impolite?"

"Absolutely," she said. "Though my actual words were only complimentary, you understand."

"What happened?"

"Lord Moorefield discovered me here in this garden with his little son and his nursemaid. He wanted the baby to bow to him—at less than eighteen months old! I intervened before he and the countess made the child hysterical with fear."

A tiny tremor touched the muscling of his jaw, as if he must negate an impulse to action, or emotions he did not want to recognize.

"You didn't like him?"

"The earl is the kind of cold-blooded Englishman that I most particularly dislike, and his wife is the same. I hope they're not close friends of yours?"

"God, no!"

Unable to contain her restlessness, Sarah stood up. "A man who's so pitiless to his own baby son is probably capable of anything."

"Hush, hush, Mrs. Callaway!" Guy Devoran sprang to his feet and murmured in her ear. "Even though we whisper, someone might be lurking behind the hedge."

He led her up to the shelter of the lion. The stone was cool to her hand. Its shadow both encompassed and threatened.

"The countess is just as brutal," she said.

He leaned his back against the plinth and folded his arms. His dark hair fell forward as he stared down at his boots.

The beast's open stone mouth breathed its empty menace into her ears. The man's keen male energy defeated her, simply because he kept it banked beneath such a clear, cool control.

"Lady Moorefield's been an invalid for years," he said calmly. "She's vaporish and occasionally hysterical, and has been known to take to her sickbed for weeks at a time over some perceived slight. She's the Duke of Fratherham's daughter, yet she's living under the domination of a harsh husband, and her family would offer her no support if she left him. *Weakness*, not *brutality*, is the word that comes to mind."

"Nevertheless," Sarah insisted, "Her Ladyship ordered little Lord Berrisham deprived of his supper simply because he'd fallen and dirtied his dress. He's barely more than a baby, and she's his *mother*."

The lion's blind eyes were crumbling beneath the etching lichen. Guy Devoran's black gaze was sharp, focused, and apparently indifferent.

"So? I don't imagine she's ever held him or fed him. Moorefield would have handed him to a wet nurse as soon as he was born. A baby's crying is ruin to any delicate lady's sensibilities. She'd have had a constant headache."

"A baby's suffering is hardly a subject for levity," Sarah snapped.

"You want me to be surprised that a countess feels so little natural affection for her own child?"

His tone seemed almost dismissive, as if he refused to acknowledge her outrage.

"No, of course not," she said. "I imagine that such indifference is common enough among the peerage, where babies are farmed out to the servants like cattle."

He gazed away at the sky. "Not always."

Sarah wanted to strike him. "Though the child was only frightened, Lord Moorefield ordered him whipped if he cried."

He glanced back at her, his eyes dark. "And was the child whipped?"

"No, thank God! The baby's nurse, Betsy Davy, loves him like a mother, and she managed to prevent his crying—"

"And the supper?"

"Betsy promised to smuggle him some of her own food, so he wouldn't go to bed hungry."

"Which the countess must have known, unless she's very disengaged from the housekeeping."

"How can you defend her?" Sarah said. "A mother who won't defend her own baby?"

"I don't defend her, but the situation is more nuanced than that. The countess may be sour and unpleasant these days, but there was a time when she might have become someone different. The heart, surely, can find room for compassion?"

"Only for the child!" Sarah insisted.

"Listen!" He spun around to face her. "Moorefield is a cruel and vindictive man. Ten years ago he married a spoiled young girl for her money. When his frail new countess didn't produce an heir right away, it was commonly suspected that he beat her, though the earl made sure to hit her only where it wouldn't show. Even angels might fear to intervene."

"So you think I took a horrendous risk, for which the baby may well suffer later?" she asked. "Perhaps I did!"

"I didn't say that."

"But you imply it. You imply that I was wrong—"

"*You!*" He seized her by both arms. His passion buffeted her like a strong wind. "Don't misunderstand me, Sarah! I do not approve of the whipping of babies. I don't defend Lady Moorefield's behavior. Any decent mother would take a whipping herself rather than see her baby terrorized—if that were the choice. Yet it's not that simple. Life is never that bloody simple, and the law allows essentially no interference in the way a peer handles his wife or his son. So what the devil do you want me to do?"

"*Do?*"

As if torn apart by lightning, he opened his hands and released her. Sarah sagged back against the plinth.

"At the thought of his ordering his little boy beaten, I've been fighting for the self-control not to take a horsewhip from the stables to give Moorefield a taste of his own medicine. Yet his wife and child would only suffer the consequences if I did."

Sarah bit her lip. "Yet Lady Moorefield is a duke's daughter. She has some influence, surely?"

"Yes, because everything changed when she eventually gave birth to a son. Moorefield crowed about it like a cock on a dung heap, ecstatic to be able to poke a stick in his brother's eye. They've been estranged for years, and at last his brother was no longer his heir. Yet his wife still lives on a tightrope. Does she care very deeply for the child? Probably not. Was she being deliberately cruel to her baby by suggesting he go without his supper, or was she trying to deflect the earl's worse impulses by suggesting a milder punishment first? I don't know. But Lady Moorefield chose this Betsy Davy, and if Moorefield ever discovered that the nursemaid had disobeyed a direct order, she'd be dismissed. Then the baby would have no one."

Sarah gazed up into his eyes, her heart pounding, and knew that she had been deliberately trying to force herself to misunderstand a fundamentally good man.

"I'm sorry," she said. "You're right. Lady Moorefield would probably have successfully softened her husband's wrath, if I hadn't interrupted."

"No," he said. "You were right to do what you could. Yet there's absolutely nothing more I can do about any of it, unless I discover that Moorefield is indeed Daedalus and that knowledge gives me a hold over him for some reason. Unfortunately, it's unfathomable that the earl would have tried to force your cousin to become his mistress *after* his wife finally fulfilled his dearest wish."

"So you think the earl cannot be Daedalus?"

He struck one fist against the lion's belly. "On the contrary, ever since I knew that we'd be looking for our villain in this part of Devon, I've thought that he's our best candidate. I just can't fathom a motive, that's all."

Sarah wrapped both arms about herself as if she could ward off disaster, and tipped her head back, half-closing her eyes.

"A man like Lord Moorefield wouldn't need a motive," she said. "I can't imagine how Rachel could have met him, but if she did and was even a little more impolite than I was, then he might have persecuted her simply for that."

"No!" Guy Devoran dug out a divot of turf with one heel, then rammed the grass back into place. "It's nonsensical that Moorefield would harass your cousin, unless he had a damned good reason."

Clouds were moving over the sun, casting brilliant halos of light about each gray center.

"That's what we came here to find out," she said.

"You shouldn't have come to Devon." Something of bitterness soured his voice. "There's nothing you can do here that I can't achieve better alone."

Angry fingers clenched in her gut. "You forget, sir! Rachel is my cousin."

"God, I don't forget that! I can never forget it for a moment."

Sarah spun about to stare up at his face. Intensity filled the fathomless brown gaze, but it was tinged with more than regret, more than rage.

Her heart began to beat faster, drumming out her anger and replacing it with another emotion altogether, until she stood as if paralyzed beside the cold bulk of the lion, gazing up at Guy Devoran, nephew to the most powerful peer in the kingdom.

Something in his eyes touched her with chill fingers of guilt and longing, yet heated her blood at the core as if she heard the ardent plunge and clash of a far-distant battle.

"What is it?" she asked. "What can't you tell me?"

He moved to pin her up against the granite plinth, then touched her cheek. His fingertips stroked once over her ear to brush against her upswept hair. A sweet, smoldering tremble followed his touch, dissolving all resistance. She wanted to faint or escape. She wanted to remain rooted here forever, encompassed only by the scorch of his black fire.

His fingertips twisted one long wisp of red hair, escaped from its pins when she had impulsively torn off her bonnet. He wove the strand around his fingers, entrapping her as if he would weave her pulse into his. His lips twisted in a small bittersweet smile as his gaze settled on her mouth.

Unless she prevented it, he was going to kiss her.

A bright shock of excitement melted her heart, as if she had always wanted it and never known with quite how much white-hot intensity, until now.

With the black flame still scorching in his gaze, he slipped his fingers deep into her hair, stroking the back of her neck as he tipped her head back—and she melted, dissolving, as the clang and crash of battle roared in her ears.

"What is it?" she whispered again—though she knew, of course, of course, just as she knew that her blood had already made its own decision.

"Perhaps, this," he murmured against her mouth.

Sarah felt his hesitation and knew in her bones how he fought, buckler and broadsword, more desperately than Ambrose de Verrant had ever battled against a host of Saxon enemies.

She could have helped him. She had one more moment to turn away, to say something brilliant or clever or sarcastic. Instead, she stood silent and craved only this one man's hot, bright, living caress.

Sarah closed her eyes and surrendered.

She opened her lips and allowed him her tongue, slipping her hands beneath his tailored coat, tracing the strength of his firmly muscled back beneath the smooth silk of his waistcoat—delectable beneath her barren hands—and a floodgate of ardor opened in her soul.

Sarah kissed him with recklessness, with abandon, and Guy Devoran kissed back, as if he would absorb her into his soul.

And she was ready—moist and hot and ready—for him to ravish her there in an earl's garden, beneath the great sleeping stone lion. To fold with him onto the sun-stark grass to allow him to take his pleasure as he would: a long, scorching pleasure that might leave her burned away to ashes, that might sear her with the white-hot rage and power of the angels.

His hands slid down to her waist, pulling her into his body, bending her helplessly in his arms, so that she clung to his strength.

She would have tugged away his cravat and jacket and shirt. She would have allowed him to tear away her dress to free her naked body to his gaze. She wanted it.

But he broke away suddenly, his lips bruised and swollen, his eyes on fire, to stare down at her like a man haunted by Sirens.

"God! God!" he said, as if the words needed to be dragged from the other side of the world. "If that doesn't drive you away, ma'am, nothing will."

Sarah scrambled for balance, knowing that her skin flamed and her tongue might never find language again. Her knees gave way. She sank down to crouch beneath the lion's open maw, her mind lost for the witticism that might put everything to rights.

He turned and stalked to the bench where she had left her bonnet, then brought it back and presented it with a bow.

She pressed both hands over her mouth—her flaming, treacherous mouth—her blood still on fire.

Guy Devoran stared down at her, the bonnet dangling from his fingers, his eyes filled with nothing but regret.

"Well!" someone said with a nicely restrained savagery.

Sarah scrambled to her feet as Guy spun about.

Lady Whitely stood beneath the yew archway. She twirled her silk parasol and tossed her pretty head.

"There's always some satisfaction when one is proved right about something, Mr. Devoran," she said. "Though the pleasure is most definitely spoiled this time, since the proof is only that our little botanist really is your whore, after all."

The silk parasol revolved with elegant fury as she turned and stalked off.

Guy Devoran bowed and offered Sarah her bonnet. "I can offer you nothing but my regrets," he said stiffly. "I'm sorry. You're all right? I must go after Lottie Whitely, before she spreads gossip."

Sarah nodded. He was obviously desperate to be gone. "Yes, of course. Please, say no more about it."

Avoiding his eyes, she grabbed her straw hat from his hand and jammed it onto her head.

She watched him walk away, lean and vigorous and lovely, and hated herself for being so absurdly, impossibly, in love with him.

GUY waited patiently in the Deer Hut, leaning his forearms on the windowsill, hands clasped, as he contemplated the dark lake and the faint hint of pearly light at the horizon. The dying summer night breathed the last of its silence, deep and still, before the birds stirred to welcome the morning.

He had set up this rendezvous while the Overbridge guests were piling into their carriages in the driveway at Moorefield Hall: five quick words, murmured into her ear from horseback, as Sarah stepped up into the governess cart.

"Tomorrow. The Deer Hut. Dawn."

She had glanced up to meet his gaze with a flash of ardent, tiger heat. His blood had roared its response, but he had wheeled his horse away to ride beside Lady Whitely. Lottie had accepted his company at first with a sulky malevolence, then flirted outrageously all the way back to Buckleigh.

Guy heard Sarah's footsteps before he saw her. Quiet, but fast, walking up through the woods. His pulse quickened. Annoyed by his own eagerness to see her, he tried to empty his mind of everything but their goal: finding her cousin.

He had thought he loved Rachel once. He had made promises. Honor demanded his fealty to that obligation.

And yet—

Sarah's shadow flitted across the doorway. She stopped at the threshold and pushed back the hood of her cloak. In spite of his resolutions, heat surged in his heart at the sharp, spicy scent of green apples, overshadowing the damp aroma of the woods.

She stepped forward. Her silhouette mutated into a warm, living woman as she sat down.

He propped his hip on the windowsill and studied her face, pale and indistinct. Her hair was braided into a simple knot. In the dim light the color was muted, like tarnished bronze.

Folding her hands in her lap, she smiled quickly, then glanced away.

Her mouth enticed like *Eria rosea*.

The memory of kissing her would haunt him till death, yet her nervous discomfort eddied through the dawn air.

"It's not very wise for me to spend much time with you, sir," she said. "I must get back as soon as possible—"

"No one else will be out of bed for hours yet," he said gently. "We're safe enough."

"I don't fear discovery."

"Then you fear that our stone lion is now here in this hut with us?"

Her head snapped up. "Our lion?"

He deliberately kept his voice free of passion. "We cannot pretend it didn't happen, and so I must apologize for so abusing—"

"Please, don't!" she said. "There's nothing to apologize for. No harm was done."

"Lottie Whitely hasn't tried to make you uncomfortable?"

She smiled with real courage. "I'm so far beneath her notice that Lady Whitely would never deign to mention it, though she very kindly warned me against you."

He folded his arms across his chest. "Warned you? Of what?"

"You're a duke's nephew and I teach in Bath. Even though my father was a gentleman and I was raised as a lady, you and I don't move in the same social circles. Thus, Lady Whitely felt obliged to mention that superior young gentlemen such as yourself will always find amusement in the ruin and abandonment of inferior young women like myself."

A flash of real anger surged through his blood. "Did she elaborate?"

"No," Sarah said with a sudden dry humor. "Other than telling me that I was—and I quote—'playing with fire,' should she have?"

He laughed and his annoyance dissipated. "How can I reply to that? I may have pursued some affairs in my time, but I've never been a rake. I don't make a habit of ruining young females. Meanwhile, Lottie Whitely is a shallow, self-centered creature, who's bored to tears with her marriage. She's flirting with me to pique her husband's jealousy, in the mistaken belief that this will force him to love her."

Sarah hugged her cloak about herself, as if to ward off the chill.

"You don't think a certain amount of possessiveness is part of love? It would be more terrible if Lord Whitely were indifferent, surely?"

"It might be, but fomenting her husband's resentment and distrust is hardly likely to bring Lottie what she wants."

"It's horrible," she said. "So much dishonesty."

"They're two equally superficial and selfish creatures," he said. "They didn't marry for love. It's simply an alliance of property and status, in which appearances are everything."

"Yet you're obliged to allow her to use you?" she asked.

"Everyone, including Whitely himself, would be offended if I didn't respond to her at all, and it would be the height of bad manners to embarrass her by spurning her publicly. So it's like walking a high wire. Whitely wants to believe that I find his wife attractive—even if I don't—while knowing that I have no intention of acting on it. Thus, both his vanity and pride may be satisfied, but without recourse to a meeting with pistols at dawn. I also avoid hurting Annabella Overbridge, if she believes that I neglect her only because I'm required to perform such a delicate balancing act with her friend. Does that shock you?"

"I don't know."

"Yet you think me equally shallow, Mrs. Callaway? Equally dishonest?"

"No! Not at all! I meant merely— Oh, goodness! I spoke entirely out of turn. I'm so sorry. I don't know very much about how such affairs are conducted in high society."

"Then thank God for that! Yet if Lottie Whitely tries to make real trouble for you, I'll bring all the power of Wyldshay down on her head, and she knows it. She may be spiteful, but she won't dare to spread gossip. Yet it was still very wrong of me—"

"—to offer comfort when I was so upset about Lord Berrisham?"

Guy jerked as if he were a marionette and Sarah had just pulled his strings. *"Comfort?"*

She clutched the front of her cloak and looked away. "Yes, I was a little discomposed, but I never thought seduction was your aim. What happened meant nothing, so I think it best that we say no more about it."

He should have been glad that she allowed him to slip so very easily from the hook, even if she had just condemned him to swim away alone into darkness.

He could not in honor wish for anything else.

Yet how long must he fight to clear his heart of the living memory of kissing her?

"As you wish," he said. "It won't happen again."

"Good. Then that's settled."

"I only wish I could offer you a more meaningful form of comfort about the child," he said. "Whether Moorefield is Daedalus or not, there's not much I can do about it."

She glanced up at him. Her eyes were brilliant, as if they gathered and reflected all the growing daylight outside. "I know you would if you could."

Guy stared out of the window, simply to avoid that fascinating gaze. Birds had begun rustling in the woods. Trees and shrubs were beginning to take shape. The lake gleamed like a silver platter.

"I thought about that baby for most of the night," he said. "My aunt can still command the king, if she so chooses, but His Majesty is a very old man. The duchess can also—to a certain extent—command Wellington. But her defense of Ryder's marriage to Miracle has cost her considerable influence in London society, and Lady Moorefield's family is almost as highly connected. Fratherham wouldn't take kindly to the Blackdown's interference in his daughter's marriage, or her treatment of her son."

"I understand, but I've still not been able to get that baby out of my mind."

"Neither have I," he said.

It was the truth, but only a part of what he could not forget. He hated the thought of cruelty to any child, yet his mind was also filled with this bright craving—for Sarah's touch, for her lips, for her good opinion—while his heart quailed at the impossibility of ever fulfilling it.

"You said you'd learned something from Mr. Croft," she said, "in spite of his reticence. What was it? I thought I might faint in his hothouse from the scent of all those massed orchids. Yet you told me that Lord Moorefield was only a minor collector?"

Guy turned his back on the view and forced himself to concentrate only on the issue at hand.

"He was, until he hired Croft away from Norris—probably from pride rather than any real interest. Moorefield hates to be outdone in anything, and his new gardener has an extraordinary gift with plants, as you saw."

Sarah relaxed visibly, setting both hands on the table. Her cloak fell open to reveal a plain, dark dress.

"And we already know that Mr. Croft went to London with Lord Whiddon's man in May, so he fits everything we know about Falcorne. On the other hand, he really loves his flowers, or he could never have created that amazing display."

Her face was shadowed, indistinct in the dark hut. Guy felt a moment's resentment that dawn was lingering so long, robbing him of the sight of her freckles, her unruly red hair.

"Which is, unfortunately, enough motive for Moorefield to steal him from Norris," he said.

"Unfortunately?"

"Yes. Otherwise, that whole business might seem a little suspicious, happening, as it did, at the critical time. Croft would probably be capable of ordering violence against your cousin, though I don't doubt that he spent most of his time in town at Loddiges."

"Which seems odd, doesn't it?" She moved one fingertip over the rustic tabletop, as if tracing a maze. "It's not a combination that makes a whole lot of sense."

Guy watched her moving fingers as if mesmerized.

"We're all a mass of walking contradictions," he said. "It's part of the human condition."

She hesitated, as if she wanted to give this statement its proper consideration, then she looked up and smiled.

"I am, certainly," she said. "And so are you."

He folded his arms. "Really? In what way?"

She brushed both palms over her cheeks and shook her head.

"Please, go on, ma'am! You cannot make such a statement, then retreat from it without explanation. Anyway, I owe you the chance for quite a bit more imprudence at my expense."

She laughed, but not with real humor. "I'm not sure that I have enough courage."

"Courage? Mrs. Callaway, you have the nerve of the Iron Duke. Pray, fire away! In what way do I embody so much contradiction?"

"Very well," she said. "You're one of the most sought-after gentlemen in the kingdom, and you're attending a house party where several very eligible young ladies are vying desperately for your attention. You've explained about Lady Whitely, yet you appear quite indifferent to all the others, as well."

"Indifferent? I've been dancing and flirting with all of them, with exactly the correct amount of attention—"

"And so little sincerity that they've all despaired of you."

"I didn't come here to find a wife," he said. "Though the invitation was long-standing, I came here to unmask Daedalus. So if we're talking about our personal inconsistencies, my neglect of the marriage mart is pretty minor. What else?"

She threaded the ties at the neck of her cloak through her fingers, as if she would smooth away invisible knots.

"You truly want me to be honest?"

"I tremble at the thought of your perspicacity, ma'am. As we've already established, it's essentially impossible for me to be candid with anyone else here. So what else have you observed?"

"I don't bring this up lightly," she said. "And if it were not for our extraordinary circumstances, this would all be none of my business, and I would never, never voice anything so improper. Yet I think that I must."

"A little impropriety now is hardly likely to offend, or reflect badly on you," he said gently. "So I would like to know what's bothering you."

"Then I must say this! When I first tried to find out about you in London, I learned immediately that you've always kept a mistress, or else you've pursued a very discreet affair with a married lady—"

He laughed, genuinely touched by her careful pronouncements, though a small voice whispered a deep disquiet that she might yet guess his secret.

"Not discreet enough, obviously! I enjoy the usual vices of my position, and female company is one of them, but where's the contradiction?"

"In your original acceptance of this invitation to Buckleigh," she said. "Lady Overbridge obviously invited you here with that express intent. She's very lovely. She's not unkind or unpleasant, just lonely and unhappy, and she's genuinely attracted to you. Yet any outside observer would think that you like orchids better."

"I do," he said. "The orchids are both more sensual and more honest—like you."

He immediately wished the words unspoken, but it was too late. Sarah stared down at her hands as hot color washed up her neck. The silence stretched.

"And this is where I prove myself equally inconsistent," she said at last. "In spite of everything I said when I first sat down, I feared something of the kind."

Guy glanced at his boots. Sarah was hurt, whatever she claimed to the contrary. He had kissed her without caring for the consequences, as if an exchange of such white-hot passion were trivial. With anyone else, it might be for him. It never would be for her.

"What exactly do you fear, Sarah?"

She pushed a wayward strand of hair from her forehead. "You still wish me to speak honestly?"

"God, yes! What the devil's to be gained by prevaricating now?"

"Then, in spite of what I thought that I wished, I suppose we cannot *not* speak of what happened in that garden." She took a deep breath. "Not because I want an apology, but because I don't."

"You *don't* regret it?"

She shook her head, then dropped her face into both hands. "Yes. No. I don't know."

"Then what?"

"At the risk of making a very great fool of myself, I fear that you in fact have some feelings for me, though you seem to be fighting your desires very desperately. Thus, contrary to what Lady Whitely seems to believe about you, it must be that only honor constrains you." She looked up. "Of course, I must have reservations about such an unwise relationship, but why—when you cannot hide your interest—would you? You're not free?"

"No," he said. "I'm not."

"Yet you still want me?"

"Yes."

"Then I was wrong to demand that we not speak of what happened, and I think we had better get it all out in the open, after all."

He strode past her to the door. Black shadows beckoned in the woods, places the sun never reached, yawning like the openings to caverns that might swallow a man into darkness.

"Very well," he said. "When a lion wakes up, it's usually best to pay it some attention. Of course, I knew exactly why Annabella Overbridge originally invited me here. She's even given us adjoining bedrooms. I don't know whether I'd ever have acted on that, because instead I find you . . ."

He hesitated as pain knifed through his heart. Sarah dropped her head forward. Her hood muffled her voice, as if she could only speak honestly to the darkness.

"As I find you?" she asked.

"God! *Attractive* is too weak a word. Fascinating. Enthralling. If circumstances were different, Lottie Whitely's warning might have proved prescient. Nevertheless I just undertook not to kiss you again, even though I don't know if I can really promise that or not."

"Yes," she said. "I feel the same way. But it's just a superficial, physical thing, isn't it?"

"Perhaps. In which case, in the circumstances, no man of honor would ever act on it. Yet I'm standing here craving you right now, Sarah."

"It's an infatuation." She cupped her forehead in one hand, as if to shield her face from the heat of his passion. "If we refuse to give in to it, it'll pass soon enough."

"We must hope so."

"After all, we barely know each other, so our feelings cannot be truly personal."

"Then why do I feel as if I've known you all my life?"

She looked up and her hood fell back. Her clear gaze pierced his heart, as if he were pinned to the wall with a rapier.

"Yes, and deeper strangers have shared a bed before, but there are a million reasons why it would be most unwise for me to begin an affair with you."

"Though you wish to?"

Sarah clenched her hands together on the table. "I don't know. Though I crave your touch as a moth craves a candle, I also know that I can't trust the way I feel."

"Why not?"

She sprang to her feet and gathered her cloak about her skirts, as if she would flee past him to escape outside. He immediately stepped back to allow her to pass, but she remained frozen in place, staring up at him.

He could not tear his gaze from her face. Heat passed between them in palpable waves. Her lips parted a little. A wave of desire shot straight to his groin.

Yet she ducked her head and walked straight past him to the doorway.

She stopped at the threshold and lifted her chin. "I'm a widow, sir, not an inexperienced girl. I can certainly choose to embark on an affair, if I wish. Yet I've known what it is to truly love a man, and these feelings are nothing like that."

"Even though this lion is roaring from its pedestal?"

"Especially then," she said.

Calling on every ounce of self-control, Guy took another step back, so that she could walk away from him unimpeded.

"Then, like Medusa," he said, "we must turn our beast back into stone."

"Thank you, Mr. Devoran. You embody such a glamorous fantasy, you see. Why should I be immune to the attraction of that flame? Yet for me to crave a gentleman's bed, when—" She broke off and glanced back at him. Hot color scorched over her cheeks. "Now that really *is* unseemly of me!"

"It's the dark," he said lightly. "It makes it too easy to exchange confidences. Yet it's almost dawn. Perhaps by shining the clear light of day on our problem, we'll find that our lion's just a toothless old pussycat, after all."

Her skin flamed, yet she glanced back at him and grinned with glorious bravado.

"*Mew?*"

Cleansing laughter washed up from deep in his heart, and she walked away down the path, releasing him.

Guy leaned one shoulder against the jamb. For a few minutes he could see her in glimpses through the trees, before she disappeared from sight.

The sky was still dim, shell green at the horizon. White bryony climbed over a stump near the hut. The flowers gleamed faintly, as if they still held reflected moonlight.

He looked up as his eye caught a hint of movement in the distance.

Her cloak flying behind her, the hood down, Sarah had walked out onto the open path by the lake.

In a flash of yellow, the sun broke over the top of the next ridge to the east.

Light flooded the landscape. Colors leaped into brilliance. The leaves were emerald and verdant, the sky and water luminescent.

Her hair caught fire in bright shades of copper and gilt. Her cloak was bottle green. Her skirts fluttered like a blue flag.

As if the sun had shouted at her, she stopped to glance back up into the woods, though the hut must be impossible to discern among the trees. She stood and stared for a moment as if she might discover the answer to some great riddle, then turned and hurried away.

Perhaps she really believed his nonsense about pussycats. Perhaps only he heard the majestic tread of the lion padding at her heels.

CHAPTER ELEVEN

ARAH AVOIDED HIM FOR SEVERAL DAYS. SHE SPENT ALL OF HER
time in the gardens with the young ladies, talking of stamens
and sepals and bracts, and showing Miss Carey and Miss Pole—who
almost seemed genuinely interested—how the calyx protected the
tender bud before the flower bloomed.

Sometimes she saw him walking with Lady Whitely, who ignored Sarah entirely, or with Lady Overbridge, who seemed content
to be pleasant, if only to please Mr. Devoran.

Sometimes he rode away on horseback, either in the company of
other gentlemen, or alone, but not again, for some reason, with Lady
Whitely. Perhaps Lord Whitely had put his foot down.

Meanwhile, Sarah was haunted: her nights restless with dreams;
her days lived in nervous starts, as if a monster might leap out at her
at any second from the back of the herbaceous borders.

The lion was the noble king of beasts, but she had begun this
quest thinking only of the Minotaur, who ate young females alive.
Absurd, of course, to refine so much about one passionate kiss.

Yet Sarah could no more forget it than she could forget that the
white bryony, which she had noticed growing near the Deer Hut,
bore poisonous fruit, or that she was only here in Devon for
Rachel's sake.

Guy had spoken to her only once since that last dawn meeting. A fast exchange near the rose garden, the air heady with bees, when she was hurrying in to fetch a shawl.

"You're all right?" he had asked.

She had nodded and smiled brightly. "Yes, of course."

"I sent a note to Whiddon, returned with a polite refusal. He doesn't wish to see anyone. The man's more secretive than the grave."

And then he had walked away, just in time to avoid Lady Whitely discovering them together.

Even that, just that one short conversation, had left Sarah feeling breathless and giddy, as if she were falling from a great height with no landing visible.

As she and the girls strolled back to the house, she tried not to think of him, not to fret about how they were ever to learn the truth about Rachel.

But how could she and Mr. Devoran uncover the identity of Daedalus, when one of their prime suspects was an elderly baron who locked himself away in his home and refused even a duke's nephew?

Miss Pole bent to examine some meadow cranesbill growing beside the lake. "Oh, look, Mrs. Callaway!"

Sarah dragged her mind back to the present.

"That's only a weed," Miss Carey said. "We ought to confine ourselves to proper flowers."

"But all plants are formed on similar principles," Sarah said, "even when we call them weeds."

"See! Those are the stamens," Miss Pole said, pointing. "That's the male part, with the pollen-producing anther at the top. Then here's the female part, where the seeds will be produced."

Miss Carey bit her lip and met her friend's eye. Both girls burst into giggles.

Perhaps botany really was an unsuitable subject for young ladies! Some other guests were approaching over the ornamental bridge. Sarah's pupils ran off to join them. The ladies clustered together in their pretty summer dresses, sleeves billowing, parasols gleaming as if silk mushrooms had sprouted from the stone.

"Why didn't you tell me," his voice asked quietly in her ear, "that you have written a book?"

Sarah spun about and looked up. Guy Devoran was standing beside her, a quizzical smile on his lips. Her visceral response was immediate. Hot color flooded over her neck and face. Her heart leaped as if she were struck by summer lightning.

"Only an amateur botany guide for young ladies," she said. "It was published over a year ago in a very limited edition."

He smiled, and her pulse launched into mad, uneven new rhythms.

"So it made you neither famous nor rich?"

She laughed. "On the contrary, it died with very little fanfare. How did you ever hear of it?"

"Whiddon sent me a stiff note this morning, asking why he had not been informed before that you were staying here. Mrs. Sarah Callaway, botanical author, is obviously more famous than you think. He read your book and he wishes to meet you."

"Lord Whiddon wants to meet *me*?"

He grinned. "We may go there this evening, if that would be convenient. We're invited to partake of a light supper and spend the night. He lives with an elderly spinster sister, who'll be our hostess and your chaperon. I can take you in the gig."

LORD Whiddon's watery gray eyes peered at Sarah through thick spectacles. Wisps of thinning white hair floated over his pink scalp. Everything about him seemed mean and pinched, except for his fabulous hothouse, where an immense collection of huge, showy cattleyas, waxy and sensual, flaunted their extravagant petals.

Sarah wandered past the orchids, her heart beating hard.

Baskets of *Aerides odorata* struggled to breathe, their perfume heavy in the moist air, their sprays of lemon-and-pink blooms clustered like butterflies.

Epidendrum conopseum added even more fragrance, though the blooms lurked shyly among the foliage like odd green insects.

Catasetum fimbriatum added both spice and color, the lips of the flowers frilled with light green around each spotted center.

Beyond the open doors, the garden faced south over a small sea inlet, trapping the sunlight.

She felt giddy, like a woman transported to some exotic wonderland, where the leaves might part at any moment to reveal Titania and Cobweb and Peaseblossom.

Guy Devoran, tall and elegant, gazed at the orchids with something close to reverence, as if they stood within the arched spaces of an ancient cathedral, rather than in the glasshouse of a reclusive and obsessive collector.

Yet as they examined flower after flower, he had subtly interrogated their host and his gardener, and achieved precisely nothing, as far as Sarah could tell. Lord Whiddon had shown them his flowers and briefly asked about her book, but otherwise barely been civil.

Mr. Hawk, his gardener—like his rival, Mr. Croft—was another blue-eyed, brown-haired Devonshire man, but he was as tight-lipped and morose as his master. Yes, he had been to London with Mr. Croft that spring, but he volunteered no more about his journey, except to agree that he had purchased several new specimens at Loddiges.

Lord Whiddon at last led the way inside the house, where his sister—tall, stick-thin, and querulous as a broody hen—waited to preside over their cold supper. Mr. Hawk tugged at his forelock and walked away, back to his potting sheds and hothouse stoves.

Seizing that one moment of privacy, Guy Devoran leaned close to whisper in Sarah's ear. "Daedalus and Falcorne?"

She watched their host's narrow shoulders as he scurried ahead of them, then glanced back at the retreating figure of the gardener. "They're both unpleasant enough, certainly. Mr. Hawk rather gave me the shivers."

"Yet, once again, what's the motive?"

"Lord Whiddon has no wife," she said.

"And wants none. He cannot have persecuted your cousin from any kind of desire for her. He has no interest in the fair sex. Furthermore, he cannot have met Rachel in society, because he takes no part in it."

"Then could she have become accidentally involved in some rivalry over orchids? Lord Whiddon's extremely possessive about his flowers."

"A passion as great as any man's for the lady who captivates him? If so, we may give him credit for that faithfulness, at least."

He gave her a careful smile, as remote as the sun god's, and ushered her into the house.

The supper was stilted and awkward. In spite of Guy Devoran's attempts to offer polite conversation, Lord Whiddon fidgeted and answered in monosyllables. The sky was still light when his sister offered to show Sarah up to her room.

"You'll forgive us, I'm sure, ma'am," Mr. Devoran said with a bow. "But we cannot, after all, enjoy your kind hospitality tonight. Lady Overbridge has planned a breakfast with charades in her Dutch water garden in the morning. So we're obliged to return to Buckleigh this evening, after all."

Sarah gave him a quick glance. It was the first she had heard of any such breakfast.

Lord Whiddon remonstrated immediately, then insisted to the point of being rude. For the first time since they had arrived, he became animated, almost shouting. He had never been so insulted in his life. His sister would take it as the greatest affront. The roads were dangerous at night. Vagabonds and Gypsies were lurking in the area.

Mr. Devoran raised a brow. "Surely you do not suggest, sir," he asked with icy softness, "that I am either remiss in manners, or incapable of protecting Mrs. Callaway?"

Lord Whiddon subsided into a red-faced silence. Within half an hour the gig was bowling back through the gathering dusk, the groom up behind, and Mr. Devoran at the reins.

Behind them, Whiddon's dull gray house huddled in its valley, the splendor of his orchids hidden as if a blanket had been thrown over a fire.

"Why did you wish to leave so precipitately?" Sarah asked.

"Only because Whiddon was so anxious to have us stay."

"I don't really understand why he invited us at all," she said. "It was not to talk about my book, certainly. He showed no real interest in my paltry literary efforts, and he already knows more about plants than I could ever hope to teach."

The horse trotted up a long lane that seemed to lead straight toward heaven.

"I'm afraid Whiddon used your book only as an excuse to try to discover why I really wanted to see him."

"He didn't believe you wished simply to admire his orchids?"

"Even if he had thought so, he wouldn't have cared. As you saw, his passion for his flowers is a private obsession, not something he normally shares with anyone. No, he had some other motive. He must have stewed about it for days."

"You think he's hiding something?"

"I'm sure of it. Yet I'm damned if I see how it could be related to our quest."

Though the evening was balmy, Sarah shivered.

Their road dipped up and down as they crossed the many brooks that ran from Dartmoor to the sea. In each little valley, humpbacked stone bridges, damp with moss, crossed running water. Birch woods clustered, whispering among the shaded rocks, before the road climbed again onto another ridge, where long shadows stretched across open fields.

In one of the broader valleys, they clattered through a small village. A handful of thatched houses straggled beside the stream, with an ancient inn hunched at one end. No one seemed to be about, though a dim light glimmered here and there from a window, and a snatch of song echoed from the inn.

They had trotted up from the village through a winding gorge to pass over the next rise, when Guy Devoran jerked hard on one rein. Sarah clutched at the rail to prevent herself from sliding into him as the gig lurched and one wheel dropped into the ditch. The horse stopped and blew nervously at the hedge.

"Alas," Guy said calmly. "We've come to grief. We may have damaged the axle, and our horse has certainly sprained a tendon." He glanced back at the groom. "Take the gig back to Stonecombe, Tom. Spend the night at the inn. Mrs. Callaway and I will walk back to Buckleigh." He tossed the man a small purse. "Make up any tale that you like—except that you'll not mention us to anyone. Is that clear?"

Tom stared for a moment, his forehead creased in a puzzled frown, then he thrust the money into a pocket, touched his hat, and nodded. "Yes, sir."

Mr. Devoran grinned at him and leaped down. "Good man! We'll rescue you in the morning."

He seized Sarah by the waist and swung her to the ground.

"I hope your footwear will allow you to stroll along a footpath?" he asked. "It's less than a mile to Buckleigh over the cliffs."

"Yes, of course! I never travel in shoes I can't walk in."

"Sensible Mrs. Callaway," he said with a wry smile.

Sarah glanced away, her heart thudding.

The groom took the reins and turned the gig back toward the village. The horse, obviously not lame, trotted away.

Guy Devoran ran up a set of stone steps half-hidden in the bank. They led to a stile in an opening in the hedge. He reached down with one hand and smiled with real gaiety.

"Come!" he said. "We must hurry, before it gets dark."

"But why are we walking?"

"To investigate a theory and to show you something."

Shadows fell darkly from the hedge, but he was silhouetted

above her against a luminescent sky, bright with the promise of sunset. A deep excitement thrummed though her blood.

"Should I be worried?" she asked.

"Not at all! It's a bit of a climb, but I believe that you'll like it."

"Then it's a mystery?"

"Better than that—the fulfillment of a myth."

There was really no other choice. The gig was gone. It would be absurd to stand in the mud and complain, and dangerous to stalk away alone, only to get lost in a network of country lanes.

Sarah tied the strings of her bonnet more firmly beneath her chin and smiled up at him.

"A nice, stomping walk before bed with something magical on the way? Yes, I'd like that!"

Guy helped her over the stile onto a path that angled up through a patch of dark woodland. He did not dare to offer her his hand again, though the occasional root made the path tricky. Yet Sarah strode confidently at his side, almost as if nothing at all lay between them.

The woods thinned. They walked out onto the short turf of the headland, and the footpath split. A stone wall with its wind-stunted hedge loomed up on their right; a field full of sheep sloped away to the left.

The right-hand path led down through a gap in the wall to the inlet that divided the Buckleigh estates from the manorial lands that ran with the village of Stonecombe. Their path ran beside the wall, straight along the top of the ridge toward the cliffs.

Guy led Sarah across the close-mown turf to a gate in the corner, which took them into an empty field, where long grass rippled in the warm breeze off the ocean.

Sarah was glowing from the exertion, her cheeks flushed, her eyes sparkling, yet she walked out like a boy, her strides vigorous and eager. Guy strode beside her and silently cursed fate. She was remarkable. She was lovely. She was forbidden.

He helped her over another stile, but this time only by allowing her to set her hand on his steadying forearm. Desire for her thrilled and demanded. He was determined never to give in to it again.

The sun dropped behind a low bank of cloud. Fat sheep lay in shadowed huddles. The air held an eerie stillness as if holding its breath in the face of the oncoming night.

When they reached the next stile, Sarah was panting.

"We can stop here," he said.

She climbed up unaided to sit on the top of the stile facing him, then tugged off her bonnet to smooth the slightly damp hair from her forehead, dangling her hat by its ribbons from the other hand.

In the field behind her, where the sheep had been moved out earlier that spring, their path wove drunkenly on toward the cliffs: a swath of springy, short turf, stunted by the trampling of feet, with the longer grass rippling beside it.

Guy leaned both forearms on the rail next to Sarah, trying to ignore the lion roaring in his heart. A little wind blew darkly off the sea to blow wayward stands of hair about her cheeks. Beneath her green cloak, her skirts shimmered: some cream-colored muslin with tiny sprigs of red petals and green leaves. Even in the dim light, her fingers were elegant and enticing, fascinating and lovely, entangled in the ribbons.

If he had wished it, he could have jumped her down off each stile with both hands at her waist, caught her against his chest and kissed her again.

If he had wished—

He clenched his fists and stepped back, just as the sinking sun broke dazzling through a break in the clouds. Yellow and gilt and green, color raced back over the landscape. Flames flared in Sarah's hair, a halo of copper and chestnut about her bright face.

Guy grinned at her and pointed to the path behind her, where it stretched ahead toward the cliffs. She spun about to look over her shoulder.

"Oh!" she said. "Oh!"

A bright ribbon of white against the longer grass, the path—and only the path—glimmered like snow.

Sarah dropped her bonnet, spun about, and clambered down from the stile. Lifting her skirts in both hands, she raced away up the white track toward the sea.

Guy reached down to retrieve her bonnet, sprang over the stile, and ran after her.

She spun about to face him as he caught up, her eyes brilliant, strands of red hair whipping about her face. Color burnished her cheeks, almost as if she saw the lion gazing from his eyes.

"It's Olwen's path!" she exclaimed.

He stood arrested as she crumpled down onto the short turf to brush one palm over the masses of daisies that bloomed at her feet. Her face and eyes were glowing, lovely.

"Perhaps," he said. "I can think of more prosaic explanations for why the flowers grow only on the path, but the effect is still remarkable."

She plucked a flower and held it up, as if she beheld a miracle. "Oh, perhaps the rest of the daisies are hidden by the longer grass, or perhaps they can grow only where the turf has been beaten down by so many feet, but I shall always choose to believe that the goddess walked here, and white flowers sprang up in every footprint."

Regret suddenly lanced through him. He had no idea why. It seemed mad.

"I thought you'd like it," he said. "Though the petals are already starting to close up. We should go."

"And so Olwen's' white track will disappear into the mysteries of the night." Sarah stood up and brushed off her hands. "Where does this path go?"

"It's one of many that leads down to the beach."

"How do you know all of this?"

"Because I've already had several days to explore. That village we just passed through—Stonecombe—is owned now by an absentee landlord, but it's part of a manor that's existed since the Conquest."

"The Conquest? You mean the Norman Conquest? William the Conqueror?"

"I don't think England's been successfully invaded since then," he replied dryly, "unless I was sleeping and missed it."

Her laugh was so genuinely merry and carefree that his heart catapulted into his throat.

How easy to catch her by the waist! How easy to tumble with her onto the warm turf! How easy to make love to her, up here on this cliff top, only a hand's breadth from heaven!

Instead, with a bow, he held out her bonnet. She nodded and took it.

A handful of seagulls broke crying up over the cliff to toss out over the water, as if they would fly straight into the setting sun.

Her skirts flared as she turned to gaze out across the Channel.

"May we go down there?" she asked. "I've never been to a wild beach."

He knew it was a mistake, for he would be forced to take her hand. Yet he could not deny the longing in her voice. *A wild beach.*

"The cliff path is both steep and treacherous," he said. "And it's getting dark. Will you allow me to help you?"

She tied the bonnet ribbons loosely, so her hat hung on her back. "Yes, of course."

Guy held out his hand and she took it.

The cliff path was damp, slippery where the rock broke through the turf. The lion circled, roaring its awareness of her small, gloved hand, her neat waist, her grace and suppleness as Guy guided her step-by-step down to the beach.

Yet he hated to rob her of such a simple pleasure as this, and they were safe for the moment. Nothing dangerous was likely to happen until well after dark.

As soon as they reached Stonecombe Cove, the breeze stopped as if shut off with a tap. Black rocks jutted up like small castles from the white sand. A stream from the valley behind them spread into a delta of tiny rivulets. Far out on the horizon, a fiery sun was sinking into the sea, sending its last long rays up across the clouds. The stream flared into a river of gold and fire, entangled with the lapping waves like skeins of her hair.

And everything changed.

Tears blurred her eyes. Distress creased her forehead.

"It's so lovely here," she said on a breath. "Lovely!"

Moisture gathered to overflow down her cheeks. Her nose tip turned pink. She bit her lip and swallowed, then covered her mouth with one hand.

Her need overwhelmed him. Without a word, Guy gathered her in both arms.

"Don't!" he whispered against her hair. "Don't! It's only the ocean."

His lips found salt as he kissed her wet face, then sweetness as his tongue found her mouth. She kissed back with simple, undiluted fervor, as if she would seek succor from his tongue for all the ills of the world.

Her body pressed against his, her breasts crushed against his chest. He stroked the tangled hair back from her face, cradling her head in both hands, and kissed her again. She clung to him with both hands, still kissing, as he sank with her to kneel on the still-warm sand.

His ardor was direct and hot, firing lust in the groin, filling him with urgent, all-consuming desire. Yet a terrible, soul-deep longing also flooded his mind: to make everything right, to heal and protect, even when he knew that he had nothing to offer her but heartbreak.

The red disk plunged at last into the ocean. Guy slipped his hands down to her shoulders to set Sarah at arm's length. They were both still kneeling like suppliants on the sand. Her eyes swam with moisture beneath her shadowed lashes.

"I'm sorry, Sarah," he said. "I'm possessed."

He helped her to stand, then he walked away a few paces. A faint glimmer beckoned far out to sea, as if the water still remembered the day. White grains, like dense clusters of stars, clung to her skirts. For several moments they both stood in silence, gazing at the breakers teasing the shoreline, listening to the grind and splash as smaller waves broke over the rills of dark slate.

Had the sun torn the heart from his body to drag it down with the daylight into the Underworld?

"The tide's coming in and it's getting dark," he said. "There won't be much moon tonight. We must go."

Sarah jammed the bonnet on her head and turned to face him. The oncoming night left her face a pale oval, her expression impossible to read.

"But how do we find our way back now? The daisies will have closed up completely, so Olwen's path will have disappeared. Are there are other paths?"

"To forgetfulness? I don't know. But there are certainly other footpaths back to Buckleigh."

They turned together, as if nothing more needed to be said. Guy led Sarah back across the sand, until they were able to step over a narrow spot in the stream. Although its entrance was hidden amongst the beds of reeds, another well-beaten path led straight up the valley beside the water.

They strolled side by side without speaking. Within another quarter mile the path plunged between high banks, so that it was like walking through a tunnel.

Should he try to offer more apologies, or should he ask why the beach had made her weep? He had no idea where to begin. He only knew that his heart was racked by tenderness.

"You're right about the dark allowing confidences," she said quietly. "Will you take it amiss if I offer a few more?"

"God! No! I'd be honored, Mrs. Callaway."

"Sarah," she replied dryly. "When a gentleman kisses a lady more than once, he may generally use her given name."

Her brave humor took him by surprise, though the lion pricked its ears, as if warning of dangerous ground.

"Mine, as you know, is Guy," he said. "In the dark we are only conspirators."

"I wished merely to say that I'm glad that I was able to tell you about John the other night. I've never been able to tell anyone the truth before."

"It must have been very dreadful for you," he said. "And a worse burden if you've had to bear it alone."

"Yes, I suppose so. I never thought about it quite like that, but, yes, it does help to pour out one's heart to a stranger."

"A *stranger*, Sarah?"

"A clumsy choice of words. I meant someone one can trust, yet doesn't expect to number among one's friends in the future."

"And that's what I am to you?"

"Ours is only a temporary alliance, sir. We both know that."

"Yet I may still call you Sarah?"

"Yes, I think so," she said lightly. "Don't you?"

They strode on up the dark path. Trees clustered now on one side, offering glimpses of the little valley where the stream dawdled into marshy pools on its way down from the hills.

She put a hand on Guy's arm, stopping him, so they stood facing each other. "And the beach—"

"It's all right," he said gently. "You can tell me."

"Toward the end John ran a fever. He cried out for the sea. He wanted to go home. He didn't mean the home that we'd shared in our brief marriage. He meant the place he'd been born. He'd described it to me once. Not a house in a busy port full of ships like Yarmouth, but a little house by a wild beach, where he'd played as a boy. That was home!"

Guy touched her cheek silently, then he tucked her hand into his elbow, and they began to walk on up the path.

"I brought him some dried seaweed," Sarah said. "I thought the scent might comfort him. But he shouted at me and dashed it to the floor. By then he wanted oranges, instead. Yet no fresh oranges were to be had. I couldn't save him! I couldn't even—"

"He had *you*," Guy said. "He knew that you loved him."

"Yet it was as if I lost him little by little. Some days he could recognize me. Other days he thought I was a stranger, then he thrashed in pain and nothing could comfort him. When he died, our housekeeper said it was a blessing, that now he was with God. But it wasn't a blessing. It was terrible."

"I'm so sorry," he said. "So very sorry. You've known too much grief, Sarah. I'm dumb in the face of it. How old were you when your parents died?"

"Seven, but I'd known the Mansards all my life, and they loved me like their own."

"But then you lost them, too."

Sarah tipped her head as if she would study his eyes, though the dark was now almost complete, leaving her a pale wraith.

"Grief is such a selfish and bitterly lonely place," she said. "It's like a labyrinth, where it's too easy to become lost in anger and self-pity. I didn't mean to burden you with my wanderings in that darkness, Guy."

He touched her cheek again. Desire burned in his heart, the aching desire to absorb her sorrow into his body, to become one with her, to share all the depths of this anguish.

And that was impossible, of course.

"No, no," he said. "I'm honored by your confidence, but I have no adequate words."

Yet she slipped her arms about his waist. "What if words won't do?"

Instantly he cradled her head in both hands and kissed her. Their lips moved delicately together, a soft, gentle kiss, desperate with tenderness.

"Alas, alas," he said at last, "but kisses are a dangerous form of comfort."

She dropped her head forward to bury her face in his shoulder. "Yet you do comfort me, Guy. I think you, too, have known some unutterable loss."

He felt it again then, the memory of so much fear and isolation, that labyrinth of loneliness and anger.

"Only when my mother died shortly after giving birth to Lucinda, my sister. I was eleven years old and I'd adored her. My father was inconsolable. Birchbrook was plunged into mourning. There was a tiny infant who needed nursing. So I was sent to Wyldshay to live with my cousins for a year."

They linked arms and began to walk together up the footpath.

"Which only compounded your loss," she said. "You were a boy robbed not only of your mother, but also of your home, your father, and everything you'd ever known. You must have been desolated."

"For a while, yes. Yet Jack and I are the same age. The duchess, however fearsome she may sometimes appear, was infinitely kind. She even came to my room every night and allowed me to sob in her arms, without ever once making me feel that a boy shouldn't cry. By the time I went home to Birchbrook, Jack and I had become as close as brothers and remain so to this day. So in the end, perhaps, I gained as much as I lost."

"Can life offer a net gain from grief?"

"Not always. I was lucky. I lost my mother, but ended up with two families: the St. Georges, plus my father and Lucinda at Birchbrook."

"And I have Rachel," she said.

His step faltered as if she had knifed him. Guy almost lost breath for a moment as the blade pierced his ribs. Sarah had Rachel and only Rachel. She had no one else left in the world. And that was all that she really wanted of him and of their odd friendship: to have Rachel—not the real Rachel, but her memory of the innocent cousin she had grown up with—restored to her.

An impossibility, unless life really offered miracles.

Sarah's head turned as if she heard something.

Numb with renewed grief, Guy stared down at her. Yet the night shifted, demanding a quite different reaction.

The sounds were barely perceptible, a faint thumping and the odd clink, somewhere ahead of them. They had lingered far too long, and now they had company.

Instantly he repressed his anguish and his desire, and set one finger gently on Sarah's lips. She nodded. Within seconds the faint noises became discernable: the muffled tread of wrapped hooves.

Guy dragged her between a break in the trees and down the slope toward the stream. He thrust her flat onto the damp grass in the shelter of a patch of thick brambles.

"Hush!" he whispered fiercely against her hair. "Someone's coming!"

CHAPTER TWELVE

OR THE SPACE OF A HEARTBEAT SARAH KNEW REAL TERROR, but Guy held her steadily within the circle of one strong arm.

The reverberation grew louder, the muted thud of feet, a slight rattle of harness. A string of ponies was coming down the footpath directly above them, though the hoofbeats sounded as insubstantial as if a fairy troop flitted by in the night.

Guy kissed her quickly on the forehead, then he squirmed back up the bank on his belly, leaving Sarah huddled beneath her cloak.

The procession continued to pass. No one spoke, no one whispered. No animal nickered or whinnied. Nothing but that furtive tread and the faint scent of horses and men slipping down to the beach.

At last the sounds faded into silence. Sarah lay as if frozen, stifling her breathing in a fold of her cloak. The wait seemed interminable before Guy slid partway back down the bank and held out his hand.

Fingers locked together, they scrambled back up to the path without speaking. The scent of ponies still lingered. A few stars had come out.

Sarah and Guy walked back toward Buckleigh in silence.

Her blood raced, in excitement, in trepidation, yet in the certain faith that Theseus strode beside her, the one man able to kill any monster. The feeling was heady, euphoric. Yet once they had entered the safety of the park, she released his hand.

He glanced down at her, still without speaking. Then he walked away a few paces to stand gazing out over the lake.

She sat down on a low wall and stared at him. Her heart pounded as if she had been running. His silhouette was as sharp as black paper against the dark shimmer of the water. His expression was lost to the night.

Yet Sarah still felt wrapped in his warm, vital presence, as if he projected security.

At last he turned back to her. Even in the dark she thought that he smiled.

"We met smugglers," he said quietly. "You'll have guessed as much."

"Yes," she said.

"I've suspected it for a while—and not simply that the local people do a little free-trading. One finds that everywhere on this coast. This is far wider and deeper than that."

"You've been actively pursuing this idea for some time?"

"Every day, since we first visited Norris at Barristow." He walked up to drop onto the wall beside her, though he still gazed out across the water. "Among other things, it explains all those orchids, glowing briefly, then dying, then being replaced at ruinous expense. Norris's estate cannot provide enough to sustain that level of spending, nor can Whiddon's. Jack's certain that neither of them has enough other investments, and neither of them gambles."

"Your cousin Lord Jonathan?"

"He and I are in constant communication, and his skills in subterfuge are far better than mine. We suspected that something like this might be relevant."

"How could smugglers be connected to Rachel?"

"Because among the gentlemen leading that pack train to the beach were both Hawk and Croft."

A shiver ran down her spine. Freebooters might claim to be gentlemen, but the trade never shrank from violence. Informers and revenue men were sometimes tortured or killed.

"Oh," she said. "Oh, I see."

Warm and solid beside her, Guy spoke with clear, quiet conviction. "Furthermore, neither gardener would have been able to do this for long without his employer knowing about it, especially when those gentlemen appear to be taking a lion's share of the profits."

She glanced toward the bulk of Buckleigh House. "You think Lord Overbridge is involved, too?"

"Probably not, but I imagine Pearse and the rest of the staff have a very good idea of what's going on and know enough to keep their mouths shut."

"So this explains why everyone's been so close-lipped." Though the air was still warm, she shivered again. "And why Lord Whiddon wished so desperately for us to spend the night, in case we saw something suspicious."

"Though I didn't exactly expect to meet the smugglers on the path." To her surprise, a little humor warmed his voice. "But this solves at least part of our local mystery. There's a general conspiracy of silence to hide a lucrative free trade, in which Hawk and Croft can easily take some of the contraband up to London."

"And did so in May, then brought orchids back?"

"Head gardeners on country estates often travel to inspect other gardens or buy new plants. It's perfect cover."

Though she knew it was ridiculous, a small disappointment knifed through her, that he had had an ulterior motive for everything they had shared earlier that night, that even his taking her over Olwen's daisy path had been just incidental to a wider purpose.

"So this is why we went to the beach? You hoped to see evidence? Recent tracks, perhaps, or some disturbance on the sand?"

"They leave no tracks because the last pony drags a thick branch to brush them away, and the boat was probably unloaded several days ago. They'll have weighted the casks to float just below the surface of the sea."

"Do you think Whiddon suspects your interest in this? Is that why he invited us to his house?"

He shrugged. "Very probably. But what I can't fathom is why he or anyone would send either Hawk or Croft to pose as Falcorne to threaten your cousin."

"Perhaps Rachel found out about this somehow, and they wanted to silence her?"

He shook his head.

"Why else?" she asked.

Guy leaped to his feet. "I don't know. We shan't solve it tonight. Come, we must get back!"

He turned and strode away toward the house, forcing her to hurry at his heels. After his previous warmth, she felt absurdly abandoned. Perhaps it distressed him to admit that they were no closer to solving the mystery of Rachel's disappearance. Perhaps he was merely anxious to escape the dangers—of all kinds—of the night.

Sarah had no idea of the time, but the house would surely be shut up. No one was expecting them until morning. The back door that she unlocked when she met Guy at the Deer Hut, then fastened again on her return, would be bolted now from the inside.

"How are we to get in?" she asked.

"Through the front door." He stopped and turned to face her. "This is good-bye, Sarah."

As he spoke, the grand double doors were flung wide. Yellow light flooded across the grass. Sarah turned and blinked.

Two gentlemen trotted down the front steps. Two ladies hovered in the lit entry hall behind them.

"Good Lord!" Lord Whitely swung his lantern to shine its full intensity on Sarah's face, then lowered it to glare at Guy. "Devoran? We were about to give up on you, sir!"

"Damme, sir!" Lord Overbridge added, panting. "We've had a search party out for you for the last several hours."

"My nag went lame," Guy said. "It was fastest to walk back. Most kind of you to be concerned!"

"But we expected you to spend the night with Whiddon, sir. What the devil possessed you to return in the dark like this?"

Guy took Sarah by the arm. His touch was casual, no more than was strictly correct.

"Having suffered through the supper his sister provided, I would not stay at Whiddon's if it were the last house on earth. I doubt that they've aired their guest rooms in thirty years."

"But to walk, sir!" Lord Whitely remonstrated. "And with a lady! Surely the inn in Stonecombe was closer? Our chaps found your man there—"

"That rat-invested hovel?" Guy turned and raised a brow. "Surely you would not suggest that this lady and I should have spent the night there together?"

Whitely spun on his heel and stalked up the steps. Guy and Sarah walked in behind him.

Lady Whitely gave them both an arch smile. "We're all most relieved to see you safe, Mr. Devoran. I trust Mrs. Callaway came to no harm? Such a sad adventure!"

"It wasn't far," Sarah said. "I am well used to walking."

"Really?" Lady Whitely pursed her pretty mouth. "Is that why you have grass stains on your skirts?"

Sarah glanced down. "I became a little fatigued and was forced to rest for a few moments on a bank. Mr. Devoran was most kind. He waited entirely without complaint for me to recover my breath."

Lord Overbridge turned to Guy. "But our fellows never found you on the road, sir, and I'd have thought Whiddon's messenger would have passed you, as well?"

"We took a short cut over the fields and didn't come across a soul." Guy bowed to Lady Overbridge and smiled. "I apologize if my decision caused you any alarm, ma'am."

"Oh, no!" Lady Overbridge said. "How could we have feared for *your* safety, Mr. Devoran? Though we were all most shocked that Mrs. Callaway was lost out there in the dark."

Lady Whitely spun about, letting her skirts swirl. "Indeed, if such an escapade were to become generally known, it could only reflect badly on her reputation. Certainly, if the young ladies' chaperons were to hear of it, they would think Annabella a very sorry hostess to have exposed their charges to such an improper influence. There has already been some talk about teaching such innocents about the promiscuous habits of flowers. We few gathered here won't breathe a word to a soul, of course, but such things have a way of getting out."

Guy glanced up at the ceiling as if to cover simple exasperation. "Not if Mrs. Callaway leaves for Bath first thing tomorrow before anyone else is up. It would simply be assumed that we had returned here exactly as planned. Will that do?"

"I've done nothing wrong," Sarah said. "I would rather not flee as if admitting that I had."

"No question of that." Guy dropped his chin and smiled at her. "You would anyway have returned home in a few days, ma'am. Surely it will cause you no great inconvenience to do so a little early?"

A wicked awareness lurked in his gaze, as if Oberon played some great joke on the forest—only this time it was at her expense.

Sarah swallowed a small rush of anger. "No, of course not, sir."

Lord Overbridge puffed out his chest. "You may take the mail coach from Plymouth to Bath in perfect safety, ma'am. And we'll reimburse you in full for your time here, of course."

Annabella Overbridge smiled shyly at Guy, then she looked back at Sarah.

"No, my own carriage shall take you as far as Exeter, Mrs. Callaway. I'd never forgive myself if your reputation were to suffer while you were in my employ, merely because of an unfortunate accident."

"Then that's settled." Guy offered his hostess his arm. Lady

Overbridge laid her fingers on his sleeve. He smiled down at her. "Though the fault is all mine, I'm devastated to think that I may have caused such a charming hostess any personal anxiety."

They walked off together, followed by Lottie Whitely and the two men.

Sarah Callaway was dismissed. She would be sent back to Bath in the morning.

He had kissed her and confided in her—but now he was sending her away.

She had run like a girl over Olwen's white track. She had climbed down onto a magical beach with a man lovely enough to die for. He had allowed her to share her deepest anguish and he had hidden her from smugglers.

They had kissed. They had kissed.

But now Guy Devoran was happy to be sending her away.

Nothing much else seemed to matter, except the desolation of that.

Yet did he really believe she would return, docile and content, to Bath? No, to go back to the school was impossible, but there was one place where she might yet be given the help that she needed—if she dared.

With a renewed sense of purpose, Sarah stalked back to her room and began to pack her few possessions. She had almost finished, when someone rapped at the door.

Her heart lurched. Sarah stared at the panels, her pulse pounding, before she called out permission to enter.

It was only a maid. The girl dropped a curtsy and held out a letter.

"I'm that sorry, ma'am! This was delivered by hand earlier with all the rest of the post from Plymouth, but I clean forgot."

Delivered from Plymouth—so it was not from Guy Devoran. Relief? Disappointment? Trepidation? The mad rush of feelings forced Sarah to sit down.

"By hand?" she asked. "From whom?"

"I don't rightly know, ma'am. Some boy gave it to our man that brings up the letters. That's all I know."

Had she really hoped that he had sent her an explanation or apology? Instead, her name was written across the letter in a far more familiar hand.

For a moment Sarah felt almost faint, but she unfolded the paper to reveal a hurried scrawl covering an endpaper carelessly ripped from a book.

As she had already ascertained from the handwriting, the message was from Rachel.

GUY made his excuses and went to bed alone. He lay awake for a long time staring at the canopy by the light of a single candle.

Whatever they discussed or agreed, whatever he admitted or promised, he still craved Sarah with an intense, bright passion—still yearned to risk the painful madness of her company—almost as if he were falling in love.

Yet Guy Devoran could make promises to no one, least of all to himself.

He closed his eyes for a moment, trying to purge his mind of the memories and the desire, so that he might concentrate instead on their quest.

He was almost certain that Rachel's disappearance had nothing to do with either orchids or smuggling. No, something quite different was going on, something that had called her away so precipitately from Hampstead, yet lay even farther in the maze of her past.

And now he had another vital clue to that puzzle.

Jack's latest letter—just delivered to Buckleigh and written by a man with a brain like quicksilver and the genius of a born conspirator—still lay on his desk. On the surface it was merely a summary of family news, but the real message lay hidden in a code they had invented as boys.

Guy sprang naked from the bed, memorized the information

again, then held the paper to the candle flame and watched it blacken into ash.

WYLDSHAY was even more fascinating than Sarah had imagined. A fantasy of medieval towers, pierced with astonishing gardens and sudden, unexpected courtyards. The castle walls soared from the spreading waters of the River Wyld, forming an island fortress.

She lay back on an ivory velvet chaise longue in an elegant morning room in the Whitchurch Wing, feeling truly relaxed for the first time in days—no, weeks! Her silk robe, a gift from Lady Ryderbourne, whispered softly over limbs languid from a long, hot bath.

Though a strong sun beat down into the little enclosed courtyard beyond the open French doors, both women were sipping tea in relaxed dishabille, their hair loose about their shoulders.

"This room is so lovely," Sarah said, glancing up at the open half-moon clerestory windows. "One feels so completely safe here."

Miracle smiled. "Then you've noticed that I've banished the dragons from this wing, though our armored hero defeats his monster almost everywhere else at Wyldshay. One would think the St. Georges were so unsure of their identity that they have to be reminded of it constantly, or they'd forget who they are."

Sarah laughed aloud. "I cannot imagine either Lord Ryderbourne or Lord Jonathan forgetting who they are for a moment—and certainly not the duchess!"

Her eyes danced with merriment as Miracle set down her cup. "I'm so glad you came to me, Sarah! I liked you right away when we first met in London, and now I know I was right. It's lovely to be able to talk with another woman without any social pressure. Alas, I'll always be a lady of questionable repute."

"Whereas my reputation is in the hands of Lady Whitely," Sarah said dryly, "so I'll be lucky to be allowed into society ever again, let alone to teach at a superior school."

"Nonsense! Her Grace could crush Lottie Whitely with a glance if she breathed a word against you. But let me tell you a tale. You've never been told my true history before, have you?"

"No," Sarah said. "Though everyone's heard of the St. Georges, of course."

Miracle walked to the open doors and glanced up at the white roses climbing over a tall trellis. In the courtyard beyond, a stone swan spilled water into the basin of a fountain.

"Then you should know that before I met Ryder I lived as a professional courtesan, earning my living by selling my favors. I had done so since I was sixteen. Have I shocked you?"

"I'd no idea," Sarah said faintly.

"I thought not, but while you're with me, you may relax about any minor transgressions of propriety. I'm still not received everywhere and never will be, in spite of the duchess's best efforts."

"It makes no difference to me, but—"

"But society isn't always so forgiving. Ryder is the beginning and end of the meaning of my life, as I am of his. Yet Anne is my only real female ally—other than Liza, the eldest of Ryder's sisters, who's not even out yet—so a new woman friend is very precious." Bright sunshine died to whispers in her dark hair as Miracle glanced over her shoulder. "Before I met Ryder I'd known times of great loneliness."

Sarah's heart seemed to be opening like a sunflower, as if the other woman offered her the key to some bright truth.

"And I've had no one but my cousin, Rachel," she said. "Though once I discovered how she'd been lying to me, I felt as if I were lost in a maze. I think I was lonely, too, more than I realized, so I'm stunned with gratitude for your generosity. When I turned up here like a waif, I was afraid that the duchess would send me away with a flea in my ear."

"Her Grace is a remarkable lady," Miracle said. "She has an eagle eye for what counts and is rarely distracted by appearances. She likes you."

Sarah leaned back to gaze up at the painted ceiling. "Then I wish

I could say that the appreciation was mutual, but I'm afraid that she leaves me quaking in my boots."

"By design, just to make sure that no one can mistake the power of Wyldshay."

Miracle strolled outside, a dark-haired woman of exquisite loveliness, framed by roses. At the back of the courtyard a wall of stone, streaked here and there with dark stains, framed an arched gateway—a remnant of far more dangerous times—that led to yet more gardens.

She touched the black streaks, before turning back to smile at Sarah.

"This gate's been here since the last visit of Eleanor of Aquitaine. It's named for her. When the Whitchurch Tower almost burned to the ground last year, we had to considering demolishing it. Yet in spite of the dragons, I didn't want to entirely dismiss the stern purpose that drove Ambrose de Verrant to build his keep on this spot." She plucked a rosebud and walked back into the room. Her eyes held only a quiet wisdom and compassion. "Wyldshay is a sanctuary, Sarah, as well as a home."

Miracle held out the flower. The petals, faintly scented with spice, were folded tightly over the secret heart.

"As I, too, came here for refuge?" Sarah said.

"And some practical help, which I'm delighted to offer. Anne's baby is bound to arrive within a few days. Then I'll take you down to Withycombe myself. Since Guy is proving so obdurate, we'll beat the truth out of Jack."

Sarah set the rose into a jug on the table, balancing it so just the end of the stem dipped into the water.

"Then you think Lord Jonathan really must have discovered something momentous?"

"Of course! If he and Guy are conspiring together, formidable forces are working on your behalf."

"Forces that would just as soon leave me out of it."

"So typical of men!" Miracle walked back outside to gaze up at some swallows, wheeling high above the rooftops. "You've not exactly said so, Sarah, but you believe that Guy betrayed you in some way?"

Heat flooded over her face. Yet if she was opening her heart to the truth, she owed Miracle a sincere answer.

"No, not really."

"Then I must ask this," Miracle said. "For Guy's sake, as well as yours. Are you in love with him?"

The hot blood burned, scalding up her neck. "I think so—but I don't really know."

"I saw something new in his eyes when he'd just met you in London, you see, almost as if he'd glimpsed the halls of Valhalla. He and I have been close friends for many years." Miracle's white robe fluttered as she strolled around the courtyard, but her voice remained quiet and steady. "A long time ago we were lovers, as well. Did he tell you that?"

Sarah stared hard at the rose. "No, though I'd wondered."

"He was eighteen. I was sixteen. He was my second. I was his first. When my first protector died, I came to London to make my fortune on the stage. Not possible, of course, unless one also sells one's favors, but I was lucky and I met Guy. We fell very desperately in love. We were children. It couldn't last. Neither of us regrets that, especially now that I've found real love with Ryder. Yet Guy's very dear to me, Sarah."

"You describe a world I don't know," Sarah said. "Which only confirms how absurd it would be for me to fall in love with him, doesn't it?"

"Perhaps. Obviously Guy has a great deal of natural power and an unassailable position in society. Yet he's not a man who ever uses women lightly. I don't believe he's ever entered a relationship without love playing some part."

The rose slipped to sink to the bottom of the jug. Water enveloped the petals, trapping tiny air bubbles.

"Do you believe in love at first sight, Sarah?" Miracle asked. "Or that we're each predestined for only one man?"

"I know I loved John, my husband," Sarah said. "Though I only really discovered it when I nursed him in his final illness."

"And did you also share passion?"

"I don't know what that really means."

Yet she did. She did. Though she was certain only that she was afraid and unsure of where those feelings might take her.

Miracle walked slowly around the courtyard. "I believe that love can take many forms, and that we can find it many times and in many ways. I loved Guy once with all the passion of a young girl finding her first really beautiful lover. I still love him now in a quite different way. I loved a couple of my other protectors, too, and each time it was unique, just as each of these flowers—though all roses— is quite unique."

"Lord Ryderbourne isn't jealous?"

"No, because my passion for him is absolute and complete, and he knows it. My having loved before—or his having loved before— doesn't diminish what we share. If anything, it enhances it." Miracle stopped by the gate to pluck another rose. She stared into its open heart for a moment. "What would this trellis be with only one flower?"

"Yet Guy told me he wasn't free," Sarah said. "He sent me away from Buckleigh almost as if he never wanted to see me again."

"I don't know how he couldn't be free, though I think perhaps he was hurt quite badly last spring. He and I have always shared most of our secrets, except then. All I know is that he kept a mistress who abandoned him. I've no idea why and I never met her, but I was afraid that she may have broken his heart."

"And so you think, if I let myself love him, he'll break mine?"

"Not deliberately," Miracle replied. "Not willingly. But love is always a risk. It can never be found without hazard."

Boots rapped hard on the path leading up to the Eleanor Gate.

Her dark hair flowed as Miracle spun about. Her face lit as if she hoped to see her husband. Seconds later, the naked passion in her eyes softened into a much simpler pleasure as a tall gentleman walked into the courtyard, his jacket slung over one shoulder.

His hair dark, his eyes brilliant, Guy Devoran stood framed in white roses and harsh stone.

He flung aside the jacket and held out both arms. "It's a girl!"

Miracle ran straight into his embrace. Guy picked her up by the waist and swung her in a half-circle, before kissing her quickly on the mouth.

She hugged him, then stepped back to study his eyes. "And Anne is well? Thank God!"

Guy touched her cheek. "Yes, both mother and baby are glowing with health, and Jack's ready to fly to the moon. Withycombe is desperate to show off the prettiest baby ever seen—except for Ambrose, of course! The duchess left two minutes ago, and Ryder will drive you down as soon as you can get dressed. He's seeing to your carriage as we speak." He grabbed Miracle's hand and towed her toward the French doors. "Come, get your clothes on! Jack will slaughter me if he thinks I caused any delay in your arrival, and your husband will be storming, booted and spurred, into your dressing room to fetch you at any minute."

He hauled her into the room and stopped dead.

Sarah stood awkwardly beside the chaise longue, flaming as if she were being martyred. It seemed absurd to curtsy, but she curtsied.

The color drained from his skin as if whitewash had been dashed into his face. He dropped Miracle's hand.

"Ah," Miracle said, glancing from Guy to Sarah. "Yes. Mrs. Callaway came to me in her hour of need, as she and I had arranged in London. Did you think that I, too, would abandon her?"

His eyes blazed in his white face. "Never!"

"Then you and she probably have some things to discuss."

In a rustle of silk, Miracle St. George, the future Duchess of Blackdown, left the room.

Sarah looked as if she were confronting a ghost. As she rose from her curtsy, her bright color receded like the tide, leaving her as pale as death.

She was dressed in some kind of silvery wrapper. The drapes caressed the warm curves of her breasts and whispered over her hips and legs. Her hair streamed in a glorious mass, crimped into deep waves where it had been released from its plaits, a dance of flames and copper, sunshine and autumn.

The lion threw back its shaggy head and roared its imperious power.

Stunned by his desire, Guy stood pinned on the spot. For the first time in his adult life he felt lost, as if he were flung blinded into an unknown forest.

Sarah sat down. Her freckles flung scattered constellations across her nose and cheeks, dark stars on skin white as ivory. Her bare feet were encased in white leather slippers, soft beneath the shadows of her robe.

"Lady Jonathan is safely delivered of a baby girl?" she asked. "I'm so glad. Of course, you'll wish to go straight back to Withycombe—"

"No! Ryder and Jack need this time together without me. Jack and I have already talked."

"You went there directly from Buckleigh?"

"Yes, but Anne began her labor not long after I arrived, and then they wouldn't let me leave. As soon as she was safely delivered, I came here with the news."

Sarah looked up and his heart turned over. Her tawny tiger's eyes seemed to be searching the depths of his soul.

"I'm not sure what else to say," he said. "You're angry?"

New color washed into her face. "Why would I be angry?"

"Because I sent you from Buckleigh in disgrace."

She said nothing, only sat beneath her magnificent hair and stared at her hands.

"Nothing more could be done in Devon," he said. "It was obvious that Whiddon would send word ahead to Buckleigh about our abrupt departure, and equally obvious that they'd be hunting for us. Surely you realized that?"

"So you took me to the front door and threw me to the wolves?"

He felt astonished. "I thought you'd understand why that was necessary."

"To insult me?"

"What the devil would they have thought if I'd announced that we were going to leave together? Be reasonable, Sarah!"

She leaped up and paced to the empty fireplace. "Yes, I understood! But that doesn't mean that it didn't hurt."

In two strides he towered over her to seize her by both arms. "Our investigation there had already reached a dead end. After I'd confirmed my suspicions about the smuggling, I needed to be free to follow other leads—"

"Did you really think I would go quietly to Bath?" She flung back her head and glared up at him. "Did you really—"

"I sent an explanation to Miss Farcey's school," he interrupted. "Since you didn't go back to Bath, you've not read it. But you know that I can pursue the rest of our quest far better alone."

"Oh, I'm sure that you can," she said bitterly. "But it's *my* quest! How *dare* you dismiss me as if I were a child?"

His blood blazed, in anger and resentment and confusion. "I don't dismiss you—and I certainly don't think you're a child! On the contrary, I'm only too aware— For God's sake! Don't you understand yet why we can't continue this together?"

The flush mounted in her cheeks until her face reflected his fire. Her eyes dilated into black pits. The scent of apples and spice and woman assailed his nostrils.

"No! Why?"

"This!" He groaned as he said it. *"This!"*

The pink tide flooded down over her neck to stain the sweet swell of her breasts. Her nipples rose beneath the fabric as if they'd been touched.

His fingers tightened on her arms. "I'm possessed, Sarah. I can't forget you. I can't have you. I try to leave you behind, but you only haunt my dreams and disrupt my days. I can't breathe without wanting you. You drag me to the brink of dishonor. You threaten me as clearly as if you held a sword to my heart. I didn't send you away from Buckleigh for your sake, but for mine!" With the last shreds of his willpower he opened his hands and released her. "Devil take it! Why won't you go away?"

"Because I love you," she said.

She reached up to cup his jaw in both hands, pulled his lips down to hers, and opened her mouth.

Nothing mattered then but the taste and feel of her, almost naked in his arms. He pulled her close against his body. His palms followed the curve of her waist and back, then roamed down over her buttocks, warm and soft, filling his palms. He found handfuls of negligee and bunched them, working ferociously to get the fabric out of the way. His fingertips roamed to find more curves: the arch of her ribs, the softness of her round belly. Her breasts fit perfectly in his hands, the nipples hard beneath the silk.

And she kissed him, groaning into his mouth, her lips a hot welcome, her tongue a ravishment, until in the end he ripped fabric and found naked flesh.

Still kissing, they fell backward onto the chaise longue. She tugged at the knots in his cravat and untied it, then pulled the linen from his neck. She snapped open buttons, pushing his waistcoat and braces from his shoulders. For a moment he was forced to surrender each hand, as she tugged the garments from his arms and threw his waistcoat aside, but he still kissed her.

She wrenched his shirt from his waistband and tugged it up. Her palms feasted on his bare flesh: his chest and waist and shoulders— even his nipples and the sensitive hollow at the base of his throat.

Hot sensation shot straight to his groin, engorging him further. Lust throbbed in his blood like a madness.

Guy broke the kiss, one bent knee balanced on the chaise, one booted foot braced on the floor, and tore his shirt off over his head.

She wriggled back on the couch, her breasts round and full, her lips swollen. Her eyes shone fiercely, like a cat's in the night.

His gaze locked on hers, he plunged both hands into her hair to cup her head and lift her, so their open mouths met again. Torn silk slipped away. Her nipples puckered against his bare chest. Her fingers spread on his shoulders, the nails scoring a faint track down his spine, until she cupped his buttocks and pulled his pelvis against hers.

Desire beat about his head, the frantic batting of wings, showers of feathers.

The insanity of leather breeches and braces! The madness of riding boots and spurs! He reached down with one hand, desperate to free himself. Something ripped: his rowels catching in long trails of torn negligee. He struggled with his buttons. A length of lace almost tripped him as he tried to change position.

He pulled back to tear open his clothes, and a swallow flashed past his head: a real bird, beating and fluttering. Black-eyed panic thumped against the ceiling, then the windows, then swept back across the room.

Guy laughed. A mad, male triumph soared in his soul. He glanced down at Sarah to share the wonder of this wild bird of desire, and his heart stopped in his chest.

She was as lovely as the dawn, her face brilliant with hilarity and the siren song of recklessness, giggling as she dodged a shower of feathers. Freckles ran in mad abandon across her cheeks, but her breasts were smooth and white, like unblemished cream.

She ducked and laughed again as the bird swooped past. Her legs sprawled in the ruin of her nightgown. Red curls spiraled like coils of copper wire where her lovely woman's belly met the flesh of her thighs.

She was willing and open and ready for him.

She claimed that she loved him.

And he was about to ravish her in an orgy of lust in Miracle's breakfast room—though their bond was based on a lie.

"No!" he said, though the word was an agony. "No, Sarah! Not like this!"

Ignoring the lure of the moving bird, she glanced back up at his face. Her laughter died as if he had strangled it, though she still looked at him as if she would forgive even that.

He gathered folds of torn fabric to cover her breasts, though he could have wept with frustration and rage at his own contradictions.

The swallow stopped to perch on the chandelier, its long pointed tail an arrow directed at his heart.

"It's all right," Sarah said softly. "I want you. I want this. I don't care about anything else."

Yet he dragged himself away and picked up his discarded clothes. He draped his shirt about her shoulders and folded his waistcoat as a cushion for her bare feet. Her slippers had fallen crushed to the floor.

"You don't know," he said. "You don't understand."

The swallow launched back into flight. Shreds of down spiraled from the ceiling.

Guy waved his arms, driving the bird to its freedom. Iridescence flashed, blue-black, as the swallow fled the half-naked man, found a clerestory window, and escaped into the open skies.

Sarah pulled his shirt over her head to cover her nakedness and hugged her knees up to her chin. Her eyes held devastation, yet she glanced up with a wry, drawn smile, as if she would never give way to cowardice.

"My virtue saved by a bird," she said dryly. "Should I be sorry or glad?"

CHAPTER THIRTEEN

ER HEART POUNDED. HER BODY FLAMED AND ACHED. RAGE and sorrow and hurt all fought for attention.

Guy strode away to the doorway, the loveliest man she had ever seen: lean and hard and fit, his arms and shoulders powerful, his spine beautiful.

His dark hair tossed as he bent to tear away a scrap of lace caught on his spur. The muscles of his naked back leaped beneath skin smooth as bronze.

Moisture rushed, deep in her core, as she were filled with liquid gold.

If she had ever questioned the true meaning of desire, she had her answer now.

She would have given anything—anything at all—for the thrill of his penetration. Traded her soul to have known him buried to the hilt in her body. Begged in the streets for the rest of her days to understand with every pore the climax of that heady contact, skin to skin, where she might seal her breasts and arms and belly against his bare body, while her legs wrapped over his rough thighs.

He turned to face her. Sunlight fired gilt on taut muscles and glistened in the line of dark hair trailing down his belly.

"I love you." His eyes offered to swallow midnight. "But this is wrong."

"Because you're already in love with someone else?"

"No. God! There's no one else."

"But Lady Ryderbourne thought—"

He strode back into the room. "Miracle? What the devil did she tell you?"

"Among other things, that she was your first lover. Is that true?"

"Yes. Though we've been no more than friends for many years now."

"Yet you've known other women," she said bravely. "Miracle thought that perhaps you truly loved the lady you lived with last spring, and still grieved the loss."

A terrible irony gleamed in his eyes. It reminded her of the expression she had once seen on the painted face of St. Sebastian tied to a tree, his flesh pierced over and over with arrows: the martyr who laughed at death, as if so much pain were ridiculous.

"No! Perhaps I once thought that I loved her. I don't think so now. She certainly never returned it."

"Yet you still feel bound to this lady?"

"Not in the way that you think!" He paced to the opposite window, then gazed out as if seared.

The mystery of his world, his being, seemed to congeal around her, as if secrets were water and Guy offered her only a winter of ice.

"But you and I had never met before that day in the bookstore. So if your secret involves this mistress from last spring, how can I be hurt by it?"

"Because love cannot be based on a lie."

"I don't understand," she said. "I love you. I don't care about any hurt to me."

"But I do." He began to pace, shadows and sunlight glancing off his bare shoulders. "Though it's painfully obvious that it's already too late. You'll be injured either way."

He stopped beside a niche to stare up at the statue of Aphrodite. The goddess's blind stone eyes gazed out toward the far-distant sea.

"Yet after everything that we've shared," she said, "every moment of hesitation only drives a dagger deeper into my heart. So, whatever you judge now about how you may wound me, you must tell me everything, Guy."

"Then first you must know this: If I'm nursing a broken heart, it's only over you." He spun about to press his shoulders against the wall and stare at the ceiling, as if he couldn't bear to look at her. "But there's no future for us, either way. I cannot bear it that I've already wounded you. Yet if I tell you the truth now, you will discover a far deeper pain. It's the devil's bargain, Sarah."

Desperate to release him, she stood up and walked to the French doors. His linen shirt covered her almost to the knees, though long shreds of torn silk trailed beneath it. The summer day boomed and laughed outside, as if it would mock her.

"Yes, because if I were to leave here now without knowing this secret," she said, "I'd only be cast into a maze of doubt and self-recrimination."

"I do realize that," he said. Once again a vicious irony overlaid his pain.

Sarah sank down until she sat on the cool tiles in the doorway, where she could look up past the roses at the summer sky.

If any other man spoke to her like this, she'd assume it was just an excess of sensibility, an exaggerated idea of the fragility of women. But this was Guy Devoran: brilliant, subtle, generous. He was trying to prepare her to hear something terrible. Though she couldn't fathom why any secret of his could be devastating to her, she dared not doubt his judgment.

In the room behind her, he dropped onto a chair and buried his head in both hands. She sat in silence, waiting in a kind of numb haze. Swallows darted, tearing their trails across a blue heaven.

At last Guy stood up. His boots thudded as he paced.

"At first I simply wanted to protect you," he began, "however foolish that may seem now. Then I was caught in a trap of my own making. While I was careful always to tell you the exact, literal truth, I only wove an impenetrable web of lies, instead. I'd have been better to have divulged everything right away, of course, then none of this"—he waved one hand to indicate the sofa, the scraps of torn lace, her abandoned slippers—"would ever have happened, but then neither would you and I—" He broke off and slammed his fist against the wall. "Ryder knows most of it, of course, and Jack."

"Then this is something you think only a gentleman can understand?"

He stopped to look at her, his gaze stark. Bitter lines of something that was not humor marked the corners of his mouth. "We'll find out."

Sarah stared back up at the sky. She was very afraid now, but if he was about to offer her the truth, then she must return that courtesy as exactly as she could.

"How did your affair with this lady first begin?" she asked.

His boots rang hollow, spurs clanking, as he skirted the edge of the room, pacing like a caged lion.

"A cold January rain was threatening to turn into sleet. It was long after dark. She turned up on my doorstep like a drowned angel, claiming destitution. I took her in to offer shelter and aid, but within a day she'd become my lover, instead. Was that my fault or hers? It hardly matters now, does it? She'd thrown herself on my mercy and that was the result."

"I don't blame her," Sarah said, simply because that was, indeed, the whole truth.

He stopped as if dazed. "You may not say the same by the time I've finished."

"Have you no idea what the very sight of you promises women?" she asked. "Go on!"

"We agreed the next morning that I would keep her as my mistress. She asked me to find her a place of her own, but it had to be in Hampstead—"

Sarah jerked as if struck. "Hampstead?"

"Yes, Hampstead. I doubt if you noticed it, but you and I drove past a vacant house crowned with chimneys like top hats, half-hidden in the trees. I leased it the next day. Her insistence on secrecy meant that we arrived there on another pitch-dark night in the pouring rain. Nobody knew about us. She never went out, and I barely left the house except for essential business. During the next couple of weeks, I slid inexorably into what I thought was love."

He had offered her an open flame and warned her of its devastating power. Sarah had insisted on thrusting her arm into it anyway, up to the shoulder, as if she had been unable to imagine how deeply it could sear her flesh.

"You don't think so now?" Her voice sounded faint in her own ears.

"No. I cannot soften this, Sarah. If it would prevent the inevitable, I would cut off my right hand rather than tell this to you. But when you suggested that you and I shared only an infatuation, I knew you were wrong. Infatuation was exactly what I felt then."

"But how can any of this affect us?"

"Haven't you guessed?" The flame blackened to ash in his eyes. "The lady's name was Rachel."

The sky turned dark, the swallows stark as white ghosts against an infinity of black space. Their twittering, only faint before, suddenly boomed in her ears as if she were being mobbed by demons.

"*Rachel?* My cousin Rachel was your mistress?"

Guy was there on one knee beside her. He held her firmly by both shoulders, or she might have keeled to the floor.

"For all of last spring," he said quickly, "from that night in January until she abandoned me without a word just before Easter. She'd been living in Knight's Cottage just as you and I discovered, but when she began to run out of funds, she came to me in London—"

"And you *ravished* her?"

"Rachel wasn't a virgin, Sarah. I wasn't the first. I'm sorry."

She stared at him with both horror and incomprehension, and pushed his hands away.

Guy flinched and leaped up to stride outside. He paced to the Eleanor Gate.

"I cannot undo or change what happened. Within a few days Rachel and I had moved into that house with the chimneys. Though I knew nothing of it at the time, Harvey Penland continued to intercept her letters, which is undoubtedly why she insisted on Hampstead. She lied to you, just as she lied to me. I didn't want you to know. I wanted to send you away, but you wouldn't go—"

The roses sprang back into focus, hundreds of white petals, each cut like a shard of glass. Sarah scrambled to her feet and collapsed onto the chaise longue, her entire body shaking.

"You blame *me?*" she said. "You blame *me* for all of this?"

Guy strode back to the doorway. "For God's sake, no! The devil took his due the minute I hesitated in the bookstore. But should I have blurted all of this to a stranger? How the hell could I have known then that I'd fall in love with you? And once I had, what choices did I have? When you told me that you loved me, too, should I have pretended indifference or dislike, and broken your heart in another way? Perhaps I'm not that good an actor."

The air in the room swallowed her in crystal clear liquid, as the rose had been swallowed, drowning as it slipped into the water jug. No, flowers didn't have feelings, did they? Flowers were numb, just like this.

Guy was trying to justify all of his falsehoods. He thought she would fall for his explanations and apologies.

He insisted that I marry him and he wouldn't take no for an answer . . . he intends to persecute me . . . I dare not imagine what he might do if he found me here alone. . . .

Rachel had written all of that about the man she had met in January, then fled in terror just before Easter.

As if it were the contaminated gift of Deianira to Hercules, Sarah tugged off Guy's shirt and dropped it to the floor, then gathered the shreds of her silk robe about her naked body.

"No," she said. "Far better at deception than any actor, Mr. Devoran, because you were Daedalus all along and you never hesitated to lead me straight into your maze."

He was still standing in the doorway, beautiful, damned, when she stumbled from the room.

THE door closed behind her. Rage and despair darkened his vision for a moment, as if thunderheads blackened the day.

Guy thrust himself to his feet, gathered his discarded clothes—even his jacket from the garden bench where he'd tossed it—and carefully dressed himself. He tied his cravat using the mirror over the fireplace. A hollow-eyed demon stared back at him, dark hair tossed about his head as if by a gale.

He smoothed it with his fingers, then unbuckled his spurs and set them on the mantel.

Once again in the guise of a gentleman, he stalked up to the chaise and flung himself back on the ivory cushions to stare up at the ceiling.

He could not have planned it better had he wanted to inflict on Sarah the worst wounds possible. He should have told her everything at the beginning. She'd have been upset to know about Rachel's dishonor, but she'd have been immediately inoculated against any feelings for him.

Now he had broken her heart and left his own shattered into fragments.

He should have known that Sarah would not be able to let him hunt for Rachel alone. In her place, he'd have done exactly the same. Her courage and determination were part of what he loved about her, further confirmation of his certainty that this love was absolutely real.

So he was facing the most bitter irony of his life. He had finally found the one woman—*the one!*—only to destroy any hope of winning her.

There was no other solution left except to go forward, of course. Alone now, if need be.

Guy sprang to his feet, but his eye was caught by something in the pitcher on the table. He scooped out a white rose and shook the moisture off the petals.

He was not Daedalus, but somebody was. He had nothing else left to give Sarah, except to solve the mystery and restore her wayward cousin. He forced his tired mind back over every shred of evidence they had all gathered: he and Sarah, Jack and Ryder.

As soon as he could escape Buckleigh without raising suspicion, he had ridden to Withycombe without bothering to stop for sleep. He had arrived to find Anne just beginning her labor. She had immediately encouraged the men to talk.

"It'll help to take my mind off these pesky pains," she had said gaily, "until we can all greet our squalling new arrival."

Jack had met his wife's eyes, then turned to his cousin as casually—on the surface—as if they were about to stroll in the garden on a warm summer's day.

"The information I sent you was useful, Guy?"

"Vital! I'm on my way to Cooper Street now. But how exactly did Rachel manage Grail Hall?"

"The earl's in the habit of signing a whole set of blank sheets, which he leaves with his secretary. Any of the servants could have gained access to them, but our culprit was one of the younger footmen, who'd also learned to forge a passable copy of his master's handwriting. The poor lad was in love with her."

"It was the blond hair and innocent blue eyes," Guy had replied with deliberate flippancy. "Deadly to any English male."

Anne had laughed, then gasped and doubled over. She and Jack had immediately retreated into her bedroom where the midwife was waiting. For the rest of the night Guy had kept vigil, his soul on fire, until their baby arrived safely early the next morning—*this* morning, less than six hours ago!

So he had brought the news to Wyldshay. Otherwise, he'd have gone straight from Withycombe to pursue Jack's information, instead of making this fatal diversion.

Guy balanced the rose carefully on the edge of the jug.

The coward's way out would be to slip away to do so now.

Instead, he lay back on the chaise and waited. Morning stretched into afternoon. Long shadows began to flow across the courtyard from the trellis.

He ordered a little food and wine, and even slept in snatches, because it would be merely self-indulgent to punish himself with further exhaustion.

The day had almost died away when Sarah walked back into the room.

Neat red plaits wound about her head. Dark green skirts swirled as she stalked with exquisite dignity across the carpet to close the French doors.

Guy stood and waited for her to sit, but she paced the room, touching objects at random.

Her face was blotched by tears, her eyelids and nostrils rimmed in red. Pain spiraled and stabbed. In spite of his vaunted concern for her, he had only made her weep.

Yet she turned to face him at last with the stark courage of angels.

"I apologize for accusing you of being Daedalus, Mr. Devoran," she said. "That's absurd, of course. Even though you hid the truth about your relationship with Rachel, I can understand why you felt you must do so, and I don't believe that you would ever have threatened or attacked her."

"Thank you," he said. "Your cousin was certainly never afraid of me."

Dying sunbeams shone through the glass to cast a red halo about her head. "But she was in love with you?"

"No! Never!"

"Yet you were in love with her?"

"No. Infatuated for a short time, that's all."

The tawny eyes burned with bitter amusement. "I don't suppose you needed to look much past her appearance," she said with remarkable, dry clarity. "Rachel's always been beautiful enough to send men into a kind of madness."

"There was that, of course," he said. "Though not—now I look back—very much else. Your cousin claimed my help. I tried to give it. We ended up in bed. Yet Rachel lied to me always, and she walked out when she no longer thought she needed me. Damaging as such an admission might be to my composure, the obvious conclusion is that she was only using me all along."

Sarah sat down in a chair, so Guy dropped back onto the chaise where they had almost made love. Part of him fiercely regretted that he had stopped, instead of proving with his overwhelming passion how much he loved her.

But then she would never have forgiven him.

The rose dropped a few white petals onto the table. Sarah picked them up and studied them as if secret writing might be inscribed on each velvet surface.

"This also explains why she couldn't tell me the truth, either," she said. "Yet when she wrote me all those letters about how she dwelled so thrillingly on the memory of first meeting you, you believe she was lying about that, too?"

"Yes, I'm absolutely sure of it."

"So you think she met her persecutor long before she met you? You said as much to me before, didn't you? I just didn't know then how you could be so certain. Now I do."

"I couldn't tell you, Sarah," he said. "I didn't want you to know. It can't have been easy to face this truth about your cousin. It's obvious that you've always thought of her as she was as a child."

She shook her head, still staring at the petals in her palm. "So why did she leave you?"

"I don't know. I go to Birchbrook every Easter. I couldn't take my mistress to meet my father and sister, so I left Rachel alone in the house with the chimneys. She wept when I left. Yet when I came back she was gone."

Sarah picked up the rose, and the remaining petals scattered. She was still pale. Her eyes still looked sore. Though he knew his judgment was no longer objective, she was the loveliest woman he had ever seen.

"Did she leave you a note?" she asked.

He leaped to his feet and stalked away. "I burned it, returned to London, and vowed never to think of her again."

"Oh, God!" The rose fell as she buried her face in both hands. "It was that pitiless?"

"If you like."

Sarah sat in silence for several minutes, before she walked across to the French doors. The long summer twilight had softened the colors outside, as if a thin gray veil were slowly being drawn over the courtyard and trellises.

"Something profound must have happened to make Rachel do that. Something we've not even conceived of, so terrible that she couldn't confide in anyone, not even me. Yet what I cannot understand—if she left you so cruelly—is why, when she turned to me for help last month, it was only to make me enlist you."

"I don't know, but I cannot regret it, Sarah. Otherwise, you and I might never have met."

She spun to face him as if she were lost in a cold, dark place, where everything was ice.

"Please don't assume, sir, that I also count that as a blessing!"

A terrible anger stirred in his soul. In his entire life, in so many dangerous ventures, he had almost never known failure—until now, when in what really counted he had failed absolutely.

"Pray forgive my presumption, ma'am," he said. "I thought you wished for the truth!"

Bright color swept up her neck to flood her cheeks. "You think I can still believe that you know what that word means, sir?"

He stalked up to her. "I know exactly what it means, Sarah. It means we must face the fact that we've both fallen into a trap of Rachel's making. I'm not accustomed to feeling like a fly at the center of any woman's web, and neither, I assume, are you. Should we simply rail at each other and have done? Or is there any way forward from here?"

"How dare you!" Rimmed in red, her eyes blazed, the tiger staring from the burning forest. "How dare you suggest that I would ever give up now! For all I know, the spider in this web is you."

"Dammit, Sarah! Rachel didn't hesitate to come to my townhouse last winter like a drowned kitten. She knew exactly where I lived and could easily have come there again this June. Yet instead, like the Norns, she's been busy spinning our fate by dragging you into her problems, as well."

"But I thought you were away? You'd only just returned to town for the duchess's ball when I found you in the bookstore."

"What difference does that make? Yes, what with Ambrose's arrival, then Jack's bringing Anne back from India, I was constantly on the road back and forth from Dorset for most of May and June. Yet there were many obvious ways to contact me, and Rachel chose to use none of them. Instead, she sent you that letter full of melodramatic hints and predictions of disaster. We've both been used—by Rachel and by each other."

She stared up at him for a moment, before she stalked to the door.

"I'm not a simpleton, sir. I only argue that Rachel must have had good cause for everything she did, even for allowing you to seduce her, and especially for leaving you once you had."

"Sarah!" he said. "I'm sorry! What the hell else can I say?"

She stopped with her fingers on the handle. A little shiver passed over her shoulders.

"I'm sorry, too," she said.

"What do you want me to do?"

The green skirts swirled as she turned to lean back against the closed door. To his astonishment, she lifted her head and laughed, though her eyes swam with bitter tears.

"I want to find Rachel. I want to discover the truth. Whatever I might feel about what I know now, I can't continue this quest alone. Ironic, isn't it? For you won't give up, either, will you?"

He strode to the fireplace. "As a matter of honor, I feel an obligation to Rachel, but—"

"But because you're in love with her, you've been prepared all along to damn your tattered claim on *honor*, and move heaven and earth to find her."

"That's not what I was going to say."

"Then why won't you abandon this quest now?"

Guy braced both hands against the mantel and stared down at the cold grate. "I can't."

"Why not? Because you still have feelings for Rachel?"

"God, no!" He spun about. "Because of the way I feel about you."

"Ah, yes!" Her braids gleamed like amber as she pointed to the sofa with one forefinger. "That wretched moment of lust. What does a gentleman of conscience do about that?"

"You want the truth?"

"From this moment on, sir, I demand that you never lie to me again, not even by omission."

"I love you," he said. "I want you. I want to marry you."

The color fled her face as if a tide retreated, abandoning its wrack of brown flecks on her skin. She almost staggered, but she gripped the back of a chair with both hands.

"That's impossible," she said. "How can you say that?"

"Because it's the truth. I don't expect you to accept me—"

"Never!"

"You may despise me all you wish, but if I thought for one moment that you'd consent to be my wife, I'd beg for your hand in marriage right now."

"Stop it!" she said. "This is madness! What can your declarations of love ever mean, when you've made them so many times before? Even to Miracle . . . and to Rachel . . . and to thousands of other women in between?"

"Not thousands."

Her eyes flashed. "Hundreds, then! Dozens!"

"For God's sake! Not even dozens! But that's hardly the question at issue."

"If you may state the stark truth, sir, then so may I! Whether Rachel ever loved you or not, no woman would ever leave you for less than life-or-death reasons. How dare you pretend the false modesty not to know that! That's the crux of this whole mystery, though I don't care one whit whether my beautiful cousin broke your wretched heart!"

Sarah wrenched open the door. Her shoes rapped away down the hallway, leaving Guy standing alone in the room.

As if dried up by weeping, her soul was a husk. Sarah lit candles and tried to force herself to think. A plain oval face, ruined by freckles and tears, stared back at her from the mirror in the guest bedroom.

He could not love her. He could not. She had no idea why he'd said it, but he could not love her. This mad, handsome, devastating cousin to the fabulous St. Georges had broken his heart only over Rachel, as any man would.

And perhaps there was some comfort and composure to be found in that. For if Rachel had succumbed in her turn, then been ashamed and tried to hide the truth, who could blame her?

Certainly not her widowed cousin, whose contentment in her own virtuous state Guy Devoran had shown to be a sham.

VITAL, unrelenting, he was drinking coffee and perusing a newspaper. Sarah studied his dark good looks for a moment before she walked into the breakfast room the next morning.

Her heart was a knot, as hard and shriveled as a peach pit.

Guy looked up, folded the newspaper, stood up, and bowed.

Though she had no appetite at all, Sarah helped herself to food from the sideboard, then sat down and allowed him to fill her coffee cup for her. His eyes were very dark, a deep, watchful gaze.

"I thought you might have already left Wyldshay," she said.

"You'd rather I had?"

She stirred a lump of sugar into her cup. "My loyalty is only to my cousin, sir. If that means that I must continue to risk your company, then so be it."

"I'm honored by your forbearance, ma'am."

Sarah cut toast and buttered it. "Very well! I still don't think that Rachel can have transformed so dramatically. It's like her to be careless and unthinking; it's not like her to be deliberately cruel. So the only question that matters is: What happened to change that?"

He pushed away from the table to gaze out of the window. Another lovely summer day, undermined, as if by a river, by their disaster.

"No," he said. "The only question that matters is how the devil you and I can go on together from here."

"Warily?"

He spun about to meet her gaze, then laughed. "Because we're still caught together in this maze—though perhaps it's been more like sharing a boat on a trackless ocean."

Sarah took a few deep breaths. When he laughed, her heart turned over. When he seemed hurt, or watchful, or angry, her treacherous pulse still resounded to his moods and his presence. Yet an abyss of pain yawned beneath all of that awareness.

She pushed her plate away, leaving her food untouched. "Either way, sir, there's no other option. Though it might be accurate to say that I, at least, have been feeling a little demented. Nevertheless—though with the utmost caution—I'm forced to insist that we agree to join forces again."

"Neither of us has much choice in that," he said.

"Yes, because Rachel's true nature lies at the heart of our problem, and we each have our different perspectives to offer. In spite of your . . . intimacy with her, I'm her cousin. We grew up together. Whatever the evidence might suggest, I refuse to believe that she's really wicked, or even entirely frivolous."

"Even though she pretended to you that she was working as a governess when she was in fact at Knight's Cottage, or living in

Hampstead with me? And before that, when she claimed to still be working for Grail, even though she'd left his house that Christmas?"

"Even then. We'll never learn the truth unless we uncover all of that past history."

"Are you prepared to face whatever that might be?"

Sarah stood up. Her heart pounded as she reached into her pocket for Rachel's last letter.

"Yes, I am. And if we're truly to go on together, we must share everything that we know. So you'd better see this."

Tall, vigorous, Guy strode around the table to take the folded paper. He glanced at the superscription and his nostrils flared.

"From Rachel?" He looked up. "When?"

"Delivered by hand the morning I left Buckleigh. It came with the rest of the post the day before. But if you remember the way that you and I parted, sir, you'll realize that you left me no way of telling you."

"I understand. I don't blame you." He flipped open the letter and read rapidly. Anger sparked in his eyes as he looked up. "How dare Rachel write you such a cavalier note! She should have known what her bizarre requests must already have cost you."

"I admit that my first reaction was as much resentment as relief. But that letter may also be further evidence of just how desperate she is."

Guy crumpled the paper in one fist. "If you can still defend your cousin after this, you're a nobler soul than I am."

"Destroy it, if you like," Sarah said. "I can still remember every word."

He took the tinderbox from the mantel, crouched at the grate, and set fire to Rachel's letter.

Dearest: I saw you driving by in a carriage with the ladies from Buckleigh. Imagine my astonishment! There's no need for you to be here, I assure you. I'm perfectly safe now and need no one. Meanwhile, I trust you're enjoying the company of the charming Mr. D.? But enough! I

must get this delivered right away, so you may return to Bath in per-
fect serenity, my dear Sarah, with no more concern for——

Your ever loving cousin,
R. M.

Guy knelt for a few more moments, watching the paper char
into ash.

"At least we know now that she's still in Devon," Sarah said,
"though we didn't find her."

"Instead she found us, though by then her purpose was only to
get rid of us again." He thrust away from the fireplace. "Why the devil did you decide to share something so damning?"

Sarah looked down. How could she still be breathing when her
chest hurt so much, when her throat was filled with ashes? She lifted
her cup, though the coffee was now getting cold.

"Because we can go nowhere unless we share all of the truth.
Miracle thought you must have learned something vital from Lord
Jonathan. Did you? You said that you and he were corresponding."

He stopped to stand with one shoulder braced against a book-
case, his arms folded over his chest.

"Jack and I have been following up every lead we could think of,
ever since the duchess's ball. I sent a man to Norfolk, who learned
nothing new, while Jack took care of Grail Hall. Before she left there
that Christmas, Rachel engaged a servant lad—just as she did at
Knight's Cottage—to intercept your letters and forward hers. Once
Jack knew who'd so abused the earl's franking privileges, he visited
the boy and exercised a little of his deadly personal charm—"

Sarah's cup slipped from her hand to crash to the floor. Cold coffee spilled across the carpet. Guy calmly rang for a footman and
pointed. The man nodded and retreated without a word.

"So now you know where Rachel was living during those missing five months," Sarah said. "This servant boy told Lord Jonathan,
who sent you the news in his last letter?"

"It's why I had to leave Buckleigh as quickly as possible."

As if all the pages opened simultaneously in a book, she saw multiple implications, none of them comfortable. "But first you wanted to send me away?"

"Do you think I should have left you to the tender mercies of Lottie Whitely?"

She dropped into her chair. "No. No, of course, you wanted me out of the way, but only because you were still trying to prevent my discovering the truth."

"Alas," he said gently, "a little late for that now."

A maid came in with a bucket and cloth. Guy watched her mop up the stains. His eyes were unfathomable. Sarah waited in agony until the girl finished and left the room.

"So where was Rachel living?" she asked. "What was she doing?"

He glanced back at her. A dark caution still haunted his gaze. "She rented rooms not far from the Three Barrels from a Mrs. Lane in an alley called Cooper Street, a stone's throw from the docks. She went there directly from Grail Hall."

"But why?"

"I don't know. Neither does Jack. He needed to get home to Anne, so that quest is now mine."

"No," she said. *"Ours!"*

He walked to the window to gaze out. "Even in the face of what else may be discovered, Sarah?"

She stood up and braced herself to face his dismissal, his scorn, or his careful excuses. Any of them would take all of her courage to fight, but more pain was irrelevant.

"The alternative is that in a vain attempt to save my sensibilities you'll leave me here at Wyldshay, while you ride off alone?"

He turned and raised a brow, then he laughed like a man on a runaway horse.

"On the contrary, ma'am! I've already ordered our carriage. Unless you have some objection, my intention—once you have finished breakfast—is that you and I shall go there together, even if we scrap like fishwives every step of the way."

CHAPTER FOURTEEN

*M*RS. LANE'S BUILDING WAS SHABBY, SANDWICHED BETWEEN a chandler's shop and a butcher's. The afternoon had already worn away to evening by the time Sarah and Guy left their servants and carriage at a busy posting house, and walked together to Cooper Street.

The Three Barrels—the inn where Guy had first met Rachel over fourteen months ago—lay closer, but Guy had said merely that he didn't think it wise that they stay there, so he had taken rooms at the Anchor on the other side of the port.

They had not fought like fishwives. They had not fought at all. One of the maids from Wyldshay, a girl named Ellen, had shared the carriage, and as the miles rolled by, Guy had led Sarah into a discussion of the Celtic myths: the casual conversation of mere social acquaintances with no history of either passion or strife.

With that same fragile amity, her hand was now tucked into his arm. Yet, however calm their conversation, her heart was alternately racing and sliding to ragged stops.

They stopped in the doorway beside the chandler's: one that must lead to the stairs up to the apartments above the shops. Her fingers closed involuntarily on his coat sleeve, the clutch of a woman about to be thrown to the Minotaur.

Guy smiled down at her. "It's all right," he said. "We may find the past, but I don't think we'll find monsters."

Sarah swallowed her apprehension and smiled. "Unless this lady approaching us from the right is the landlady. In which case, you're entirely wrong, sir, and we have a monster by the tail."

He glanced around and laughed. A heavyset woman was fast bearing down on them, her face flushed with annoyance. She stopped, panting, to glare at them.

Guy bowed with exquisite charm and indicated the door they were blocking.

"Mrs. Lane? These are your premises, ma'am?"

"Might be!" She looked him up and down. "Perhaps that depends on who's doing the asking!"

"Not the taxman," he said gaily. "Merely an idle gentleman on a quest, who believes you may help him. The name is David Gordon, ma'am. Perhaps we may further our acquaintance over a jug of brown ale?"

The woman laughed, and her face creased into a quite different shape.

"Well, I'd not say no to that, sir! Especially when the gentleman doing the asking is such a well-set-up young fellow as yourself." She nodded at Sarah. "Your lady wife, sir?"

"My dear companion, for better, for worse, Mrs. Lane," he said, patting Sarah's gloved hand. "Married six years last Friday."

She could hardly object to such an obviously necessary ruse, yet his words resounded very oddly in Sarah's heart: *For better, for worse . . . for richer, for poorer . . .*

"Then you've caught yourself a pretty fine fish, Mrs. Gordon." Mrs. Lane grinned crudely at Sarah. "No offense, m' dear, but— plain as you are—you've done very well for yourself and anyone would be a fool to deny it."

Guy clamped warning fingers over Sarah's hand, but her trepidation had given way to an absurd temptation to hilarity.

She gave the landlady a conspiratorial wink. "Then you must be a very good judge of a pretty face, ma'am, since neither you nor I have ever seen one in the mirror."

Mrs. Lane tossed back her bonnet and roared with laughter.

Five minutes later they all were comfortably seated in her cluttered parlor, cracking open a jug of brown ale. Guy flirted and charmed until Mrs. Lane was twinkling and smiling.

They broached a second jug.

"I was a good-looking woman in my day, I'll have you know," Mrs. Lane said.

"You still are, ma'am," Guy said. "And, as it happens, your sound judgment in the matter is most fortunate."

She dimpled like a girl. "And why would that be, sir?"

"We're looking for news of my wife's cousin, a very pretty lady indeed. We believe she stayed here last year: Rachel Wren, or perhaps Mansard?"

"No, I'm sorry, sir!" The landlady wiped ale from her mouth. "I've never heard of anyone of that name on Cooper Street. And I never forget a tenant. Never!"

"But my cousin is quite remarkable, ma'am," Sarah said. "Hair like sunshine and eyes like the sky. No one ever forgets her. She'd have arrived here at the end of 1827, around Christmas."

"Ah! And then she left, sudden like, that next May?" Mrs. Lane downed another draft of ale. "Well, now you describe her, dearie, I know just the lady you mean. Always very quiet. Kept herself to herself. Would that be her?"

Guy sipped his ale casually, as if their inquiries were merely idle curiosity. Sarah damped down her impatience, though her heart raced.

"Very likely," he said. "So what name did this lady give you, ma'am?"

"Why, that would be Mrs. Grail, sir."

The word slipped out before Sarah could stop herself. *"Grail?"*

"Well, I suppose I should have guessed that was a false name, shouldn't I?" The landlady chortled. "Not likely you'd find one of that family lodging here, is it?" She leaned forward as if sharing a huge secret. "Lord Grail's family seat's not more than fifty miles from here, a great fancy place. You can't miss it."

Guy set down his glass. "And how did she spend her time here, ma'am? I'm sure any landlady with such a kind heart takes a personal interest in all of her tenants."

Mrs. Lane simpered. "Well, indeed I do, sir, even if I say so myself! Poor little thing spent all her time writing letters. Then she walked to the post office every day, rain or shine, as if her life depended on it."

"Did anyone write back?" Sarah asked.

"Only some female relative in Bath, or so she said. So she was disappointed in that, wasn't she?"

Gentle, solicitous, as if they really were married, Guy slipped one arm along the back of Sarah's chair. She glanced up at him, and her heart skipped a beat. Belying his light smile, his eyes were grim and bleak, as if he looked into darkness.

"Did she seem to be expecting letters from someone else?" he asked.

"Well, it stands to reason, doesn't it, sir?" the landlady said. "She hoped to hear from the father."

"Oh, no, that's impossible!" Sarah said quickly. "My cousin's father died long before she came here."

Mrs. Lane gave her a look of withering pity. "Not *her* father, dear! The baby's father! But the rogue left her in the lurch. Not the first time that's happened and it won't be the last. So I always thought it was lucky for her that the babe was born dead."

Sarah's stomach contracted as a painful spasm caught her beneath the ribs. The room went white. Demon voices shrilled as if screaming very far away—somewhere on the edge of Hades—though she could barely make out the sound, because all the cheap china figurines and pottery jugs in the room were clattering together in her ears.

Yet Guy pulled her firmly against his own body, his palm warm on her shoulder.

"Hold on, Sarah!" he murmured in her ear. "Lean your head against me! Do it now!"

His other hand found her fingers under the table and squeezed hard.

She gulped down her nausea and dropped her head against him, while she locked her fingers on his like a drowning woman clinging to a rope.

His heart beat steadily. His strong pulse throbbed against her palm.

At last Sarah found herself emerging into a vast silence, eased only by the calm cadences of Guy's voice, still speaking softly to Mrs. Lane.

"Then she was already with child when she first came here?"

"Why, yes, sir! Must ha' been! A good six months gone. Though she hid it very well, or I'd never have given her the room to start with. Yet she always paid her rent on time, and when her belly got big I felt sorry for her, poor little thing. No, she definitely carried that baby full term, though she ought to have gotten rid of it long before, for it was obvious she was in trouble."

Sarah swallowed hard, tasting cheap ale and the dregs of heartbreak as she clung to Guy's hand.

"Yet her baby was stillborn?" he asked quietly.

"Dead as a drowned sailor. I'm very sorry, Mr. Gordon, sir, if that's upsetting to you and your wife, but it's the plain truth. Would have been a boy, too, so the midwife said, but what use is another bastard to the world? So, like I said, she was better off."

"And exactly when did all this happen?"

"Let me see, now! That would have been in March of last year—1828. She was poorly afterwards, poor lamb, for quite two months, though she had her color back by May. Lucky for her that she did! For she'd entirely run out of money and she asked if I would let her stay another month on credit."

"Of course, you couldn't do that," Guy said. "No one could."

"I work for my keep," Mrs. Lane said, bridling. "There was no reason she couldn't do the same. She took a position at the Three Barrels—though I doubt if that would have kept her, and if she'd turned to the street, as so many girls do, she'd have had to find another place to live. I keep a respectable house, sir. As I said, if I'd known she was in trouble when she came, I'd never have let her have the rooms."

"But did she give you any reason to hope that she expected further funds?"

"She said that she did. She still thought that her lover would come for her, you see, even after all that time. And I suppose he must have done, for she walked in here the very next day, merry as a grig, and paid up in gold. Then she packed up her things and was off. I've never heard hide nor hair of her since."

"So your kindness was well rewarded." Guy slid a small purse across the table. "I'm sure you won't take amiss this small token of our personal appreciation?"

The landlady slipped the purse into a pocket and dimpled. "Not at all, sir! Most generous! I did no more than my Christian duty, I'm sure."

Guy helped Sarah to her feet. Still dizzy, she clung to his arm.

"You recall the midwife's name, Mrs. Lane?" he asked.

"Why, yes, sir! I knew her very well." She laughed. "Bess Medway would have delivered the devil for a bottle of gin."

"And her address?"

Mrs. Lane shifted her large bulk and sighed. "I can tell you where she is, sir, but it won't help you. Bess died last April, not two weeks before Easter, and she's buried at St. Michael's."

"Lie back," he said. "It's all right, Sarah. I'm here."

She glanced up. His eyes were dark with concern, his lips white at the corners as if he knew some terrible, heart-wrenching pain. She turned away as hot tears choked her vision again.

Somehow, they had walked back to the Anchor. Guy had supported her every step of the way with a silent, absolute compassion.

He pounded a pillow into shape for her head and helped her onto the bed.

"So I'm proved wrong," she said bitterly. "I should have gone back to Bath, as you wished."

"Hush," he said gently. "No one's to blame. However hurtful, we can handle this truth, Sarah."

Her throat hurt. Her eyes stung with sand and salt, as if she had been staring for hours into the teeth of a storm.

"Yet Rachel was in such deep trouble and she never . . . why didn't she trust me to help her? Instead, she wrote all those silly letters about still living at Grail Hall—"

"Don't!" He untied ribbons and set her bonnet aside. "What, really, could you have done? You were already sending her all the funds you could spare. And she really believed, if Mrs. Lane's correct, that she'd hear any day from the father of her baby."

"Daedalus?" She shivered. "She met him at Grail Hall?"

"Perhaps." He lifted her feet onto the cover, then sat down on the end of the bed to tug the laces from her boots. "We'll sort all that out later."

"She must have felt so ashamed," Sarah whispered. "And then— after all of that—to lose the baby!"

Guy eased away her boots and set them on the floor.

"You need to rest," he said.

"I've been wrong," she said, "about so many things, though of course I can handle this truth. It's just that—"

"Hush! You need to cry and you need to sleep. You can do both quite safely right here. No one will disturb you."

Sarah turned her face into the pillow. Anguish choked her.

Would have been a boy, too, so the midwife said, but what use is another bastard to the world—

She closed her eyes, lost in grief.

He sat in silence for a few moments, just his presence a comfort. But then he began to tug away her hairpins, gentle little tugs, easing away the tight plaits that bound her head. His fingers began to massage her scalp and the back of her neck. The gentle, soothing rhythm spread through her veins to spread balm into her aching heart. Little circles, little circles, undermining tension and anguish, taking away pain.

At last she slipped into sleep.

Guy watched her steady breathing for a few moments.

In spite of his grief for her, for himself, for Rachel, he still desired Sarah with a bone-deep passion. Everything about her was lovely to him. The pretty curl at the corner of her reddened nostrils. The shading of color in her lashes, from chocolate to sand with amber at the center, like the coat of a tabby cat. Her fair, frail skin, even when blotched by tears. The dusting of freckles marked her cheeks like shreds of leaf shadow.

What the hell was beauty, anyway? The porcelain doll he had been obsessed with in Hampstead? Or this passionate, sensuous woman, all cream and warm amber? A woman whose face betrayed every impulse of her heart: clever and caring and witty?

She sighed in her sleep and snuggled into the pillows. Her hair was glorious, rich and soft, a copper mass rippling across the pillows like red sand just abandoned by a wave.

All ladies combed out their hair at night, then braided it again into one long, loose plait.

Guy found her brush lying on the washstand, but he didn't see a ribbon and he would not go through her bags without permission. So he tore a thin strip from the edge of his handkerchief. With infinite care, his heart bruised and open, he brushed her hair until it lay even and smooth, then he wove a single plait and tied it with his makeshift ribbon.

Because he had thought it simpler to appear to the world as man and wife, Guy had reserved adjoining rooms. The door between them could be locked, and he had made sure earlier that the key was on her side. To remove her shoes and brush out her hair was improper enough. To undress her further was quite out of the question.

Guy pulled the coverlet up to her chin and closed the shutters over the window to plunge her room into darkness. No doubt Sarah would wake again later, so he left a single candle burning beside the bed before he strode into the adjoining chamber, where his own bed waited.

How the hell had he ever thought for one moment that he might be in love with Rachel? He pulled off his cravat and opened his shirt collar, then stood for a long time at the window as the summer night slowly stole color from the day.

Beyond the port buildings, a thin web of masts and rigging, where the tall ships rode at anchor out in the deep water, wrote their mysteries across the sunset.

GUY woke to a glimmer of starlight, a slight rustle, and the click of a latch. Instantly he was fully alert. He reached out silently to the table beside the bed, where his pistol lay next to the unlit candle. He froze, his heart thundering.

His pulse launched into a quite different rhythm of alarm as his eyes began to focus.

Something white wavered in front of the open doorway of the adjoining bedroom.

His nostrils opened on a faint hint of green apples.

He pushed up in the bed, keeping the covers wrapped about his waist. He was naked. He always slept naked.

Ivory silk fell in long drapes to her ankles. The single, fat plait hung over one shoulder. She stepped forward, her bare feet soft on the rug, and closed the door behind her.

As the White Lady had moved over the waters of the lake, Sarah walked up to his bedside.

The lion roared.

Her breath came fast and light. The nightgown rose and fell

over her breasts. Her gaze locked onto his bare shoulders, and her eyes opened like a tiger's in the dark.

"Guy?" she asked softly. "You're awake?"

He thrust tousled hair back from his forehead with one hand and sprawled back against the pillows, desire and shock coalescing into one white-hot center.

"More than awake."

"Ah," she said. "You realize, then, that I did not come to talk?"

Choked by the question, he reached out to seize the tinderbox. The darkness was too dangerous. Her fingers closed about his wrist. Impetuous, his penis throbbed into life, flooding him with rash desire.

"No," she said. "The dark is better."

He lay still for a moment, all of his senses concentrated on her touch. His tendons and bones jutted harshly against the yielding flesh of her palm. Hot blood pumped through his veins.

"Sarah."

He heard her name as if someone else spoke it: a stranger, a man standing on the edge of a precipice. Yet his shoulders sprouted wings, and power coursed through his limbs with the strength to fly him straight into the fiery core of the sun.

For another split second she stood without moving, her breath ragged on the night air, her fingers cool on his wrist. He brought them to his lips. She surrendered her hand softly as he unfolded her fingers, one by one, to kiss the palm. Softly, softly—though his pulse thundered—he tasted the sweetly resilient inside of her wrist.

Green apples and woman.

Her breath caught. She closed her eyes and dropped her head back. He cupped her hand against his cheek, and she spread her fingers to push them back into his hair, the tips tingling across his scalp.

His erection tented the covers over his lap, and his heart soared. *She had come to him. She loved him. She would marry him.*

He could scarcely believe it.

"This means yes?" he asked.

Her smile ghosted in the dark. Her breasts moved softly beneath the loose nightgown.

She slid her palm over his bare shoulder and down his arm to clasp his right hand. She, in her turn, brought his hand to her mouth. Her lips pressed into the center of his palm, finding the one vulnerable, miraculously tender spot in any human hand.

Her tongue touched. Wet and warm, erotic as hell.

"Yes," she whispered against his palm. "Of course this means yes."

She released his fingers. Starlight glimmered over the white gown as she grasped it in both hands and slowly pulled it up over her head.

Small white feet, the arch erotic and shadowed. Neatly turned ankles and smoothly curved calves. A passionate swell of female thighs and perfect female belly. An arch of ribs and the profile of a breast that rose and fell, white and round and tipped with a nipple that puckered in the cool air. His gaze riveted there in an explosion of desire as she dropped the gown to the floor.

Guy thought he might climax on the spot. He heard himself draw in a harsh breath, as if wounded.

She was lovely, lovely, lovelier than orchids in starlight, yet just as ephemeral, just as voluptuous, and he had wanted her for such a very long time.

Her braid swung as she sat down on the edge of the bed. A pearly sheen of starlight caressed her naked shoulders and arms.

Ringing with a bright, wild joy, he flipped back the edge of the covers.

"You'll get cold," he said.

"No," she replied. "Somehow I don't think so."

His soul resounded with craving as his body thundered its eager demands.

Yet as she slipped beneath the covers, her chill skin burned his hot flesh, so Guy caught her in his arms to cradle her head on his shoulder. She draped one leg over his. He trawled his fingers down the long curve of her flank, over the enticing swell of her hip.

Words fled, thought fled, to be replaced only by this stunning indulgence, the single-minded male delight in softness and woman and curves, everything perfect, everything right.

She ran her palm across his chest and over his arms, as if she marveled at his body. She trailed her fingertips down the centerline of his belly, as if she wanted only to intensify his pleasure.

In an agony of desire he caught her head in both hands and kissed her: rolled her onto her back, her head nestled in pillows, and kissed her hot, open mouth. Her breasts pressed beneath his chest. Her legs sprawled beneath his. His erection thrust, hot and firm, against her belly, seeking an almost unbearable pleasure.

Desperate that he might yet fail her, he tried to make himself wait, breaking the kiss while he filled his hands with her breasts, heavy and full. Like pebbles, her nipples rolled beneath his seeking fingertips. On the edge of control, he lowered his head to suckle them: sweet, sweet, rough beneath his tongue, all puckered feminine resilience.

She sighed and writhed and cried out, her fingers gripping his hair. Her breathing broke, laboring for air, as she gasped.

"*Yes, yes, yes . . .*"

His mind blank, his ears filled with the roar of the pride, he found her moisture. She opened to his plunge and encompassed him.

She was honeyed and swollen and slippery. In every sweet spot where flesh touched flesh, flames burned, scorching him. His skin on fire, Guy tossed back the covers and reared up on his knees, lifting her hips to meet his.

Her plait had unraveled, spilling her hair over the pillows. Her head was thrown back, her eyes closed, her mouth open in the slightest of snarls as she panted in rhythm with his thrusts. Never, never, had he seen anything so lovely.

He had desired her for so long. He wanted it to be perfect. Yet she moaned and lifted her hips to grind against his body, and—as his lungs emptied and his head fell back—his pleasure culminated in an intense rush of ecstasy, and it was over.

Damnation! Damnation! Like a callow boy, he had finished too soon and left his lover behind: his lover, his affianced wife, his Sarah.

Guy felt like laughing and fighting, bawling and cursing. Bliss and disappointment and mortification all concentrated into one wildly imperfect delight.

Sarah sighed and pulled him down to lie on top of her with her arms tight about his back, her head turned sideways on the pillow. She still held him deep inside her body, slick now on their combined moisture. Her breath puffed fast and hot in his ear.

"I'm sorry," he whispered, bracing himself on both elbows so that he wouldn't crush her. "I wanted that to be the most memorable—"

She wriggled and smiled up at him, her face hazy in the starlight.

"Yes," she said. "It was. It still is. Don't stop now!"

He dropped his head forward onto her shoulder and laughed.

He was still hard.

His desire still flamed, unabated. In spite of that humiliatingly fast climax, he wanted her so much that he was still hard.

Without withdrawing, he began to thrust again. This time every moment dawdled and danced. Every exquisite sensation lingered to be savored. Guy was a god of potency. A man-bird soaring on waxen wings to the sun.

She trembled and gasped, hot breath, hot flesh, as she climaxed.

And though he felt the intensity of her pleasure, he was still hard: a lion roaring his triumph across the hot plains of a secret, dark country, filled with rapture.

He was still hard.

Guy rolled her on top to let her ride him, his hands on her hips to help guide her movements. She dropped her head back and worked for her own pleasure as he caught her breasts in both hands, supporting their weight, flicking his thumbs over the hard tips, until she cried out and climaxed again.

She fell forward to press herself against him and kissed him, open-mouthed. Her body burned against his, sliding where slick flesh met slick flesh. Her nipples rubbed against the hair on his chest. And he was still hard.

He felt like shouting at the top of his lungs. He ached with bliss—sweat ran down his spine—yet sweetly, sweetly, she began to move against him again, drawing him even deeper into her body.

This time, just before his climax started to build its impetuous demand, he pulled out and turned her over. Her hair rioted across the pillows, the mutiny of crinkled waves glinting faintly in the starlight. Yet she glanced shyly up at him over her shoulder, a faint puzzlement in her eyes. Her obvious confusion only fired his desire.

He leaned forward to whisper against her damp hair. "Trust me. You'll like it."

"Like what?"

"Kneel here," he said gently. "Like this."

He nested the pillows and positioned her. She hesitated for only a moment before she did as he asked. Then, cupped against her back, his belly against her buttocks like two spoons in a drawer, he slid into her again, once again seeking the mouth of her womb.

Lovely. Lovely. Lovely. Carnal and wicked and passionate. Her erotic intensity stunned him. He feasted on the sight of her round woman's bottom curved like the waist of a violin as it sloped up into her slim back. Her pretty spine and shoulders and arms, white beneath her mass of tangled hair.

Guy leaned forward and lifted her, supporting her in his arms. He whispered his ardor and love—a jumble of meaningless syllables, broken by his roaring breath—into her ears.

And this time he was too late to stop himself. Pleasure spilled in a concentration so great that he shouted. And she was there with him, convulsing and convulsing deep inside. Dark sensations rippled up and down the length of his shaft. He had taken her with him to ecstasy.

Slick with sweat, they collapsed together to the bed.

Guy pulled up the covers and gathered her softness against his own body. Wonder filled him so deeply that he didn't know if he could ever be coherent again.

She nestled her head into the hollow of his shoulder.

"I didn't know," she whispered. "I didn't know that it could be like that."

Was there something guarded, almost frightened, in her tone? He didn't know. He was long past any kind of subtlety.

"Memorable?" he murmured. "Perfect. I love you, Sarah."

Bright with triumph, defeated by love, he cradled her until they both fell asleep.

HE woke again, perhaps five or six hours later, just as the summer dawn began to stain the room with pink light. Blackbirds had begun their faint twittering outside.

In shades of red and orange and amber, Sarah's hair crinkled over her breasts and shoulders. Her lips were parted a little, showing a small glimpse of white teeth.

With a strange kind of reverence, Guy woke her with soft, fleeting kisses, his heart aching. She opened tawny, wildcat eyes and gazed up at him.

He did not want words. He wanted only to demonstrate once again how much he loved her, how desperately he desired her. So before she could speak, he kissed her soft, open mouth, then trailed his lips over the smooth, creamy softness of her arms and legs as if he traced the secrets of a maze.

His heart filled with wonder, he lingered in curves and crevices, worshiped the shapes of her flank and breasts. Each nipple was a pale, dusty pink, darkening and puckering as it contracted beneath his tender tongue.

The hair at the apex of her legs flamed as bright as the hair on her head. He parted the little tangle of copper with two fingers and let his mouth explore her slick folds. She gasped in surprise, but her breath came faster and faster as she lay back and allowed him to do it.

Guy pleasured her until her breathing shattered and she cried out, then, potent, exultant, he made love to her until the birds had called up the day.

A clatter had begun in the inn yard. Light streamed into the room. Yet, ignoring the sun, Guy fell asleep once again with Sarah still cradled in his arms.

HE opened his eyes on a gray room and rain pelting the windows.

Sarah was already sitting up in the bed, her knees drawn up to her chin, the covers wrapped about her legs. She was gazing at the wet glass, streaked with runnels of silver.

Her back curved, lovely. Dulled to amber in the dim light, her hair tumbled about her shoulders.

"It's raining," she said.

Guy reached up to wrap a long tendril around one finger. He was an empty ocean bed, as vacant as the far reaches of space beyond the planets, yet joy danced and sang in his heart. As her hair coiled about his hand, a new erection began to demand his attention, filling him with the bright anticipation of more pleasure.

"So dawn made a false promise?" he said. "Never mind! I pledge to order the sun to shine on our wedding day, but right now even the rain seems blessed. I love you, sweetheart. Dear God, how I love you!"

She dropped her forehead onto her folded arms and said nothing.

He tugged gently at the long strand of hair, until she turned her head. Her expression was stark, her eyes bleak with—what? Guilt? Fear? All joy imploded, as if he had been gored.

"Sarah," he said again, like a man who thought just the words could convince her. *"I love you."*

"No," she said fiercely. "Don't say that!"

Numb with shock, Guy swung his legs over the side of the bed and walked naked to the washstand. He dashed cold water over his face and head, then rubbed his hair brutally with a towel. His incipient desire had died as if slain. He stepped behind the screen to use the piss pot, then wrapped the towel about his waist before he strode back to the bed.

Her eyes darkened as she looked up at him, but she turned away to gather her hair in one hand. Her fingers fumbled as she tried to braid it.

"Don't say what?" he asked. "The truth?"

"No! Let us always speak the truth!" Her voice was ragged. "I admit that what happened last night was what I thought I intended. However, I never meant that I would marry you."

Anguish roared in his ears. "But you said *yes!*"

"I meant yes to wanting you . . . wanting your body. That's all! I'd be insane to marry you!"

His pain transformed into a kind of rage in the blood—though surely he wasn't truly angry? Just distressed and confused, his mind flooded with bitterness.

"Sarah, for God's sake! We must arrange a wedding right away. I took no extra care last night. You might be with child."

She turned away, her half-made plait straggling over her spine, and shook her head.

"You cannot take that risk!" He tried to soften his voice, but he heard it grate, full of fury. "I love you. I want to marry you."

"No." She lifted her head. "There won't be any child."

"You've started your courses?"

"No, not that."

"Then what?"

Her eyes gazed up into his with stark courage, and crimson spread over her cheeks.

"When I was first married, Mrs. Mansard thought it would be wiser if I delayed starting a family. Until things were more settled, she said. Perhaps she already guessed that John might not live very long, and wanted to prevent my being widowed with a tiny baby to raise alone. So she showed me how to use a little sponge with vinegar and—"

"You took *precautions?*"

"Yes, of course. I'm not entirely out of my mind."

"So you planned all this ahead of time?"

As if to escape him, she climbed from the bed, dragging the cover with her and wrapping it about her body.

"Yes! Please see reason, Guy! Anything else would have been madness!"

"Not if we were about to be married—and what the hell else was I to assume? But if you had no intention of marrying me, why did you come to my bed?"

Draped in the bedcover, she plunked down onto a chair. Her freckles marched in dark array across her shockingly white cheeks. Her eyelids burned red, as if she were about to weep.

"I already said why: I wanted you. I wanted your body. That's all!"

He felt as if she had just poured arctic ice into his soul. He strode up to the bellpull and tugged it.

"By why *now?*"

"Perhaps I just wanted to know what Rachel knew."

He spun about to face her. The towel slipped off his hips. Guy kicked it aside.

"You made love to me from *revenge?* You thought that since I'd used your cousin like a harlot, it would be interesting to know exactly what that feels like? But I love you. I want to marry you."

"Do you think"—her voice was barely above a whisper, firm but quiet—"that you can browbeat me into marriage by shouting at me?"

His anger collapsed as if punctured. "A naked man who shouts at a woman is usually already married to her," he said.

She was surprised into a half laugh. Fresh pink washed into her cheeks. "Not this time, though you're very beautiful naked."

Embarrassed, he bent to retrieve the towel, though she was just Sarah, afraid and brave and lovely, and he loved her.

"And that was enough reason for you to come to my bed last night, though it's not enough to marry me?"

"Yes—no—you know perfectly well it was for no kind of revenge."

He tore into his cases to find a clean shirt. "Then why did you suggest—"

A rap interrupted them. Guy stalked to the door and sent the inn boy off to fetch hot water for his 'wife.' He could almost have laughed at the irony.

Sarah glanced away at the wet window. "I don't know. How can I answer you? The truth is that I came to your bed because I felt . . . I don't know . . . desperate, or lonely, or mad? I woke panicked in a dark room. I'd been dreaming that I was caught in quicksand, while Rachel was running away across a great beach into a dead-end cove while the tide was coming in. She was about to be trapped there and drowned, but she was too far off to hear my shouting, and I couldn't move. My skirts were wrapped about my legs."

"I could not—" He took a deep breath. "However absurd it seems now, I didn't want to ring for Ellen, and I could not remove your dress or petticoats, Sarah."

"No, of course not. I didn't blame you for that. I simply undressed and put on my nightgown, intending to go back to sleep. Then suddenly I couldn't bear to be alone. Rachel had a *baby*, Guy, and she was all alone among strangers when her little boy was born dead, like a drowned sailor."

"So you came to me for comfort?"

"Perhaps. I don't know. Though obviously I wanted more than that and planned accordingly." She stood up, draped like a statue of Aphrodite. "But would it have happened if I hadn't known about Rachel? Probably not."

Not bothering to wait for hot water, Guy scrubbed himself all over, then rubbed his cold flesh with the towel as if he would punish his muscles and tendons just for existing.

"You don't think that all of this breaks my heart, too?" he said. "You don't think that I feel equally helpless in the face of all this chaos and tragedy? Yet I love you and I refuse to believe that you don't love me, too, at least a little."

She walked toward the door into the other room, trailing the bedcover like a bridal train.

"Love you?" she said. "I've been *in love* with you ever since I first saw you."

He pulled his shirt on over his head. "Then I don't see why we shouldn't marry."

"Because it's not the same thing, at all." She stopped with her hand on the latch, her neck bent, her back graceful enough to bruise his heart. "Rachel is still lost. We still don't know why she went to Cooper Street, or who's the father of her baby. All we know is that she was alone and afraid and desperate, and probably still is, and that you didn't hesitate to take advantage of that. Meanwhile, you and I have been caught together on this quest, and I, too, became caught in that heady infatuation. Perhaps that's natural enough. I don't know. But if we'd met in the normal way—at a local assembly, say— you'd never have given me a second glance."

"I love you," he repeated.

"Yet you can't deny the truth of what I just said, can you?" She wrenched open the door as he tugged on his trousers. "I don't doubt that you think that you love me, Guy, but—"

"—but you still can't believe me. Why? Because of Rachel, or Miracle? Yes, I've loved before, but not like this! *Never* like this!"

The tawny eyes held nothing but pain. "Don't, Guy! You're talking about passion, not love."

He grabbed his cravat and draped it about the collar of his shirt. "How the devil can you refuse to acknowledge what I proved to you last night with my body?"

"I don't. You tore open my soul and destroyed all my preconceptions. I had no idea what a man like you . . . what would happen to a woman like me, if she opened her heart to a man like you. I didn't know quite how profound . . . I didn't know quite how profoundly you would make my heart ache. So if I came into this room last night out of curiosity, or loneliness, or even lust—or anything else that I might now deem trivial—I learned a very bitter lesson."

"Trivial?" He dropped the ends of his cravat, flung one arm wide, and pointed. "So you still can't accept the truth of what happened in that bed? Then I'm damned if I see how I can ever convince you!"

Color rushed back over her skin, staining her cheeks with crimson.

With a rattle of cans, the inn lad carried hot water into Sarah's room. Guy stared at her in incredulity as she wrenched open the door.

"No, because that's the way a man beds his mistress," she said. "Not the way any gentleman ever makes love to his wife."

Chapter Fifteen

ARAH WALKED INTO THE INN'S BREAKFAST PARLOR AND SAT down opposite him. A web of narrow plaits was woven neatly around her head, as if to mock his memory of her red hair streaming in damp tangles over her naked breasts.

She was pale, but she faced him with admirable composure.

Guy ordered eggs and hot rolls and coffee, then watched the beauty of her mouth, the grace of her movements, in deliberate self-torment.

Soft color washed back into her cheeks as she drank her coffee, until a gentle pink stained the freckled cream over her cheekbones. Yet she toyed with her breakfast and ate almost nothing, until she pushed aside her plate and leaned back.

Her tawny gaze studied his face, as if she needed to make up her mind to something.

"I'm sorry, Guy," she said at last. "I'm sorry for the way everything happened last night. I think we should agree to forget all about it."

He attacked a roll with both hands, tearing open the soft core. "Since we can be certain that no child will result from our unwise coupling?"

The color in her cheeks deepened to crimson. "I don't know what else to do, Guy. I don't understand anything about the way I feel. I don't even understand why I can't regret what I did, and yet at the same time repent it with every fiber of my being. I don't expect you to understand."

"It's more usual for a gentleman to beg a lady's grace when he oversteps the bounds of propriety," he said.

She smiled, though her eyes were filled with desolation. "Nevertheless, I fear that I was more cruel than I intended. We can't go on together unless I admit that I was, indeed, in the wrong."

"Not at all, ma'am." He stirred a little cream into his coffee. "No blame attaches to you."

"Then can't we simply be friends once again?"

He glanced at her over the rim of his cup. "No."

"Why not?"

"Firstly, because you and I were never simply friends. This lion has been stalking us ever since I first saw you in the bookstore."

She pushed a few crumbs about on her plate with her fork. "But we discussed all of that and agreed—"

"Secondly, whatever we agreed then is completely irrelevant now. Perhaps a woman can share that kind of passion and still see her lover as nothing but a friend. A man never can."

She stared at the rain still streaming down the windows. "You did so with Miracle."

"Yes, but that took the best part of ten years."

Sarah glanced back at him. "You still desired her, even after your relationship ended?"

"I was only eighteen when we met and still eighteen when I left her. My emotions and understanding were those of a boy. It took a year after we parted for us not to fall into bed together upon occasion, then another two before I shed every element of that awareness, though neither of us wished any longer to act on it. I cannot do that with you."

"Miracle is unique," she said. "There's no one else like her in the world."

He poured more coffee. "There's no one else like you either," he said. "I never offered marriage to Miracle, and I'm no longer a boy."

She set down the fork. "But I'll be gone from your life within a few weeks. Now we know the real nature of her trouble and that she's definitely still hiding in Devon, we're bound to find Rachel soon."

"And in the meantime?"

"We go on," she said, "as if last night never happened."

Rage and despair fought like tigers in his gut, but he would never again deny her the truth, however stark.

"You're not such a fool, Sarah, as to truly think that possible. I can't look at you without recalling every sensation, every pleasure, and with a ferocity that takes my breath away. If those feelings were mine alone, as a gentleman I should be forced to curb my desire and treat you with nothing but a proper courtesy. As it is— Hold up your hand!"

Her brows drew together. "What?"

"Like this." He propped one elbow on the table and held up his right hand with the palm facing her.

Her pupils expanded, like a cat's in the dark. She drew back and shook her head.

"You don't need to touch me," he said. "Just hold your hand up, with the palm facing mine."

"No!"

"You cannot, because if you do we'll strike sparks. The lion will break from his cage right here at this table, and we'll scandalize the other guests and frighten the horses."

She clenched her hands together in her lap. "Though I can barely begin to comprehend what happened between us, I can't deny that it was important and wonderful. Yes, of course there's part of me that craves the chance to do it again, but—"

"But you still don't think that a passion like this is any basis for marriage?"

"Not if it's forcing me to fall in love with you against my better judgment, Guy! What basis for marriage is that?"

"None, obviously," he said. "Because true love is evidently only the gentle, respectful admiration that you shared with John Callaway."

Sarah pushed up from the table to stare down at him. Tiny tremors shook her fingers. A fast pulse vibrated in her speckled throat.

"Yes, if you like. Yes!"

"As you wish!" He stood up to escort her from the room. "Yet you still insist that we continue our quest together?"

"We must," she said. "We can't give up now."

"Nevertheless, I shall ride alone today to Grail Hall to find out exactly who was staying there nine months before Rachel's baby was born. One of those guests must have been her lover."

"But she'd been living there barely more than a month," Sarah said. "I can't understand how she could have done it."

They had reached the privacy of the corridor. Without touching, Guy cupped the side of her jaw, holding his palm an inch away from her skin. His fingertips began to tingle.

"Yes, you can," he said.

Sarah wavered for a moment, but she closed her eyes and leaned her face against his palm, her soft cheek filling his hand. A small moan escaped her lips.

"Don't!" she said softly. "Please, don't!"

His heart began to race. He lifted his hand as if she burned him.

"Shall I kiss you?" he asked. "If I did, would you deny me?"

Her eyelids lifted heavily, as if she were drugged. Yet she looked up at him with the gaze of a tigress.

"No," she said. "No. You know I would not. In spite of everything, I cannot deny you."

Guy stepped back, forcing himself not to touch her again. "Then what the devil do we do about this, Sarah?"

She braced her shoulders against the wall, almost as if she could no longer stand without support.

"I don't know," she said, then with that splendid, deep-seated bravery, she met his gaze again and laughed. "I would think that the normal thing in the circumstances would be for you to make me your mistress."

SARAH walked almost to the edge of the port, where the paved streets gave way to dirt lanes. Rustic cottages nestled here and there in a network of kitchen gardens and orchards.

Guy had called for a fast horse and ridden away, though the heavy rain had soaked his cloak and streamed off his mount's coat like water over slate. Sarah had watched his lithe figure from the inn window—watched him manage the powerful horse as it pranced, eager to be off—and known a pain like a burn.

She felt stunned by her own naïveté, stunned that she had not consciously understood that no woman could ever give herself to a man like him and not become instantly enslaved. She had already been desperately, hopelessly in love, but last night—in a moment of weakness, or stark need, or madness—she had gifted him with possession of her soul.

And so he had felt obliged to offer marriage.

She didn't doubt that he meant it, or that he had felt equally in love with her *at that moment*. Yet he had felt the same way—he must have felt the same way—with every woman he had ever taken to his bed, even Rachel. And each time the woman must inevitably have felt even more.

Whether Guy Devoran wished it or not, he could never take a mistress without forging unbreakable chains of passion that tied that lady to him forever. As soon as they made love, Rachel, too, must have been robbed of her soul and her liberty, and she and Guy had lived together in that Hampstead house with the chimneys for over two months. So what could possibly have happened to make Rachel leave him?

Impossible to sit and do nothing, fretting over the idea of Guy riding hell-for-leather for Grail Hall, or burning with images of his sharing his bed with Rachel or Miracle, so Sarah had donned her thickest cloak and also plunged out into the downpour.

Now, two hours later, the rain had stopped. Ellen trailed a few steps behind her, carrying a folded umbrella. Thin, watery sunlight soaked into the shabby thatch on the cottage roof as Sarah walked up to the front door, swallowed hard, and pounded on the knocker.

It was, without question, the right place. The description had been accurate in every detail. As promised, a plump, comely woman opened the door.

"Mrs. Siskin?" Sarah asked.

"Why, yes, ma'am!" Bright hazel eyes assessed Sarah's face. "Can I help you?"

"I fear distressing you, ma'am, but I understand that your sister was Bess Medway, who was buried in St. Michael's churchyard last spring?"

Consternation darkened the hazel eyes for a moment. "Why, whoever told you that, ma'am?"

"Mrs. Lane in Cooper Street, just this morning," Sarah said. "Your sister delivered my cousin's baby there, and I wondered— Might we talk?"

Mrs. Siskin clucked like a mother hen. "Come right through into the parlor, dear! I don't get too many visitors these days." She peeked over Sarah's shoulder at Ellen, who was shaking drops from the umbrella. "And your maid can take a cup of tea in the kitchen with my Ursula, if she'd be so inclined."

Sarah followed the midwife's sister into a cozy little room. Leaded windows stood open onto the garden. Outbuildings and trees steamed gently, filling the air with damp scents.

"So what was it you wished to know?" Mrs. Siskin asked as soon as they had exchanged preliminary courtesies over a hot teapot. "Bess died right here in this house, bless her soul, but she brought many babes into this world in her time and probably forgot most of them."

"Yes, but I hoped perhaps in this case . . . Rachel—my cousin— is very beautiful. Everyone always remembers her. Her hair's a true gold and her eyes are the deepest blue, like the best velvet. Your sister would have been called to assist her a year ago last March. Did she ever mention such a lady to you?"

Mrs. Siskin's eyes became wary. "Well, I don't know," she said, looking down at her pretty china. "I don't know what to say. What was the name again?"

"My cousin was calling herself Mrs. Grail, but she wasn't married. Did your sister ever say whether Rachel told her anything about the baby's father?"

Her teacup rattled as Mrs. Siskin set it down hard in the saucer. Her eyes filled and her chin wobbled, as if she were about to weep.

"It was all so long ago," she said. "Perhaps I did wrong trying to set things right!"

Sarah leaned forward, her heart thumping. "What things, Mrs. Siskin? No one could have known ahead of time that it would be a stillbirth, and if the baby had lived, he and Rachel might have become wards of the parish. So I wondered whether—"

Mrs. Siskin rose abruptly and walked to the window. She pulled out a handkerchief and wiped her eyes.

"No," she said. "No, I know nothing about the father. It's not that."

"But something happened? Something important?"

Mrs. Siskin crushed the handkerchief in one fist. "Yes, but Bess was dying, poor thing, before it all spilled out. It had weighed on her conscience something dreadful, and she was desperate to make her peace before she was taken. She feared she'd burn for all eternity, and she wanted it made right."

"Though it seems terrible, it would have been her duty to demand the name of the father while Rachel was in labor," Sarah said gently. "No loving God could condemn her for doing only what the parish required."

"No, no!" Mrs. Siskin collapsed onto a chair by the window. "You've got the wrong end of the stick entirely! Bess sinned very terribly, though she'd never have done it if Mr. Medway hadn't put her up to it."

"Mr. Medway? Her husband?"

"Ronnie Medway was from Devon, a Stonebridge man," Mrs. Siskin said, as if that explained everything.

Sarah's heart contracted as if a ghost had laid a hand on her arm. "From the village of Stonebridge, near the south coast?"

"Yes, he and his half brother both. Medway was a fisherman."

"Is he still living?"

"God rest him, no! He was taken not three weeks after Bess delivered your cousin. His boat went down in a storm. Divine retribution—that's what Bess feared, and that's when she took to drink. Though she could never tell me what the matter was, not until she was dying, right up there in that bedroom above our heads. She said she couldn't die easy unless she first tried to put things to rights, and she charged me to do it for her, if I could."

The sun slipped behind a bank of cloud, plunging the room into a damp gloom. Sarah felt ill, though she didn't know what she feared.

"What did she want put to rights, ma'am?" she asked.

"Why, that she and her husband had taken so much money to keep such a terrible secret!"

Mrs. Siskin pressed her crumpled handkerchief to her eyes and burst into tears.

GUY arrived back at the Anchor the next day seething with impatience and wet with rain. He had been forced to spend the night at Grail Hall.

The earl and countess had covered up their surprise at his astonishing arrival with well-bred ease, so he could hardly respond to their hospitality with a brusque demand for the guest list from almost two years before. Yet he had hardly slept. Even though he had just ridden the best part of fifty miles in half a day, he had lain awake for hours staring at the bed canopy and thinking about Sarah.

She haunted and obsessed him. His hands ached for the touch of her skin. His groin ached for the depth of her embrace. He wanted to see her laugh and hear her talk. She was extraordinary—perfect and imperfect, human and real and maddening—and he loved her.

Yet a fierce battle raged in his heart.

Could it be true that Sarah wanted only his body and his protection—and not his heart—just as Rachel had? And if that was the case, could he blame her? He had deliberately ensnared her in a web of lies. He could hardly, after that, demand her trust.

He strode into his bedroom at the inn and tossed aside hat and gloves, then rapped at the connecting door. His boots were splashed to the knees. Dirt speckled his breeches and the tails of his coat. Had Ambrose de Verrant come home to his wife like this, fresh from combat, and demanded his marital rights? And had his lady spurned him or welcomed him? After all, she would probably have been forced into marriage—

Sarah opened the door. Her cheeks colored like the petals of an orchid reflecting the setting sun.

Guy made himself step back, or he would have seized her and kissed her and carried her straight to his bed. He brushed one hand over his face, rubbing away flecks of mud.

"I'm sorry to come to you in all my dirt," he said. "I had to make sure right away—"

"Yes," she said. "Yes, I'm fine. You saw Lord Grail?"

He nodded. "Twelve guests stayed there that June to attend a scientific convention on the latest ideas about Egypt."

"*Egypt?*"

"Pharaohs, pyramids, hieroglyphics. Ancient Egypt, long before Alexander. Grail is a patron." He held out a slip of paper. "One of these men must have been Rachel's lover."

Sarah read rapidly through the list, before she glanced up. "But several of these names are Italian or French, and this—is this German?"

"Dutch. If the baby's father returned home from Grail Hall to somewhere in Europe, that might explain why Rachel came here to a Channel port."

Sarah walked back into her own room, poring over the list again. "None of these names rings a bell, but then why would it?"

He tore his gaze away from the sweet curve of her back, her red plaits, the vulnerable nape of her neck—as smooth as a speckled egg—as a new awareness struck him like a thunderbolt: something in her voice, something both of excitement and fear.

It held a shadow of deep happiness, yet she was not happy.

"You have news of your own?" he asked immediately. "Something that's both pleased and upset you?"

"Yes," she said, looking up. "Yes. I know now exactly why Rachel left you, Guy."

He gazed at her for a moment as if the answer to all mysteries was written in the depths of her eyes.

"What's happened?" he asked.

She sat down on a hard chair beside the window, so her face fell into shadow. "I couldn't just sit here yesterday doing nothing, so I went to see Mrs. Lane again. Then Ellen and I walked to St. Michael's to visit the midwife's grave—"

"You doubted that she was really dead?"

Sarah shook her head. "No, I just wanted to see it. There was a touching verse on the headstone about repentance and the hope for salvation. However, Mrs. Lane also told me that Mrs. Medway had died at her sister's cottage, just outside of town. So Ellen and I walked there next to see this sister—a Mrs. Siskin."

Fifty miles was a fair distance to travel on horseback, especially for a man in a hurry. Guy's pulse resounded through his veins as if he were still riding. He should have realized that Sarah would not rest idly at the Anchor while he was gone, yet he still felt astonished.

"You're simply the most remarkable lady I ever met," he said quietly.

She turned her head. "Am I? In what way?"

He dropped onto a chair, stretched out his tired legs, and closed his eyes. "Never mind! Pray, go on!"

Her skirts rustled as she stood and rang the bell. "You need food," she said, "and coffee. I'll order some."

"Thank you. So what did you learn from this sister?"

Small neat shoes rapped as Sarah paced. He knew exactly how she must look: the graceful walk, the tawny eyes, the copper-and-bronze hair with just a few strands escaping over her cheeks.

"The baby was born alive," she said.

Guy jerked upright so abruptly that he almost fell from the chair.

"*Alive?*"

A servant appeared at the door. Sarah ordered food and drink, then sat down again at the table. Guy pulled up his chair to join her, so they sat facing each other.

"If that's true, how could Mrs. Lane not have known? Or did she lie to us?"

"No, she didn't know," Sarah said. "Rachel's labor lasted well into the night, and the landlady was asleep long before the baby was born. However, if Mrs. Lane hadn't kept silent to start with, Rachel might have been carried across the parish line as soon as her pains began."

"God, it's barbaric!"

"Yes, but no parish wants to take on any more fatherless infants, so it's the midwife's duty to demand the name of her lover while the mother's in labor. That's why I went to see Mrs. Siskin, though that isn't what happened this time."

Guy ran both hands back through his damp hair and tried to swallow his anger. "Then I suppose we must be grateful for the kindness of those women."

Sarah ran her fingers over the tabletop as if her nerves were unraveling. "It wasn't all kindness. Mrs. Medway already knew that she was going to steal Rachel's baby."

"*What?*" He met Sarah's gaze, staring into the depths of her devastation, barely aware of his own. "How the devil was that done without her knowing?"

"Quite easily, I think." She propped her forehead on both hands. "Mrs. Medway had deliberately allowed the lamp to burn down, and by the time her baby was born Rachel was barely conscious. It wouldn't be hard to smuggle a newborn out in the dark and say that he'd been born dead."

Guy tried to recall his fragile lover, who had turned up on his doorstep like a wounded bird in the night, her flippancy always hiding some dark sorrow in her heart. *This was it. This was it.*

"Dear God," he said. "I'm so sorry, Sarah. Rachel didn't hear the baby cry?"

"No, because Mrs. Medway handed him straight to her husband, who was waiting in the hall, and he carried him right out of the building. There was a great deal of money involved. If her baby cried then, Rachel heard nothing but her own tears."

The list from Grail Hall lay on the table. Guy crushed it in one fist. "And one of these twelve men abandoned her to face this fate all alone."

"Yet Rachel never betrayed him," Sarah said urgently. "She must really have loved him—"

"Because she spent her days in Cooper Street writing frantic letters to this swine, until she feared, at last, that his abandonment was final?"

They were interrupted by the arrival of a maid carrying a tray with hot coffee, beef, and bread.

Guy filled two cups. "Mrs. Medway and her husband were paid to steal the baby?" He looked up at Sarah. "By whom?"

"By his half brother. But that terrible night weighed on the midwife's conscience. So on her deathbed she told her sister all about it."

"And the husband?"

"Had drowned three weeks after the baby was born."

"Any chance that he was murdered?"

Sarah's face blanched beneath the freckles. "I don't know! His boat went down in a storm. I assume it was an accident."

"But a convenient one. Never mind! Obviously, this brother had arranged everything long before that, and no one attacked the midwife, who'd have been an even more damning witness."

"No, not as far as I know. Mrs. Siskin only said that the gentleman behind the whole scheme was a lord who was prepared to pay very good money for a healthy baby boy, especially one with blue eyes and golden hair—"

"Oh, God! Don't tell me!" Guy's chair clattered back against the wall as he leaped up from the table. "This man took the baby down to Devon?"

"Yes," Sarah said. "Mr. Croft and Mr. Medway were raised together in Stonebridge: same mother, different fathers."

"So Croft was Falcorne!" Guy spun about to face her. "Did the child die later?"

"No," she said. "I believe that he's still very much alive, and so does Rachel—because Mrs. Siskin wrote to tell her so, right after her sister died last April."

"And Rachel left me the day the news of that fact arrived in Hampstead?"

Sarah smoothed out the list of names, her fingers stroking the crumpled paper, though Guy had already committed each one to memory. "She had to go after her little boy as soon as she knew. Any woman would."

"What the hell difference would another day or two have made? If I hadn't been away at Birchbrook—if she'd waited, if she'd told me—I could have helped her!"

She looked up, her eyes desolate, but she cut a slice of bread and beef, and set it on a plate.

"You should eat," she said. "Men always need to eat."

Guy laughed, but not from mirth. "Thank you—I'll eat later. Let me get this straight: when the baby was first stolen, Mrs. Medway and her husband were sworn to secrecy, but as she lay dying—over a year later—the midwife begged her sister, this Mrs. Siskin, to contact Rachel to tell her the truth?"

"Yes." Sarah refilled Guy's coffee cup. "Mrs. Siskin swore to all of this on her Bible."

"How the devil did she know where Rachel was living?"

"She didn't. But Mrs. Medway left her sister a little legacy for the purpose, and Mrs. Siskin hired an investigator, who discovered that Rachel's letters were being sent via Grail Hall."

"And no one ever forgets her." Merely from habit, Guy sipped at his coffee. "So this investigator found the servant who'd been acting as Rachel's go-between—the same one Jack interviewed—and that boy sent him to Bath, where he discovered that Rachel's letters were now coming from Hampstead. After which, he managed to unmask Harvey Penland, and the rest was easy. The man should work for British Intelligence."

"Apparently he did, years ago," Sarah said with a dry smile. "On the Peninsula, under Wellington. So Mrs. Siskin was able to tell Rachel that Mr. Croft had taken the baby to Devon, which is why she went down there that Easter."

Guy set his cup on the table and choked down some bread. He must keep up his strength. He was going to be forced to do some more very hard riding very soon.

"Yet she didn't know who had the baby?"

"No," Sarah said. "Mrs. Siskin only knew that he was being raised as the son of a very wealthy man, who could give him every advantage in life. Yet how can that compensate for stealing a new-born from his mother and telling her he was stillborn?"

"It can't," Guy said. "Because the child must be either Lord Berrisham or little Master Norris. However, Croft would never have admitted to anything, and as soon as Rachel confronted him, he warned his master. So that's when Rachel first came to the attention of the man we've been calling Daedalus—"

"It's Lord Moorefield," Sarah said. "I'm certain of it."

Guy strode back and forth, vaguely aware that his wet boots squelched on the carpet.

"Why?"

"Because of the way he treats Berry."

"That's not enough, Sarah! Both Norris and Moorefield have sons about the right age. Both employed Croft at about the right time."

"No," Sarah insisted, standing up. "It's Lord Moorefield! And if Rachel managed to get one glimpse of the toddlers, she'd have known right away that Berry was hers."

"For God's sake, Sarah! Even if you're right, the earl would never have agreed to see her, let alone allow her anywhere near the little boy. No, she must have returned to London defeated, then hid in those lodgings on Goatstall Lane, where either Moorefield or Norris soon sent Croft—calling himself Falcorne—to terrify her into silence."

Sarah blazed like the setting sun. "Why won't you accept that Lord Moorefield is Daedalus?"

"Because you're relying on intuition, not facts. We've no evidence that Rachel's ever even seen the child."

"Yet—even though she was afraid—she went back to Devon again. After writing to me as she did, that must have taken enormous courage."

"Courage? More like foolishness!" Guy ran both hands back over his hair. "Why the *hell* didn't she come to me for help, instead?"

Sarah crumpled back to the chair. "I don't know, but Rachel didn't leave the house in Hampstead because she didn't love you, Guy. She left to go in search of her son."

"Even that's a huge assumption!"

"Yes," she said. "But at least the baby lives."

Guy stopped dead. His rage evaporated.

"I'm sorry! I didn't mean to shout at you." He strode back to the table to set his chair upright, then stood with one hand resting on the rail, gazing down at her. "I know you're happy about that, so why do you still feel so much dread?"

She shook her head. "It's all right. We're both upset."

"I shall avenge your cousin, Sarah. Daedalus has finally flown too high."

"No," she said. "Only his son Icarus flew too close to the sun and was drowned."

"In this case, our villain may still lose his child, but I swear to you that the little boy won't suffer for it, either way."

She pushed away from the table to walk restlessly about the room.

"Yet there are so many mysteries left. Obviously, Rachel left Grail Hall that Christmas when she could no longer hide that she was with child, then she fled to Cooper Street to be near the coast." Sarah picked up the list of names. "Yet her genuine letters from Grail Hall mention nothing about any of these men. Instead, she only wrote glowing accounts of remembering her meeting with you at the Three Barrels. Why?"

A horrific suspicion flashed into his mind that Sarah thought he was still hiding some desperate truth.

"Do you think that I was there at Grail Hall, as well? That I could be the father of this child, and am hiding that from you?"

She looked so startled that he immediately wished the words unsaid.

"Goodness, no! I don't doubt your word in that." She dropped back to her chair. "Yet don't you see? In all those first letters when she was writing about you, Rachel must really have been inspired by falling in love with the father of her baby."

Guy sat down and leaned back to study her face. Sarah was still afraid and he wasn't sure why.

"I've already realized that," he said. "Not very flattering to my pride, is it?"

"Nor mine!" She laughed with a flash of bravado. "Why she didn't tell me the truth? Why did she hide her real feelings for this unknown lover and pretend it was all about her memory of one day with you?"

"Perhaps the man's married," he said. "Perhaps she knew he would abandon her."

Sarah stood up and began to pace the carpet again. "Why does life have to be so chaotic and unpredictable, Guy?"

Not sure why he felt so bloody uncomfortable, he glanced out of the window. The sun had broken through the clouds to sparkle on the damp cobblestones.

"I don't know. Perhaps there are always hidden patterns, though sometimes we can't see them."

She laughed again, though he feared it was only the laughter of a heartbreak that he knew no way to mend and wasn't even sure he understood.

"Because it's a maze," she said. "So all we have to do is find the end of the right ball of string, and we'll be led straight out into the sunshine."

He felt desperate to comfort her, but had no idea where to begin. With perfect timing, the rattle of cans and the clank of metal announced the arrival of hot water and a tub in his room next door.

"You ordered a bath?" she asked.

"When I first came in. It appears to have arrived. I must get back to Devon right away, and clean, dry clothes wouldn't hurt."

"And then?"

"I'll be off to beard Daedalus in his den."

Sarah picked up her cloak. "Then go and bathe. I think I'll go out for a walk."

He leaped up to seize her wrist. "Not without me!"

She gazed up at him. The burn of their contact began to melt through his bones. He yearned to pull her into his arms to kiss her— a need so intense that it hurt.

Yet Guy released her and stepped back.

"There may be danger," he said. "Even here. Whether Daedalus is Norris or Moorefield, either way he's no fool. People talk. He may have guessed why you and I were at Buckleigh. We may even have been followed here. If suspicions were already raised, it's not so hard to find out that you're Rachel's cousin."

Sarah tossed the cloak aside. "Very well. I'll take no risks and remain inside like a chick in the nest. Meanwhile, your bathwater's getting cold."

He laughed, just because he loved the brave, wry humor in her voice, and strode away into his bedroom.

The door closed behind him.

Sarah stood for a long time at the window, staring down into the courtyard. She longed to stride down to the docks to the clear air of the sea, yet Guy was right. It might be dangerous, and anyway he would—just from gallantry—be worried.

Yet whatever he said, he couldn't really love her. He was still hurt by Rachel's desertion in Hampstead, even in the face of such a compelling reason—no, especially now that he knew the real reason.

If it hadn't been for Mrs. Siskin's letter arriving at the house with the top-hatted chimneys in the one week that Guy was away from home, Rachel would never have left him. Perhaps in the end they'd have married.

He was not free.

Yet anyone who read Rachel's letters with this new knowledge could be certain that she had been very desperately in love with her baby's missing father all along, and very probably still was. In which case, Guy had never been more to her than a means to find protection when she ran out of funds—exactly as he had feared—and now he must be certain of it.

How could that not hurt? Sarah closed her eyes and tried to remember John's face. In the months before he died, they had achieved a frail, fragile love that she would treasure till she died. Yet she had still lied to him and told herself it was for his sake, not hers. So who was she to insist now on the truth? Or even claim that she understood much about the true nature of love?

Meanwhile, her future stretched bleakly before her: long, barren years with Miss Farcey in Bath, teaching the daughters of the gentry about geography and botany. And after that? A lonely and impoverished old age. How could the memories of nursing John be enough to sustain her, now that she had tasted real passion?

Without making any clear decision, Sarah walked up to the door separating the two bedrooms. She hesitated for a moment with her hand on the latch, hearing the little splash of water through the door as he bathed. Her bones turned to liquid gold, melting in the furnace of her own desire, telling her exactly what she wanted.

Her pulse beat in mad, excited rhythms as she turned back, stripped off her dress and corset, and prepared the little sponge as Mrs. Mansard had shown her. If she had deeper motives than pure lust, her heart was too exhausted to know them, so this time she didn't hesitate at all as she opened the door dressed only in her shift and walked in.

Guy had just stepped from the tub. Ebony-dark hair slicked over his head like the coat of an otter. Tiny rivulets ran down over his naked body to soak the towel beneath his feet.

Without making any attempt to cover himself, he turned to face her.

Beautiful. Beautiful. The beauty of a fit young man in his prime, as muscled and lean as a racehorse.

Her blood burned. Her bones caught fire.

The towel in his hand dropped to the floor.

She stepped forward into his open arms. Cradling her head in his fingers, he tipped her face back to ravish her mouth with his own.

Moisture steamed where his damp, hot flesh pressed against the shift that covered her body. She rubbed her belly against his, feeling the thrust of his arousal and the power of his naked thighs. Desperate, molten, as he broke the kiss she caught his jaw in both hands and stared up into his eyes.

"You cannot go to Devon without me," she said.

A shadow darkened his eyes. "We can continue together only as lovers, Sarah."

"Yes," she said. "I'm prepared to take that risk."

"Then you win," he said. "It would take a better man than me to defy what's happening between us. Since you insist on it, we're in this together from this moment on, and may the devil help us."

He wrenched the linen shift off over her head, then stepped back to gaze at her naked body. Ardor flamed in his eyes as if she, too, were divine.

Her blush scorched, but he swung her up into his arms to carry her to the bed.

As the coach rolled back toward Devon they made love on the padded seats, contorting their limbs to fit in the awkward space, laughing and fervent and entirely without inhibition. They made love every night—over and over again—when they stopped at the posting houses on the road.

They laughed and joked and feasted together.

Yet a shadow traveled with them, like an impenetrable barrier of smoke. However much he tried to hide it, Sarah caught glimpses of that darkness in his eyes. Some vital part of Guy's soul had withdrawn into some deeply private place, as if—whatever physical passion they shared—his real essence could no longer be touched.

Nothing more was said about marriage and nothing was arranged about how a gentleman might usually set up his mistress. Guy bought her no gifts and offered her no money. Neither did he try to press a ring on her finger, or persuade her that they were meant to be together for all time. And never—not even in their deepest ecstasy—did he say again that he loved her.

Guy simply ravished her with the power of his body and his mind, and said nothing at all about the future.

Sarah tried to calm the panic hidden in her heart and savor him, because these strange days out of time would never come again.

Until Rachel was rescued, he was not free.

July had almost slipped into August when they rolled through Exeter and headed for Dartmoor.

Satiated and fully clothed for the moment, she leaned back to study his dark hair and eyes, to drink in that lithe, almost fey grace as he turned his head from the window to meet her gaze. She knew his power and his tenderness in every pore of her being, and was helpless in the face of it. Yet he still guarded his most private thoughts from her, and she had forfeited any right to trespass.

"Where, exactly, are we going?" she asked.

"To a cottage on the moor. Knowing I'd undoubtedly be coming back, I rented it secretly before I left Buckleigh. They're expecting us."

"Who is?"

"The men I left here on Dartmoor to watch events and gather information while I was gone. We arrive under an assumed name, just as we've traveled."

She had paid it no attention on the journey. Guy had arranged their rooms and their meals.

"You're Mr. David Gordon again?"

"No." He gave her a quizzical smile. "We're Mr. and Mrs. Guido Handfast."

Sarah laughed, but her pulse stumbled and the ache in her heart opened like a wound to throb with new pain.

She glanced from the window. They were travelling up into a thick white mist that blanketed the top of the moor. Great blocks of granite, stacked like huge, abandoned toys, loomed and faded. A troop of wild ponies suddenly broke across their road, then scattered in a clattering of unshod hooves to disappear as if they had been swallowed.

Yet the silhouette of something more ominous wavered darkly in the mist ahead of them.

"There's a horseman coming our way," she said.

Guy leaned across her to look out. He rapped on the carriage ceiling.

The horses pulled up as the approaching rider came into focus: a wiry, thin-shanked man on a brown pony.

"It's Peters, sir," he said, doffing his hat as soon as he drew level. "I've bad news."

"Important enough to meet me out here?"

"Well, someone's waiting at the cottage, sir, and I thought you might like to know this first: Croft's dead. Killed in a fight with the revenue men above Stonebridge Cove."

Sarah's heart stopped dead, but Guy seemed perfectly calm.

"When did this happen?"

"Last night, sir. Word is that someone tipped off the authorities, and the officers set up an ambush."

"Anyone lost besides Croft?"

"No, sir. The others all got away safe, though the goods were all seized."

"Thank you. You were right to come out here to tell me," Guy said. "Who's waiting at the cottage?"

"Not one of us, sir. Never seen the fellow before. But he was most insistent that you'd want to see him right away. Since he already knew your real name, we thought it best to let him stay and keep an eye on him."

"This man knows me as Guy Devoran?"

"Yes, sir, but he's not much more than a boy, truth be told. We're keeping him cooling his heels in the stables."

"Then tell our mysterious stranger that we're on our way and will be delighted to meet him. You may send him in as soon as we arrive."

"Very good, sir!"

Peters jammed his hat back onto his head, turned his pony, and rode away into the mist.

Sarah did her best to crush her sense of dread. The carriage jolted forward.

"Do you think Daedalus arranged it?" she asked.

"Croft's death? Possibly, but why turn murderer at such a late date? No, it's probably just a damnable coincidence, though I'm sorry for it, because I'd planned to interview the man again."

"You think you could have made him tell you who Daedalus really is?"

"Yes."

Sarah pressed her hands to her cheeks as if she could rub away her distress. She could imagine the skirmish in that narrow, deeply cut path from the beach. The revenue officers springing down the banks, swords and pistols drawn, the smugglers scattering like leaves or fighting back, and Croft the gardener meeting a sudden, brutal death.

"Daedalus is Lord Moorefield, Guy, and I believe him capable of real violence."

"Very likely. But I cannot act against him until I have proof."

"Why not?"

"Because if we confront the wrong man, the secret will be out and Daedalus will become truly desperate for the first time. What the devil's he thinking right now? He knows that Rachel discovered that her baby was stolen, but also that she can't be certain of his identity. Since he sent Croft to town to arrange those attacks, he must have trusted his gardener absolutely. Now, much to his gratification, Rachel's disappeared and there's been no shred of rumor since then that his son and heir is an impostor. Thus, he's feeling wary, but safe."

"What if he knows about Mrs. Siskin?"

"I don't think that's likely, though just in case I left a couple of lads to surreptitiously watch over her. Meanwhile, the midwife and her husband are both dead, and Croft's just joined them. So no one's left to bear witness to Rachel's mad tale. If she publicly announced her claim, Daedalus could dismiss it as the ravings of a madwoman. All that would change immediately if we were to create the scandal of the age by accusing one of his innocent neighbors of stealing Rachel's child."

"Especially if the accuser was Blackdown's nephew?"

"Exactly. Meanwhile, perhaps he suspects us, perhaps not. But right now he can't know that we've come back to Dartmoor, which gives us a tiny advantage."

"So who's this stranger waiting at the cottage?"

Guy sat quietly for a moment, as if listening to the horses' hooves on the stony surface of the road.

"I hope it's the lad who delivered Rachel's note before you left Buckleigh," he said at last. "I've had men looking for him ever since I left."

Sarah swallowed her trepidation, though she had no idea why she felt so desperately afraid.

"Then you think that this boy may be our only link to discovering where Rachel's been hiding?"

"Yes," he said quietly. "Precisely that."

CHAPTER SIXTEEN

THE HORSES STOPPED IN FRONT OF A BUILDING. THE MIST had thickened to soft, heavy cotton, but two flambeaux wavered beside a doorway, staining the air as if it were soaked with yellow dye.

"Our new abode," Guy said, leaping down.

Sarah took his proffered hand and climbed from the carriage. The facade of an elegant stone house loomed up in the mist.

"You call this a cottage?"

"It was a rectory once, but the parish is depleted these days. Mr. Handfast was able to rent the whole place very reasonably. In pursuit of his hobby, you understand: studying lichen."

"Lichen?" she asked. "Rather a comedown from orchids, don't you think?"

"I have my own orchid," he said. "Why the devil would I care to look at any others?"

Guy swung her up into his arms and kicked open the door to carry her over the threshold.

Though she was living every day now in a haze of uncertainty, Sarah squealed and laughed, and he kissed her as he set her down in a small parlor.

Perhaps all her fears were for naught. Perhaps nothing could stand in their way now: no mystery, no past, no buried grief, no doubts, not even Daedalus.

A single lamp cast its warm glow over the room. A fire burned merrily in the grate to ward off the night chill from the moor. In front of the single tall window the table was already set for supper. A tray on the sideboard held wine and glasses.

Guy helped Sarah off with her coat, then bent to light a taper to set a flame to more candles.

"A hot meal should appear at any moment from the kitchen," he said. "But the staff understand that they're otherwise to make themselves scarce."

"I am," Sarah said, "starving."

"So I am," a light, musical voice said behind them. "May I join you for dinner?"

They both spun about. A young man stood awkwardly in the doorway. A shabby greatcoat enveloped his body. A shapeless hat shaded his forehead.

Yet his chin tipped with something like defiance.

He gestured over one shoulder. "Peters said you wished me to come in straightaway."

Sarah felt as if she had been knocked in the jaw and were spinning away into an ashen mist. Glad? Yes, of course she was glad! Yet a huge sorrow had also crashed over her, pressing her down like a rogue wave, a wave that snapped great ships in two and sent them straight to the bottom of the ocean.

She clutched at the back of a chair, holding on until her vision cleared and the gladness surfaced through her selfish distress like a cork—until she saw Guy's face and heard the bitter shock in his voice.

"Please, don't hesitate," Guy was saying. "Pray, join us! I must say that you make a very pretty boy, though I suppose we must all regret the loss of so much golden hair."

The newcomer ducked his head to pull off his soft cap—and Rachel looked up, her eyes brilliantly blue beneath a halo of cropped golden curls.

"I didn't know how else to hide," she said. "I don't care about my hair. I care only about my little boy. Please, don't be angry!"

Sarah sank onto the chair and sat pinned beside the fireplace. Rachel dropped her cap to the floor, walked straight into Guy's arms, and burst into tears.

He held her, cradling her head against his chest as if he comforted a child. Candlelight glistened over Rachel's gilt hair. The short cut only emphasized her perfect bones. Her throat and jaw were as pure and clean as an angel's.

"Hush," Guy said. "It's all right, Rachel. I'm not angry. I was a little taken aback, that's all, but we're here now. We'll rescue him."

Sarah met his barren gaze above her cousin's fair head. His eyes held nothing but darkness. Limned in candlelight, he and Rachel made a flawless couple, so striking that any observer might feel breathless to see them together.

Still clutching Guy's sleeve, Rachel turned to face her cousin. "I knew you'd get Guy to come to Devon, Sarah. I couldn't go to him myself. You do understand?"

"Yes," Sarah said, though the knots had tightened in her stomach. "We both understand. Come and sit by the fire. You look frozen."

Rachel stumbled to a seat. As if suddenly returned to life, Guy strode to the sideboard. Sarah had no idea what he was thinking or feeling. He seemed shuttered, entirely self-contained. She knew only that something in him had shattered and that he fought to hold himself together.

"We already know all about your baby, Rachel," Sarah said. "We spoke with Mrs. Siskin and Mrs. Lane, and we've pieced together most of the story since then—about Knight's Cottage and Goatstall Lane and why Lord Jonathan found you in that kitchen in the Three Barrels. I'm so sorry."

"I thought I could steal him away by myself." Rachel pushed slender hands back through her curls. "But when I first arrived here from Hampstead, I had no idea who had my baby. I tried to talk to Mr. Croft—he was at Barristow Manor then—but he claimed to know nothing. When I insisted, he laughed and said that Barry Norris's little boy was his own and he could prove it, and I'd be hauled away to Bedlam if I tried to insist otherwise. No one else would see me."

Guy poured wine. His eyes seemed almost terrifyingly calm, like the water in a deep well that might hide unknown ghouls.

He gave Rachel a glass. "Did you show Croft Mrs. Siskin's letter, or mention her at all?"

"No!" Rachel's long lashes swept down over her eyes as she stared into the glass. "He frightened me. I just said I'd heard a rumor."

"But why didn't you wait for me to come home from Birch-brook? You know I'd have helped you."

"I didn't want you to know the truth. Sarah understands."

Perhaps she did. Rachel may have believed that Guy loved her, but she loved another man and always had. She'd been alone in the house with the chimneys when she'd first learned that their baby had lived, after all. Any woman might have thought it better to make a clean break in the circumstances, though perhaps not such a cruel one.

"So when you couldn't get anything further out of Mr. Croft, you hid in London?" Guy asked.

"Yes," Rachel said. "I didn't know where else to go. And I did try your townhouse, Guy, but they said you'd gone down to Wyld-shay and they didn't know when you'd be back."

Guy leaned both shoulders against the wall, his gaze hawk-dark. "You could have written."

"No! I couldn't write, not after the note I'd left you in Hamp-stead. And I am sorry about that. Truly! When I read Mrs. Siskin's letter, I felt frantic, desperate. I couldn't think. All I could imagine was getting down to Devon as fast as possible to find my baby."

He tipped his head back and closed his eyes. Tension drew taut lines at the corners of his mouth.

"Yet I think what you wrote was the truth," he said. "Though it's best forgotten now."

Rachel had the grace to blush, a charming warm glow that suffused her peerless skin like a sunrise.

"So Mr. Croft rebuffed you and you came back to London empty-handed," Sarah said quickly. "Then when someone began attacking you, you wrote to tell me how frightened you were."

"Yes, because I realized then that Mr. Croft must have talked about me to the man who really had my baby. I thought he must want to kill me in order to keep his secret." Rachel's blush deepened and she set down her wineglass. "I didn't mean to deceive you, Sarah—"

"Yes, you did," Sarah said. "But it's all right. I understand. When you first fell in love at Grail Hall, it must have felt far too overwhelming to share with anyone, even me, though you poured out all those feelings into a tale about remembering Mr. Devoran on the yacht. But once you'd begun to spin such a network of falsehoods, at what point could you possibly retreat?"

"It was like falling into a well," Rachel said, "where all you can do is keep falling."

Sarah met her cousin's gaze, filled with genuine remorse, and fought to find her higher self. Whatever it cost her, she could not let herself give way to ignoble jealousy or resentment. Especially not for the cousin she'd grown up with!

"And a great love can feel very private," she said. "Something to treasure secretly deep in one's heart, especially if you fear that a future together may prove impossible."

Rachel dropped to her knees at Sarah's feet. "I knew you'd understand!" A new note of excitement colored her voice. "A love like that! I'd never imagined, never known— Can you ever forgive me, dearest? Though I did make up stories, my heart's always been true!"

Sarah caught her cousin's hands. "I've never doubted your heart, Rachel."

"His name's Claude d'Alleville," Rachel said. "His father owns a chateau in France."

Guy's dark eyes, fathomless and quiet, met Sarah's gaze. They both recognized the name from Lord Grail's guest list.

"He was at Grail Hall for the Egyptian gathering?" Sarah asked.

"Yes. I was asked to attend the meetings to take notes. Claude's English is perfectly fluent and I speak as much French as any other lady, but we fell in love before we'd even spoken. He's the handsomest man you ever saw, Sarah! It was love at first sight. Can you believe that?"

"Yes," Sarah said. "Yes, of course."

Guy walked up to the table. "I'll ring for dinner," he said. "And an extra plate."

Rachel rose with a small, nervous laugh, and allowed him to help her to a seat. Sarah followed. His hands brushed briefly over her shoulders as she sat down, sending a little shock like an electric current through her veins.

Some of Guy's men brought in the supper dishes, a slightly rough crew to serve at table. As soon as they left the room, Guy turned back to Rachel.

"Monsieur d'Alleville disappeared, though you wrote to him every day?"

"He said when he left England he was going on a new expedition to Egypt, but his father would forward my letters. I don't doubt him," she added. "He'll come for me as soon as he can."

"But it's been over two years," Sarah said gently.

"So? He's probably in Nubia by now, and my letters won't reach him until they all arrive together in a bundle—carried on camels!"

Guy seemed fascinated by the candles on the table. "Meanwhile, in your reluctance to seek me out directly, you sent Sarah those letters filled with panic. Though you traveled back here to Devon from Goatstall Lane several days before she arrived."

Rachel pushed some boiled cabbage to the side of her plate. "I was too afraid to wait. A wall fell down and almost killed me. And the man who had my baby would never suspect that I'd come here to live right under his nose, would he? So I sold most of the rest of my jewels and dressed like this—only more respectably, of course—then rented a little out-of-the-way place on the moor. No one suspected me."

"And you visited Barristow as soon as you could?" Sarah glanced at Guy. "Mr. Norris said that a young man had met his little boy in the garden."

"Yes," he said. "I overheard. I just didn't know at the time that it might be important."

He poured himself more wine and turned back to Rachel. "Thus you hid in plain sight. Which of my men found you and didn't tell me?"

Rachel pursed her mouth like a rebellious child. "It was my fault. You can't blame him."

"I don't. No male could ever resist you. I assume it was Oliver?"

She colored. "He probably guessed you'd understand."

"Then he's right. And, fortunately for him, he's young enough to be unafraid of my retaliation. So was Master Norris your son?"

"Oh, no! That's why I never went back there, and anyway the nurse panicked. No, when I did find my little boy, his nursemaid never breathed a word to anyone."

"Which nursemaid?" Sarah asked.

"Betsy Davy, of course! I went to Moorefield Hall next, because I discovered that Mr. Croft had moved there from Barristow Manor. As soon as I saw my little boy, I knew for sure."

Guy had become very still, as if his heart had slowed. "How did you get access to the child?"

"I hid in the gardens. Betsy was scared the first time she saw me, but I pretended to have wandered into His Lordship's grounds in pursuit of a goldfinch. Though she soon realized that I wasn't really a boy, she didn't mind. She's lonely."

"You told her who you were?"

Rachel shook her head. "No, I just made up another story about running away from a vicious husband: a terrible man who beat me and threatened my life. I said he'd sent my own babies away, so I'd never see them again. It wasn't so very far from the truth. Betsy even cried a little when she heard it. She doesn't have any real friends at the Hall. After that we met almost every week, whenever she could sneak out with Berry into a concealed part of the grounds."

Guy pushed his chair back from the table. "Then you're quite sure that Lord Berrisham is really your son?"

"Oh, yes!" Rachel bit her lip and blushed. "He looks just like Claude."

"We believe you," Sarah said gently. "But don't you see? All the witnesses to what really happened are dead."

"Why does that matter? I know that he's mine and I already have a plan to take him."

China rattled as Guy sprang up and strode away across the room.

"For God's sake, Rachel! There's no proof. Successfully steal Moorefield's baby by yourself, and you could end up on the gallows. Make the attempt and fail, and at the very least Betsy Davy will face dismissal, when she's all the little boy has."

"But I *know* that he's mine!" Rachel's eyes filled with tears, as if for the first time she was on the verge of hysteria. "I *know* it, Guy!"

Sarah caught her cousin's hand and squeezed her fingers.

"We're all worn out," she said. "We'll finish talking in the morning. It's time to go to bed."

To bed! As she said the words, she felt that white, sick pain and tasted her wine in her mouth again. She'd been sharing Guy's bed ever since the Anchor, but her cousin had no idea of it. Would Rachel assume that she could ensnare Guy again, body and soul, exactly as she had in Hampstead in the house with the top-hatted chimneys?

The situation was hideous: hideous and scandalous and excruciating.

"I have a slight headache," she said and realized it was true. After all, she and Guy had been traveling for days, and though she'd been unable to eat much, she'd had four glasses of wine. "I think I'll go up right away."

Giving Guy an awkward smile, Sarah fled the room.

Once in the hall, she had no idea where to go, but the man who had met their carriage on the moor stepped out of the servant's hall, carrying a tray with some sliced fruit.

"I need to go up to my room," Sarah said. "Is there a woman who can show me?"

"Third door on the right at the top, ma'am," Peters said, jerking his head. "Your boxes have already been taken up."

She stumbled up the stairs and pushed open the designated door. A large four-poster dominated the space. Her cases sat in one corner. Guy's trunk sat next to them. Some helpful lackey had already unpacked his shaving kit and laid it out on the washstand.

Sarah crossed to the window and opened it. Mist still hung low over the moor, shrouding the entire world, trapping her in this nightmare.

A great love can feel very private.

It could undoubtedly grow privately, and perhaps it ought to die the same way?

But what if one knew now with absolute certainty that this love would never, never die, not until verses of repentance and the hope for salvation were engraved on one's tombstone? What then?

The summer night wasn't truly cold, but it was damp. Sarah shivered and closed the window. The bed waited, fresh sheets already turned back. Her nightgown lay across the pillows. But what if he didn't come to her? What if, right now, he and Rachel—

Sarah couldn't lift her boxes by herself, but she pulled out the bare essentials for the night and grabbed her nightgown from the bed. Carrying the small bundle in her arms, she walked out into the hallway and opened door after door.

There were five decent-sized bedrooms, and the clean linen was stacked in a cupboard at the end of the hall. She chose a pleasant chamber facing east, made up the bed, and crawled exhausted between the covers.

Yet she lay awake for a long time. It was horrific to contemplate

Guy's finding her in his bed if he were secretly wishing she wasn't there. Even worse to wait for him there, her heart eager, her blood on fire for him, then have him never come at all.

This way, if he wanted to find her, he could easily do so. The choice was his.

At last she fell asleep, dry-eyed and desolate, and in the morning he still hadn't come.

BRILLIANT sunshine blinded her when Sarah woke up, as if to mock her misery. She washed and dressed, then stood at the window for a moment, gazing out at the purple heights of Dartmoor basking beneath a clear blue sky. In spite of the bright sun, it was still early. A small band of native ponies grazed in the far distance.

She had been madly, overwhelmingly in love and let those giddy emotions cloud her judgment. It had all been remarkable, wonderful, as if Guy had magically transported her to the wood near Athens ruled by Titania.

Now, however much it hurt, she must return to dull reality. She could allow herself some grief at the wrenching loss, yet she must also find the determination and courage to stand aside and let Guy rescue Rachel once again.

If Sarah Callaway had not initiated it, he would never have taken a plain widow to his bed. Contemptible to let anger or pain override compassion for the fragile cousin she had grown up with, and especially for the innocent baby Rachel had borne and lost in so much agony.

Yet it hurt, it hurt, and her heart burned with indignation and pain.

No one else seemed to be up, so Sarah walked downstairs and into the unkempt garden. Water gurgled somewhere out of sight. She followed the sound, winding along a stone path through the dense greenery. Flowers and shrubs struggled against a rampant growth of weeds.

A little stream trickled over rocks into a damp, mossy hollow, thick with watercress, the banks brightened by a clump of purple loosestrife.

Guy sat on a fallen log staring at the water.

Her heart failed. She turned to flee, but he spoke without turning his head.

"Sarah! Please stay!" Sunlight fired highlights in his dark hair and danced over the entrancing lines of his face, though his gaze was lost in shadow. "Does that take so much courage?"

Courage? Perhaps it was only weakness that prevented her from turning and running away.

"Where's Rachel?" she asked.

"Presumably still in her bed. You'll notice that I said *her* bed, not mine."

"But I thought—"

"No, you didn't *think*, you feared." He rose and gestured to the log. "Will you sit here with me?"

She forced herself to walk forward, one foot, then the other, and sat down. The stream plopped and rushed merrily as it wove between the stones.

He dropped down next to her and rested a forearm on each thigh, his fingers relaxed, his hands shaped so beautifully. A desperate longing seized her heart: to undo the past, to undo everything, to spin life into a fairy tale, where a redheaded schoolteacher might truly win the heart of a man like Guy Devoran.

He gazed into the water in silence for several more moments, making no move to touch her. Sarah sat in a kind of suspended agony and waited.

"You should know this," he said at last. "I told you once that I had been infatuated with your cousin. I was certainly hurt when she left me. In fact, I was enraged by her desertion, but I know now that it was the hurt of wounded pride, not that of a broken heart."

"Yet you felt desperate?"

"I certainly felt responsible. I told you the truth about our day on the yacht. I did not tell you that afterwards I hunted for her for several months. The memory of Rachel standing in that breeze at the bow of the boat haunted me. Jack knows all of this—and Ryder. They might even tell you that I was a little demented when I couldn't find her."

"Because she was hiding in Knight's Cottage by then. How could you have known where she was?"

He picked up a pebble and tossed it into the stream. "I couldn't. I don't blame myself for that. With the money Jack paid her, she could afford to live anywhere, until—though you were still sending her what funds you could spare—she ran out of money and turned up on my doorstep."

"That winter must have been terrible for her," Sarah said. "To be alone with her grief, while writing to me as if she were still working as a governess."

"I know it hurts, Sarah, that Rachel didn't confide in you—just as it hurts that she and I became lovers, though I discovered very quickly that I'd built up an image of her based on a fantasy. Yet she seemed so damned fragile, standing there in the rain on my doorstep, trailing a broken wing like a ringed plover."

Sarah stared at the stream, the delicate froth of bubbles where the water was trapped for a moment behind a rock, though it was the stone that would be worn away.

"But she's not fragile, Guy. She's brave and resourceful, and it took great courage for her to come back here to Devon as she did. I've been used to protecting her all my life, yet now I think that Rachel may be pure steel at the core."

"That's one way of putting it." Guy tossed another pebble. "But what your cousin is at the core, Sarah, is self-centered."

She felt flayed. "No! If Rachel's been selfish or deceitful, it was only for the sake of her baby—or sometimes for her own survival after her lover abandoned her."

"I don't deny that she's suffered very terribly, or that she deserves our care. But the plover is a trickster, offering an illusion of broken feathers. As soon as she thinks she's safe, she flies off. This is not to my credit, Sarah, but what I felt for your cousin was always a great deal closer to pity than love, and it still is."

"Then you deny her courage?"

"No, but I assume that you fled my room last night because you feared that I wished to be with Rachel, instead of you. I can imagine no worse fate. I shall protect your cousin to the best of my ability from the results of her own foolishness, but my heart—unreliable as you seem to believe it—is yours and always will be."

Sarah closed her eyes against the sun, then glanced back at the tumbling stream. The water laughed and sparkled as sudden tears blinded her.

"You didn't say so on our journey," she said. "Not once."

He glanced down at her and smiled. "Did I need to?"

She hugged her arms about her waist, remembering, remembering. "Perhaps not."

"I rather thought that I'd been proving my love for you day and night ever since we left the Anchor. Or do you still believe that a man's passion can have nothing at all to do with his heart?"

A little breeze moved along the stream. The tall spikes of purple loosestrife swayed.

"No, it's not that. Not any longer."

"Then you're abandoning some very basic female wisdom," Guy said dryly, "for that's very often true—except in this case."

Sarah dropped her forehead onto her knees and laughed. "Yet when you tell me that you love me, it's as if the sky parts to show me a glimpse of heaven, though a new trap yawns at my feet, one I can't begin to fathom." She looked up. "I can't explain it, Guy. I only know that I'm afraid."

A third pebble splashed into the water. "Because the best, deepest love can only survive on a foundation of courage and trust?"

"Yes, but I would trust you with my soul." Heat seared her cheeks. "Though last night I was indeed racked by doubt, I still couldn't flaunt—I couldn't! Not with Rachel in the house."

He laughed. "Not even in secret?"

"Guy, even if I admit that I love you with all my heart, I'm still afraid that the gods may be planning some terrible punishment for such hubris. I can't really explain it."

He lifted her hand and pressed it to his lips. "My beautiful Sarah, don't you know that I came to you last night? Alas, when I discovered where you'd hidden yourself, you were already asleep."

"You couldn't have come in," she said. "I'd have known."

"Because you and I are tied together now as if bound by Ariadne's thread? No, I stood staring down at your sleeping face, then crept away to my own lonely bed. It wasn't easy, but you and I should never come together in confusion and fear. I love you."

He closed his fingers gently over her palm. Her blood surged in deep waves of desire, even at so simple a contact. She knew she would step blindly from a cliff top, if he held her hand like this and asked her.

"I believe you," she said, but she released his fingers.

He stood to gaze down into the rushing water. "Rachel and I talked for another hour or two last night. She never once expressed any sorrow for the pain that she's caused you. She takes it for granted that you'll always defend her and fight for her happiness."

"I shall," Sarah said.

"And so, I suppose, will I." Guy held out a hand and helped Sarah to her feet. "I wrote this morning to d'Alleville at his family chateau in France—that's the only address Rachel's ever had—and sent the letter to Ryder to forward for me. A plea to an absent lover, if he lives, may make a stronger impression if it's franked at Wyldshay."

Cold fingers touched her spine. "If he lives? You think Claude d'Alleville may be dead?"

"If he really went to Egypt, I think it very likely. The Nile has a habit of eating Europeans alive. Dysentery, ague, local violence—"

Sarah stared down at their linked fingers. "Yet he anyway ignored all of Rachel's letters."

"Not quite. He wrote to her several times after he first returned to France, though all correspondence stopped as soon as he learned she was with child. However, she insists that she knows he still loves her."

"Though he cannot," Sarah said. "Not after all this time. Even if he didn't die in Egypt, he's proved ten times over that he's only indifferent."

"Exactly. In spite of the Blackdown dragon seal on my letter, I have no real hope of ever getting a reply."

"So what shall we do about Berry?"

Guy released her fingers and strode away a few paces. Sunlight warmed his broad shoulders and glinted in his dark hair.

"That question kept me awake for the best part of the night. Even if we get him back from Moorefield, what then? I can provide funds for Rachel to raise her baby alone, but he'll still be a bastard, instead of an earl's son and heir. There's also the uncertain fate of the countess."

"Lady Moorefield's not a helpless child, and we cannot leave a baby in such a cruel household."

Guy turned to smile dryly at her. "So—unpleasant as His Lordship's disposition may be—it's rather fortunate in the circumstances?"

She met his eyes. In spite of her trepidation, she laughed. "Yes, I've already thought of that, too. I could never condone tearing a baby from the heart of a loving family."

Guy held aside a hanging branch. They began to walk back to the house together.

"There's also the matter of justice to the earl's brother, illegally excluded from his right to inherit the title, assuming Moorefield never has legitimate sons. As for the countess, I can't promise to protect her, though I'll do what I can."

"How on earth did she pretend to give birth without anyone finding out?"

"I don't imagine it was that difficult, though I intend to interview the local gossips this afternoon to find out."

Sarah stopped to look up at him. "So we will recover Berry?"

"I intend to use all the power of my family connections to do so. Thus, while I pursue my more nefarious purposes, you and Rachel will go shopping in Plymouth."

"Shopping?"

A dark flame flared in his eyes. For a moment she thought he would kiss her. Yet he only smiled.

"Of course," he said. "If we're to impress Moorefield with our massed strength, we must arrive in style."

SARAH watched him ride away. Nameless fears still fluttered like a flock of dark crows, but she was no longer afraid that Guy didn't truly love her—or that she didn't truly love him. They had proved it with passion. They had also proved it many times with their unspoken understanding, almost as if they knew each other's thoughts.

Yet she felt as if they stood on the brink of some great chasm filled with treacherous waters, while only the most fragile of bridges stretched across to the other side.

She turned to go in and met Rachel just stepping outside. She was wearing one of Sarah's best gowns. Though the dress was neither fashionable nor new and didn't quite fit, her cousin looked breathtaking. The bright morning sun sparkled on her golden curls. Her blue eyes were as guileless as periwinkles.

"Guy's gone?"

"Not for long," Sarah said. "He promises that we'll get Berry back from Lord Moorefield tomorrow, after we both buy some new clothes."

"Yes, I'd love a new dress." Rachel plucked at her skirts. "Your things are so plain, Sarah. Hardly fit to impress a peer of the realm!" She bit her lip as she gazed away down the drive. "He would have married me, you know."

Sarah gulped down her little rush of pain. "In the house with the chimneys in Hampstead? Guy asked you?"

"Not in so many words, but he would have done. He was in love with me."

"Of course he was," Sarah said gently. "But you were already in love with Claude."

Her cousin's white fingers dashed away a sudden welling of tears. "I'd have waited for him forever, Sarah, but it was so hard when he never replied to any of my letters. I even had to sell the locket he'd given me. Then all those months in Cooper Street and all the rest of that year after I thought I'd lost our baby. It was terrible! Yet I tried not to distress you, even when it was almost unbearable to carry on alone."

Sarah caught Rachel's hand in her own. "Yes, I know, dear. I know. But why did you go to Hampstead?"

"Mrs. Lane had already threatened to evict me, so I couldn't stay in Cooper Street. Then a kitchen girl at the Three Barrels told me about Knight's Cottage. Her sister had worked there, and Guy had just given me all that gold. Since I was sure by then that Claude must be in Egypt, what difference did it make where I lived?"

"But when your money ran out again, you went to find Guy?"

Rachel nodded. "What else could I do? Hampstead Heath was miserable in January, and Guy's townhouse wasn't hard to find. Though there was the nastiest storm that night. I was soaked to the skin and shivering like a willow leaf. You can't imagine! Yet I knew that he'd take me in. Then I thought that he deserved something in return, so I went to bed with him."

"That was your idea?"

"Oh, yes! Did you think it was his?" Rachel glanced down and colored a little. "And it was really very nice, too. After all, he's very handsome and incredibly caring. You do understand, don't you?"

Sarah swallowed her mad impulse to laugh. "Yes, I understand."

"If I'd had a heart left to share, Guy might easily have won it. Yet in that terrible dark winter as I stared at the frost on the windowpanes, I began to fear that Claude might have died. It made me feel a little mad. If Guy had asked me to marry him then, I think I might have done—though I never loved him and I never will."

"But that letter came from Mrs. Siskin, instead. If you were so sure that Guy loved you, weren't you concerned that you might hurt him very deeply when you left him like that?"

Rachel pulled out one of Sarah's best handkerchiefs. "No! Because the truth is that though Guy may have thought that he was in love with me, he never knew the real me, not as Claude did." She tried to stifle her sobs, but they came out in little hiccups. "I made up all kinds of wild stories about myself and never shared anything real. Guy knew that, I think. Yet he gave me jewels anyway, like that bracelet I sent you. Then one day when I was feeling particularly frantic, I made him promise that he'd always take care of me, whatever happened."

"And he promised?"

"Yes, yes, of course! I insisted he make a solemn vow on his honor. He couldn't have refused me!"

"But now you're quite sure that Claude is still alive, after all?"

"Oh, yes! After I found out about Berry, I dreamed about him. The most vivid, startling dream! Then I knew with absolute certainly that Claude lived, after all, and that if I could only recover our baby he'd come for me."

Hot tears—of pain, of grief, of a kind of terrible compassion—blurred Sarah's vision as Rachel spun about and rushed back into the house.

GUY rode back to the Rectory across the moor. Granite outcroppings clustered on every rise. The warm afternoon sun shimmered in myriad small puddles, winking like small mirrors lost in the heather. Butterflies danced. Golden flowers crammed the branches of the gorse.

A bright flash of copper almost stopped his heart dead.

A redheaded woman in a cream dress had just disappeared between two of the huge granite stacks.

Guy turned his horse and cantered straight for the rocks, then leaped down and threw his reins over a bush. More gorse bushes crowded against one side of an almost hidden green space, enclosed and private among its rock walls, like an outdoor room with the sky for a ceiling.

Sarah stood on a patch of short turf, her shoulders leaning against the warm stone. She was swinging her bonnet lazily in one hand and staring up at the sky.

"They say that when gorse is out of bloom, kissing's out of season," Guy said.

Sarah glanced around to meet his gaze.

Naked desire sizzled in the warm summer air, heady and impetuous.

Bright color washed over her cheeks. "But gorse blooms almost all year."

"Well, exactly!"

Guy strode up to her, seized her shoulders in both hands, and kissed her. Her lips parted and her tongue met his. He kissed her with blazing fervor, a frantic, pulsing ardor, as if he might yet be called away on crusade and be forced to leave his true love forever. Yet Sarah kissed back with mad abandon, as if by her absolute surrender she could convince him just how much she loved him.

They came up for air, breathless, and Guy gazed down into her eyes. "No more doubts, sweetheart?"

She touched his cheek. "No, Guy. No more doubts."

Hot need coursed through his veins. He slipped his hands to her waist and pulled her close against his body.

"Then let's pledge our sacred sacrament. Right here. Right now."

Her face flaming, Sarah glanced about. The lichen-streaked rocks trapped the sunshine like champagne in a glass. Bright golden gorse bloomed. The blue sky soared. His horse snatched at blades of grass. They were completely private.

She laughed and shook her head. "We can't," she said. "Not here!"

"Yes, we can. No more doubts."

Guy stepped back to peel off his jacket and waistcoat. He tossed them aside, then slipped his braces from his shoulders. His riding breeches sagged a little to settle loosely on his hips. Pleasure fired through his blood, throbbing into his erection.

Sarah stared at him, her face on fire, her eyes fierce and wide.

"We can't, Guy!" she said again. "Not here!"

He laughed and tugged off his cravat, then pulled his shirt from his waistband to pull it away over his head. Her gaze caressed his naked flesh. The shirt dropped from his fingers.

Guy stepped closer, pinning Sarah against the rock. Her blush stained her neck and the tops of her ears. Intimate. Passionate. As if he touched her.

"God, sweetheart!" His voice was already husky, whispering in her ear. "It's been over twenty-four hours. No one will find us here. You don't even need to get undressed."

He stroked gentle fingers over her nape and the base of her throat, then teased the tip of one breast through her dress with his thumb.

"I can't—" She gasped. "Ah, dear God! No, Guy, I can't deny you!"

His blood flamed, his pulse thundered. His arousal strained against the flap of his breeches. He pinched her nipples a little harder, following the depth of her response, knowing in his soul the intensity of her pleasure and exactly how to heighten it.

Sarah sighed and shivered. She closed her eyes.

Beloved, beloved, how could I ever deny you?

As he kissed her again, she slipped her hands around his waist, then ran her hands up and down his naked back. His flesh was sun-hot, ardor-hot beneath her palms. Firm muscles arced smoothly from his spine, then softened into vulnerable little hollows beside his taut belly.

Guy broke the kiss, tipped his head back, and swallowed hard as she ran her fingers around his waistband.

"What exactly do you have in mind?" she asked softly.

Reckless, headstrong, he dropped his chin to grin at her. "Turn around," he said.

Reckless, trusting, Sarah did so.

He bent her forward over a little ledge of rock and lifted her skirts to her waist. With both hands he stroked her bare thighs and kneaded her bottom, then he knelt on the short turf to follow his hands with his mouth.

Desire pooled and throbbed. Giddy with pleasure, she spread her legs further. Kissing and licking, he brought her to the brink of explosion, until she sagged forward helplessly against the rocks.

She was swollen and open, desperate for him, when he stood at last and dropped the flap of his breeches to slide his erection deep inside her body. Gratification rushed and flooded, intense and liquid.

His palms cupped her breasts, supporting her, while his thumbs flicked over her nipples.

Sarah surrendered, body and soul, in absolute trust.

Guy murmured in her ear as they made love beneath the blue heaven. She didn't know what he said. Words of love? Wicked sins? Promises? Vows? She didn't care. Breathless and enchanted, she climaxed again and again.

She was already satiated and helpless when he suddenly stopped moving, pinning her to stillness with both hands now on her hips.

They stood locked together for a moment in silence, all consciousness centered on the overwhelming sensations. Warm sunshine, rough granite, her legs sprawled apart, his black boots planted between them, and the intimate joining of their bodies.

"I don't suppose," he said, panting a little, "that you're wearing your little sponge?"

Sarah shook her head. "No, no! But it doesn't matter anymore."

"Yes," he said. "Alas, sweetheart, yes, it might."

So he would protect her from the most scandalous consequences of their love, even now!

He kissed her bent nape, and withdrew slowly, slowly. Bereft, suddenly shy, Sarah dropped her skirts to her ankles and turned around. Her legs trembled. Her belly ached with pleasure.

Dark hair fell damply over his forehead. His eyes were wild and ecstatic. He was still erect, throbbing with unfulfilled arousal. Desperately, she wanted to help him, use her hands and her mouth on him, just as he had brought pleasure to her.

Guy stroked the wild tangles back from her forehead, then began to turn away. His erection brushed against her skirts.

"No," she said. She caught him around the waist with both hands. "Let it be my turn now." Intense pleasure fired through his blood as she stroked her fingers tentatively over his naked flesh. "You will show me how?"

He gazed down into her eyes for a moment, before he laughed a little, then nodded.

She smiled back, shy and hot and eager. "I want everything to be equal between us, Guy—"

He stopped her words with his mouth, then murmured in her ear, his very soul on fire with excitement.

"If you truly mean it, my love, this is hardly the moment for conversation."

Sarah met his gaze and laughed as she sank with him onto the short turf. Fired with desire Guy sprawled back against the rock, while she knelt over him to explore the ultimate wonder of his ardor for her.

His moans filled his ears. His excitement built again into a white-hot intensity. It was the strangest of surrenders, to allow her to touch him and lick him, to be the passive partner abandoning his body to her hot exploration.

Tentative, bashful, she pleasured him as he had so often done for her. His glans throbbed with a life of its own. His pulse thundered. All thought dissolved in the face of such intense pleasure.

She glanced up—her eyes euphoric, dark and hot beneath her lashes. His heart swelled. With a choked groan, Guy lifted her to press his open mouth over hers—musk and salt and sweetness. Yet her fingers still palpated, and his head fell back, the kiss broken, consciousness fled, as he climaxed in her hand with blinding power.

Her fingers slipped away. Sarah chortled from pure bliss. His rapturous laughter joined in, swallowing his whispered sounds— both formless and heartfelt.

Still giggling, she collapsed to stretch out beside him on the grass.

Sunshine beat hotly through her closed eyelids, staining her world scarlet. Soft sounds betrayed that he was gathering his clothes and shrugging into his shirt.

Overwhelmed, Sarah drifted, almost on the edge of sleep, until she felt the cool touch of his shadow once again and knew that he was standing over her, shading her from the sun.

"You'll get burned," he said softly. "The sun will give you the most unfashionable freckles."

She shaded her eyes with one hand and smiled up at him. He had already buttoned his breeches and tied his cravat.

"That was—"

"Ah, sweetheart!" He thrust his arms into his coat sleeves. "Say nothing, unless it's to say that you love me."

Tears burned. She sat up. "I love you."

Fully dressed, he dropped down to sit beside her on the grass, his back against the rock, one arm about her shoulder. Her head cushioned, Sarah leaned into his strength and stared up at the sky.

"You're still hesitant to make a baby?" she asked.

He stroked wisps of hair from her cheeks and nodded.

"Then, even now, you're afraid for our future?"

"Yes, because I know now for certain that there's absolutely no way to prove that Berry is Rachel's child."

A shiver passed down her spine, as if a cloud passed over the sun. Sarah pulled away to look at him. "Yet you still believe you can take him from the earl?"

He tugged her back into his embrace and pressed his lips to

her hair. "Of course. I just don't know how high a price may be exacted."

"Whatever it is, we must pay it."

"Do you really mean that?"

Sarah nodded.

"At whatever cost to us?"

"Yes, of course. Why do you ask?"

His fingers stroked gently along the back of her neck. "Because Lady Moorefield claims to have given birth at the Hall helped only by her own women, so no local midwife was in attendance. A doctor from London was called to assist, but he arrived too late—by design, obviously. He found the new mother a little tired from her ordeal, and the baby already at the breast of a wet nurse."

"This doctor made no examination?"

"According to the servants' gossip, both mother and child were glowing with health. So the doctor refrained from imposing on Her Ladyship's modesty. Instead, he joined the earl to toast his new heir and returned home."

"All of which could have been arranged ahead of time," Sarah said. "Were none of the servants suspicious?"

"The lower staff believe she was genuinely with child, and Her Ladyship's personal women will be absolutely loyal. Two of them have been with her since she was born. Thus, all the witnesses would only swear to every circumstance of the lying-in, and the earl would see me damned for questioning it."

The bit jingled as his horse tossed up its head to stare off into the distance.

Her heart lurched in alarm. Guy leaped to his feet and strode across to the gap in the rocks. Sarah scrambled up to join him.

The Rectory roof glimmered faintly in the valley far beneath them. Rooks wheeled over distant woods. The horse shook its ears and began grazing again.

No one was coming.

Yet Sarah felt filled with foreboding, as if the monster came to life again at the center of the maze.

"Then all we really have is Mrs. Siskin's story?" she asked.

Guy lifted his mount's reins from the bush and gazed out over the shimmering summer. Something close to heartbreak lurked in his eyes.

"I love you," he said. "Whatever comes of all of this in the end, never forget that, Sarah. I love you and only you—deeply, absolutely, and with all my heart and soul—and always will."

MOOREFIELD Hall basked benignly in the sunshine, a beautiful house that deserved to ring with happiness. Sarah's new gown was the most elegant she had ever possessed. The deep blue set off her pale complexion, robbing attention from her freckles to emphasize the smooth, creamy texture of her skin.

While they had all prepared in the grandest inn in Plymouth for their assault on Lord Moorefield, Guy had also produced a lady's maid, who had dressed Sarah's hair into a flattering new style. She knew she looked her best and there was great confidence to be found in that, even when in the presence of her far more beautiful cousin.

Yet Sarah felt only dread.

Radiant in ivory and white, Rachel clung to Sarah's arm. Her blond curls framed her face in breathtaking perfection. She looked fragile, wide-eyed, and innocent—*trailing a broken wing like a ringed plover*—in spite of her obvious underlying excitement and determination.

Elegant and deadly, Guy walked beside them. They were all shown up into a fashionable parlor to wait for His Lordship.

Lady Moorefield already stood at the window. She turned to greet her unexpected guests and give them all a tight smile.

"The earl will be here presently," she said. "Pray, won't you sit? Though if you have business to discuss, Mr. Devoran, it can only be with my husband, surely?"

A vision of masculine perfection, his impeccable coat exactly fitting, his waistcoat a glory of subtle—but ruinously expensive—white-on-white embroidery, Guy bowed over her hand.

"I would never insist that a lady remain in any situation that makes her uncomfortable, Lady Moorefield, especially in her own house. However, while we await the earl, may I convey a message from my aunt?"

The countess glanced up at his face, then folded into a chair. "The Duchess of Blackdown?"

"I understand that Her Grace knew your mother quite well?"

She frowned. "My mama has been with the angels these ten years, sir."

Guy sat down and crossed his legs at the knee. "Nevertheless, the duchess extends an invitation for you to stay at Wyldshay, whenever you might find convenient."

"I must own myself quite startled," Lady Moorefield said. "I had not been aware of the duchess's interest."

"Perhaps because you've not made many friends since your marriage," Guy said blandly. "Also, as it happens, Lady Crowse will be taking her own townhouse throughout the next Season. Should you find the idea appealing, she would enjoy another lady's companionship. In which case, you would never lack for friends or protection."

Lady Moorefield stumbled to her feet, forcing Guy to rise also. "Please offer all appropriate appreciation to the duchess and Lady Crowse for their kind invitations, Mr. Devoran. However, if I wish to stay in London, I may do so with my own family, though I cannot think why anyone should imagine that I should not wish to remain with my husband and our little son."

Guy bowed his head. "As you wish, ma'am."

"What the devil is this about, Devoran? I'm a busy man, sir."

Sarah glanced over her shoulder as Lord Moorefield stalked into the room, his face thunderous.

Guy bowed. "Just a friendly call, my lord. We've just come from

Wyldshay. The duke and duchess convey all that is proper. You re-member Mrs. Callaway, of course?"

Lord Moorefield looked Sarah up and down as she curtsied. "I can't say that I do, sir!"

"Perhaps you didn't notice me, my lord," Sarah said. "I was here with the house party from Buckleigh."

The earl dismissed her with the wave of one hand. "Of course, ma'am. Charmed."

"Mrs. Callaway is a close friend of the St. Georges," Guy said. "This is her sister, Miss Mansard."

Giving the earl an angelic smile, Rachel curtsied. A servant en-tered with wine and cakes. Everyone sat down.

"May I offer my condolences on the unfortunate loss of your gar-dener, Moorefield?" Guy continued. "A skilled man, sadly lost, so I hear, in a local brawl?"

The earl leaned back comfortably in his chair. "Killed by rev-enue officers, sir, as you've no doubt already heard. There's not a man in Devon that doesn't take part in the local trade. Impossible to stop them, I'm afraid."

Guy stared vacantly at the wine in his glass. "Then Croft has taken many secrets to the grave with him."

"Secrets, sir?"

"So I understand," Guy said mildly. "Though nothing, fortu-nately, that's lost forever."

Lord Moorefield stared at his guest's impassive face. "I don't imagine for one moment that this is a simple social call, Devoran—"

He broke off as Rachel leaped up and dropped her plate, scatter-ing cake across the carpet. She lifted her chin like an avenging angel, a vision of gold-and-white fury.

"No, it's not! Mr. Croft stole my baby and gave him to you, and I demand to have him back."

Sarah caught Rachel's hand. The countess set her plate on a side table, her fingers shaking, but Moorefield threw back his head and laughed.

"So the St. Georges befriend madwomen now! Who is this creature, Devoran?"

"I'm the baby's real mother," Rachel insisted. "That's why we're here, to get him back, however much you try to claim him as Lord Berrisham."

"Rachel!" Sarah tugged hard, and her cousin sat down, her face mutinous. "Don't!" she whispered. "You promised!"

Ignoring the ladies, the earl took a delicate bite of cake, then shook crumbs from his fingers. "You support this unfortunate woman in her outrageous claims, Devoran?"

Guy stared absently at the ceiling, though a small muscle had tightened in his jaw. "Since they are true, yes, of course."

"Hah! I'm not sure whether to dismiss this as an inappropriate jest, or call you out. The charge is obviously preposterous!"

"I wish that were so," Guy said. "Of course, all the direct witnesses—Croft, who paid for and stole the baby; Mrs. Medway, the midwife who delivered him; your wife's maids, who concealed her false pregnancy—are all either sadly deceased or loyal to the point of death."

"You're mad, sir!" Moorefield surged to his feet. "You insult me to my face in my own home?"

Guy leaned back and stretched out his legs. "I also, unfortunately, insult your wife, so you may be certain that I would never bring such charges without proof."

"There is no proof," the earl replied with deadly calm. "Furthermore, in spite of your care in reminding me of your illustrious relatives, you would be wise to remember that Fratherham is my wife's father, and I'm a peer of this realm." He snapped his fingers in Guy's face. "I can break you like this."

"Dear me," Guy said.

Moorefield flushed with anger and stalked away. "I'm also at a loss to know why you would take any interest in this chit's wild claims, except perhaps from some personal malice toward me. Out of jealousy?"

"Over your orchid collection?" Guy asked lazily. "Or over your happy circumstances in life?"

Moorefield struck one fist into the other. Sarah held her breath. *Guy wants this! He wants the earl to lose his temper!*

Yet Rachel tore her fingers from Sarah's grasp and flung herself into Guy's arms, forcing him to explode from his chair to catch her.

Sagging dramatically in his embrace, Rachel turned to face the earl. She looked magnificent: beautiful, wronged, all fragile porcelain and gold, her hair a gilt halo against Guy's dark jacket.

"You don't understand, Lord Moorefield," she said. "Mr. Devoran is my baby's father."

CHAPTER SEVENTEEN

ILENCE SHOCKED THROUGH THE ROOM AS IF AN EARTHQUAKE had struck. Sarah flinched. Huge, blinding birds dived at her head and tore pecking into her heart. Yet nothing moved, except for Guy helping a white-faced Rachel to a seat.

"Berry is Mr. Devoran's son," she repeated. "We were cruelly parted, but we're to be married now and the wedding's to be held at Wyldshay at Christmas. You cannot gainsay the claim of the baby's real father, Lord Moorefield."

The earl sat down, his face white. "Is this true, sir?"

Guy glanced down at him and smiled. "Alas, truth is a strange commodity, though my wedding arrangements are not quite so precisely arranged as yet."

"Then you do not deny it," the earl said. "Yet you can hardly—"

"Yes, he can," Rachel interrupted. "Though I was his mistress, I cannot be ashamed of it. Even my cousin knows it. Look at her! You'll see the truth of what I say in her face."

The earl gazed at Sarah for a moment, while her heart pounded. Then he sat back, arms folded, and laughed.

"So I perceive, ma'am."

As if ceding the field, Guy strode away to the window. Dark and elegant, he stood quietly gazing out. Rachel dropped her head into both hands and started to weep.

"Good God!" Moorefield said. "Tears!"

Furious, devastated, Sarah walked over to her cousin and sat next to her. Rachel took her proffered handkerchief and sobbed quietly into the little square of cotton.

There's a child at the heart of all of this, Sarah reminded herself, *an innocent little boy!*

Still laughing, the earl poured himself more wine. "So your mistress comes to you with a wild tale of losing your little bastard. I'm amazed that you would choose to marry such a careless chit, sir. But I will certainly not give up my son based on such bizarre speculations."

Guy spoke over his shoulder with icy precision. "You will not—however tempted you may feel—insult Miss Mansard. It is not my wish to meet you at dawn, Moorefield, but I will if you insist."

His face still creased by his grin, the earl pushed to his feet and marched up to the fireplace, where he stood with his hands clasped behind his back.

"Then as I guessed, sir, you cannot answer me and I believe we've said enough. You'll be pleased to leave my house before this absurdity gets out of hand, and you may take your two harlots with you."

Guy stared casually out through the glass. "You will, in particular, not insult Mrs. Callaway. You may feel secure in your claim to the child, but the grave often speaks in unexpected ways."

The countess shivered. "No! How can you prove anything?"

Guy turned and smiled at her with what looked like real kindness. "I regret to embarrass you, Lady Moorefield, but such are the vagaries of fate. The midwife's sister wrote out a complete account of what happened."

The earl guffawed. "A forgery, if such a document even exists! You'll have to do better than that, sir, before you attempt to steal my son."

"This sister lives," Guy said.

"But the midwife herself is dead, and any of a thousand dockside bawds would tell a lie for three shillings."

"I did not mention," Guy said quietly, "anything about the midwife's sister's location. And we stray, most unfortunately, into dangerous ground once again. If you imply that I would pay for false witness, you impugn my honor far more than I intend to insult yours."

"Nonsense! You have no proof worth discussing, Devoran, and you know it." The earl tugged hard at the bell cord. "If you persist in this gibberish, we may indeed name our seconds and I shall kill you."

Guy bowed. "It's to your credit, my lord, that you haven't tried murder thus far—unless Croft's untimely death was not a coincidence, after all? However, I don't believe we'll need to resort to violence, or not quite yet. I can prove that this lady is the child's mother, and I don't believe you would wish the world to know the whole story by indulging in anything as public as a duel."

Sarah pressed her hand to her mouth. She felt ill. *He's bluffing. He's bluffing. No one will believe Mrs. Siskin or Rachel, and Lord Moorefield will call Guy out and kill him.*

"And it *is* all nonsense!" Lady Moorefield, her skin chalk white, pointed one trembling finger at Rachel. "Lord Berrisham will be an earl one day, but this woman would publicly brand him a bastard, instead? What mother would rob her own child of such an inheritance?"

Rachel looked up, her lovely hands clenched into fists, her face stained by tears. "I would, because Moorefield Hall isn't my baby's true birthright; Birchbrook is!" She glanced toward Guy. "Mr. Devoran's inheritance isn't entailed. He can leave it in any way that he wishes."

The earl raised a brow. "That so, Devoran?"

Sarah gulped down a fierce pain. *He must have told Rachel this in Hampstead—*

Yet Guy's eyes remained quiet and dark. "Yes, as it happens, but if we're to fall back on the judgment of Solomon, there's a far better test than the wealth or position the child may inherit." He flashed a bright smile as if to share a wicked joke. "Though that might be quite soon, should either of us die in a merry little meeting at dawn."

The earl chortled. "So what the devil do you have in mind, sir? Shall we threaten to cut the child in two with a sword?"

"No," Guy said. *"Bring him in here and let him choose his own mother."*

"No!" Rachel cried faintly. "He's not to be frightened!"

"Ah," the earl said. "Thus speaks true maternal devotion, or are you afraid of the test, ma'am?"

A footman appeared at the door. "You rang, my lord?"

"You will show these persons to their carriage," the earl said. "But first you will instruct Miss Davy to bring Lord Berrisham in here without delay."

His face impassive, the footman bowed. "Very good, my lord."

Guy strode back to Lord Moorefield. "The child is not to be frightened or coerced. You agree?"

"Why not? The test will only demonstrate to the persons gathered in this room that you've completely lost your mind."

"Nevertheless," Guy said. "We shall try the experiment."

The room lapsed into silence, until a tentative knock sounded at the door. The earl called out permission to enter. Betsy Davy walked in, leading little Lord Berrisham by the hand.

She glanced at the assembled company, then bit her lip and curtsied to the earl. "Yes, my lord?"

He ignored the nursemaid and spoke to the child. "You see three ladies in this room, sir. One of them is your mother. You will please go to her."

The little boy's mouth quivered and he buried his face in the nurse's skirts.

"He's afraid!" Rachel gave Guy a pleading glance. "Don't you see! He's afraid!"

Guy shook his head at her, walked up to the little boy, and crouched down.

"It's all right, Berry," he said quietly. "You don't need to do anything and no one's going to hurt you, but perhaps there's a lady in this room that you'd like to have tell you a story, or sing you a song?"

His eyes derisive, the earl stalked back to his chair, where he sat down, legs crossed, and tossed back more wine.

"A charming scene," he said. "Solomon wasn't nearly inventive enough!"

Betsy Davy picked up the child and whispered soothingly to him. Berry looked round-eyed around the room, then he smiled and pointed at Sarah.

"Lion!"

The nurse laughed nervously and set him down. The child toddled forward a few steps, then ran straight up to Sarah to grasp hold of her skirts.

"Lion!"

Sarah glanced up at Guy and bit her lip, but the little boy had already turned toward Rachel. He held up both chubby arms and an angelic smile lit up his face.

"Mama! Mama *skween*! Song! Song! Berry up!"

Meeting his smile with her own, Rachel lifted the toddler onto her lap. As if oblivious to anyone else, she began singing softly in her baby's ear. His golden curls were exactly the same shade as her own.

Lady Moorefield wavered to her feet, then collapsed back to her chair. "It's true!" she wailed. "It's true! I cannot have children of my own. I cannot!" Her face crumpled and her eyes filled with tears. "But my maid discovered that Croft's half brother was married to a midwife—and in a port city, too, where babies often die in the poorhouse. Why shouldn't I save one of them? So I paid Croft to move here from Barristow Manor. I paid everyone to keep silent—"

The earl was towering over his wife, his face thunderous. "You've said quite enough, ma'am!"

"No!" The countess flinched, but she pointed a shaking finger at Berry. "It's too late for that, sir! Look at them!"

Guy caught Sarah's gaze and gestured with a quick tilt of his head. She reined in her own emotions, nodded, and spoke quietly in Rachel's ear.

"Go! Take Berry outside. He doesn't need to hear any more of this."

Rachel looked up, her face pale but composed. Still crooning in her baby's ear, she carried him from the room. The nurse gazed after them, but she bit her lip and stayed.

Lady Moorefield stared up at her husband with a desperate defiance, her eyes swimming with tears. "No, they must understand, sir! If they understand, they'll see that we've been in the right all along, and they'll leave the boy with us."

For a moment Sarah thought the earl might strike his wife. Instead, he stalked away and stood in rigid silence, while the countess continued.

"That child's had everything of the best, Mr. Devoran. Croft kept him happy on the journey with a rag dipped in brandy, until we hired a stout, healthy wet nurse with five sons of her own. I told her that I'd tried to nurse him myself and failed. Imagine my humiliation!" She wrung her hands together. Tears streamed openly down her face. "I even hired that girl—Betsy Davy—to be with him day and night. Don't you see? He's had everything a child could want!"

"But he was a helpless infant," Sarah said, "and you took him from his *mother*."

Lady Moorefield dabbed at her eyes. "So? If I hadn't, he'd have died from neglect. Now he'll be an earl."

"No, I'm sorry," Guy said gently. "He's going to leave now and go to Wyldshay with his mother. You'll forgive me, I trust, if I also steal his nursemaid? You will come with us, Betsy?"

Betsy Davy curtsied. She looked shocked to the core, but determined. "Yes, sir, I thank you. I'd not be parted from that little mite for all the tea in China."

"No," the countess said. "You must let me keep him!"

The earl brought his fist down on the table. The tray slid to the floor, shattering glasses and plates.

"Keep him *now*, madam? With the Blackdowns knowing the truth! Are you mad?" He spun about and flung out one arm to point toward the door. "Take him, Devoran, and get out! For God's sake, it's obvious the brat's no son of mine! His blood's tainted. He was born in squalor. In the end he'd only have disgraced my name and my title. So take your whores and your bastard, sir, and get out of my house!"

Guy nodded to Betsy Davy, who fled the room. He offered Sarah his arm. "You have my word of honor, my lord, that no hint of this incident will ever escape this house. When the Earl of Moorefield tells the world that his little son has died unexpectedly, I can assure you he'll be the recipient of society's condolences, not its censure."

The earl's mouth twisted in a sneer. "I'm supposed to be grateful for that?"

Guy's dark eyes held only sorrow, yet his voice was calm and emotionless. "I merely point out what's in everyone's best interest. There is, unfortunately, also the potential for a very damaging scandal to leak out about certain gentlemen in this area being a little too deeply involved in the local trade."

Lord Moorefield scowled and dropped back to his chair. "You also accuse me of smuggling, sir?"

"You and Norris and Whiddon," Guy replied blandly. "A little embarrassing should that become too widely known—especially when you Tories set such store by the law!"

Lady Moorefield bent down to pick up a china figurine—slightly chipped now—that had been standing on the table. She was crying in soft little hiccups.

"For God's sake!" the earl snapped. "Don't pretend a grief you don't feel, madam! It's bad enough that I married a barren woman, without her making a spectacle of herself."

Guy led Sarah toward the door, but he paused with his hand on the latch.

"And one last thing. If, after a decent interval, Lady Moorefield decides to live apart from you, but does so from any cause other than her own whim, my aunt will know about it."

"You'd also rob me of my wife?" the earl asked.

"No, sir, because that's not within my power, only yours. However, if you should ever feel bereft of a legitimate heir, you might remember that your brother and his sons also carry your father's blood."

The earl's lip curled and he stretched out his legs. "Then we'll plan on a family reunion at Wyldshay, when Lady Moorefield and I come to your wedding."

"Alas," Guy said. "You forget: You'll be in mourning for your little son, and I fear that my nuptials are likely to be postponed—"

"No!" Lady Moorefield leaped up. "No! I won't see Berry raised as a bastard, not after all I've done. I won't! You must marry that poor girl, Mr. Devoran, and at Wyldshay with the whole world to witness it. Otherwise, I'll renege on everything I just said and I'll tell everyone that a hysterical madwoman stole my baby. Then she'll be hanged, and if you breathe a word, the earl will indeed call you out and kill you."

"Alas," Guy said. "What a very uncomfortable threat, ma'am! After all, His Lordship is a far better shot than I am."

Lord Moorefield spun to his feet and snatched the figurine from his wife's fingers. He crushed it in his fist, tossed aside the pieces, and stalked up to Guy.

"I don't really believe, Devoran, that you're any more that by-blow's father than I am, and I'm damned sure that you cannot prove it." He pulled out a handkerchief and wiped a trace of blood from his hand. "As for your charge of smuggling, you may have the backing of Wyldshay, but Fratherham will see you ruined and Blackdown be damned. Thus, you will indeed be pleased to give that child the legal protection of your name, sir, or I swear on my honor I shall recover him—simple enough when his mother is nothing but a harlot—and he may grow old in my pigsties!"

Sick fear enveloped Sarah as she clutched hard at Guy's arm. He set his palm firmly over her hand.

"Wyldshay has its own pigsties, my lord," he said. "However, the child is indeed mine to safeguard, so you may look forward to reading next week's newspapers."

He bowed his head. The door shut behind them. They were out in the hallway. Guy supported Sarah with an arm around her waist as he led her down the stairs. Whiteness filled her head. Her legs felt flayed.

Sunlight blinded her as they stepped out into the courtyard where Guy's coach was waiting. Sarah pulled away from him and leaned against a tall marble pillar beside the grand entrance. The sweet summer day seemed to mock her.

"What have we done?" she asked faintly.

His boots crunched on the gravel as he strode away a few steps. "We have rescued Berry, Sarah."

"But how could you—? Did you plan for Rachel to do that?"

"Do what? Trap me into offering for her? I'd certainly guessed that she might make whatever wild claims she hoped would foster her cause. She just took it one step further than I expected."

A frantic fear battled beneath her ribs. "Then how could you risk it?"

"Because we had no real proof, and Moorefield knew it. Mrs. Siskin wouldn't stand by her story for a moment if she were threatened. Playing on emotions was our only hope." He stared away into the distance. "You didn't believe Rachel, did you?"

"That you're the real father? No! Yet you didn't deny it."

Guy slammed his fist into the other side of the pillar. "How the devil could I?"

"But how dare you risk Berry like that?"

His gaze filled with shadows and ghosts. "I don't believe that I did so any more than was absolutely essential."

Sarah yanked her bonnet ribbons into a tight bow beneath her chin. The sickness still hammered at her skull, blinding her, but a white dread burned her heart.

"The earl really could make good on his threat?"

He spun about, ignoring his scraped knuckles. "Yes! Yes, of course! The countess rejected my offer of a way out, and the man's a mortal enemy. He's a bloody earl, for God's sake! Even without the aid of his father-in-law, he'd be formidable. With it—simply for political reasons—the Blackdowns would be forced to back down. Wyldshay's already been weakened by Ryder's marriage to Miracle."

The fear intensified, filling her with anger and madness. One of her ribbons tore away in her fingers. Sarah threw it aside.

"Yet in a test of love, not even Solomon chanced the infant," she insisted. "That's the whole point of those stories. And your cruel little test could have gone wrong so very easily. Berry's known Lady Moorefield all of his short life. What if he'd chosen her, instead of Rachel? There was no telling what he might do! He's just a baby."

"I am," Guy said with icy control, "well aware of that. In fact, I thought it was the crux of the whole issue." He glanced down at his scraped hand. "As it was, it was a risk I simply had to take, though it was less hazardous than you may have feared. Rachel was coming here every chance she could get, ever since she fled Goatstall Lane. She's been singing to Berry in the gardens, the same song every time. She sang it to me."

The pain intensified in Sarah's heart and she closed her eyes. "After I'd gone to bed and left you alone together?"

He seized her arm and forced her to face him. "Yes, Sarah! I told you that Rachel and I had talked. There's no conspiracy against you."

She pulled away, holding onto the rage, because if she stopped being angry she might die of grief.

"No, but it was madness to rely on it! Rachel had met Berry only while she was dressed as a man. He was confused and scared. He almost chose me."

Guy stalked past her to the waiting coach and flung open the door. "Yet he didn't! What difference would clothes ever make to a child still in short skirts? Fortunately, Rachel always sang the same ditty. She's crooning it right now."

Sarah looked around. Rachel and Betsy Davy were hurrying around the house. The nursemaid was carrying a small box, presumably containing her few personal possessions. Berry's golden head lolled on Rachel's shoulder. Her baby had fallen asleep in her arms.

The words floated toward them on the breeze:

> *Hush-a-bye, baby, in cradle of green!*
> *Papa's a nobleman; mama's a queen;*
> *Sister's a lady who wears a gold ring;*
> *And brother's a drummer who drums for the king.*

Berry stirred in his sleep and murmured. "Mama *skween*."

Sarah gazed at the child's golden head, and her anger collapsed into an abyss of grief, inexorable and vast.

"Dammit, Sarah!" Guy's voice held nothing now of anger, only anguish. "Do you think for one moment that I'm not aware of all the implications of that pretty little scene upstairs?"

"I know, I know," she said quietly as her heart shattered. "I know we'll never hear back from d'Alleville, but I agreed—in fact, I insisted—that whatever the price, we must pay it."

"Even this?"

She glanced into his eyes. "Yes, Guy, even this!"

"Then honor has demanded its due," he replied with terrifying calm. "And justice, at least, will be satisfied."

Rachel and Betsy walked up. Berry, fast asleep once again, sagged heavily in his mother's arms.

"Thank you, Guy," Rachel said with a quiet new dignity. "You didn't really mind what I said upstairs, did you? After all, none of that will matter once Claude comes for me. So where are we going now?"

Sarah met Guy's dark gaze for one stark moment. Like hers, his sorrow had intensified into real pain.

"To Wyldshay," she said, holding out her arms to take the baby, so that Guy could help Rachel climb into the carriage. "Guy will take you and Berry to stay with Lady Ryderbourne and the duchess, and on the way you'll leave me in Exeter, where I shall catch the next coach back to Bath."

*   *   *

FOR the first time in his twenty-eight years, Guy rode up to Birch-brook without unqualified joy.

His father's rambling brick home fronted onto a courtyard shaded by a stand of tall trees in full, glorious green leaf. At the back of the house the remains of the moat had been filled in long ago by his great-grandfather, a younger son of the first Earl of Yelverton, in order to plant a formal garden and shrubbery. Then his grandfather had added the orangery, where his father and sister now grew their exotic plants.

Meanwhile, the title had passed to the first earl's eldest son, Thomas Devoran, and then through his second son to the present fourth earl. The third earl had died with no sons, only daughters: the Duchess of Blackdown and Guy's mother, Lady Bess Devoran.

No one was in the parlor, so Guy strode into the hothouse. Her dark hair dressed in a simple knot, his sister sat surrounded by greenery, reading.

"The latest novel?" he asked. "Dare I interrupt?"

Lucinda tossed aside her book and threw herself laughing into his arms.

Guy kissed her and admired her new frock, then suppressed his burning sense of urgency while she showed him the new additions to her orchid collection. Whatever the state of his heart, he would always give Lucinda his undivided attention.

Why should his troubles be allowed to spoil her pleasure in his unexpected homecoming, or his in being with her?

"Ah, Guy, it's so good to see you," she said at last. "But of course you want to see Father. He's down at the home farm, poking about with Foster and some new spotted pigs. Though unless you fetch some gaiters, you'll ruin those boots, because it rained yesterday and the Birch Brook overflowed its banks again."

He kissed the top of her head. "Not to worry, it's time I gave these boots a taste of the real country. So please tell Cook there'll be a third at dinner, while I'll wade down through the mire to marvel at Foster's latest litter."

Lucinda giggled and hugged him again, then ran off to see to her duties as lady of the house. Guy stared after her for a moment. Fine-boned, beautiful, and painfully young, she'd be going to London for her first season next Spring and no doubt be engaged within three months.

Henry Devoran was deep in conversation with Mr. Foster, master of the pigsties, but he glanced up at the sound of squelching boots and his face lit up like a lamp. Father and son threw their arms around each other. As Henry pounded Guy heartily on the back, Foster touched his hat, bowed, and walked away.

"Look at this, sir!" With one arm still linked in his son's, Henry waved a hand at the animals rooting about in their pen. "Now, there's pigs for you!"

Guy laughed. "The handsomest shoats I ever saw in my life, sir."

"Best in the Home Counties!" His father dragged Guy over to another sty. "Take a look at this sow!"

"A beauty, sir, but I fear that I didn't come down here to talk about swine, or at least, not directly."

Henry gave him a shrewd glance. "Very well, sir! Out with it!"

Guy turned his back on the sow to meet his father's open gaze. "I came to tell you that my engagement to marry at Wyldshay this Christmas will be announced in the newspapers next week."

"Good God, boy!" The pig grunted as Henry grabbed Guy's hand and shook it. "Then I must congratulate you! But Wyldshay? Why not right here in your own home? Don't tell me! The girl's that high-and-mighty? What d'ye do, sir? Nab a German princess?"

"No. Nothing like that." Guy guided the older man toward a stone mounting block. "Please sit down, Father, and listen carefully. Miss Rachel Mansard is a gentleman's daughter from Norfolk. However, it's my most earnest desire that she will jilt me long before the wedding."

Henry Devoran sat down with a thump. "Well, sir! If you wished to leave me speechless, you've done so. You'd better explain yourself."

Guy paced the flagstones, telling his father just enough while trying to distress him as little as possible, then stood with his hands locked behind his back.

"So though you never intended marriage or declared yourself, you allowed this young lady to form expectations? You made promises you now feel obliged to keep?"

"Yes, sir. There's also the child to consider."

Henry mopped at his brow with a handkerchief. "Though he's not yours? So you hope to provide grounds for this Miss Mansard to jilt you with no loss of honor to anyone?"

"That's my sincerest wish, yes."

Guy's father slumped into himself, as if he had aged ten years. The pigs snuffled about in their pens.

"You know how very much I loved your mother, sir. I've never looked at another woman since the day that she died." He glanced up and blinked away a trace of moisture. "You're just like her."

"Yes, I remember her."

"You know I'll support you, Guy, in whatever you wish. Yet what if this Miss Mansard doesn't cry off—?"

"Then I'll be obliged to go through with the wedding, of course."

Henry pursed his mouth as if he swallowed grief. "Not even Wellington could escape a similar situation, though it's well known that he never really loved his wife. I just never thought to see my only son trapping himself into a loveless marriage."

"I hope most sincerely that it won't come to that, sir," Guy said. "But if it does, you have my word of honor that I shall never deliberately bring pain to her. I will not ignore her while I follow other interests, nor entertain a mistress, while abandoning her alone in the country. Rachel may always count on my civility and courtesy—"

"Though not your love?"

"No. She knows that."

"Then how can you promise that neither of you won't find love elsewhere?"

"She may, but I shan't."

Henry Devoran stood up and grabbed his son by the arm. "You cannot promise that, sir!"

Guy smiled at him. "Yes, I can, because I love another lady just as deeply and absolutely as you loved Mama, and shall till the day that I die. Yet if I marry Rachel, this other lady and I will not see each other privately ever again."

"Then I foresee tragedy," his father said quietly. "And you'll break your heart, just as surely as you're breaking mine."

GUY leaned both hands on the medieval parapet at the top of the Fortune Tower and gazed out across the Blackdown estates. Woods and fields stretched away toward the distant Channel, where breakers beat steadily at the cliffs.

Sarah had not written. Neither had he, except for the short note that still lay in his pocket.

A group of figures crawled along one of the paths far below: Rachel and Miracle with their babies, two of Ryder's young sisters, and a retinue of nursemaids and footmen.

He could not, for the first time in years, confide the depth of his feelings to Miracle. She was still very dear to his heart, but she, too, was a mother. She, too, would put any baby's happiness ahead of her own, and expect the people she loved to do the same.

Guy dropped his forehead onto his folded hands and closed his eyes. The temptation to cast honor to the wind and ride hell-for-leather to Bath hurt like a burn, yet he knew exactly what Sarah would say.

"We're not free."

In the privacy of his room the previous evening, he had filled sheet after sheet with the distraught contents of his soul, then just as carefully burned them. It would only be a cruelty to commit to the impersonal post such a reminder of what they risked losing. Neither of them wished to bring the other that much anguish, and words were anyway unnecessary. Yet he had led his first true love straight into disaster.

Alas, alas, he had—in what now seemed like another lifetime—made Rachel a solemn vow on his honor that he would protect her for as long as she might ever need him. And she needed him now. Worse, the innocent child might need him forever.

Even if he seized Sarah and carried her off to the Antipodes, they could not build a future together on the ruins of that baby's life.

So in the end he had written her just two lines: *Beloved, I leave Wyldshay today to do what I can. If I fail, you know exactly what is in my heart and always will—G.D.*

As if they drowned together in the cold Atlantic, they might each cling to this one last straw—that he would find Claude d'Alleville alive and bring him back—even though they were both almost certain that it was a wild-goose chase.

He would never forget his father's face as Henry Devoran realized the extent of the trap that his only son had woven for himself, but at least Guy did not have to face the distressed gaze of his elder cousin, a man whose natural chivalry was inseparable from his soul. Of course, Ryder would understand, yet he would be equally pessimistic about the likely outcome. So it was fortunate that he was away, seeing to business in another part of the far-flung empire of the duchy.

Meanwhile, Jack was basking in the quiet company of his wife and new baby daughter in his own home at Withycombe. However painful it might prove, Guy would visit Jack and Anne before he left for France, even knowing that it would be impossible to hide the truth. Instead, he would have to rely on the depth of their love for him, and trust that they would not trespass any further than he could bear.

So only his aunt, the duchess, remained, with her clear green gaze, as penetrating as that of any goddess.

"Good heavens!" she had said when Guy's carriage had first arrived from Devon, bringing her such unlikely guests. The mildest of reproofs. Yet it was always impossible to escape the challenge of her cool assessment.

Footsteps shuffled behind him. Guy glanced around.

"The carriage is ready, sir," the footman said.

Guy ran down the spiral stairs to take the shortcut through the rose garden. As he reached the wrought-iron gate it swung open.

The duchess's leaf-green eyes darkened to forest shadows in the shade of her parasol. Her gaze flickered over his clothes: designed for fast traveling, not fashion.

"You have taken it for granted that I will cooperate in your plans for this imprudent marriage, Guy." She walked away a few steps. "Do you think I will do so without exacting the truth for a reckoning?"

He bowed and fell into step beside her. "What truth do you seek, Your Grace?"

"I seem to be in the habit of arranging unsuitable marriages for the young men in my life," she said. "Firstly, for my beloved sons, and now for my equally beloved nephew. However, this time there would appear to be neither social advantage, nor true love, though there is already a child. Charming, but a bastard. And, I fear, not even yours?"

Guy took the parasol from her hand and held it to shade her face as she bent to inhale the scent of some roses.

"Perhaps, but either way it's of no consequence. If I return from this journey alone, I will marry his mother."

She took back her parasol and turned away. "Even if I have no desire to be complicit in arranging a catastrophe?"

"If Rachel and I must marry, I promise to maintain as loving and civil a match as I can manage."

The green gaze had never been easy to read and now it was entirely opaque. "Ah, yes! For the sake of the child."

"Berry is the only innocent party in all of this. And, unfortunately, the Earl of Moorefield, with the most extreme of the Tories at his tail, has an interest in the outcome."

"You believe that this wedding will poke a stick in Moorefield's eye? Then you are fortunate, sir, that he is an old enemy of mine."

Guy plucked a red rose that she couldn't quite reach and gave it to her. *"Enemy?"*

She held the flower up to the sun to admire it. Light soaked into the petals like blood.

"The earl has been cruel since childhood. No dog, horse, or servant was ever safe in his hands. Why else would I have agreed to tolerate his wife here as my guest, if necessary?"

"Yet she wouldn't leave him," Guy said.

"Of course not. She fears that he, or her father, will kill her if she does."

"Then you must agree that I had to remove the child from his grasp, irrespective of the cost."

Twirling the rose in her fingers, the duchess strolled away along the path. "I am not sentimental about children, sir, yet I am very fond of you."

"So you will arrange the wedding?"

"If you are so determined to sacrifice your own happiness." The summer afternoon heat beat down, trapped by the encircling stone walls. "And not only your happiness, I fear," the duchess continued. "There is another lady, is there not?"

"Yes."

Long ivory ribbons trembled against her gown. "With whom you are quite desperately and very seriously in love?"

"Yes."

"And her impulse to protect this child from the earl's wrath equally overrides her attachment to you?"

"Yes, it does. It must. We freely make the same choice. We could not build a future together on Rachel's unhappiness and her baby's destruction."

"Then your journey is Mrs. Callaway's last hope," the duchess said. "Though I fear that you do not in truth expect a happy outcome?"

"No," Guy said, "and she knows it, but I must try."

His mother's sister tucked the rose into his jacket pocket, and touched him briefly on the cheek.

"Then Godspeed, Guy!" she said quietly. "If I must arrange a wedding, I would far rather it was for the correct bride."

He bowed, kissed her hand, and strode away.

SARAH came in from her walk and removed her wet bonnet. She had been soaked by a sudden thunderstorm. Strands of damp hair coiled miserably on her neck. She caught a glimpse of herself in the hall mirror and made a face, determined not to give way to self-pity. Yet the eyes that gazed back at her were haunted.

Guy's note was engraved on her soul: *If I fail, you know exactly what is in my heart and always will.*

As he knew hers.

So there had been no need to trouble him with any more correspondence, especially with half of France between them.

His absence filled her heart with a wrenching pain, infected with the dread that—despite his best efforts—their parting would be forever. Yet, while her days were racked by fear, her nights were tormented by memories: of his touch, his smile, his scent, his passion.

If he failed and never came back for her, she would live the rest of her days like a ghost, an empty shell drained of spirit.

"Ah, Mrs. Callaway!" Miss Farcey stepped into the hallway. "You have a visitor—from Wyldshay, no less! Though from His Lordship's manner, I fear it may be bad news. I've shown him into my private study. It won't do to keep— Oh, my! Are you quite well? Pray, sit down for a moment and collect yourself."

Sarah gulped down her sudden sick fear and excitement. Had he come for her? Had something happened?

"No," she said. "Thank you. I am quite well. We mustn't keep this gentleman waiting."

She hurried into the small study, then stopped dead. In the dim light the resemblance was uncanny. Yet she knew Guy's scent in her blood and his touch in her bones. Her hope to see him imploded instantly.

"Lord Jonathan?"

"I didn't mean to startle you, Mrs. Callaway," he said. "Pray, sit down!"

"Miss Farcey feared there was bad news. Is Guy—?"

He caught her by both elbows, then helped her to a seat. "No! As far as I know, my cousin is perfectly well in body, though probably just as sick as you in spirit." His gilt-brown eyes searched her face. "May I ring for some wine, or some tea?"

"No, thank you," Sarah said. "Guy spoke to you about me before he left?"

Lord Jonathan perched one hip on the corner of the desk. "I know that your memory haunts his dreams and persecutes his heart with every breath, as his does yours."

"Please, my lord," she said. "Don't say that! If he and Rachel must indeed marry, he'll never, *never* allow himself to be disloyal to her."

He folded his arms across his chest and stared down at the floor. "Mrs. Callaway, you may think this none of my business, but I'm an expert in noble self-immolation—or at least I used to be, before Anne cured me of such nonsense. Our cousins don't love each other, and they both admit it. Yet Guy has no natural gift for choosing honor over happiness, and he'll despise himself if he fails—"

"He won't fail!" Sarah said.

Lord Jonathan leaped up and rang the bell. A maid answered and he ordered tea.

"No, perhaps not. Yet I believe he has hoped—as you have—that you and he would never need to be tested so sorely."

Sarah smoothed her hair back from her forehead. "Yes, we have hoped that, though all the evidence is to the contrary. Yet if he could persuade Berry's real father—"

"A man named Claude d'Alleville, from the Chateau du Cerf in the Dordogne?"

Sarah began to long for the tea. Her mouth tasted like a desert, and she still felt faint and sick, but she nodded.

"Guy wrote to him there while we were still in Devon," she said. "Why? Is there an answer?"

With a soft rap at the door a maid arrived with the tea tray. While the girl bustled in, Sarah studied Lord Jonathan's face. A new, unnamed fear threatened to engulf her, as if she stared into the heart of tragedy, but he turned and strode away to the window.

He waited there quietly until the maid left and Sarah had poured tea, then he walked back, took her cup, and stirred in plenty of sugar.

"Here," he said. "Drink this!"

Sarah sipped at the strong, sweet tea, while dread stalked her heart. "Rachel writes to me every week about the child," she said desperately. "And sounds well enough in herself, but—from kindness, I think—she never mentions Guy. Of course, she knows what he's doing and where he's gone, and she's absolutely certain that he'll bring Claude d'Alleville back to England to marry her. Though if Guy and I are right in our fears, Guy cannot stop this marriage, Lord Jonathan, and I will not."

"I understand," he said quietly.

"But there's no word from Guy?"

"No, he's still somewhere in France. Meanwhile, Miracle and Ryder have left with our sisters for Wrendale in Derbyshire. They won't return for several weeks. The duke is in London, and my mother is still staying at Withycombe with Anne and me—"

Alarm surged through Sarah's veins. Her teacup clattered into the saucer. "So Rachel's at Wyldshay alone, and there's bad news from France? Monsieur d'Alleville repudiates both her and the child?"

"No, it's not that. I'm sorry. I stopped at Wyldshay this morning on quite other business, only to find that the letter Guy wrote in Devon was returned unopened two days ago. Your cousin was in the hall when it arrived. No one could prevent her seeing what was scrawled across the outside—"

"On the cover?"

His eyes were dark with compassion. "I regret that I cannot soften this, Sarah, but Claude d'Alleville is dead."

Sarah pressed her palm to her mouth. An agonizing rush of tears burned her eyes and closed her throat. A faint, faraway screaming filled her ears, though she sat locked in an absolute silence.

Lord Jonathan sat beside her to put one arm about her shoulders.

"I'll do whatever I can," he said gently. "This news is a terrible blow, I know, the death of all your hopes. I already sent for Anne and my mother, but I thought you'd also want to go to your cousin."

"Yes, yes, of course." Sarah wiped her eyes. "What's happening now?"

"She locked herself into her room and is refusing all food and drink. Betsy Davy is taking care of the child, but the windows are shuttered and barred, and the servants fear that Rachel may injure herself. I would have broken down the door, but I thought perhaps—"

"No, no, I'll come right away," Sarah said.

"My carriage is waiting outside," Lord Jonathan said. "I'll make your excuses to Miss Farcey."

Sarah clung to his arm as he helped her to her feet. The room had disappeared as if it were filled with white fog.

"He'll get to the Dordogne too late," she said. "As soon as he arrives at the chateau, he'll discover that Claude cannot save us. Then he'll begin to slowly die inside like a plant deprived of water. I don't know if he can . . . But, no, I must think of Rachel—"

"Hush!" he said softly. "The death of hope is very cruel, but Anne will help you as much as she can, and as soon as I've delivered you safely to Wyldshay I'll go after Guy myself."

Sarah swallowed hard and the mist cleared. She no longer felt faint. She felt cold, as if winter's frost had already frozen her blood.

There was no way out now. She would grow old here in Bath, a spinster schoolmistress, who had once known a few glorious weeks in the company of the one extraordinary man to whom she had given her soul—and her body. While he would spend the rest of his days married to Rachel.

"I'm most obliged to you, my lord. I see now why Guy loves you like a brother."

To her surprise Lord Jonathan Devoran St. George, long known to the fashionable world as Wild Lord Jack, took both of her hands and kissed them.

CHAPTER EIGHTEEN

⟡⟡⟡

The door to Rachel's bedroom was solid mahogany. Her gray eyes filled with concern, her pale hair dressed neatly, Anne—Lady Jonathan Devoran St. George—stood quietly to one side as Sarah knelt and called through the keyhole.

She thought she could hear muffled sobbing, but perhaps it was only the sweep of swallows' wings echoing down the chimneys.

In the end Sarah stood aside, her heart racked by dread, as two burly footmen broke down the door, shattering the lock. Anne pressed Sarah's hand briefly, then gathered the servants and took them all away.

The room smelled foul, the air stale with grief. Only one thin shaft of light leaked between the closed shutters. The bed hangings were drawn.

"Go away!" Rachel muttered. "Leave me alone!"

"It's only me," Sarah said. "I'm so sorry, sweeting. Words can't even begin—"

"No! Go away!"

Sarah crossed to the windows, lifted the bars, and threw open the shutters. Yellow light flooded into the room. A litter of torn clothes and broken china lay strewn across the floor.

She walked to the bed and pulled the hangings aside.

Rachel's face was buried in the pillows, her hair a tangled mat.

Sarah swallowed her rush of grief, sat down, and put her arms about her cousin, lifting Rachel's unresisting head onto her lap. She smoothed the fine curls back from the hot forehead, and rocked her as if she were a small child.

"It's all right, Rachel. You're not alone anymore. I'm here now."

"He's dead, Sarah! Claude's dead!"

Her tears burned dryly in her throat. "Yes, I know, dear. My heart breaks."

"I cannot bear it. I don't want to live in a world without him. Everything's gone wrong."

Sarah rocked steadily. "Hush, hush! Yes, I know it seems more than we can bear. Yet we must bear it, because there's Berry to think of and he needs his mama."

Rachel looked up. Her face was blotched, the eyelids swollen. "Claude will never see his baby son now. He loved me, Sarah. I was the love of his life."

"Yes, yes, I know. Of course, he loved you!" *And God please forgive me for the lie!*

"He'd have come for me and Berry and taken us back to France as soon as he'd been able. So Guy went to fetch him, to tell him I was here waiting for him, but now—" Rachel sat up, her face a ruin of sorrow. "Is Berry all right?"

"He's with Betsy," Sarah said. "She's wonderful with him, but you're his mama and he needs you. Do you think Claude would want you to grieve like this, if it meant that his little boy would be left crying for his mother?"

"No, no, and Guy will really have to be his father now," Rachel said. "Or else Lord Moorefield will ruin me and take Berry away."

"Yes, I know. Lord Jonathan has gone to France after Mr. Devoran to bring him back to you."

Rachel wiped her eyes with an already sodden handkerchief. "I know Guy thinks he's in love with you, Sarah, but I can't lose Berry again. I can't!"

"So Guy will marry you at Christmas, just as he promised, and take you back to Birchbrook, where you and your baby will always be safe."

Rachel flung herself back onto the pillows. "I can't help it," she said. "I can't manage alone. I'm not as strong as you are, Sarah. When Mama and Papa died, my whole life came to an end, but I went to Grail Hall and did my very best. How was I to know that I'd meet Claude there and fall in love? But after I thought that my baby was dead, I didn't really care if I lived or died. It was like living in a fog—until that letter came from Mrs. Siskin. But now it's all ruined and I don't have anyone left—"

"Yes, we've lost so much, you and I," Sarah said. "But you'll always have Berry, and Guy Devoran will stand by you forever."

Her cousin looked up, her profile flawless, her eyebrows perfect over her bruised, swollen lids.

"But he doesn't love me, Sarah, and I've only ever really loved Claude."

"So you'll both marry with your hearts torn open by loss. Yet if you treat each other with kindness, in the end you'll find happiness together. Perhaps there'll even be more children."

Rachel grasped Sarah's arm. "I never meant to hurt you. Truly! I was waiting for Claude, and I—"

"It's all right," Sarah said. "It's not your fault. You didn't intend this to happen. None of us did. But Guy will never be forsworn, and he'll love you and be true to you. If you allow it, in time you'll come to love him, too."

"But what will you do?"

Sarah took Rachel's hand and tried to smile, though her heart lay burned to ashes.

"You know how I've always longed to see some different country? Well, I thought I might find a place at a school in Yorkshire, perhaps, or in Scotland."

"But if you go so far away, I'll never see you!"

"Not often, perhaps, but we'll still write." Sarah dredged real compassion from the depths of her heart—for where else could she find comfort now?—and smiled at the cousin she loved. "And you must promise in future to always write the whole truth."

Rachel smiled back with heartbreaking bravado. "I should have told you about Claude when I met him. Yet when we first fell in love it was so overwhelming, and then when we . . . well, I knew you'd be so disappointed and shocked—"

"No, I understand," Sarah said. "Now, it's time you let the maids set this room to rights. Come, let me order you a bath and get you a fresh dress. Berry needs you, and you can't let Guy return from such a sad journey to find his bride still weeping in her bed."

SARAH sank exhausted onto the window seat in her own room. Her eyes burned as she stared out at the remains of the sunset.

I have lost him forever!

Yet Rachel's one great love, Claude d'Alleville, was dead. Guy lived. So how could she allow herself to mourn such a selfish loss in the face of her cousin's far more terrible grief?

At least Rachel would never discover now that her Frenchman had never really loved her. She would never have to recognize that no man who loved a woman would ever have abandoned her for two years and left her to bear their baby alone.

Instead, Rachel would go to her grave believing that Berry's father had always adored her—though she would do so as Guy's wife.

For Sarah's sake and for the sake of his own honor, Guy would do his best to make Rachel happy. Whatever secret passion he might carry in his heart, he was far too fine to allow his heartbreak to damage his marriage.

So he would share his wife's bed and they would inevitably create children together. Eventually his past loves would fade into bittersweet memories—as would Rachel's. Then her letters would fade and eventually fail.

They would all want to avoid any visits.

And in the end, perhaps, Guy would find happiness.

So Sarah must make a new life. For Guy's sake, she would do her best to make it fruitful and fulfilled. Yet as the sinking sun finally plunged her room into shadow, she dropped her head onto both folded arms and wept.

THERE was no word at all from Guy, and only one short, cryptic message from Jack, which Anne read out—*I'm close on Guy's heels. More later!*—buried in his private communication to his wife.

The duke was still in London, though the duchess had returned from Withycombe with Anne and her new baby girl. Miracle and Ryder had offered to come back from Derbyshire, also, but the duchess thought it best that they remain at Wrendale and keep her daughters well removed from the disaster that was unfolding at Wyldshay.

After talking to Sarah, she had written to Miss Farcey, who was most flattered to hear from Her Grace. If the duchess needed Mrs. Callaway at Wyldshay, Miss Farcey was honored to give her botany teacher an extended leave of absence, though she hoped she might be remembered in the future, should Her Grace ever wish to recommend a young ladies' academy to any of her friends.

Meanwhile, Rachel walked through the days like a ghost, incapable of either eating or sleeping, her face gaunt, clinging only to the knowledge that Guy was coming back to marry her. The golden curls became as dry and brittle as straw. Except for her sore, reddened eyelids, Rachel's once perfect skin was like chalk, though two bright crimson spots burned in each cheek.

Sarah choked down her own distress and quietly nursed her stricken cousin. Whenever she could spare the attention from her little baby, Anne assisted her, though the duchess kept her own counsel.

Yet Sarah lay dry-eyed in her room every night, her heart full of longing, her soul winging its message of love to Guy, while she bottled up her own heartache as if she imprisoned demons.

Meanwhile, Berry laughed and played, safe in the care of Betsy Davy. Even Rachel bravely hid from her baby the weight of the grief that had struck her down, finding the courage from somewhere to play happily with him and sing to him. Eventually, she began to talk about her marriage and tell her little son that he was going to have a new father.

Then Sarah knew the agony of discussing the wedding plans.

"Will Guy like me in blue?" Rachel asked one morning. "I've thought of getting a new blue gown with silver ribbons. Her Grace says I may order anything I like, and Claude always liked me in blue."

Yet at the mention of her lover's name Rachel's eyes filled with new tears. Sarah helped her to a seat.

"Guy will take one look at you in any color you care to name and fall in love with you all over again," she said. "Don't think that he didn't love you in Hampstead, Rachel, because I know that he did."

Two tracks of moisture traced down Rachel's cheeks. "You know, you might be struck down by lightning for saying such things, Sarah. I enticed Guy into bed, because otherwise I thought he might not take care of me. Yet Claude—"

Rachel broke down into hysterical sobs, leaving Sarah holding her in both arms, while her own heart was racked by despair.

"Mrs. Callaway?"

Sarah looked up.

A footman stared across the room. "Her Grace requires me to inform you, ma'am, that a carriage is approaching the front entrance at the gallop."

"*Guy!*" Rachel leaped up, picked up her skirts in both hands, and ran off.

For the first time, Sarah's courage failed her absolutely. Her heart had lodged somewhere in her throat. She sat in stark fear staring blindly at the wall, while her heart thundered.

After a few moments Anne came into the room, her eyes clear and calm. She walked up to Sarah, took her hand, and sat quietly beside her.

"You should go down," Sarah said at last. "If Guy's returned, then Lord Jonathan will be with him, and your baby might need—"

"She's sleeping," Anne said. "And Jack will understand."

Sarah smiled at her and forced herself to walk down with Anne into the Great Hall.

Rachel had already followed the duchess out into the courtyard, where two footmen had flung open the great oak doors. A commotion of horses and iron-shod wheels echoed into the castle as a carriage raced up and stopped.

Sarah clung to Anne's hand, but Rachel ran back inside, her face white.

"It's not him!" she said. "It's not Guy's carriage from France. It's Lady Moorefield!"

Anne's fingers closed on Sarah's, steadying her against her desperate rush of grief. Both of them sat down.

With immaculate self-control, the duchess walked back into the room, supporting the countess on her arm. She helped Lady Moorefield to a seat, then walked away to stand at the great fireplace.

The countess sat stiffly beneath a tapestry of St. George and glared defiantly at the duchess. Her face was swollen with bruises. A bloody cut stained one eyebrow. Another cut cracked her lower lip.

"This is what you wanted, isn't it? I've left him."

A green fire burned in the duchess's bright gaze. "Then we offer you the sanctuary and protection of Wyldshay, Countess."

Yet the doors to the courtyard still stood open. Another carriage clattered up. Someone was shouting.

Lady Moorefield cowered back in her seat as her husband strode into the room.

The earl stopped and glanced around, then laughed and slapped his thigh with a riding crop.

"The protection of Wyldshay, Duchess? The duke is not at home, I believe, and neither are your sons or your nephew? I see only five females and two of them weeping. I have every right in law to chastise my wife. Neither you, nor these protégés of yours, can stop me."

Green flames blazed in the emerald eyes. "Several dozen of my menservants are within earshot, Moorefield," the duchess said. "Since the countess is my guest, I advise you not to take another step."

"I can hardly imagine that you will dare to interfere, madam, when I am merely fetching home my own wife." The earl laughed, still slapping his thigh. "No unarmed footman would have the nerve to lay hands on a peer of the realm——"

"Perhaps not, but I, on the other hand, am both armed and dangerous," another man's voice said. "So you will not raise that whip, Moore-field, unless you really wish to give me the excuse to kill you."

Rachel looked up as if the gates to Heaven had just opened. *"Guy!"*

Sarah's heart had skidded to a halt, then lurched into a mad, un-steady rhythm, like a horse galloping over stones. Joy and fear and relief surged through her veins. Yet she sat clutching Anne's hand as if she were frozen.

Guy ignored all of them and walked farther into the room, his dark gaze fixed only on the earl. He was soaked with muck, his boots ruined, his clothes spattered. Even his hair was filthy, falling forward as he threw aside his hat and riding crop. A bone-deep fatigue marked his face, as if he had not slept in weeks.

The duchess lifted her elegant brows. "My dear nephew, what impeccable timing! You chose to return from France on horseback?"

"It was faster."

Moorefield slowly lowered the whip, but his eyes looked mur-derous.

"You should leave, my lord," Guy said quietly. "Even without calling on the footmen, you are outnumbered."

The earl guffawed. "By you, sir—in your present state hardly fit to be called a gentleman? And these females?"

But two more equally bespattered young men strode into the Great Hall.

Lord Jonathan wiped the mud from his face with a handkerchief. His eyes met Anne's for a moment before he walked up to stand beside Guy. His face was equally drawn.

The third man was a stranger. He stalked proudly into the room, removing his gloves as he did so. Unlike the Wyldshay cousins, he was as fair as Adonis, yet bruised shadows circled his red-rimmed eyes.

Rachel promptly fainted. Anne and Sarah ran to kneel beside her.

As if unaware of them, Guy strode up to the earl and took the whip from his hand.

"This gentleman is Lord Moorefield, Jack," he said over his shoulder. "You may remember him from some unfortunate prior encounters in London."

"A long time ago," Lord Jonathan said. "But I'd be happy to kill him for you, if you like."

The blond stranger walked forward. "No," he said with a slight French accent. "The pleasure of killing him is mine."

The earl looked the Frenchman up and down. "Who the devil are you, sir?"

In spite of his obvious exhaustion, the stranger smiled with open menace. "My name is Claude d'Alleville. I am given to understand, sir, that you have persecuted that unhappy young lady." He gestured toward Rachel, now lying insensible in Sarah's arms. "You threatened her and frightened her and drove her into hiding and despair. Your other crimes may be upon your own conscience, but there is also the matter of a child. I intend to kill you, sir, just for that."

The duchess walked forward. "Welcome to Wyldshay, Monsieur. I do so adore all this high drama and vengeance. However, my first duty is to my guests who are already discomposed. You will forgive me, I am sure, if I leave all this unpleasantness to you gentlemen?"

Claude d'Alleville bowed with impeccable grace and kissed her hand.

"Meanwhile, Lady Moorefield is about to accompany me to my

private suite to take tea." The duchess cocked her head as more wheels rattled on the cobbles outside. Another carriage had arrived in the courtyard. "Ah! I suspect that the duke has returned a little earlier than expected. So very fortunate! Good day, sirs."

Lady Moorefield's face remained frozen as the duchess led her away. Two footmen carefully carried Rachel from the room. With unspoken understanding, Anne and Sarah took a seat together in the corner. Lord Jonathan strode across the flagstones to stand beside his wife.

A whirlwind of footmen ran to assist as the Duke of Blackdown stalked in, several other gentlemen trailing behind him. The duke stopped in his tracks. His penetrating gaze coolly assessed the ongoing drama.

And at last Guy glanced at Sarah. She met his tired, burning gaze and tried to smile, but the Frenchman stalked up to Moorefield and slapped him across the face with his wet gloves.

"I demand satisfaction, sir!"

The duke raised his eyebrows. One of the guests at his shoulder murmured softly, "Good Lord!"

"An affair of honor, Your Grace," Lord Jonathan said calmly, walking forward. "Perhaps some of these gentlemen may agree to act for Lord Moorefield? Guy and I will be delighted to offer the same service for Monsieur d'Alleville, of course."

Anne squeezed Sarah's hand. "Come," she said softly. "Apology is impossible now. We must leave this to the men."

Sarah swallowed her sick fear and allowed Anne to lead her from the room.

The duchess met them at the bottom of the stairs. She was a little pale, but her composure was absolute.

"Well?" she asked. "We are to host a duel?"

Anne nodded. "Yes, and immediately, I fear, even though Monsieur d'Alleville can barely stand."

"Then we must hope that this Claude d'Alleville is less tired than he looks and is a better shot than Moorefield," the duchess said.

"Or that he will demand rapiers. Frenchmen love to fight with swords. However, I fear that Mrs. Callaway needs to sit down before she faints."

The duchess led the younger ladies into a private sitting room and rang for tea.

Sarah collapsed to a sofa, her soul an ocean of exhaustion, as if she stared hollow-eyed over the remains of a sea battle and had no emotion left. They all knew what this meant. If Lord Moorefield killed Claude d'Alleville and emerged triumphant, a devastated Rachel would still have to marry Guy. If the Frenchman killed the earl, he would be forced to flee the country. Either way, disaster stalked.

The duchess stood quietly at the fireplace, her ribbons trembling. Anne closed her eyes as if she retreated into some quiet private place, where perhaps she prayed. Sarah folded her hands and gazed numbly from the window.

Sunshine streamed through high clouds. Swallows gathered on the rooftops. The last of the summer roses nodded lazily in a small breeze.

She could not pray. She could not even hope. Lord Moorefield had cheated and manipulated and threatened, yet they had no evidence that he had ever murdered. She could not actively hope for any man's death, simply in order to secure her own happiness.

The minutes ticked by, marked by the steady beat of the gilt clock on the mantel. A stifling hush blanketed the room.

We all love him! Sarah thought suddenly. All of us!

The duchess loves her sister's son as if he were her own child. Anne loves him like a brother. Jack and Ryder love him, as does Miracle and his own family. Berry will love him just as much, and Rachel will come to love him in the end.

If Lord Moorefield walks out of Wyldshay alive, I am the only one who will lose him. Yet though I love him more than I love my own soul, I cannot hope for a death in order to win him. I cannot!

Boots thudded at last in the hallway. The door to the room burst open. Anne opened her eyes and met her husband's bright smile. Guy strode in behind his cousin, brushed the hair back from his forehead, and bowed to his aunt.

"Well?" the duchess said. "Am I to arrange a wedding or a funeral or both?"

"Not dead," Guy said. "It was pistols. Moorefield's badly wounded. But in front of a half a dozen witnesses—including the duke, Lord Grail, and Lord Ayre—he apologized to d'Alleville and renounced all claim to the child."

"Then a wedding," the duchess said, smiling. "No, two weddings."

She glanced at her son and his wife, and the three of them left the room.

His eyes dark with passion, Guy's met Sarah's gaze. Her heart soaring, she stood up and walked straight into his embrace.

HE slept heavily, his newly washed hair spilled on the pillow, his freshly shaved jaw sharply defined in the candlelight.

Somewhere in Wyldshay, Anne and Jack, similarly reunited, were no doubt sleeping together with equal delight.

Lord Moorefield, bandaged and disgraced, had been driven away in his carriage. Lady Moorefield, against every entreaty, had decided to go with him.

Guy, Jack, and Claude d'Alleville had ridden across France without stopping and then galloped straight to Wyldshay as soon as they reached land. Yet in spite of his fatigue, the Frenchman had prevailed. Not with swords, but with pistols. A duel decided by first blood. The earl would walk with a limp, if he ever walked again, for the rest of his life.

It was over. The duchess had quietly sent up food and drink and a bath, after which Sarah had allowed Guy to fall unmolested into bed. Further explanations could wait until morning.

Meanwhile, Rachel had begun to weep piteously as soon as she recovered her senses and saw the father of her child and love of her life. And so Claude was very likely sitting by her bedside, watching her sleeping face, as Sarah watched Guy's.

Sarah woke next to the ticking of the clock and the light sound of Guy's steady breathing. A high moon rode the clouds outside their tower room. Restless, she slid from the bed and walked silently to the window.

At the base of the castle walls, the River Wyld spread into a calm lake, shimmering with silver and shadows in the moonlight. Sarah leaned on the sill, her heart entirely at peace, and gazed down.

Warm fingers touched her nape. Her blood leaped. She turned her head and smiled.

Guy kissed the back of her neck, then enfolded her in his arms.

"The goddess walks," he said quietly. "The White Lady of moonlight and flowers."

"And the god has returned," she said. "Oberon, king of the wild realms of Faerie."

He laughed with that uniquely wry appreciation for the absurd and stroked her hair back from her cheek.

"I drove to the Chateau du Cerf entirely without real hope," he said. "Jack had caught up with me by then, so I knew that Claude d'Alleville must be dead. I tried to take comfort in the knowledge that Anne and the duchess were both here to support you, but at that moment—"

"Yes," she said. "At that moment, when it seemed that all real hope was lost . . . Yes, I felt the same way. Yet you didn't give up?"

"God, no! How could I give up, feeling as I do about you? So Jack and I drove on and arrived at the chateau to find the place in chaos. Claude d'Alleville shared the same name as his father. Claude *Père* had indeed just died, but Claude *Fils* had been called back from Alexandria as soon as the old man first became ill." His arms tightened about her. Sarah leaned her head back into the warm hollow of his shoulder. "Yet my letter arrived in the days soon after the father's death, and his secretary assumed it was once again for him."

"And so returned it unopened to Wyldshay? Meanwhile, Berry's father was on his way home from Egypt, and he arrived to find you there in his home. How did he react?"

"At first he was inclined to send us to the devil, but then he found Rachel's letters amongst his late father's papers. He brought them down into the grand salon—"

"The chateau is imposing?" Sarah asked.

Guy chuckled in her ear. "Very! Which may be the reason why Claude *Père* had been so hysterically opposed to his son's marrying a penniless Englishwoman. He apparently couldn't bring himself to actually destroy Rachel's letters, but he'd kept them without sending them on to his son. Claude believed his father's suggestion that Rachel had found a new lover. He never knew about Berry."

His fingers gently stroked the hair away from her nape. Sarah wished she could purr.

"Until you told him. After which, he agreed to come back here with you to marry Rachel?"

"Not exactly. He was furious that he'd been so betrayed by his own father. Yet he was still inclined to believe that Rachel might just be some kind of hussy, after all—until he was able to take the time to read her letters. Of course, Jack and I were frantic with impatience by then, knowing the havoc that the returned letter must be creating here at Wyldshay. We'd written to you and Anne as soon as we knew Claude was alive, but when he agreed to come back with us we rode across France like the devil, told him the rest of the story on the journey, and obviously arrived here ahead of the post."

He felt so solid and real and ardent, enveloping her in his warmth and strength. Sarah caught one of his hands and kissed his palm. "So Claude no longer believes that Rachel never really loved him?"

"My dear Sarah, I don't know what the devil he believes. Yet he will marry her and take her back to France. He's filled with determination to rescue his little son and agonizing over the fate of his damsel in distress. So they'll be mad romantic fools in a home full of drama. Fortunately, I believe he'll be an excellent father. Betsy Davy will go, too, so Berry will always be safe."

"And Lord and Lady Moorefield?"

Guy became very still and took a moment to answer. "May stew in their own misery down in Devon. Yet I believe the earl's pride is finally broken, which may make him a better man. He'll have to accept now that his brother's his heir, and he'll have a hard time beating his wife again, especially if he can only walk with assistance or not at all."

Sarah closed her eyes. "I cannot feel too sorry for him when I think of the misery he caused, yet I'm glad that neither you nor Lord Jonathan had to shoot him."

"So am I," he said. "But enough about everyone else. What about us?"

She rubbed her cheek against his hand. "I rather hoped that you and I could continue to be mad romantic fools here in England," she said.

He spun her about. Moonlight glimmered in his dark hair and outlined the fine bones of his cheek and jaw. "Why? Because you and only you stir my soul in a way that I'd never imagined possible? Because I would lay down my life—not just as a figure of speech, but my very life's blood—if it were ever required, only for you? Because I burn for you as ardently as any man ever burned for a woman?"

"Well, yes," she said, "if you like."

He laughed in real joy. "Then will you marry me, Sarah?"

She reached up to cradle his face in both hands, so the moon silvered her fingers and glimmered on her arms. "Yes. Yes. Yes. Yes. Yes, I will marry you. Yes, I want to give you babies of your own. Yes. Yes. Yes. Yes, if you'll have me, with all my heart and soul I will marry you."

Guy laughed as he swung her up into his arms and carried her back to the bed. He slid in beside her, then tugged her nightgown off over her head.

His fingers trailed in erotic little patterns over her hot skin. "This is what you want?"

Desire flared as her palms feasted on his firm flesh, and she laughed.

"I've wanted it forever, Guy. Don't you know that?"

EPILOGUE

Chateau du Cerf, February 1830

My dear Sarah,

Claude and I are just thrilled with your news. So Berry will have a cousin before next Christmas! You know that any baby of yours will be as dear to me as my own, and we're very, truly happy for you, dearest, and for Guy. I'll love him forever for rescuing Berry, and so will Claude. I can't tell you what it means to both of us to know that you and Guy are so happy together. I'll wager you're almost as happy as we are! Living here at the chateau really is like living in a fairy tale.

Is Birchbrook just heartbreakingly lovely right now? Remember the snowdrops at our house in Norfolk? How very brave those little flowers were to defy the winter frosts like that, poking their white faces up through the snow in the woods, so confident that spring was coming, in spite of all the evidence to the contrary!

We both did that, didn't we? Defied the threat of winter to find the perpetual summer in our hearts.

Berry is quite the little master now. He can talk French just as well as English, and Claude is as proud as a peacock. He'll always be our firstborn, so it's nice to know that there's none of that silly business with entailments. Even if we have another son, Berry will one day inherit the estate from his father.

Meanwhile, I can't say that I'm sorry to hear that Lord Moorefield's faction was so soundly defeated in the House of Lords. Though I'll never understand politics, whatever the Duke of Blackdown's party proposed must be right!

Oh, and there's news that will amuse you about Betsy Davy. She loves Berry as dearly as ever, of course, but she's also been walking out with one of Claude's grooms. Though her French is still lacking and his English more so, the language of love must transcend all of that, for they're to marry next April, and will no doubt set up a nursery of their own. Claude doesn't mind, since he indulges his little English wife in everything, and Betsy and her new husband will be given their own cottage in the grounds as soon as they're wed.

I regret nothing now, dearest, except that I ever lied to you and Guy, and caused you both so much pain. But all's well that ends well, they say!

In the greatest affection, believe me your ever-devoted cousin,

Rachel d'Alleville

Author's Note

Jack and Anne's story was told in the bestselling *Night of Sin*, first released in January 2005, where Guy first met Rachel to take her out for that fateful day on the yacht.

Games of Pleasure followed in November 2005. Ryder plunged his horse into the sea to rescue a lady cast adrift in a small boat, only to find her unconscious and half-naked. That lady was Miracle, though Ryder had no idea then what she'd been doing for a living.

And Olwen's daisy path? That's an exact description of a footpath I discovered in Devon while researching *Clandestine*.

Further details may be found on my website at www.juliaross.net.